-REVOLUTION CITY-

-By-

-D J Bott-

I

PROLOGUE - DOWN WHEN THE WALLS START SHAKING

Once upon an apocalypse...

The end, just like the beginning, turned out to be a whole load of nothing. A complete absence of anything. Those who had once been, who had suffered through the lingering agony and the fleeting ecstasy of existence, had finally found solace in the bosom of oblivion, with no memory of what had been before.

But, just like the Big Bang before it, this tranquil state of limbo was to be ruined by the unfortunate intrusion of Life, though this time heralded without so much as a bang or even a whimper. One second there was nothing, then suddenly there was far too much of every single thing that had ever been or ever would be.

This was particularly alarming to one individual, because - just as he was getting used to not existing at all - he suddenly found himself plummeting towards a big ball of *everything*.

He could only assume that this vast example of *something* was the Earth itself, which was inconvenient because he was scorching and screaming towards it. Not only had this confused young man been unwillingly dragged back from the lukewarm comfort of the void, but he had no idea how he came to be attempting planetary re-entry without a vessel. This concerned him precisely because that's the kind of situation that usually demands total comprehension.

The young man reasoned that he must have blacked-out, if only for a second or two; the only explanation for his current recollection displacement. The urgency of his predicament meant that he would have to take stock of his situation, and fast. He was wearing an armoured space suit, which was a relief in the short term, but wouldn't do him much good in the long term. If he were to believe the information provided by the neural-interface operating system, and he had no other options, he was forty-one thousand miles from making potentially fatal contact with a random city street, whether he was ready or not.

Which he wasn't.

'Hello?' His words were muffled by the helmet's padding. 'Anybody?'

Despite the lack of response it turned out that he was not alone. A military unit drifted in the scorched stratosphere around him, a team that he could only assume he belonged to. Their armoured orbital-drop space-suits left trails of steam in their wake, following them down towards a vast, mountainous cloudscape. In the far distance the young man could see even more free-falling soldiers, drifting in clusters towards the peaks of bright white and valleys of charcoal grey between.

("Dyce?") A name floated through his head in a feminine voice that he was sure did not belong to him. As Hudson's eyes scanned clusters of data he realised that the calm and sincere voice had been transmitted through a hardware-assisted pseudo-psychic connection between operatives. ("You're having a panic attack.")

It actually took him a moment to realise that the young lady was addressing him, and that "Dyce" must be his own name. That name certainly sounded familiar. He tried it on for size, using it to refer to himself in the third person, and it seemed to fit.

Dyce tried not to yelp as a large metal dome loomed into view, a complicated system of automated locks and latches perched between the shoulders of another drop-suit. Those shoulders rolled back as the arms reached out to grab him. The dome was actually the helmet's heat shield, and it snapped open so that Dyce could see his compatriot's face through the transparent visor that it had protected.

("*Breathe!*") The young lady's lips didn't move. She ordered Dyce to open his own heat shield so that she could observe and approve.

According to Dyce's neural interface the lady's name was Macalister Breaker. She was taking long, slow, exaggerated breaths to remind Dyce how controlled, circular breathing worked to help him relax and focus. She lifted her head and flared her nostrils as she inhaled, holding, then exhaling through her mouth. Though Dyce was mimicking Breaker's breathing, he was actually focused on Breaker's eyes. He remembered them clearly. It was not the first time that he had gotten lost in them, and this formed a psychological bridge to his temporarily absent identity.

For a moment that felt like a millennium, before those wide eyes disappeared behind a reflection of the curved horizon, nothing else existed...

("*Focus!*") Breaker ordered, she looked as if she would slap Dyce's face if she could. ("*We are nearly there! Remember – breathe deep, stand tall, aim true. And don't close your fucking eyes!*")

Dyce felt his heart sink when Breaker locked her heat shield before she let him go and spiralled away, disappearing into the clouds that consumed them all a moment later.

Blasts of static electricity danced through the pressured mass of vapour, pinging between ice crystals, twisting around water droplets. These flashes triggered brief memories of rotating yellow warning lights within a ship's hanger, belonging to a solar frigate cruising through a shallow orbital trajectory. He had been surrounded by his squad, intermittently bathed in bronze by the spinning lights, in the moments before they had been launched down toward the globe beneath...

But he didn't have time to dwell. The cloud was thinning, revealing solar ships floating beneath them, framed by a vast, devastated landmass below. These gravity-defying military mega-structures were roughly seventy-two-thousand tons of brutalist oblongs and edges, solar sails protruding from their sides like fins, reflecting the exploding munitions that filled the air between them.

It quickly became apparent that Dyce and the rest of the team were an a collision course with a solar destroyer. Over the neural com-link he could hear his teammates panicking. At least he wasn't the only one experiencing *squeaky bum time*. According to the others this was an enemy vessel, not that it mattered who it belonged to if they hit the hull, smeared across it like bugs.

Dyce involuntarily broke one of Breaker's rules, closing his eyes tight, though he had the good sense to focus on his breathing...

Inhale, one two three... Hold, one two three four... exhale, one two three four five. Inhale, one...

(*"Dyce! Pay attention!"*) Breaker admonished him over the com-link.

(*"Okay!"*) Dyce gritted his teeth, shook his head, then opened his eyes.

But no amount of controlled breathing could prepare Dyce for the fact that the solar destroyer beneath was suffering a cataclysmic engine failure, the result of a successful breach. A cluster of explosions from within the solar destroyer caused its spine of anti-gravity generators to fall out of synchronisation. The physics defying devices started to compete with each other, pushing and pulling until they cracked the ship in two.

'Oh shit, oh shit...!' Dyce shouted into his helmet, because that was the only sensible response.

The solar destroyer's momentous gravity bubble still held its two crumbling halves aloft as Dyce and his teammates fell between eighty-two levels of doomed crew members. This created a lot of obstacles; water rushing out of the vessel's ruptured cooling tanks, spilling out like waterfalls; an avalanche of unmanned vehicles tumbling out of the exposed hanger bay; flailing, free-falling figures. Dyce somehow managed to dodge between a lot of what was cascading out of the scuttled ship, at least until a displaced vending machine hit him and sent him spiralling away.

Luckily, though, someone caught him. At least, that was what he thought had happened, a body had definitely mashed against his. It took a few beats for both entangled parties to realise that they were not on the same side.

Dyce's anonymous armoured adversary was obviously far more competent, stabilising their tailspin by evacuating several canisters of compressed air simultaneously. When Dyce dared to open an eye he found himself staring down the barrel of a handgun, scraping a jagged line across his visor. He squirmed like a kid avoiding a fork full of vegetables.

Breaker came chasing after, using her compressed air canisters to steer through the ever splintering muddle of metal, a very delicate operation considering that the obstacles were subject to the bewildering vagaries of the pseudo-physics that existed within the malfunctioning gravity bubbles.

But before she could catch up, Dyce and his foe were suddenly snatched by the artificial pull of another vessel, a troop carrier. The enemy hit the hull first, the force of it smashing their armour and momentum mangling their body. Dyce still held on to what was left of that enemy soldier, his breathing galloping on ahead of his sanity.

The troop carrier was descending rapidly, rotating slowly, it's burning engines drawing a double helix of smoke and popping embers in its wake. Dyce pulled himself up on to his knees and grabbed a handle in the hull. With the cascading carnage now above him he could see the districts by the bay popping with munitions, alive with movement, the landscape shifting as explosions churned up the scenery and tore down buildings. He found some solace in the ocean , shimmering from the shore to the horizon, unmoved by the petty, macabre machinations of man. The entire panorama was given a silver sheen as the sun was slowly swallowed by the massing grey cloud.

Suddenly, from somewhere above, a rain of ammunition ripped up the hull and the broken body beneath him, pummelling the grenades it was carrying. The explosion sent Dyce flying. He was lucky that his body hit an antenna array instead of spinning out into the sky. Of course, he didn't feel all that lucky.

A small magnetic anchor grabbed hold of the hull, and on the other end of the anchor's cord was Breaker, the spindle on her hip reeling her in. She detached her rail rifle from the mag-lock on her black, aimed back up and opened fire. Somehow she had managed to attract the ire of a a fully armoured automaton circling above. Luckily the failing gravity bubble was warping the trajectory of her opponent's onslaught, it's mechanical mind not programmed to deal with such unexpected anomalies. But when Breaker retaliated she was able to compensate for the gravitational warp through trial-and-error, unleashing round after round at her pursuer with adequate precision.

The enemy machine unfolded its many limbs across the carrier. On its belly, multiple mobile turrets spun, unleashing a barrage of bullets. The antennas Dyce held rattled until he could bear it no longer, collapsing.

("Dyce!") Breaker shouted over the com-link. ("Shoot its legs!")

But Dyce's fingers froze on the trigger. He couldn't trust himself to hit the target and not hit his friend.

("Dyce!") Breaker insisted, clearly running out of patience.

So he panic pulled the trigger, and, though his armour

buffered the recoil, each successive shot went wild, until he was lucky enough to hit a leg joint and put it out of alignment. The machine unbalanced, swinging it's bulk into the array and demolishing it around him.

Dyce didn't see clearly what happened next, only glimpsing Breaker's counterattack. Chunks of flaming machinery barrelled past him, he could only wonder how Breaker had managed that. It obviously had not been easy - Breaker hit the hull hard in a whirlwind of smoke, holding on to her anchored smart cord.

The troop carrier started decelerating in the most excessively violent way, hitting the side of a skyscraper, decimating floor after floor, turning the shattering windows into projectiles, tearing through Breaker's helmet and wrecked the mechanisms, sensors and cameras.

The troop carrier finally slowed to a stop when the opposite end hit an adjacent building, throwing Dyce backwards along the ship. Breaker removed her ruined helmet and discarded it, chasing her friend to the edge. That was the last thing that Dyce saw as he fell away...

Perhaps concussion or stress had made Dyce pass out again, because his perception of the world fell away, too, and all that remained was darkness...

Once again, there was the bliss of nothing. But he remained completely conscious, completely aware of the void and his place within it. It was so quiet that for a moment he could hear his own organs move, until that too vanished. From everything to nothing.

He was free to muse on how useless he had been during that fight, how completely devoid of agency he was.

What a waste...

Soon, though, it appeared that this limbo was not actually entirely empty. Shapes floated into view, objects from the real world completely devoid of their surrounding context, like the void was glitching. Parts of ships, parts of people, frozen explosions suspended in time, near and far. He had to wonder if everything he had just witnessed had been a simulation or an immersive re-creation corrupted by systemic failure.

A cross-section of the riser reappeared without the embedded ship or his friend. He could see in the glass the reflection of the grey sky punctuated by drifting red embers, drifting around his body, plummeting in slow time.

So there he was.

Pathetic. Useless. a Disappointment. No future. No direction but down.

But then...

'*I'm sorry,*' said a soft, androgynous voice. '*I'm trying to help...*'

Dyce tried to have an anxiety attack, which seemed like a reasonable reaction, but without a body or it's organs that was nigh on impossible.

'*I wanted to aid your mental recovery, but this memory was all that I was able to reconstruct with the limited time available. Considering my geographical distance from your smouldering, disintegrating body and brain I'd need access to a processor-stack capable of...*'

Dyce's meta-conscious id screamed at the existential insanity of what he was hearing.

'*You know what? I'm getting ahead of what you're currently capable of comprehending. Too technical.*'

There was a pause whilst the mysterious benefactor reaccessed their tactics. Dyce had to admit that they were right about his current cognitive ability. What he heard next was easier to understand, but even harder to process.

'*You died. That's the important part. Maybe I should have lead with that. At some point between your orbital drop and where you are now, your life came to an end. I did what I could to rectify that, found help where I could. It wasn't easy, especially by remote, but I was able to bio-hack your brain and force-boot your latent...*'

Another pause. Dyce tried to access a lot of different expressions, all of them some variation of confused or horrified, but realised he didn't have a face.

'*When you wake you'll have to finish reconstructing your*

memories yourself. There are plenty of commercially available software solutions, I'm in no position to make recommendations. But full recollection isn't actually a prerequisite, its not necessarily gonna help you in the trials to come. You could always start fresh, be any one you want. Build a new you out of the people you admire. Or not, I'm not the boss of you. But I've been observing your life for a while, and, personally, I wouldn't recommend you being entirely the old you. Like, try a twenty/ eighty split.'

Dyce could not help but find himself agreeing with the sentiments of the mysterious voice.

'You have to be ready for what's to come. It's gonna be tough, You have to prepare yourself. Be better. Get ready.'

But Dyce had other intentions. He was trying, through sheer force of will, to reconstruct that memory and the people in it, to retreat back in to the safety and comfort of being unexceptional. No fear of having to live up to expectations, no fear of failure if you never set a high precedent in the first place.

'There are others... find them, because as hard as I'm trying to hide you from him, *he is trying to hide* them *from me.'*

Him?

'He calls himself Riot, and he intends to manipulate every path to trigger his ideal scenario. Riot would not hesitate to tear this world down to get what he wants. Find the others, head for the Shard, defeat Riot.

But...

'They're coming for you...'

Who?

'Wake up!'

THE BALLAD OF ME AND MY BRAIN

The final year of the Centenary War.

They're coming for you...
Get ready...
'*Huh?*' Dyce Bastion grunted in response, waking himself up.

He was so detached from reality and his own current situation that he was actually alarmed to find that he wasn't falling down the side of a building with a sky full of flaming debris above him, a fluctuating carpet of combatants moving amongst the city beneath him, and a mysterious voice in his ears. He put out a hand to steady himself and found that he was indeed safely lying on a solid floor.

Every atom ached, he could barely move. Rational thought was an irrational struggle. To top it all off, he felt as if something huge and heavy had slapped its arse down on his head and farted.

In his ears there was an overwhelming hum, entirely the result of whatever lingering trauma had rendered him, *well...* according to the voice from his dream he had expired, past on, no more, ceased to be, pushing up daisies, an ex *whatever-his-job-was...*

But as the hum eventually, gradually, mercifully subsided it was replaced by the wind whistling through this level of the structure. He could hear how high up he was, and he could smell the ozone. He could also sense his isolation, confirming that no one else had survived, his team mates were gone.

What had happened after the troop carrier lodged itself between those risers?

Free-fall, firefight...

Her...

He opened his stinging, dilated eyes, first focusing on a white smudge of light scattered on the surface of a shallow puddle, separating into an oily spectrum as he lifted his left hand up out of it, ripples spreading through it as drips fell from the fingers. He could see that he was wearing nothing but a tattered muscle-feedback suit, the synthetic musculature snapped and withered, exposing the tips of several of his fingers.

With a tremendous effort he pushed himself up, pausing in an awkward position to look around, ascertaining that he was many storeys up a random riser. A prone, pathetic silhouette against the gloomy skyline.

'Hello?' He managed to ask, his throat stinging. He could taste copper as if gargling blood. He half expected to hear the unidentified disembodied voice but it now seemed so distant that he doubted that he had ever really heard it at all.

He was gradually regaining some semblance of self, though a patchwork of random images and unfinished thoughts. All he knew for sure was that something devastating had happened to him on every conceivable level. Mentally, physically and spiritually. His body and mind had been damaged by a massive concussive force, he knew this because he could still feel it lingering in his muscles and organs. *The soul clinging to the bones.*

He shuffled closer to a window, following the ambient sounds of the city, though the lunar light was too much for his sensitive eyes right now. He pulled himself across a vast carpet of stones, though they clattered like chips of metal, poking and prodding him, nicking his skin, irritating him immensely.

He pulled himself up the window's frame and let it take his

weight. His gaping mouth collected damp air, condensation gathering on his cracked lips and arid tongue, slithering down his throat. The city was taking hard, heavy breaths, the wind moved in and out in waves, tickling his hair and brushing his skin.

Fragments of knowledge coalesced into something useful, a little basic intel on his location. This was an unnamed satellite town, part of Contact City on the west coast of Alcyone, a man-made continent. He hated that he could not yet remember his own personal history but could apparently remember the vague location of some crusty old buildings. Perhaps he recognised the skyline from reconnaissance footage shown during some mission briefing, perhaps downloaded directly into his cranium.

He turned his attention back to the shadow-filled room and immediately regretted it. He saw something so unexpected and twisted that his brain sent an order to his legs to leap back in shock, which they absolutely failed to do. Perhaps the message didn't get there, perhaps his mending muscles couldn't find a solitary fuck to give.

Something was there in the room. A shape. As his eyes adjusted to the dark, the moon's light - reflected off nearby buildings and refracting off puddles, battered metal and scattered glass - highlighted skeletal details, familiar yet twisted. He had not been alone, after all.

What sat there, cross-legged amongst the metal gravel, was an amp. These were semi-sentient automatons, but to call an amp a robot was a gross oversimplification, though this particular one was more humanoid than most. Hudson could not tell if it were on his side of the war or not, though the machine seemed devoid of what one might call life.

It sat crossed legged as if deep in meditation. Behind it was a path carved through the sparkling gravel by dragging something human sized, from the stairwell door to its perched rump.

In its hands, resting in its lap, it held a small device the size of a lighter. A small LED display on one edge of the device was flashing blue.

Dyce crawled over to it, a mammoth task in his current state. He attempted to brush the clattering *stones* aside, to make a path to the amp, but there were too many and the task seemed insurmountable, his irritation multiplying exponentially.

He propped himself up with one hand, stretching out with the other, gingerly taking the offering from the amp's hands. The machine's fingers were slack, though a few digits stuck to it like a dead spider's legs, stretching out until they either snapped loose or broke off at the knuckles.

Punctuated by a yelp that unfortunately channeled a clumsy puppy he lost his balance and face-planted the jagged carpet of pain incarnate. He initiated a scream that escalated into a roar of unfettered frustration, though the severity of the stabbing pain peeked his curiosity, and the metallic clack of the stones backed up the suspicion. From down here he could see that they were actually crushed bullet casings, an absurd amount of them. He gave a curious grunt through gritted teeth as he picked more discarded shrapnel out of his face.

'*This is fun...*'

He sat up and crossed his own legs in a sloppy mirror of the meditating amp, though he couldn't help but slouch. He had a better view of the automaton now. It looked as if it was wearing padded black armour over the top of its navy blue carapace which seemed semi-opaque when it caught the light at the right angle. Curiously, it's joints were turning charcoal black, misshapen like mould, flaking away.

'What happened to you?' Hudson asked.

But there was no glimmer of life in those seven small eyes dotted around its head. Dyce was confused by the fact that he could see that each of those orbs had a different coloured mechanical iris, he shouldn't have been able to differentiate in the low light, but they were only appearing more opulent the longer he looked, as if his eyes were tuned to some obscure ocular frequency. He could see defects in the mechanisms, could count the minute scratches and hairline cracks. He was mesmerised for a moment, before his head started to hurt. As he averted his gaze he noticed that the sockets around the eyes were caked by that same crumbling charcoal as if the synthesised muscle were rotting.

Hudson half hoped for some sign of life, though the other half hoped the dead machine and its unnerving bio-mechanical appearance remained dormant. It's unexplained presence led him to wonder about his mysterious dream-dwelling benefactor, about whom he had not one single clue.

He inspected the small device that he had taken from the amp and instinctively knew it's purpose, in fact it dredged up many mundane memories. It was a tabris, an essential piece of equipment that most people owned and used, a neural link that had many essential applications. It linked the user to their armour, weapons and powered fraymes amongst many other machines. It also connected people to local and global networks, and facilitated non-verbal communication between operatives.

He was happy to see it, fractions of his old self psychologically realigning as he rolled it between his fingers. He had spent a lot of time lost in these things, apparently a bit of a tech-geek, and felt that a little tinkering never hurt. Through the haze of soggy synapses he recalled his previous self hunched over a cluttered desk with a plastic container full of illicitly sourced precision tools, working on personal projects, things that would get him in a lot of trouble and definitely void the warranty. It was fine as long as no one found out, just a bit of fun...

With understandable suspicion he considered the tabris. Was this a gift for him? Was it safe to use?

He passed the small device from finger to finger, distracting the restless monkey part of his mind so that the subconscious could take stock of his situation. His powered orbital drop armour was missing, though he suspected that some of his aches and pains were caused by fragments of it embedded within him. He still didn't know how he had died, but the patterns of pain told a story that couldn't be ignored. He had no weapons. He was on the top floor of a derelict riser, no idea how he had come to be there. Maybe he had been dragged up here by this empty amp. What else...? He was unknown miles away from... *from...*

Wait... Where was *home?*

He knew this place, though. Alcyone, a man-made continent consisting of five huge cities filled with unfinished architecture. This landmass had been fought over constantly for the last century, changing hands on a regular basis. Right now it didn't belong to his side, he was on deadly ground.

'Shit,' he said to the unresponsive android. 'Shitting arseholes.'

Zoning out, he held the tabris between two fingers, moving it around through the air, imagining it was the spinning troop carrier from his dream. He lifted it higher above his head and imagined it was the solar ship that he had dropped from.

The Pulse In The Machine, that was the orbiting solar ship's name. He ran back through the memory, the drop, the enemy ship breaking in two beneath him, fighting on the carrier's hull, being thrown from it...

Then there was more, he saw a blur of images set to a tangle of sound. Footfalls and cracks, bangs and chatter. Nothing he could grab a hold of and bring into focus. He saw himself surrounded by figures, comrades perhaps, faces looking up in unison, the sky opening up to reveal a cascade of light that scorched the earth and everything, *everyone*, around him.

'But I came back...' He directed his confusion at the meditating amp. 'Why?'

Breaker was the only one he could really remember. She was so much better qualified than him, she could have handled this situation better than he ever could. Not that he really had a firm grasp on his predicament.

'Why me? I'm no one...'

His heart ached when he thought of Breaker. What would

she do if she were here? She'd be on top of this mess, she'd have a plan. If only he could get inside her head…

'I can't do this.'

The tabris was the key to rebuilding his memories, to reclaiming his old self. There was a small LED screen built into a small recess in one corner of it, flashing still.

'I dunno, maybe if I could…' He started talking to the amp, just for something to bounce ideas off, but stopped for a moment as he felt foolish. Then he felt foolish for feeling foolish because he was essentially alone. 'If I can remember them, see how they handled things, tried to get… to get inside… No, no not me. Stupid stupid. I'm shit. I'm not them. So… fucking…'

He rolled his eyes, clenched his teeth. He felt sick to his stomach.

Through the moisture collecting within the LED's recess it showed that it was fully charged and ready to go. What worried him though was that it was already synced to someone, transmitting and receiving data packages.

He tried to read the data displayed on the flashing LED display with his aching eyes. Not that he couldn't see it, it was that his brain wasn't entirely functioning on an adolescent level, let alone an adults level. He stared at it until his mind started to recompile the symbols into words, feeling like a caveman holding a smart phone, an unintentional impression complimented by the sniffs and snorts emitting from his snotty nose. He realised that the device was already synced to him, and it had been this entire time, even before he woke it had been connected to his cross-firing synapse. That explained the commandeering of his slumber and the forced deployment of a recompiled memory within it.

There he was, cautious about connecting to it and opening himself up to the unknown and the hurt it might bring, but it transpired the first step had been taken for him. So, it had already begun without his consent or knowledge, and he had to come to terms with the fact that it was time to take control.

With a few subconscious gestures he ordered the tabris to open the Minds Eye operating system, it booted up, and its logo span through his vision.

He closed it immediately.

He wasn't ready. He scrunched his eyelids tighter, creating a rolling cascade of tension that became more intense with every revolution.

But the more immobile he remained the more sounds he became aware of, things that he should not have been able to hear, inside and out, near and far. He assumed the auditory escalation was due to concentrated, unchecked stress, that why he could hear his heart racing, thumping, his breath labouring as his chest tightened. He improbably heard his organs moving, heard broken skin mending. Just beyond that he could make out the wind whipping remnants of yellow and black warning tape on the window frame by him, on all the windows all around him, glass rattling, bothering the putty that held it in place.

He noticed the dirt gathered beneath his fingernails, could see every granual of it and he wondered if he had clawed his way out of the ground, from some impromptu grave, and in that moment he just wanted to crawl back like a dying dog and bury himself back in that hole. Someone else could take his place. Anyone else. Everything was so muddled, so confusing, so *wrong*. He felt the tabris in his hand as he squeezed his hands into fists, and for a moment he wanted to crush it, to feel it's shell crack, to destroy his only means of communicating with the outside world or rebuilding his former self.

He wanted, *needed*, to unleash a primal, guttural scream that would shake the foundations of reality, but all that he could do was choke on ash.

That's when he saw a chunk of shrapnel apparently forcing its way *out* of his chest. He sat up straight and watched it for what felt like an eternity, until finally the massing blood pushed it out to land upon his lap. He ran his fingers over the skin, brushing the blood aside to see that it was already healing. In an awed daze he studied the crimson smear over his exposed fingers, pooling in the glove's snapped and receding synthetic muscle.

Something powerful and agonised was welling up inside him and wanted to leak out of his eyes, but his tear ducts were still mostly fused, denying him an outlet he badly needed. Phlegm, though, managed to mass in his mouth. He was unworthy, at least that's the story he was telling himself. Perhaps that was the story he had always told himself.

There were letters and numbers etched on the piece of freshly ejected shrapnel, beneath the blood and sinew. He picked it up and wiped the gore from it, revealing it to be a metal ID tag, along with a couple of fused links of the chain that had previously held it around his neck. He read the tag to refresh his memory but had to re-read it several times before his mind made sense of it, an indescribable jumble to his broken brain. There was the insignia for the League of Nations - the side of the war that he had previously fought for - above his name, serial number and barcode.

As he stared at the name he remembered something else from his dream. A voice telling him to find something called Riot, which was responsible for his death... was that real? He also had to find some others... whatever that meant. Find the Shard... Was that a person, a thing, or a place?

He fancied he could hear that voice again, like cut content getting reused. *'Imagine yourself stepping into another's body, moving as they move, standing as they stand, talking as they talk... reProgram yourself with the best of others, upgrade your self-esteem, your skills...'*

'Dyce Bastion,' he read off the ID tag, but his mouth was so dry it hurt to speak.

What kind of a person were you, Dyce J Bastion? He asked himself, suspecting that the question was irrelevant. The important thing, he was starting realise, was finding out what kind of person he would become.

THE DEVIL TAKES
CARE OF HER OWN

Three city blocks from Dyce Bastion's lonely vigil stood the exposed skeleton of a building. Only the first seven levels were close to complete, ceilings, floors and all, beneath the riveted steel bones of the thing.

The only sounds were the old unexplained noises that buildings made, like creaking old muscles, and the assorted whooshes and rattles performed by the elements as they passed through.

Sand from the nearby coast had gathered on those half completed floors, the wind whipping up it up in little spurts, funnels and twirling dust devils. These inconsequential things made more sound than a lone figure traversing the colossal tower crane whose arm had long ago crashed into the riser. The figure hopped down from the adjacent riser onto the arm's counterweight and skipping down the length of it, her steps too quiet to echo through the vast latticework of exposed girders.

Trip Kosheen of the Unified American Military was skipping along the arm of the massive construction equipment, heading in to this unfinished riser, abandoned decades previously.

She was attempting to retrieve an old song from the depths of her memories to distract herself from the fact that she was seven floors above the riser's only completed levels and focus her mind. The ballpoint-tips of her prosthetic legs dodged the bioluminescent fauna that had grown along the crane arm and each of the girders. She lightly brushed a bulb which popped, sending a cluster of its fizzing, voluminous seeds up and out, twirling in the breeze, drifting down like lanterns towards the mostly completed levels far beneath.

Without losing momentum for a moment she reached to the quick-release lock on her back and released her hefty gravity-rifle. The weapon was temporarily compressed for increased mobility, its true length and mechanical complexity revealed as she unfolded it one handed, spinning it around a finger by the trigger guard, well timed bumps and jerks of the load-baring arm at key moments locking the mechanisms into place, a technique that she had mastered through repetition and persistence.

Chatter filled the neural com-link as she skipped over more of that sensitive fauna, each delicate tap of the tips of her prosthesis against the iron triggered a change in the colour of the luminous buds from blue to pink.

("Is everyone in position?") Asked a gruff masculine voice that she knew all too well, and that her Minds Eye operating system unnecessarily identified as Private B. K. Reaver.

("Five seconds.") Trip Kosheen replied.

("A pincer movement requires everyone in position, Kosheen.")

("I know.")

("Well, I'm fucking glad you know, now demonstrate comprehension through action.")

("I am on my way. I'm not -fucking- magic, Reaver, I can't teleport.")

("Reaver, Kosheen,") Another disembodied voice, belonging to their commanding officer Paris Oshii snapped at them. *("You two need to knock that shit off before I knock you both out. With extreme* fucking *prejudice. Now get ready.")*

Kosheen stopped and knelt down at the end of the tower crane's arm, where it was forever resting upon a crossbeam crossroads, its weight warping the girders. She carefully placed the sniper rifle down between two glowing masses of the unearthly fauna. As she unwisely let the big man's taunts percolate in her brain, she slowly shook her head, accompanied by the grinding of tension cracks, resisting the urge to decimate something brittle with her fists, knowing the network of metal would ring like a cathedral full of bells.

She had to remember to be stealthy despite Reaver belittling her and attempting to push her to the edge of her patience. She mentally disconnected herself from the com-link channel that included the rest of her team, and shook her head.

'Go fuck yourself, you big dumb ox,' she mimed to herself.

She released her fist and flexed the fingers, feeling the push and pull of the prosthesis bolted to each digit as she tried to shake out the tension. She placed a hand down upon the crane arm, and she was actually delighted to find she could still feel the hum of the battle, that attempted incursion by the League of Nations forces, lingering in the *soul* of the city, it's foundations, reverberating up through the tower and along the network of pulleys that still somehow held the tensile cable, playing a sustained note like an overplayed guitar string.

Kosheen sat with her posterior amongst the alien plant-life growing through the girders and the crane, swinging her kinetic prosthetic legs over, letting the ballpoint-tips dangle over the long drop. She waited for the order to come from Corporal Oshii, for the rest of their team to breach a room seven floors beneath her, a synchronised pincer movement against an unsuspecting enemy encampment.

She had her headset resting on her forehead, held tight by an adjustable strap. She pulled it down over her eyes and synced it to her tabris interface device so that she could see details human eyes could not using the seven tiny, beady cameras set into recesses all over the headset. Reality seemed to warp into the uncanny as layers of digital data augmented her vision.

She could now see the target floor of the riser, presented to her as a wireframe image built using data collated from not just her own headset but also equipment belonging to every other member of her team, each one of them taking point, preparing to breach. One by one her Minds Eye was filled with figures, furniture and assorted objects represented as green silhouettes. Kosheen activated a glo-stick and placed it between her lips, taking a deep and satisfying inhalation of its ill-defined, illicitly sourced chemical compound. Inside her Minds Eye she moved through the virtual space, tagging human targets.

She attempted deep breaths to regain additional composure, shuddering as a little more anger and resentment slipped out. She absently ran fingers through her short, spiked hair, a cluster of which she accidentally yanked from the follicles after catching it between the minute floating bolts that pinned her exo-skeleton through the skin to the bone. She swore through grinding teeth.

The tiny servos and artificial joints caught the natural neon of the non-terrestrial fauna as they moved. She had rarely resented the mechanisms themselves, but she lamented the revulsion and pity that she often suffered in the eyes and actions of others at the sight of them, as if she were trapped in a cage built for her bones. But the frame was one with her, the motorised brace her only means of locomotion. Born with tetraplegia, she was unable to move without this mechanism, surgically pinned through her skin, macro-bolted to every bone. From the base of her head down to the stumps where her knees would be, and along her arms to the tips of her fingers, it was powered through biologically-generated kinetic energy, battery-banks in its spinal stack recharged through the movement of her own body and its organs. This also helped her handle the heft of her almost comically large high-velocity long-range gravity-rifle with its selection of sniper scopes.

She realised that she had to get her head back in the game. She forced her attention back into the target floor of the riser and looked at all those souls wondering around, oblivious to the organised chaos about to be unleashed upon them.

This wasn't really necessary, of course, this had already been a busy day. They had enjoyed a few hours of fun hunting enemy stragglers, survivors of the battle. Some of them had even put up a decent fight and proven themselves to be enjoyable sport, but this had only lasted so long, numbers dwindling. Perhaps some had gone to ground. Perhaps they should have set up camp for the night, but they had already planned to make a move upon this enemy encampment, one of many that they had been observing for a while. Oshii wanted this one gone before they could absorb any more of today's survivors. These were lost, broken people hiding amongst the many lost and broken places. The city of lost things. Kosheen called it sport, but really it was more like foxes decimating a henhouse, a brief moment of chaos and fury, entirely controlled by the aggressor, turning their sanctuary into an inescapable abattoir.

("So,") Kosheen asked, reconnecting to the group chat, talking as she virtually walked the wireframe room, pinging the anthropomorphic outlines. ("When we're done with these asshats who wants to get Chinese?")

("Where you thinking?") Asked a younger soldier named Darius.

("I forget the name... The restaurant hidden in the scrubbed out tanker in the third district.")

("Oh yeah. Best noodles in all Alcyone.")

("Reaver, don't flay anyone alive.") Kosheen asked. ("It puts me off my beef chow mein.")

("I promise nothing.")

("You know that's not really beef?) said Darius.

("Don't care.")

("You seen many cows round here?")

("What's a cow?")

("Jeezus, read a book!")

("No.")

Kosheen selected an old song from her tabris to entertain herself as she checked out the figures in the target room. She learnt what she could from their body language, noted how well armed each of them were.

'I'm gonna fuck *you* up,' she sung this threat, though barely more than a whisper, to the general tune of a song that floated at the periphery of her memories, a song whose title and lyrics had refused to coalesce into anything more than a frustrating ode to her lost life. She directed her improvised ditty to one of those victim-shaped virtual representations in her Minds Eye. 'Then I'm gonna fuck *youuuuuu* up...'

("The doors are booby-trapped,") She said, as she zoomed in upon their wooden frames. ("I recommend a wall breach.")

("Well, thank you for telling us how to do our jobs.") Reaver replied, sarcastically.

("Why?") Kosheen sounded exasperated. ("You just had to acknowledge.")

She stopped her virtual tour through the room when she found that one of the targets had an odd signal. Double heartbeat. Pregnant. She moved the glo-stick from one side of her mouth to the other and grunted, curious. Kosheen wondered if the woman knew. The target placed a hand on her belly,

But these quiet moments alone always gave her too much time for reflection. She hated that. More and more often she was having thoughts that contradicted her prescribed world view. But soon there would be violence, and she *liked* that, because she was good at it, and it could be useful for silencing those little dissenting voices inside her head, helping to drown out that annoying sense of morality that had recently, inexplicably, returned to bother her after so long absent. Maybe it had always been there, had never really gone away. It had been there at the edge of her sanity, a nagging little bug that nibbled at her façade. That wasn't what their glorious, legendary leader had taught them - Paris Oshii expected them to have no empathy for the enemy, nor restraint for anyone different from them.

Kosheen's face contorted and constricted, unsure what to

think. It was best not to think at all.

'Two for one,' she whispered to herself, getting herself back in to character after a small, insignificant bump. She felt much better.

Suddenly a notification popped up in the corner of Kosheen's vision. She scowled at the flickering oblong of text, primarily because of the comparative rarity of this level of notification compared to other types of communication she would normally receive. It was a message from back home, a high level Priority Request, and they had not received one of those in a long, long time.

They had not heard from home. They had not been home.

("Anybody else checking out this order?") Kosheen asked the group.

("It's not an order, it's a request,") Said a man named McMorrow.

("They want someone to check out some riser, they need to visually confirm who or what is in there,") Reaver added, clearly he had skimmed through the details of the communication which was more than Kosheen had done, his sub vocal communication still translating his disinterest. *("That's some rookie runaround bullshit right there.")*

Kosheen opened the notification and was presented with a virtual representation of a nearby riser, and on the building's top floor was a cluster of heat signatures.

("So, they think all those heat signatures are enemies?") Kosheen read the details that accompanied the virtual diorama. Something didn't seem right to her. *("It doesn't make sense, why would so many soldiers, stranded in enemy territory, camp out at such an altitude with no visible means of escape? What are they gonna do, leap out the window?")*

("Cuz they're all fuckwit inbreeds,") Reaver said.

("That is a ludicrous quantity of cockroaches, like someone baited a trap with a king's banquet,") Corporal Paris Oshii agreed, and what she said was usually the last word on any subject. *("I'm not risking my people on that. That communication*

had a city-wide dispersal, let someone lesser do it.")

Kosheen reached out and idly spun the digital representation of that suspect riser, staring at those blobs of red that supposedly represented enemy soldiers. Then she mimed scrunching it up and threw it into her Minds Eye's virtual trash can. It had probably appeared in the notifications of every UAM soldier within five city blocks, let them deal with it. Reconnaissance missions were beneath the Augmented Fourth.

("Kosheen,") McMorrow suddenly interjected with a warning. *("There's someone heading for your position! They just passed us.")*

("What the fuck?") Kosheen panicked. *("There's no one showing up on the scan!")*

("Walked past us, full body hidden beneath a hooded cloak.")

Kosheen hopped back up to a crouch, gyroscopically balanced on the ballpoint tips of her prosthetic legs. She cycled through her headset's visual filters to see if this mysterious enemy showed up. In the end she lifted her headset back up, the strap holding it in place on her forehead, and used her homegrown eyes.

She spotted the figure sneaking across the half finished floor seven storeys beneath Kosheen. He was wearing a shimmering raincoat that hid him from their equipment, hood up. The figure stopped in a nondescript area, hesitant, looking shifty. Kosheen had to decide whether she was going to take him out of the equation, and she had only a small window of opportunity. He hadn't seen her, or so Kosheen thought. If she took him out it might spook the other targets, there were too many variables – He could be in com-link contact with them right now, they might be waiting for him at a specific time...

("Best laid plans ruined by a walking cliché,") Kosheen groaned.

But Kosheen saw another figure moving in on the mystery man's location, a bulky figure wearing triclops armour that she recognised purely from his body language.

("Reaver?")

("I've jammed his signal.")

("Right, you want me to...?")

Reaver had terminated verbal communication. Clearly he didn't want anyone to object to his actions and spoil his fun.

Kosheen switched to Reaver's neural feed in time to see the viscera. This was such a jarring transition for the banality of her own vantage point that she was unable to decode the flesh from the form. As was his modus operandi, Reaver did not just eliminate the straddler, he chose to eviscerate him, ending him in the most drawn out and sadistic way that he could realistically make time for.

'This is what you people deserve, fucking *league-tards*.' Kosheen didn't just hear Reaver say this, she could feel Reaver's lips form the words, his smug, superior grin widening, *their* face ached from the exaggerated nature of it.

'Not league,' the straddler said, so proud of this that he had to say it through his agony. 'I am free.'

'Bullshit...' snapped Reaver, as he tortured the straddler a little more. 'Being free makes you no better than animals, you're less than league.'

'We're all just animals. Some more then others,' the man spat blood through gritted teeth, he crimson-inflected spittle covering two of the seven small camera eyes over Reaver's helmet. 'Life is pointless, and you're just afraid that all there is to it is eating, drinking, sleeping and fucking. Like animals, only we're just aware enough to be bored shitless. Hold on tight to your beliefs, your patriotism, your tribes, to make it all *worth...whi...le...*' He was about to squeal in agony as Reaver clamped his mouth shut with his gauntlet.

Kosheen snorted through a derisory sneer. *Free,* how pathetic. If you're not in a tribe, what do you have to live for? It sounded so pre-rehearsed, like the man had to convince himself that it was true. But, for the briefest moment, she realised that she heard that tone in the others, maybe even in herself... she shook the thought off. Blasphemous.

Pathetic, she thought, because that was way less troubling than dwelling on the word *free.*

Reaver dropped the body when there was no more resistance left in him.

Kosheen returned her attention to prepping the targets in the room beneath. Her inner monologue was oddly subdued, monosyllabic, and this bothered her simply because she didn't know why.

("No survivors,") said corporal Oshii. *("Leave them breathing long enough to data-mine their minds for anything useful.")*

The targets began acting strangely, extinguishing their lights and fires. Reavers actions had tipped them off.

Suddenly Kosheen felt an ache in her stomach that she could not explain, something from deep inside, and her attention returned to the zigzagging lines that represented the heartbeats of the expectant mother and her future offspring.

Potential offspring...

Unless...

She held her breath for a second, though she didn't know why. It wasn't something that would usually bother her, but *something* had changed and that bothered her. She wanted to scan through the last few weeks, days, hours, minutes...

'*Why...?*' She breathed.

Kosheen stared at that visual rep of that heart beat...

She had been born different, with only one full leg, the second stopping just beneath he knee. To the military that owned her - that owned all newborns of her social status - this actually made her an asset, a body that could be augmented. On her third birthday her only leg had been surgically removed, too. So, from the knees down she had a pair of permanent prosthesis, kinetic anatomical appendages with tiny gravity orbs at the tip of each. She was built for speed and agility, she could acquire tactical positions no matter how improbable they should be to reach.

Kosheen's fate had been sealed from inception. She'd had no choice. The tiny heartbeat, this foetus was already more free than her, born to deserters and those abandoned by an uncaring system.

Kosheen decided to tag the pregnant woman a different colour, though she wasn't even sure why, or what she was going to do. It was too late, though, the woman had already been tagged by McMorrow. Kosheen grunted, then shrugged. She told herself that she didn't really care. She had gotten good at lying to herself.

("It's go time.") Corporal Paris Oshii said on the com-link. *("Be ruthless. Be legendary.")*

With unlimited pride they all concurred with a hearty cheer that they could hear only within the wireless, sub-vocal network through which they communicated.

Kosheen grabbed her ID tags, turned them over so that she could see the laser-inscribed flag. She kissed it and silently gave thanks to the higher powers in their government and military, to their infallibility and grace. With her head bowed, eyes closed, her lips moved as she recanted the words of their national anthem as if it were a prayer.

Then Kosheen picked up her gravity rifle, nestled the stock into her right shoulder and stared down her weapon's scope. Instantaneously, her Minds Eye overlaid the digital representations of the targets. She was aiming *through* that room's ceiling, right at an armed guard stood in a corner, near to where one of her teammates intended to make their entrance.

Kosheen pulled the trigger. The gravity rifle spun up and fired. She felt the push against her collarbone. Behind her the bioluminescent fauna reacted to the kinetic force, causing a chemical reaction to spread through the petals in waves, transforming them from luminous pink to neon blue.

Kosheen switched from target to target, firing again and again, her gravity propelled projectiles piercing the plasterboard panels above the hideout, letting pinholes of dusk into the dark space, whipping through the wisps of smoke from the extinguished campfires.

It was time for the rest of the Augmented Fourth to breach the walls. Chunks of wall all around the room became clouds of decimated masonry with synchronised precision. Kosheen observed it through the eyes of her compatriots, slipping from one set of eyes to another. The room was lit by muzzle-flash, as the Augmented Fourth moved through the room eliminating their selected targets.

Kosheen stood up, disconnecting herself from the com-link for privacy, unlocking the body of her gravity-rifle, folding it up and stowed it on the magnetic lock on her back. She drew her custom handgun and jumped, plummeting seven floors, crashing through the plasterboard, rolling through the splintering chaos of the battleground that the hideout had become.

One of her cohorts, McMorrow, was moving towards the pregnant target, and Kosheen shot his shoulder before McMorrow could do anything. Though the bullet didn't pierce McMorrow's armour, it did a good job of distracting him as it bounced up and knocked a chunk out of his respirator. McMorrow held his hand up to his breathing apparatus, confused, then looked around in an attempt to identify the culprit.

Kosheen hurtled straight past McMorrow, dropped to her triple-plated knees and skidded right around her target, grabbing the pregnant lady and putting a gun to her head.

'Do not fucking move,' Kosheen warned the stranger.

Then, almost as soon as this violent incursion had begun, it was over. Someone tossed an incendiary grenade into a campfire, reigniting it in the most over the top way. The flickering fire illuminated all twelve members of the Augmented Fourth, standing over their prey.

Kosheen always felt a little under-dressed compared to her compatriots, and as she looked around at the fire-lit silhouettes, today was no different. They were wearing bulky, full-body Triclops armour, and she wore only a tactical, padded, sleeveless spider-silk-weave armoured jacket

– bullet and blade proof, specially designed to fit around her mechanical brace.

The only one of them that wasn't simply stood there was Reaver. This imposing individual – an effect that was mostly achieved by the bulkier variant of armour that he wore, which he had gotten professionally adjusted to his expanding, protein-fuelled expansion – lifted a victim up off the floor, holding the mortally injured man with one hand. His grip tightened around the victim's neck, watching the blood dribble from his lips, his legs kicking at air. Reaver dropped the victim and placed a foot upon the man's face, shifting his considerable weight down until the skull beneath the flesh started to splinter. Reaver did things like this so that he could feel as big on the inside as he looked on the outside. This was a final indignity upon the doomed, just to reinforce Reaver's ego.

Through the crowd Kosheen glanced at Oshii, the Augmented Fourth's leader, both because of the awe that she felt for her commanding officer, and the fear of what Oshii's reaction might be her little insubordination. Kosheen could see - through her visor and Minds Eye – that her prisoner's heartbeat had increased, but not to a dangerous degree, not yet. Kosheen leaned over her, lifted her head, and began a well rehearsed speech, one that each member of the Augmented Fourth had said many times, though none could recite it with the theatricality or authority of Corporal Paris Oshii herself.

'You're lucky,' Kosheen said. 'You get to tell others about what happened here. We are the Augmented Fourth. We decimated the eleventh mobile infantry at the Battle of The EvanMoor Industrial Complex. We were the only ones to walk away from the Liberation of Vermillion Plaza. These cities are our playgrounds and our kingdoms. Every single person within is our own personal...'

With a sudden and unexpected bang of bone and blood, the pregnant woman's head popped, the skull imploded and her brain splattered out on to Kosheen's own face.

'Oshii's orders - no survivors,' said Reaver, as he snorted and wiped his nose on his right gauntlet.

Reaver was stood there, looming over Kosheen, the offending rail rifle in hand. Kosheen wanted to wipe that smug, superior look off Reaver's face. Any feeling of superiority that this oaf of a man felt was completely unearned, no matter how much effort that he put in to maintaining his ego. Kosheen wanted to tear the nose from Reaver's face and feed it to him, which was the sort of torture that she usually reserved for their enemies, but now she wanted to turn those tactics upon one of their own.

'You absolute prick,' Kosheen said.

'Now,' Reaver said, his eyes widening in barely contained anger. 'I *know* that you did not just say that to me.'

'Oh, I definitely did.'

Reaver casually unleashed a few more rounds into the dead woman's body. Then Reaver leaned in towards Kosheen and pointed a finger at her to emphasise his point.

'You are going to learn to respect me, *child*.'

'Excuse me?' Kosheen asked. Reaver had never called her *child* before, and she was dumbfounded. 'I really fucking doubt that.'

Reaver must have liked something that he had seen in Kosheen's eyes, because he grinned and walked away. Kosheen had never quite seen him like that before, not towards her at least.

Kosheen stayed, crouched down beside the body, for longer than she should have. She opened her right hand and let her beloved bespoke handgun sit in her palm. It was custom built and rather ostentatious, and it meant more to her than anyone knew, having a part of her old life baked into the resin grip, mixed with rainbow glitter, for a little razzle-dazzle.

The group's chatter subsided. They all looked in reverence to Corporal Paris Oshii as she floated through the room – their beloved leader, saviour, guru, teacher, idol... She was surveying the aftermath of the mayhem that her followers had wrought. She was the kind of person who would saunter through any battle as if her aura somehow repelled bullets.

'The Augmented Fourth have baptised this League hive in your own heretic blood and written a gospel with your entrails!' Oshii spoke loud and commanding, knowing that this was the last thing many of their dying victims would hear. She was theatrical and overblown when she needed to be, and her people loved it.

'That's right,' said Reaver, to the victim he had beneath his armour's metal boot. 'The Augmented Fourth. You losers never stood a chance.'

Reaver pressed harder and harder upon the man's chest until he heard a crack. He lifted his boot to have a look at the mess. He had clearly intended to play with *his food* a little longer, *you might say,* and had gotten over-excited trying to impress their commanding officer. Like a hyperactive child or puppy.j

'We all kneel at the alter of Unified American Military, the glorious dead and the powers that be!' Oshii continued, and her team lapped it up. 'We are their preachers and their inquisitors, and you are our sacrifice!'

Kosheen stood up and walked away from the body. She felt a little numb and she wasn't sure why. She found herself at the furthest end of the room, where a patchwork of rags hid a large window. She glanced back, with envious eyes, as she heard Reaver speaking to Oshii. The big man had been working his way through Oshii's ranks for a long time, trying to gain grace and take a position by her side.

'No real resistance,' Reaver said. 'Nothing but pussies.'

'They're not pussies,' Oshii said. 'Pussies can take a pounding.'

'Nothing but sweaty, sensitive ball bags,' Kosheen added.

Something caught Kosheen's attention, a drumming of rain on glass. She looked over at a large, long patchwork of scavenged rags that hid the windows, hanging from the ceiling from industrial staples, rusty from the damp. She stepped over a few bodies and grabbed the smelly rags. She held them for a second, her right eyelid twitched for a second as she stared vacantly at a stain that was developing a seam of mould, tightening her grip on the fabric as if it were a throat. Then she yanked the makeshift curtain down, revealing the window itself and the dilapidated building across the street and the tower crane that was resting against it. It was still early evening, gradually going dark, a fine rain pattering against the pane.

By the deep blue of the evening light, Kosheen could see the life that these people had made for themselves here. They had clearly been hiding here for a while, perhaps going native, the first step towards being drawn to one of the Stray tribes.

Kosheen turned back to the window and placed a hand upon it, watching the raindrops leave trails down the dirty glass. It was a mawkish moment of reflection that was quite out of character for her, or at least the character that she had created when she chose to become a fully engrained member of this team. When she had made the choice to be a survivor and not a victim.

'Victim...' She mimed the word, eyes vacant.

The clusters of micro-sensors in her gloves picked up a reverberation through the glass, almost imperceptible at first, escalation almost imperceptibly, but her exo-frame relayed it to her nerve endings. It got more and more intense until she could hear it shake.

'Something's coming!' She warned the others, backing away and taking her custom handgun back out of its holster.

Then, through the window, trouble crashed inevitably into view. Two fraymes – ten foot tall, human-piloted, gyroscopically balanced mechanical monsters - were locked in a life or death struggle out in the street.

One of the fraymes was a mass of black and grey armoured plates, the other frayme had a dirty blue hue. These bulky machines were in the middle of a brutal brawl, laying into each other with their large mechanised fists, each punch and posture an approximation of the pilots' muscle impulses redirected from their spinal stack to the machine via their tabris.

The blue League of Nations frame seemed to roar in defiance before the its rival. The black and grey UAM frayme drove it back with a succession of successful blows.

Kosheen and her cohorts whooped and hollered as if they were watching a boxing match. A couple of them, Kosheen included, were miming throwing punches.

'What model is that?' Asked Darius, pointing enthusiastically at the American frayme. 'Is that a Simian Tsunami?'

The UAM frayme grabbed its adversary by the head and squeezed with all the force of a hydraulic press, until the head cracked and the eye sockets splintered, forcing out a camera eye, swinging free on its fibre optic stalk.

But the big blue League machine retaliated, forcing it's full weight into the UAM frayme over and over again until they crashed through the window and into the lobby. The League frayme straddled its prey and punched its head over and over until it was completely decimated. The League of Nations frayme reared back, victorious, like a gorilla.

Then, apparently buoyed by their success, the League pilot pushed their frayme on and up, climbing over its fallen enemy, further into the hideout with a murderous desire .

Whilst the rest of the Augmented Fourth opened fire upon the League frayme's thick-plated armour, Kosheen took her gravity-rifle from her back and unfolded it, automated mechanisms locking it into combat configuration. With the high-velocity weapon's weight against her shoulder and it's nitrogen-cooled superconductor-stack humming on its back end, her tabris rapidly gathered data from her visor's various sensors, which it collated to present her a variety of targets, angles and vectors via her Minds Eye system.

All of this deep-math took place within a fraction second, a brief moment in time that reached a crescendo with pull of a trigger. A hair-thin electrical discharge followed the gravity-rifle's projectile all the way from the tip of the barrel into the enemy frayme's exposed eye-socket. The chemicals within the round mixed upon impact, forming an unstable compound with a catastrophic reaction, decimating the frayme's head and scrambling its senses.

The room fell silent. The enemy frayme was frozen in an agonised pose. Every member of the Augmented Fourth stood and watched both of the fraymes for signs of life, vigilant, crosshairs on the League frayme's cockpit.

They were all surprised when it was the enemy frayme that was the first to show any signs of life, as the League pilot opened up his cockpit. Either that took a lot of balls, or, more likely, an interior electrical fire had forced him out. He would no doubt surrender, which Reaver would see as a sign of weakness and an invitation to do whatever vindictive thing that he liked to the stranger.

But the enemy pilot was not fleeing, nor surrendering. Able to see again with his cockpit open, he was targeting them by eye.

He unleashed a torrent of ammo from a rotary chain gun, a percussive onslaught so powerful that the room seemed to shake, Kosheen could feel her teeth rattle and the noise made her brain spin. Everyone leapt for the ground, ducking behind fallen enemies and pillars, as the indiscriminate spread of metal hail tore through anything it touched.

The bombardment struck the encampment's weapon stash, igniting anything volatile and causing a chain reaction. The explosion sent Kosheen rolling and bouncing back through the room. The relentless percussion became a muffled drone as she blacked out.

In the darkness she heard a voice...
There you are...
I found you...
Hidden too well...
Even HE doesn't know... don't have long... stay hidden...

Kosheen shook herself awake in time to see the enemy frayme pilot fleeing past her, on foot, using the chaos as cover as he left his compromised machine behind. He was running through the chaos that he had created, just an angry, swearing, sweaty blur.

Kosheen reached for her sniper rifle first and found that it had been blown to the other side of the room, then she found that her beloved custom handgun was missing, too, and she could see no sign of that.

'Where's my...?' Kosheen panicked. 'Did he...?'

'He took your gun!' Darius shouted, pointing at the pilot.

The enemy frayme pilot was heading through out of the room past a door blown from its hinges when the pilot's salvo inadvertently triggered the trip-wire at the door's base and detonated the hidden grenade. Kosheen got a glimpse of the pilot stumbling through the hallway beyond.

Well, that really made her mad. That custom handgun had a lot of sentimental value and it was certainly not cheap, meaning she was not going to let some random prick sully it with their grubby hands. She could have wasted time running back to grab her sniper rifle, but for a crime this heinous she craved the tactile thrill of a physical assault. That's what Oshii taught them; be ruthless, be legendary.

Kosheen leaned forward like a sprinter getting ready for a race, her prosthesis contracting, gathering kinetic energy. Then she launched herself, bounding across the bodies of their enemies, and the decimated remnants of their camp, and into the hallway behind her quarry.

The enemy turned to fire, but Kosheen used the hallway to her advantage, elevating herself above her target by bouncing from wall to wall, using a combination of momentum and the tiny gravity orbs at the tips of her legs, until she was scraping the high ceiling with the exo-skeleton's knuckle guards. Then she dropped, speed and gravity turning her fist into a projectile, the fingers' braces acting as a knuckle-duster that cracked the pilot's helmet and sent him spiralling across the floor. Kosheen skidded after her quarry on sparking knees.

The frayme pilot rolled onto his back and fired Kosheen's own beloved custom handgun back at her, but the shot was wide. Kosheen pinned the pilot's arm to the ground with a scorched, double-bolted knee, grabbed the gun by the barrel, attempting to wrestle it free, but the enemy was putting up a good fight.

'Kosheen!' Shouted a voice from behind her, to alert her to the fact that another handgun was spinning across the floor to within arm's reach.

Kosheen grabbed this plain, ordinary handgun, pushed it up underneath her adversary's helmet and blew out both sides of his respirator with one shot. As compressed air ignited and the breathing apparatus exploded, it pulled chunks of bloodied bone and tattered ribbons of skin and muscle with it. The man's tongue flopped out through the gap where the jaw used to be, hanging over his throat like a neck tie.

Kosheen sat back on her knees and took a moment to catch her breath, admiring her fresh kill, high off the adrenaline rush. She looked at the gun that had been slid across the floor to her, and recognised it as soon as she saw the unpleasant name that had been given to it, inscribed roughly into the side of the barrel using the tip of a progressive blade on a low power setting. It belonged to Reaver, and she could hear him advancing down the hall towards her. With a flick of the wrist she tossed the gun over her shoulder to the big man, who managed to catch it. She did not want to turn to look at him.

'I guess I should thank you,' Kosheen begrudgingly said, as she checked her own gun for damage.

'I guess you should learn to take better care of your shit, *child.*'

Kosheen was, understandably, triggered. She did not know why Reaver had taken to demeaning her with the word *child*, but it made her entire body contract, starting in her organs, out through her chest and culminating at her grinding teeth.

Reaver was close enough that Kosheen could feel his breath on her neck, but she chose to not give Reaver the pleasure of knowing the depth of her displeasure.

Reaver stood there for far too long, not saying a word, until finally he turned and walked away. Kosheen felt as if she could sense the big man's malicious grin. She shuddered.

Kosheen took her own handgun from the pilot's grip and admired it, moving it around to watch the rainbow shimmer move in waves through the glitter that had been baked into the custom grip's bespoke moulded resin. The weapon had not been cheep, a custom-spec work of art, made from a lightweight polymer-based material; semi-automatic; large magazine capacity; ambidextrous controls; buffered recoil; chambering the largest centre-fire cartridge ever handled by the eighty-two-year-old Green Stray gunsmith responsible for its creation.

What made it special to her, though, was the special ingredient baked into that resin grip, suspended alongside that glitter were the ashes of her old life, a significant part of who she used to be. She briefly thought about a boy she used to know...

However, this was not the time for sentimentality. She had suddenly become aware that the enemy frayme pilot had been in possession of a progressive blade, and that he had apparently managed to unsheathe it during their tussle and embedded it in Kosheen's thigh.

'Oh wow,' she deadpanned, wide eyed, stunned. 'How did I miss that?'

She bit her lip, sighed and gingerly pulled it out. There wasn't much blood, so it must have missed any arteries, but still, she decided that she wouldn't be activating that cluster of nerve-endings any time soon. She grabbed a small medical aerosol from a compartment on her jacket, and sprayed its foam into the messy incision.

From the main room she could hear a voice she didn't recognise, someone with an upbeat tone. She wiped her blood off the blade and took it with her as she re-entered the main room, where some of the others were assisting the Unified American Military pilot out of his irreparable frayme. It was the UAM pilot who had the upbeat tone, loud and brash. Kosheen picked up her sniper rifle, checked it and folded it back up, before stowing it on the magnetic plate on her back, where tumblers spun around it, locking it in to place.

'Girl, *YOU*!' Exclaimed the American pilot. He was pointing at Kosheen. 'You are one hell of a shot!'

A couple of the other members of the Augmented Fourth were cutting the American pilot from his safety harness, the locks broken during the battering his frayme had received. They helped him to his feet and held him upright. His inability to stand was not due to any injury, it was that the bio-feedback from the frayme to his brain had allowed him to feel every blow, including the assault that had broken his machine's back. But now that faux pain was fading away, and the combat high had him laughing maniacally.

'That takedown was extremely fucking cool!' exclaimed the youngest, newest member of the team, a teenager named Darius.

'Yeah, I know,' Kosheen said. She gave a slow shrug, frowning, as if she knew this was too obvious for anyone to bother stating.

The boy Darius was still trying to acclimatise to the Augmented Fourth's barbarian ways, as Kosheen had done so long ago. Kosheen didn't know what to make of the fact the Darius was clearly in awe of her.

Then every member of the Augmented Fourth received an update from their Minds Eye system, as it identified the UAM pilot and showed each of them his name, ID number and the highlights of his service history. His name was Bruce Rosario, and he was a lieutenant. He outranked their beloved Oshii.

This would be a problem.

Rosario frowned as he stared at Oshii. His own Minds Eye must have identified the Corporal, because he looked more than a little intrigued by her. But then he started to look concerned, and this was no doubt because everyone had heard of Oshii's legend.

Then Rosario noticed the logo that each of these soldiers had sprayed on their armour, a red "*A*" that could also have been a number four, each logo painted in crimson red, like blood, but each had identical splatter as if created with a stencil.

Rosario let out a grunt that terminated with a stutter and splutter triggered by a nervous energy.

'Yes, she is *that* Corporal Paris Oshii,' Reaver took great pride in saying.

'So, the famous Oshii is only a corporal?' Rosario asked, practically muttering it, his mood suddenly changing drastically. He must have realised how disrespectful the Fourth would have found that, because he grunted again.

But Oshii didn't speak, she didn't say a word. She simply stood there, arms crossed, head bowed. Thinking. Clearly she did not like the way that this was going.

'The cogs turn slow around here,' Reaver said, on Oshii's behalf, by way of explanation.

'Well, I guess that puts me in charge,' Rosario continued. He had the common sense to nod at Oshii before adding - 'With all due respect, of course.'

There was a general murmur of disdain from the group, though nobody vocalised. Nobody except Kosheen, who displayed her dissent with a question, after she had checked out the officer's highlighted biography again. He had been in charge of a lot of different units. Too many, in fact. Kosheen had already decided that the lieutenant was bad news and worse luck.

'Lieutenant Rosario?' Kosheen asked. 'What were you doing in that frayme? Where's your unit? With all due respect.'

'Surviving,' Rosario said, sharp, defensive. 'That's what I was doing.'

'Watch your tone!' Reaver suddenly snapped at Kosheen. 'You're addressing a superior!'

'It's okay, Little miss *Sharp-shot* is still on a combat high, making her brash and cocky, I'll let it slide,' Rosario winked at Kosheen. 'Just this once.'

'Am I the *little miss?*' Kosheen scowled, looking as if she were chewing son something nasty.

Kosheen made the mistake of looking in Reaver's general direction, and the bastard was staring at her, scowling at Kosheen for her blasphemy. Kosheen had seen Reaver give his various victims many different looks over the last thirteen months, from malicious, mischievous joy to intense hatred, but she had never seen a look quite as unnerving as the one that Reaver was giving her right now. Something was changing in the dynamic of their relationship, and that was probably by Reaver's design.

Rosario looked around at the group, and clearly he could feel that the resistance to his command could become a problem. He tentatively tried to stand under his own strength. Rosario thanked McMorrow for propping him up, complimented McMorrow on his well maintained beard, then attempted to stand up as straight as he could. To Kosheen's eyes Rosario looked as if he were constipated.

'When was the last time you had any communication from home?' Rosario asked the group. 'I bet it's intermittent these days, right? If at all? When was your last supply drop? Or are you fending for yourselves? Is destroying these little encampments for supplies worth it, or was this all just for *shits-and-giggles?*'

'It's been pretty intermittent...' Darius muttered.

'The lack of communication is an error,' said Reaver. '*We* don't just get brushed aside like the League's heathen hoards.'

'Indeed,' Rosario said, then let out a little laugh. 'Well, I can still call for supply drops, airlifts, airstrikes... Anything you need.'

'Really?' Reaver asked.

Rosario hobbled around the group, slowly regaining his strength.

'So,' Rosario stared at the A stencilled on Kosheen's armoured vest. 'You're the Augmented Fourth...'

He looked as if he were realising that he was potentially out of his depth. But, for all his bravura, it was clear that his ego wouldn't let him back out now.

'You guys are...' Rosario began, no doubt thinking of all the stories that floated around this continent about them.

'Infamous?' Kosheen asked.

'Legendary,' Reaver added with pride.

The way that Rosario looked at Kosheen suggested that he thought her answer had been more appropriate. Kosheen grinned.

'I, *errr...*' Rosario struggled to find words.

'Well,' said Kosheen. 'You're only human.'

'What?' Rosario asked. 'Look, anyway.... You need to finish up here, then we need to go check out this nearby target. I assume you saw the notification, the request to check out a potential threat on the top floor of a riser.'

'We saw it,' Oshii finally piped up. 'Looks like a trap.'

'Could be a trap,' Rosario conceded, though he sounded as if he were only humouring her. 'Could be a large amount of League soldiers.'

Rosario returned to his frayme, grabbing it by one of its petrified, inactive arms to steady himself, then disengaged the rail rifle that had been locked into the machine's arm. He checked it over, lifting up the top like an office stapler to check the magnetic rail. Then he took some extra mags from his frayme's auto loading mechanism.

'Finish up here,' Rosario ordered, stern, slinging the rail rifle over his shoulder. 'Five minutes. I'll be waiting outside.'

Kosheen unsheathed her new progressive blade, wiping the smears of her own blood off it on the back of her jacket, turning it around so that the blade itself was hidden behind her forearm, then advanced on Rosario. She wanted nothing from this potential usurper, she wanted him gone.

But Oshii herself grabbed Kosheen's hand, took the blade

from it and slid it back into her pet zealot's own holster.

(*"No,"*) Oshii said, over a private com-link channel, so that Rosario wouldn't hear. (*"He has been anointed, chosen by the powers that be. It is not for us to judge. But if somehow he is not worthy, if he fails, then he will be hung by his own incompetence. That's how it's always been."*)

Kosheen stared deep into Oshii's eyes and was, as always, overwhelmed by the corporal's *iron-clad aura*. Oshii was right - of course she was, she *always* was - but this seemed like a waste of time on a deadly detour. The next few hours would be interesting, at least.

'I guess we're not getting Chinese then?' Kosheen asked.

'What do you think?' McMorrow asked, rolling his eyes.

'I think I want beef chow mien,' Kosheen replied.

She looked around at all the bodies. All of them. Something didn't feel right. Somehow, nothing felt right anymore.

They finished up, and headed out into the dusk...

CROSSFIRE
HURRICANE.

Darkness, nothing, emptiness. A complete absence of...
Its time...
'*Huh?*' Grunted a groggy young woman, roused from the deepest, darkest, emptiest slumber by a mysterious, powerful voice that somehow managed to fill a never-ending void. Foreboding as it may be, she was not lucid enough to appreciate its gravitas and failed to tremble, repent or anything that may be deemed appropriate.

It was so dark and silent that for the longest time she hadn't even realised that she *had* woken up. Everything was so empty, including her mind, that she wondered if the universe had ended. It was a kind of limbo, a perfect *Nothing* which, somehow, shuddered.

This shudder became a quake in the foundations of infinity, as the void suddenly filled with a hundred million stars followed by a hundred million more. Each pinprick of white burned as bright as a billion nuclear explosions, flickering and pulsing. There were as many stars being born and dying as there were neurons and neural pathways in the human brain.

With a sudden, unexpected stutter it all went into reverse, and the stars started compressing back together until every single one of them formed the sharpest point on the dot at the bottom of a single high-resolution question mark at the end of a sentence presented in a boring font, white words upon a black background.

This certainly confused the young woman observing all of this, because she was still trying to get her head around the fact that the stars were not really stars at all, the concussion-addled brain of the observer was fabricating a *universe of fusion* from a handful of pixels.

WHO ARE YOU? That was the question presented to her, all in capitals.

'Well, that's a stupid question,' the observer thought aloud, her cracked voice stumbling over the the first sounds her dehydrated throat had formed for a long while. She supposed she had better answer. *'I'm... I'm...'*

The question vanished, replaced by three dots that appeared next to each other, blinking in turn, over and over, as they waited for the response.

'Well, I'm...' She really needed a drink.

HYDRATION IS NOT A REQUIREMENT OF COOPERATION.

'How did...?'

THIS SYSTEM REQUIRES VERIFICATION OF MENTAL STABILITY TO ANALYSE PROGRESS... PROCESS INTERRUPTED. STATUS UNKNOWN. COMPLETION PERCENTAGE UNKNOWN.

'You're in my head right now, so you're a diagnostic system. Am I in an infirmary?'

WHO ARE YOU?

'In an existential sense, or...?'

IDENTIFY YOURSELF.

'My name...'

This shouldn't have been a hard question. *Was this concussion? From what?* She briefly remembered the feeling of being in a vehicle as it tumbled over and *over, people yelling...*

'Nico?' She asked, unsure, as a name floated up from the murky depths at the back of her mind. 'I'm Nico..'

She hesitated for too long.

'Shikari?'

CONFIRMED.

'What kind of name is that?'

PHYSICAL TEST: COMPLETE. RESULT: ACCEPTABLE..

'I passed a test? I've never so much pride,' she didn't sound like she was proud of herself. Her real feelings were exemplified by her following remark. 'I need a drink.'

NEUROLOGICAL TESTS: COMPLETE. RESULT: ADEQUATE

'*Adequate?*' She asked. '*Adequate*? Ex- *fucking* -scuse me? I'm not okay with that diagnosis. Can I speak to a registered, corporeal, human doctor, please? *Hello?* Which hospital am I in?'

Systems activated and the Minds Eye Operating System flooded her consciousness, layers of data filled her visual cortex, but it was all just a muddle to her aching mind.

'I can't read all that, I've just witnessed the birth of the universe. My mind's been blown. Or maybe it was just my miss-firing synapses over analysing some punctuation, either way... Where even am I?'

ALCYONE - CONTACT CITY. THE WASTELANDS.

SEPTEMBER TWENTY THIRD.

TWENTY-ONE NINETY-SEVEN.

EIGHTEEN THIRTY-ONE HOURS.

'Could you be more be a little more precise?' She rolled her eyes.

ONE HUNDREDTH YEAR OF THE CENTENARY WAR.

'Centenary War? When did they start calling it that? I guess the good people in marketing have something to sell .'

The words faded and images appeared in their place, a mosaic constructed from live video feeds that were being layered one on top of another until they eventually coalesced into a single clear image, relayed directly to her mind from a set of cameras matching the movements of her eyes with pinpoint precision.

'So, I'm *not* in any infirmary,' she realised, deflated. 'And you are just my armour's diagnostics, and I'm... Where? The middle of nowhere? The wastelands, you say. Well, *shit.*'

It dawned on her that her body was tightly packed into the cushioned interior of a suit of powered armour. Systems were rebooting and recalibrating as her Minds Eye operating system showed her a visual representation of her armour, highlighting any damage.

She yawned and stretched what muscles she could, and the armour moved with her, a thousand tiny servos matching every minuscule muscular movement. Rows of valves opened down the armour's spine as the system test-fired the pressure exchange system.

The armour relayed physical feedback to her, allowing her to actually feel that a great weight was pinning her down. She tried not to panic. With the help of her powered armour she was able to shimmy herself from under the shifting mass. A limp, lifeless human arm fell into her field of view, and she froze for a second in surprise, but the pale, rigid fingers did not move.

She pulled herself free, looked around the mass and realised that it was a pile of, perhaps, ten or eleven different bodies, some still suited and booted in powered armour, many stripped of parts, some bodies just dumped there, exposed and rotting.

She picked up a discarded helmet and looked it over. It was the triclops variant of armour worn by the Unified American Military, so-called because of its three camera eyes, only each one of them were missing from this one, deep scrapes around the sockets hinted that they had been prized out. The respirator beneath them had also been roughly excised. Scavengers had been here looking for parts for profit, and they would probably return.

She had been conscious for literally five minutes and thirty-seven seconds and already she realised she needed to fortify her position against enemies unknown.

'That must have been a hell of a party,' she coughed out the words, realising she needed water.

One by one, her Minds Eye system placed a marker above each body, identifying the deceased, and one by one her heart sank a little lower, hope diminishing through systematic labelling.

The green hue of the camera's night-vision filter revealed that she was inside some sort of military vehicle, its features and furniture mostly bolted down. There were more signs that someone or something had been in here and removed things of value. Something must have spooked them because they had left the job unfinished.

Nico Shikari decided to check her weapons, which turned out to be an easy job because she didn't have any. She checked the compartments on her armour, empty. She had to arm herself and fast.

'Hydration is not a prerequisite of... yadda yadda...' She mocked the voice in her head as her dehydration clawed at her throat for attention. 'Know-it-all AI bullshit.'

There was a water dispenser set into one of the walls, which she hoped was in good working order. She took a metal canister from where it was locked into her hip, unscrewed the top and connected it to the dispenser. Once activated she could only watch with unlimited disappointment as the H20 trickled into the bottle. Not what she had wanted or expected, but at least there was something happening. She rested her aching head against the wall as she watched the container's water level slowly rise - *drip, drip, drip* - trying not to close her eyes, and drifted in and out of memories of her journey here. She had no idea how long this was taking, could have been minutes, could have been hours. Once the canister was reasonably full, she tightened the lid back on and reconnected it to her suit, rotating it until the proprietary connection on the bottom of it lined up with the pipe inside of her armour with a satisfying click. She sipped at it through the plastic straw that ran all the way up her suit from her hip to her mouth, via a small pump and filter that would be worth a lot to a scavenger, and tried to convince herself that she felt better already.

She pulled at the sliding door on the vehicle's side, but it would not budge an inch. She checked the seals, found that the locking mechanism had fused shut in some sort of electrical fire. Or perhaps, she wondered, someone had welded the door shut to keep something out. Or something *in*. She immediately wished that she had not had that thought.

'It's going to be one of those days, isn't it?' She groaned. She foolishly, groggily, expected the diagnostic system to answer her, but that had clearly served its purpose and shut down.

A ladder was set into the back wall of the vehicle between an air-processing unit and an open refrigerator, empty except for a single broken bottle. She climbed the ladder one rung at a time, which most people agree is the best way to climb ladders, finding that the hatch at the top was ajar and the lock broken and bent out of shape, impossible to close fully. She threw her back into it, pushing it open all the way.

She disengaged the locks on her helmet, the components sliding apart to release its grip on her head. As she removed it, real unfiltered oxygen hit her hard, so intoxicating that it made her head spin and she had to grab at the hatch to stop herself falling back in. She stopped and took a few more deep breaths and attempted to centre herself. In three seconds - hold four seconds - out five seconds – repeat.

She pulled herself up and out and was immediately overwhelmed. The sky was a broken kaleidoscope, the clouds a cacophony of colours, some she couldn't even identify, lit from within by explosions. The separating spectrum almost seemed to move around the black shapes that darted through them like paint in water. Her eyes focused, revealing the wastelands around the ship and, above this, the appeared to be igniting the chemical-tainted clouds, creating layers of reds, oranges and yellows. The air was scored by arcing munitions, detonations blooming and lingering on as ghostly afterimages.

Structures shook, coughing out fountains of smoke and burning dust which the small aircraft pulled into spikes and spirals as they darted through them. These were aero-mechs, and the gravity-generators nestled deep inside their bellies allowed them to perform amazing acrobatics. They launched missiles from arrays nestled beneath their stubby little wings that left parallel lines of scorched propellant that fixed the horizon.

Nico felt like a child watching fireworks as she spun around to absorb the spectacle, her heart beating faster with every explosion. She saw huge tank-like amps of competing nationalities striding across rubble or climbing risers like spiders, firing ballistics that rumbled like thunder and flashed like lightning. Some would occasionally pull back their heads and let out a thunderous cacophony of roars, fierce battle cries - warnings to all of those who dared set foot upon their battlefield.

'Looks like there really is a party,' she said to herself, gutted that she was missing it. She was trained for battle from birth, as was every conscript, it flowed through her blood. It was – she believed - inscribed in every patriotic soldier's DNA.

She could not tell if her side, the Unified American Military, was winning against the League of Nations, she didn't know whether to holler or howl. She would charge into battle, but it might take an hour or two to reach the fray.

'So, where are we, Private Second-Class Nico Shikari?' She asked herself. 'Time to investigate my personal predicament, I guess.'

The crashed vehicle was partially dug into the ground by the banks of a babbling river. The detached tail fin was standing upright out of the water a few metres away from the rest of the ship. There was a marker sprayed on the ship, next to the hatch, a tribe of scavenging Strays had staked their claim on the vessel, and this was a warning to the other tribes to stay away.

She felt the weight of the triclops helmet in her hands as she turned it over. The helmet was still connected to her brain wirelessly through the mental link, so she switched back to its trio of eyes and used them to check out her own face, to see if there had been any damage when this ship crashed.

'Well, there I am...'

She hardly recognised the green eyed girl staring vacantly through thick rimmed glasses. She somehow hadn't even realised she had been wearing the spectacles, which surprised and concerned her, though this could probably be explained away due to their light weight. She focused on a single, lonely drop of rain from those chemical-infused clouds running down her glasses, its route diverted by a hairline crack in the lens.

'How long was I out?' She wondered aloud, but not too loud. She watched her lips move through the helmet's eyes which was incredibly creepy and unnatural. The breeze teased her short red hair.

As she inspected her mush, re-familiarising herself with herself, she saw no ethnic or familial heritage in her appearance, no shade of shadow of a family tree. Spending a good chunk of your short existence on the battlefield meant that monogamous relationships were rare, to some they were a vague outdated concept that they saw in movies or read about in books. Battlefield hookups were driven almost exclusively by basic animalistic urges, and the dutiful need to procreate and replenish the ranks, keeping the army in a fresh supply of new soldiers. The military crèches were where they were prepped for training from the moment they could walk. No child knew their parents, not at Nico's level of society.

She cut the optical connection, her eyelids fluttering as her real eyes took over. Then she accidentally dropped the helmet down by her feet due to a severe case of *morning-fingers,* cursing as it clanged and bounced along the hull.

'*Somebody must be coming. Must be...*' Nico said to herself as she took her glasses off. She felt very tense indeed as she kneaded her forehead with her knuckles, then massaged her closed eyes with her fingers.

She pushed her glasses back up the bridge of her nose in time to see two nearby risers shake with the sound of persistent destruction as two rival aero-mechs tussled between them.

Both unbound by gravity due to the oscillating gravity orbs

cradled beneath them, between cockpit and tail, the aero-mechs flew sideways between the risers, facing each other, unleashing a sustained onslaught at each other but hitting the adjacent buildings more than they hit each other, scattering shattering glass and spent bullet casings.

But then one of the aero-mechs was victorious, scoring a critical hit that sent its opponent spiralling down into the ground where it bounced and rolled, until it finally came to a stop not far from Nico's ship, burying its nose deep in the dirt. Nico quickly realised that it was definitely not one of the UAM's Bullet-Witch aero-mechs, it was instead an enemy fighter, a League of Nations' Rabid-Banshee.

With a sudden hiss the cockpit blew open and the seat dislodged a little, an attempted emergency ejection, moments too late. It amused Nico to see that the Leagues' equipment was as old and unreliable as the UAM's own. The subsequent miss-timed deployment of the pilot's parachute seemed to rouse him from his shock, and as the rectangle of nylon drifted down behind him the pilot grabbed his pistol and opened fire at Nico.

But for the pilot the world must still be spinning, as it had during the crash, and his targeting was messy. Nico threw herself off the top of the ship and sprinted along the ground as bullets whipped past her head or buried themselves in the ground around her feet. The pilot's pistol emptied with a succession of impotent clicks. Nico bounced up into the cockpit, pushed the pistol aside and threw her armoured fist at the pilot's face.

But her knuckles didn't reach the pilot's face, her entire attack brought to a holt by a sudden blow to the crown of Nico's own head. She tried to pull away, but it became clear that the cockpits canopy had crashed down upon her, leaving her to forever wonder whether the pilot had managed to grab the canopy and pull it down somehow or he had control of a mechanism. She yelped in pain, cursing. Perhaps she wasn't yet firing on all cylinders, maybe she'd missed a moment. She felt the weight of the frame upon her, pushing at it, too distracted to notice as the adversary pistol whipped the side of her head.

As the world span around her crunched cranium, she wound her fingers back into ball-busting business mode and struck back at the pilot. Her target, foolishly, instinctively tried to catch it and broke every bone in his hand and wrist as the gauntlet hit it like a wrecking ball. His body spasmed, causing him to inadvertently fire the gun he held in his other hand, ricocheting off the armour over Nico's shoulder, lighting up the air by her head. Flashing up her eyes, the sound almost deafened her.

She screamed as a primal rage rattled through her. She grabbed the gun by the barrel with one hand and pulled it away, the pilot refusing to let go even as she hit him over and over again.

But then she was shocked to find that it took a frightening amount of will to stop. She had turned his face into raw, bloodied steak. Forcing her fist open took just as much effort, and it was shaking, crimson running down the gauntlet. She was shocked by her own aggression, having no idea where that had come from.

Her hand ached, not from the punches but from the tension that had locked it. The knuckles were bone white beneath the blood.

The man's eyes seemed to linger like headlights in her mind. Why? The emotion there, it seemed almost... But what he was and he felt didn't matter. He wasn't like her and her people. *All the same... Less than... No more than... Only a...*

Hmmm, she grunted, as she turned her fist over and watched the crimson trails spreading down and around and following the creases in the skin.

'Sorry about that,' she said to the bloody mass that had recently been a face, and as she said it she was surprised to find that she really meant it.

But what was causing her to think this way, to re-evaluate her prescribed perception of *others*...?

'No, no, no... Can't think like that...' she told herself. *They wouldn't show us any mercy... not at all... because they are all... everyone one of... every one...*

She shook the hand, attempting to disperse more of the tension. The anger slithered back deep down inside her mind, where it found somewhere dark and dank to hide, but the monstrousness of the act - that she had almost committed - lingered like the copper taste of blood in the back of the throat.

She took the pilot's pistol from his lifeless hand and, after some rummaging around, found that he had only one spare clip of ammunition. She saw that part of his roll-cage had come loose and attempted to embed itself in his abdomen, and a closer examination revealed that this safety feature had been held together by several layers of duct tape, now ripped and frayed.

Slowly, carefully, she pulled the empty clip out of the pistol's grip then she placed the spare one in. There must be a good fifteen bullets in there, if she could get it working; there was a biometric identity scanner built into the grip that would allow the gun to be used if just one of its many security checks was passed, and that included fingerprints, pulse, voice, biometrics, body language...

She took the pilot's progressive blade and activated it. There was a hum from the blade itself, a resonance that no normal human should be able to perceive, but somehow, she could. As it vibrated at a microscopic level it would cut through almost anything.

She tried to prise open the guns handle, where a PCB would be squished next to the ammo clip, holding the microprocessor and data shard that controlled the security checks and held a database of all the active UAM or, in this case, active League soldiers' meta data. This would, in a millisecond, cross-reference the wielder with millions of potential users and instantly authorise the use of the weapon. This list would be updated every time they passed within the range of a satellite or any wireless data point, even sharing and updating lists between other geopolitically affiliated weapons met in the wild. They would, essentially, talk to each other, spreading the information like an airborne disease.

But her finger slipped, the knife veering catastrophically off course and decimating the security device, sparking a succession of misfires, over and over again until the weapon was empty. Every single bullet embedding itself in the League pilot or the seat he was sat in.

As a final *kick-in-the-ovaries*, distracted by the emptying clip, Nico failed to notice that the progressive blade was still gliding through the gun like a hot knife through butter, striking the final bullet. The bullet popped like corn and the vibrating blade shattered.

She leapt up off her butt and onto her heels, holding but of the weapons at arm's length, gritting her teeth. In one hand she held an empty, broken gun and in the other she held a handle and hilt with no blade.

She stared in shocked, shamed silence for a few seconds.

She slumped down onto the aero-mech's nose cone and stared back at the ship that she had woken up in, that could have potentially been her tomb, but now was the only shelter that she had available. She could have run, someone would return for their salvage. But she wondered then how anyone would find her if she didn't stay static. This would be her fortress, then. Stencilled on the side of the jump ship was its name, the *Nilin Remix*.

'Pleased to meet you, *old-girl*. I guess its just you and me for the time being,' she whispered to her temporary abode whilst she longed for the land she called home.

MEMORY GOSPEL

Dyce Bastion – formerly of the League of Nations; formerly deceased - sat within the branches of a tree into which he had been deposited by a high, wet drop. This painful landing had been the punctuation mark at the end of a long, violent and frightening chase through an underground service tunnel. The ones doing the chasing had been the tunnel-dwelling cannibalistic locals, threatening to tenderise and eviscerate Dyce, until he had reached the tunnel's abrupt end, an opening as jagged as the cliff-face from which it protruded. Given no choice, he had leapt out and had been taken by the force of a waterfall, caught by the tree.

Dyce rubbed the damp air from his face and felt refreshed by it. He also picked the leaves and twigs out of the open wounds on his cheeks, glued in place by blood. He looked up at the cliff face and the broken-open service tunnel that protruded from it – from which he fell, from which the water was falling – to gauge the distance of his drop. He was, as always, lucky to be alive.

In that rock face he could see the building blocks of the entire manmade continent of Alcyone on full display, its history mapped out on the face of that rock. The recycled materials were diverse - brilliant white coral; various alien ore mined from meteorites and asteroids; the frames of old vessels both vast and small. It was all cemented together by compacted sand dredged from the deep. The rock face had been created by whatever catastrophe had flattened a massive chunk of the city, forming the wasteland.

'Well, at least I finally got a moment to myself,' he said. He had needed some time to gather himself, to recuperate, after escaping the Augmented Fourth, an angry amp, the Red Strays...

And *her*...

Worst of all, *her*...

'Don't do that to yourself, don't allow her the pleasure of getting into your head...'

The waterfall was feeding a river that glistened with the light of the twin moons, looking like a winding ribbon of silver that ran into the wasteland. During the time he had spent in the tree he had watched a gravity weapon lift a Goliath into the sky, high above the wastelands, then drop the humongous war-machine amidst an earth-battering bombardment. Rubble had been shaken from the cliff face and debris had tumbled from the risers that sat high up on the cliff edge. For a terrifying moment he had feared that there would be an avalanche of abandoned architecture that would have buried him forever.

'*That's what* she *does...*'

The wasteland was currently shrouded by the thick, brown cloud of dust which still lingered from the Goliath's destruction. He could see glimpses of the chaos taking place behind that ethereal shroud, flashes of gunfire and explosions which illuminated fleeing figures and malfunctioning machines.

'Why can I remember *her*, but...' But then he sighed and realised that, despite the awe-inspiring view in front of him, all he could think about was Corporal Paris Oshii, the spectre from his past. She had a new band of zealots to swoon over her, since the last time he had met her, the Augmented Fourth.

The central web of districts that made up the hub of Contact City were still some way down the river, on the opposite side of the wasteland, but he could still make out the pattern made by the bridges that connected the risers. There were forests growing in the abandoned city, some even sprouting out of the risers themselves, a mixture of terrestrial and non-terrestrial nature. From here Dyce could not see as far as the capital, Absolution City, but he could see its centrepiece, a huge tower called the Complex Shard, a glass needle at the country's heart. It was the continent's mind, it's spine.

Above the Complex Shard were the two moons, Lunar and Terminus, lighting the sky. Terminus moon, where he had been trained - he was starting to remember a vertical slice of that time, now. Where he had met all the people he had ever known. Where he had met Breaker...

Ignorance might have been bliss, after all, because rebuilding the memories of all that he had lost was its own special torture.

His tabris beeped, the sound muffled. He had made a conscious decision to disconnect his mind from the network, he hadn't wanted to dwell on the things that it was processing.

He unlocked the compartment that housed and charged the small device, taking it out delicately. Scrolling text on the small LED readout informed him that the memory defragmentation program had completed its final cycle. It was ready to be viewed, to be re-experienced.

He swore and seethed. *Now? Really?* The timing was impeccable, just as he was lamenting the sense of loss triggered by the *natural* recovery of a simple shard of his old life in came a bigger chunk, as if he were being mocked by the universe. A big missing chunk of his memory was now there, inside the tabris. The events that led him from those moons to the battlefield where he died, then to the top floor of that riser where he had been reborn.

That riser was also where he met Oshii and her men, of course. *How can she be here?* The universe must have a strange sense of humour, bringing Oshii back *into* his life after bringing *him* back to life. This could have been a fresh start for him, but apparently that wasn't to be.

He wirelessly synched the tabris to the interface devices implanted in his head. The Minds Eye system booted with a crackle of mental feedback that rather upset his psychological constitution for a moment, before everything settled down. The system augmented his view of reality by overlaying his scenic view with fast-scrolling reams of developer credits, preceding the most *important* detail of all, the developer's trademarked logo, so large that it appeared to eclipse the cliff and even the risers standing upon it.

Deep breath in, which turned to a shudder on the way back out. He started the memory. It began as a flat image, before becoming more tangible – becoming, as far as his senses were concerned, *real* - so fast that it was overpowering. He felt as if his consciousness had capsized and been doused within perfect recall, as if living it again...

Dyce was inside of a drop ship, surrounded by his military unit, each one of them wearing drop suits over their armour, locked into deployment bays...

Two seconds in to reliving the memory, he killed the connection. Being back there, knowing that he was about to witness everything that he had lost, it hurt harder than any explosion. He sat there, amongst the branches of the tree, shaking his head.

'*I can't, I can't...*' He said to himself. 'But... No come on, *boy*, come on... You gotta... No guts, no glory...'

It was time.

'It's not time,' he shook his head and put the tabris down next to him. 'Nope.'

He looked up at the horizon, and found himself staring into it, his mind making recognisable shapes out of the drifting, billowing dust clouds like an animated Rorschach test, but he saw nothing good in those shifting shapes.

He wanted to throw the tabris into the water, to break it on the rocks at the base of the water fall and never see its broken parts again.

'Torturing myself,' he muttered. 'There are plenty of people who want to do that for me. Apparently. *I guess I need to know why.* Come on, Dyce. No guts, no glory.'

He activated playback once again, and his consciousness was saturated by the terrible tsunami of reconstituted recollection.

I remember...

He remembered...

Twenty six hours and fifteen minutes ago.

The stifling feeling of the full body, powered armour in which he was encased, readouts reflecting off the visor, the blurred, out of focus figures around him, the shake of the ship, the Skinny Puppy, a League of Nations drop ship dispatched by the Pulse of the Machine, a solar ship in deep orbit above Alcyone. Inside the ship there were at least forty soldiers locked into hydraulic bays, lined up in parallel to each other along the inner walls. They were each wearing disposable orbital drop suits attached to the powered armour that they would be fighting in.

'He's a slave to his bowels,' said a twenty-something, her accent was a watered-down Welsh.

Laser etched into this soldier's identification plate was the name Macalister Breaker – Dyce's friend, his role model, his hero, *his...*

My...

No...

No, I have to get through this, I have to witness this memory...

Her Identification plate read Macalister Breaker, and a long string of numbers beneath a barcode and a laser etched representation of the League of Nations insignia.

'I'm not, I'm fine,' Dyce Bastion said, snapping back. He didn't like being the centre of attention, especially not when he was this nervous, mere moments before his first real drop into his first real battlefield insertion. Banter wasn't exactly a second language to him.

'Is it nerves?' Asked the twenty-something man locked into the next drop-cage beside Dyce, a man improbably named

Cuxwill.

'I'm fine,' Dyce repeated. He was younger than his two friends, chronologically circling the farthest edge of seventeen.

'Bastion, mate, I would not want to be you right now, locked up in your drop-suit,' Cuxwill said. 'Marinating in your own farts.'

'*Fucksake*,' Dyce muttered.

'Loosen up, *mucker*, you'll linger longer.' Cuxwill gave Dyce a wink.

'Okay,' said their commanding officer, sergeant Solomon. He was locked into a seat next to the hatch that led to the cockpit. 'Run one last check on your seals and air supply, we're about to clear the oxygen out of this chamber.'

This is it... Dyce thought. He didn't like his chances.

Dyce should have known that he was not alone in his mortal malaise, but he felt truly that he was, completely self-absorbed in this moment, collectively processing the slow march toward the inevitable. With the air slowly vanishing from the chamber, their only conversations were com-link transmissions.

("Bastion, do you want Cuxwill to hold your hand?") Breaker joked.

Choosing not to answer, Dyce snapped the metal blast-shield shut over his air-tight visor, mostly featureless except for the four beady camera eyes at each corner of the helmet. His existential dread was making him irritable.

("Bastion,") the Captain's voice came through the com-link. *("You're shadowing Cuxwill. This is your first live battlefield insertion and Cuxwill has higher test scores than you, so he'll be holding your hand.")*

("Shit,") Dyce thought.

("I heard that, soldier; the com-link IS on.")

Dude may have believed that he had kept his expletive to himself, but the problem with *thought* was that the com-link could easily turn it into a *transmission*. He wanted to ask if he could shadow Breaker instead but kept his sub-vocalisations to himself.

'Bollocks,' Bastion said aloud, to nothing but his helmet. 'Big fat sweaty hairy man bollocks to thee and thine.'

He then glanced sheepishly at the captain to see if the man had somehow heard those words, if somehow he had failed to block the com-link. The captain was staring intensely back at him, or at least he appeared to be. The helmet made it hard to tell. The silence was becoming unbearable, and Dyce realised that he had to answer.

("Yes, sir, I will shadow Cuxwill, no problem. Sir.")

("Good man,") the sergeant said.

Sergeant Solomon began a speech, designed to rouse his team, but Dyce zoned out, staring into the subtle, ghostly reflection of his own eyes within his own visor, wide and scared. He could hear his own breathing, loud and laboured.

The captain finished his sermonising and the group returned to their private conversations. Dyce surveyed the room. All around, people were reacting to their pseudo-psychic conversations, but not actually moving their lips – though force of habit occasionally made a few of them mime random words or bob their heads in time with the rhythm of their internal dialogue.

("Talking of hand holding, Bastion,") Cuxwill said to Dyce. *("Did you ask out the girl from Supplies?")*

("I... No...") Dyce didn't want to talk about it. *("Maybe...")*

("And...?") Cuxwill seemed eager to know.

("Doesn't matter.")

("Come on, dickhead.") Cuxwill sounded a little whiney as he insisted.

("She told me she had better things to do") Dyce said, sheepishly. He was, he had to admit, very woolly generally.

("Better cock to do,") Cuxwill said. *("I think that's what she meant.")*

("Cuxwill, for fuck-sake,") Breaker reprimanded her square jawed associate. *("Have some respect, you colossal cock-womble.")*

("Breaker!") Cuxwill was surprised to hear her voice. *("I didn't realise you were connected to our private line!?")*

("Cuxwill,") Breaker said, despairing. *("Your last conquest said you were hung like a scientist with the brain of a donkey.")*

("That's smart people racist,") Cuxwill complained. *("Though, I suppose some of them must have small...")*

("Fucksake...") Breaker lamented her association with this muppet. *("So, I guess it must be true, Cuxwill.")*

("What's that?")

("I hear your two imaginary friends will only speak to each other now. No one wants to listen to your fluff.")

("Hey Breaker, what are you doing tomorrow night?") Cuxwill asked her, playfully.

("I'll be helping you to locate the last charred remnants of your battered ego, after I turn you down,") Breaker replied. *("Again.")*

("Harsh,") Cuxwill's tone suggested that he was taking this as flirtation.

Dyce grinned harder than he expected to on a day like this, even if he was trying to figure out if his two friends were indeed flirting. He enjoyed listening to them *chatting-shit*, as they called it, even if his own *self-esteem-tank* was too empty to allow him to participate.

("Dyce, do you think Cuxwill was actually just asking me out?") Breaker asked on a private line between herself and Dyce.

("At this point, does it matter?") Dyce's grin tightened into a grimace.

("Bastion, relax,") Cuxwill said, placing a hand on Bastion's shoulder. *("No point in getting wound up. If anything goes wrong, there's a strong chance you'd be dead before you even realised.")*

("Thanks,") Dyce replied, sarcastically. *("That was so inspiring that I almost unclenched.")*

("That's the spirit! It's all about perspective, mate, how you see the world, how you filter it. If you change the way you look at things, the things you look at will change.")

("Huh...") Dyce said, genuinely mulling that over.

("See, I'm smarter than you'd think. Up HERE for thinking,")

Cuxwill tapped his head before pointing down at the lower end of his body. *("Down THERE for dancing.")*

Dyce rolled his eyes.

("Up here for drinking, down there for tinkling.") Breaker added.

("That was poetry") Cuxwill chuckled.

("Cuxwill, you're just a wannabe playa,*")* accused Breaker.

("Excuse me?") Cuxwill placed a hand to his chest as he gasped. *("I'll have you know that I'm a red-hot stud.")*

("He has a high score,') Dyce added.

("Only because he lowered his standards.")

("Lowering my standards was the only way to include you,') Cuxwill fired back. *('I got a lot of love to give!")*

("You wanna pace yourself, Cuxwill,") Dyce added. *("You only get a bucket and a half.")*

Before anyone could process Dyce's advice, sergeant Solomon gave them the bad news in the most inspiring tone that he could muster.

("It's time,") the commanding officer said. *("We're opening the drop door now.")*

A series of clanks rang through the floor beneath them, the sound snaking through the multiple locks, hinges and hydraulics within it. Flashes of amber chased each other down a parallel set of LED strip-lights down the walkway between them, which was actually one long hatch masquerading as solid, safe flooring. Between those lit lines, the remaining air was vacuumed out of the ship and into the blackness of space, a visible hiss that drew a cascading line of vapour all the way down the length of the floor. Then it opened down and out, the door's edges glowing red hot as they faced the Earth's atmosphere.

Dyce scrunched his eyes up in pure, unfiltered terror, his feet now dangling over that open door beneath them. The image that lingered behind his eyelids was of Breaker, her face gradually obscured behind her visor, as that heatproof glass reflected the brilliance of Earth's vast kaleidoscopic cloudscapes, shimmering turquoise oceans and distant shores of grey and green.

The drop-cages released them...

Gravity took them...

They fell...

We fell...

I fell...

PROGRAM PAUSED

Back to the *here* and the *now*, back out of the recovered memory, back to the real world. It was a shock to come back, the replay had been so convincing. He had been able to feel, taste and smell the inside of his old armour as if it were really happening all over again. It took a moment to get his bearings back, but he was still sat amongst the branches of the tree.

He tried to ground himself in what was real right now. A moist mist drifted up from the base of the waterfall, the leaves of the tree were glistening with damp. He took a deep breath of real air and, infinitely preferable to the filtered air of the drop suit in his memory. There was a slight breeze against his face, he closed his eyes and allowed himself to experience it in a way that he never had before.

'Breaker...' Those two syllables tinged with regret and longing. He tapped one corner of the tabris against a branch, then against his forehead, trying to knock the emotions out of his head, like salt from a shaker.

'*Come on, Dyce,*' he said to himself with a sigh.

The last frozen moment of the memory hung in front of him, the Minds Eye Operating System had turned what he had been experiencing into a two-dimensional image that appeared to be floating in the air, exactly the way memories don't. The words PROGRAM PAUSED flashing across it.

'Okay,' he said to himself, with absolutely no enthusiasm at all. 'Let's do this thing.'

He reactivated the program and that flat, frozen image

started to develop some depth; the Earth beneath him, the other falling soldiers ahead of him. It became more and more potent as *the past* wrapped around him, until he was again experiencing the sights, sounds, smells and physical sensations.

He had just been released from the drop cage and gravity had pulled him from the drop ship...

He found himself tumbling away from the Skinny Puppy, a drop ship that had itself come from The Pulse of the Machine, a League of Nations solar frigate stationed in deep orbit. Within his battered and used drop-suit, various complex systems kicked into life, systems too complex to be understood by these purposefully under-educated *cannon fodder.*

("Bastion, did you sleep last night?") Cuxwill asked over the com-link.

("A little...")

("More than me, truth be told. It's understandable. Stick with me and we'll live ... tell tHaT ... FrOM supPlies... tO...") then Cuxwill cut the line, leaving Dyce to wander what words of wisdom that brief burst of interference had robbed from him.

("Bastion?") Breaker's voice came to Dyce now. *("How you doing?")*

("I've never been better.")

("Liar,") Breaker's voice was strangely muted. She wasn't her usual self-assured self. *("Look, forget what the CO said, ditch Cuxwill, stick with me, you'll be fine.")*

("Thanks,") Dyce said, gratefully accepting Breaker's concern, convincing himself that it was genuine affection, and placing it, metaphorically, between his heart and the chest-plate's emergency defibrillator.

The Earth seemed to be coming up at them, as the thunder of atmospheric re-entry overwhelmed them. They dropped towards the magnificent cloudscape - the swirls, curves and static waves of the nimbus resembling the troughs and peaks of mountain ranges.

("Did you sleep last night?") It was Cuxwill's turn to private message Breaker. He had failed to block Dyce out of the chat, and Dyce listened closely.

("Jeezus,") Breaker said.

("Is that a yes? Did you sleep alone last night?")

("Cuxwill, go fuck a blender.")

("Harsh.")

("Bye, Cuxwill.")

("...Bye?")

Their armour started to break apart, but this was supposed to happen, an automated purge of the orbital drop suit components attached to the outside of their combat armour. As the components spun away they drew lines of smoke through the scorched air.

Breaker grabbed Dyce and tried to remind him how to breathe. She had been monitoring his vitals and had seen his increased heart rate and inconsistent breathing. He had been on the verge of passing out.

As Dyce stared through their heat resistant visors into Breakers eyes, it was not making it any easier to unwind his crippling tension. Despite this, he somehow managed to get himself to a point where Breaker was satisfied enough to let Dyce go, spinning away a moment before they entered the cloud. The immense pressure within conjured blasts of static that bounced around them, their bodies crackling like Tesla-coils...

Dyce pulled himself back out of the memory again, but this time it was to skip ahead. He knew what happened next, he had dreamt it before he woke alone in that riser - as his body had rebuilt itself; as a mystery voice spoke to him as a decaying amp sat in a lotus position before him. He already knew that they fell through a disintegrating solar destroyer, it all went to shit, Macalister Breaker saved him. The spinning troop carrier broke apart when it became lodged inside the side of a riser, and he fell. *Again...*

What next...?
He hit *play...*

Dyce immediately felt a jolt of concussive pain through his entire body, followed by the weightless sensation of free fall. He had been thrown from an out-of-control troop carrier, which had become embedded between two risers. He tried to catch a glimpse of Breaker upon that disintegrating ship, but all he saw was his own body reflected in the windows of the surrounding risers, tumbling backwards in slow motion. He had a date with the dirt, and he had to do something about that. Before he hit the ground, a blast of compressed high-density gas erupted from his armour to cushion the impact, smothering him in a thick, heavy cloud.

He did not, as a result of the gas, see a UAM bull-amp wander into his drop-zone and certainly did not plan to land upon it. The bull-amp, as dumb as it was, seemed to be vaguely aware that something had hit it, in the same way that an elephant might be aware that a bird had landed on its back. It swung its back-mounted turret around to throw the pest off. It worked, Dyce hit the ground and rolled across it.

The bull-amp lifted a hefty leg to stamp Dyce out, casting a shadow over him. But, luckily for him, a missile launched from a passing aero-mech embedded itself into a joint in the amp's lifted leg and detonated. The machine stumbled; its legs buckled under its displaced weight. The ground shook as it hit.

Dyce lay there on his back, momentarily shell-shocked, staring back up at the sky. But the bull-amp had its revenge upon that aero-mech, unleashing a salvo from its back mounted cannon, causing the airborne pest to lose control and spiral into one of the risers, rolling through it catastrophically.

Far beyond the resulting hale of shattered glass, Dyce saw even more soldiers falling from orbit like shooting stars, breaking the cloud, identified and clarified by his Minds Eye. More meat for the grinder.

'*No...*' He said, emotionally battered by the unjust nature of this futile endeavour. *What is the point?*

Dyce rolled over and pulled himself up to his feet, seconds before a random soldier stumbled into his back, knocking him right back over. The passing soldier glanced back, his eyes burning with a madness that came from having absolutely no idea what was going on but knowing that he was going to die very soon.

Dyce sat where he fell, overwhelmed. His legs refused to move.

Fucking senseless...

A grenade hurtled through the pulsing mass of soldiers, arcing over his head. It was close enough for Dyce's Minds Eye system to capture an image of it and present it to him with abridged information and sterile warnings. The image showed that the grenade had a Kalamari Industries logo down one side.

The grenade indiscriminately struck a fellow League of Nations soldier, dispersing the Kalamari branded nano-spores within, spreading like a virus, through the armour, the skin, bonding to his cells. The chain reaction was rapid and magnificent, the cells themselves expanding, twisting and mutating as the microscopic nano-machines turned them into seeds designed to rapidly take root within the body, where they germinated and bloomed. The victim's body became a bouquet, erupting through the atomically compromised armour. Hitting the floor in an explosion of petals and leaves, each and every one of them the colour of metal, flesh, muscle or blood.

Amongst all of this, through the shower of horrendous horticulture, Dyce spied a figure, stood in the deep shadows of a doorway, framed by the decimated, rotting wooden frame. The figure did not move, holding as still as a statue, wearing a long cloak with a deep hood that hid their face. But still, Dyce felt as if that figure was staring right at him, *through* him, *into* him...

Dyce had to look away, however, as Cuxwill stormed into

view from stage left, the gunmetal-and-flesh coloured petals embedding deep into the treads on his armoured boots with a satisfying crunch. Cuxwill had his rail rifle in one gauntlet, and he offered out the other to help Dyce up.

'You could look happy to see me,' Cuxwill said.

Dyce took the hand and said nothing as he was helped up, and continued to say nothing as Cuxwill lead him through the exploding, screaming chaos and into a riser, climbing in the through a shattered window. They stepped into an open plan office, a dark space filled with overturned desks, broken partitions and filing cabinets whose draws were open. Breaker believed that he was leading them through a shortcut to their rendezvous coordinates. They moved through the building staring down the barrels of their rail rifles, checking every corner and shadow for movement.

'What happened to Breaker?' Cuxwill asked.

'Did your Minds Eye not show you?' Dyce asked, as he checked behind a desk for enemies.

'I was distracted,' Cuxwill said, then seemed to think of a good explanation that served to transfer of blame. 'I was looking for you! You were supposed to be following me!'

'I got hit by a vending machine!'

'During a free fall?'

'It's going to be one of those days.'

The pair of them stepped over ancient booby traps and trip wires that the beady camera eyes marked out instantly. There was a skeleton reclining in an office swivel chair, its head hung back and its jaw wide open, held in place by calcified sinew. Dyce focused upon a water cooler, there was a rat inside, treading water. Living its best life, no doubt.

Cuxwill eliminated an enemy hidden behind a partition-wall by shooting through it, the cheep wood exploding like confetti. They found the fresh kill slumped over their weapon, clinging to it still, like a child holding a soft toy for comfort. They seemed to have been alone, hiding.

They stepped out of the riser and into the middle of a

bullet and blood ballet. The earth was churning, the buildings were breaking. But they were nearly at their rendezvous coordinates, at least.

("I hope you're not leading my boy astray,") Breaker's voice suddenly came in loud and clear over the com-link, not that either of them could see her, and she wasn't sharing her location on the display in their Minds Eye.

("Your boy?") Dyce asked, confused but delighted at the wording.

("Seriously, Cuxwill, don't get Bastion killed by being a complete fuck-nugget.")

("Oh, take your bra off and give your tits a rest!") Cuxwill snapped back.

Breaker was understandably unable to compute Cuxwill's retort. *("...What?")*

("Where are you, Breaker?") Dyce asked, after a short, bemused silence.

Breaker transmitted her location for a moment, and it was down a side alley. Dyce and Cuxwill jogged on, turning a corner to find a good proportion of their team mates congregated here. Breaker turned to them and smiled.

'Well, good of you two recycled spunk-splotches to finally join us!' She said.

'Did the enemy deploy some interference, Cuxwill asked. 'We're barely getting any info from you lot.'

'This whole city is a meat grinder,' Breaker said. 'They knew we were coming.'

The commanding officer stepped up to Cuxwill, barging past Breaker. The majority of their team stood behind him.

'Where were you two gob-shites hiding?' Asked the commanding officer.

'An onslaught of tracer fire complicated my descent,' Cuxwill explained. 'Then I went looking for this *nonce*.'

'Hey!' Dyce snapped.

'Just banter,' Cuxwill winked.

'Just a wanker,' Dyce replied.

'You two dickheads missed your landing zone by a mile...'

'That's an exaggeration...' Cuxwill interjected.

'That was the worst display I've ever seen, and if you don't watch your mouth I'm gonna have you shot!' Their commanding officer was fuming. 'But luckily for you, we are all in the shit, so our imminent deaths have gotten you off the hook.'

'Well, that is a relief,' exclaimed Cuxwill.

'We're going to have to fall back to a nearby building, fortify it, and wait for fresh orders,' said the commanding officer.

Solomon lead the way, and the team followed, cutting through dark alleys and making their way across a street strewn with abandoned vehicles, ducking from one vehicular chunk of cover to the next, making their way towards an abandoned bank building down the street.

They took a narrow alley that lead around the back of the bank building, then burst in through a fire door. One by one they filed into what would have been the staff break room.

'I've gotta use the *little-boys-room*,' Cuxwill joked, as he absently picked up a coffee pot and sneered at the solidified and putrified coffee within.

'You've gotta shut *the-fuck* up,' Breaker said, not in the mood.

But, though they all spread out with the intention of prepping the building, it soon became apparent that they did not have the time. There was an unexpected bang that shook the building, the ceiling cracked and chunks of dry-wall and dust fell. Then another bang, and another... The abandoned break-room's equipment and furniture jumped, the coffee pot smashed. The door to the main lobby fell off its hinges and clattered to the ground.

Mutters of confusion echoed around the room. Dyce, Breaker and Cuxwill looked at each other, found no solace, then looked at their commanding officer. Solomon was staring at the cracks in the ceiling, breathing slow but heavy. He had nothing to say.

Dyce noticed, almost immediately, the way that the dust was

floating up instead of down. Such a subtle thing, perhaps a trick of the light, or a trick of the mind brought on by stress. But it escalated, as bricks and mortar shifted along the ground, skipping. Then the break-room's equipment and furniture became weightless, spinning on their corners, levitating in pirouetting clusters.

The roof was breaking up and crumbling *up*wards, letting in shafts of light, illuminating curtains of dust. Dyce's unit stood around, hopeless. Static crackled through the air around them.

("*Dyce...*") It was Breaker on a private channel.

("What?")

("I got a bad feeling...") Dyce had never heard Breaker sound so scared. ("There's something I should tell you...")

Dyce froze up. What could it possibly be, and why now? For a moment he was almost afraid that she was about to declare her undying affection for him. Which would have been awkward, awesome and, ultimately, heartbreaking in its timing.

("There's something I...") The connection was starting to falter. ("...Not supposed... to...")

An unnatural wailing came through the door that led into the bank's main lobby. Splinter by splinter, the door began disintegrating, drawn back into the room beyond, where an unusual, indescribable absence of *anything* waited for them. Then the wall around the door started to crumble out into that void. Too, and the ceiling above them collapsed *up.* Everything was being pulled up, towards a swirling ball of perfect white that had appeared in the air above the building.

There was an eery silence, as if the entire population of the battlefield had stopped to look, all the sound eliminated from the area. They could hear their own heartbeats, the movement of their internal organs, the grinding of bone on bone as they moved.

Then, one by one, they noticed a single string of light had appeared in the centre of the room. From the ground to the clouds, not much wider than a hair. Pulses of white energy flowing through it, becoming more and more intense with every cascading phase.

They could all feel it, closing in on them. This was the end.

The silence was eventually filled with a whistle that began on a wavelength inaudible to humans, escalating until it was so loud and unbearable that it overwhelmed everything else. Their visors and blast shields began to rattle and hum, some even cracked.

Then came a detonation. The string of light expanded exponentially, engulfing them, becoming a force that shook their atoms and warped their particles.

Those who didn't die immediately, who were not crushed, mashed, blended or flayed by the initial strike, those were the ones who decayed within an agonising dilation of time. Skin tore, bones shattered, organs burst, a cocktail of faecal mass and blood pushed up through every tube and out of every orifice. Brain matter microwaved until the cross-firing of synaptic systems became a delirious charge of random static...

They all died, of course. Every single one of them...

The thing is, not all of them stayed dead...

One of them came back...

Intermission...

Dyce Bastion drifted in and out of consciousness, these waking moments trigged by bursts of pain, endured for seconds, then ended by subsequent assaults of pain, more than anybody could endure. The armour, destroyed by the blast, had torn through his skin and chunks of it remained inside his body, the built-in defibrillator was now embedded in his chest, amongst his broken and mangled ribs. The copper flavour of his own blood filled his mouth, his lungs struggled to take in enough air...

Intermission...

Amid the cacophony of agony, he nearly missed the simple sting of a needle piercing his skin. Of course, he hadn't really noticed it at the time, his attention elsewhere, but now, with the benefit of digitally-assisted recall, it was so clear. The software isolated the sensation for him, identifying it as a suspicious event.

Dyce caught a glimpse of the syringe, being held by thin, robotic fingers. The fingers were fizzing, as if being within the blast radius was affecting their integrity. Dyce recognised this amp, it was wearing the tactical armour that *he* now wore, in the current time...

The meditating amp, as he had come to know it, the burnt out husk that had been sat across from him, when he had been reborn...

Intermission...

Dyce came to consciousness again, and found himself in the eye of a storm, surrounded by a whirlwind of fusion. Swirling, fizzing, popping yellows and reds, as if the particles themselves were expanding, igniting then bursting.

There was a figure stood amongst this chaos, a black silhouette against the glorious light show. The figure was wearing a long hooded cloak, the wind attacking it, until the hood was blown back, revealing a face that existed nowhere in nature, the cold metal of a machine's narrow head. This amp reached up towards the sky with both arms, as if in thanks. But then, as it turned around to face Dyce, a second pair of arms reached out, too, from its waist, pushing the cloak aside.

The Emissary... The name floated through Dyce's head, though he didn't know from where.

The Meditating amp was still there, too, buried beneath a pile of rubble, from which it launched itself – how it had gotten under there, Dyce did not know – and attacked the Emissary. The two amps threw fists at each other, the Emissary grabbing the Meditating amp's limbs, with all four of its own hands, yanking them apart, painfully, splaying them....

Intermission...

Dyce must have blacked out again, but returned to the light just in time to see the Emissary retreat back, away from its adversary. A seraph-amp landed between the two amps, the hulking machine setting itself down with a contraction of its lower limbs and a mighty expulsion of compressed air that threw up a cloud of burning brown earth that whipped around it. The Emissary leapt upon its back, then it fired up its thrusters and spirited them both away.

The "Meditating amp" stood there, watching, making sure that they had definitely gone. Then it returned to Dyce, wrapping its arms around him, helping him up…

That was the last time he was conscious, until he awoke in the top floor of that riser…

ILLUMINATE

What now?

Dyce Bastion had a new problem to add to the list.

Unless he was having some sort of lucid mental health issue, his five senses seemed to be torturing him by randomly recalibrating their limitations, pulsing back and forth from barely functional to super human and unbearably overwhelming. As a result, he was suffering from vertigo, clinging to a window frame, too dizzy to move away from the humungous drop before him.

His eyes were closed as tight as possible because even glimpsing the world beyond the window was too much, but he couldn't do anything about the audio onslaught, however, as he refused to let go of the window frame and cover his ears. And as for the smells... All of the smells...

Why won't it stop?

He could somehow hear raindrops pooling and dripping from surface to surface both near and far, from a puddle on the opposite side of the room to an upturned, blood-stained helmet collecting droplets in the cockpit of a crashed vehicle by the shoreline. Next he heard broken glass crunching under someone's foot, somewhere in some distant riser, then the unidentifiable whir of machinery and the hiss of pistons. Things scurried and scattered in dark shadows - insects, rodents, and even things that were not native to this world. He could *feel* some of them, their movements reverberating through a network of everything, and it was nauseating.

Dyce became anxious, his heartbeat sped up, his breathing became shallow. He took deep circular breaths, as he had been trained to, breathing in for three seconds, holding it for four seconds, then breathing out for five seconds. Gradually he managed to calm down, his headache receded.

Are my senses actually hyper or am I imagining things? Is my brain broken, or is something different?

There was only one way to find out, and that was to...

One, two, three... here we go...

He dared to open his eyes, and what he saw overwhelmed his senses in a much more profound way than the previous auditory bombardment. Because, all at once, it seemed as if he could see everything, right down to the most minute detail, an endless overlapping collage of detail and movement.

Dusk had crept up upon Alcyone and its five cities, the night chasing the light back towards the horizon. He could see that nearly every rain-slick surface in the coastal town had a gold sheen and a silver lining, smoke and steam drifted up from downed vehicles, broken robotics, burnt bodies and discarded weapons in distant rooms and litter-strewn streets. In the distance, a riser had broken open, perhaps long ago, the fractured frame fanning out like the rotten branches of some vast weeping willow, casting long shadows over the nameless streets. The kaleidoscopic sky, stained by a century of chemical warfare, was trying to make silhouettes of the decimated risers, but in the space between them he could see the wine-dark sea, shimmering as it caught the moonlight. Ash and embers drifted through the streets like spirits, carried by the continent's rasping breath. Then there was the alien fauna, a bioluminescent forest of alien origin that grew through and around the buildings and the *broken things,* and the vibrant life forms that were drawn to it, or born from it, thrived off it...

So, he concluded, he really had been destroyed and reborn, after-all, and he believed that his hyper-sensitive senses were evidence of this. because it seemed as if these were his new eyes and he was using them for the first time, and his muddled mind was unable to regulate and filter the over-abundance of information.

No... No... This is impossible...

He still took his circular breaths, calming himself down. He focused on a piece of yellow and black warning tape the clung to the window frame, watched it fluttering in the wind. Gradually he calmed down, and his senses seemed to do the same, reaching a more manageable plateau.

He turned back to the meditating amp that sat in the middle of the room. It appeared even more lifeless than it had before, it's metal skin looked darker, the blue pigment become black with a hint of green around the edges of each panel.

'I bet you had some idea what's happening, right?' He felt his lips and tongue form the words, the teeth help control the airflow out of the mouth.

This was all too much for him. He had never had control over anything, his life, his career, and now whatever was going on with his body. He was a conscript, like everyone else down in his lower social class. Stood accused of being born without a silver spoon. He wasn't a warrior, not by nature, he was a worrier. He knew so many who would have excelled in this situation, left alone in a hostile environment with only their wits.

But, of course, he soon identified another issue. It was one of *those* days. As he loosened his grip on the window frame and tentatively looked back out, he glimpsed a large and well-armed machine standing on the roof of the smaller riser across the road from his position. It was an amp, a mechanical life form, and he could only assume that this was an enemy unit, though from this angle he could see no identifying markers, recognising the outline. It was completely different from the meditating amp that accompanied him in this room, having a more animal form, with four long legs carrying its weight and its weaponry. This particular model was called a sentry-amp.

He backed away from the window, out of the machine's line of sight.

Dyce began to feel uneasy. Someone or something was, apparently, coming for him. So, where were his exits? Well, there were two, the stairwell and next to that, the long dead elevator shaft that formed the riser's spine. Of course, there was a third way out, but that involved leaping up of a window. He hadn't quite reached that level of desperation.

He could only assume that all seventy two floors were as desolate as this, with weeds growing from cracks in the concrete. The entire floor of the building was absolutely covered in spent bullet cases, rusted and misshapen. The source of this metal gravel was possibly an old aircraft that had long ago crashed into this floor of the building and become lodged between ceiling and floor. It was of a type that Dyce had only ever seen in films, broken rotary blades on the top and the tail led him to believe that this was what he thinks they used to call a *helicopter*, and the armaments and the shape of the canopy looked like a precursor to the gunships and jump ships that he knew. The cockpit appeared to be empty. Upon impact, parts of the rotors had evidently cart-wheeled through the room, one had lodged itself into a pillar which bore the scars of countless bullet impacts.

This antique reminded him of the movies he used to watch, and by association the music that he would absorb, both illegally, as so many of them did, on their hacked and modified tabris interface devices. He would spend his downtime searching the dark recesses of the Comscape network for glorious lagoons of banned entertainment, excitedly sharing whispered tales of what he had found with his friends. Remembering this made him feel a little more human, and he found that some of the songs would play through his memory in astonishing detail, much clearer than he could remember the voices, words or names of lost friends and coworkers.

Then something useful caught his attention, a campfire that had not been lit for many years. He tried to get up and walk to it, and he immediately collapsed, letting out a cry as metal dug into his hands and knees.

He reassured himself that he could do this, even if he had to crawl ,which, of course, is what he had to do. The bullet cases crunched under his hands and knees. He persisted, no matter how many times he collapsed, and with every hard-won inch he felt himself getting stronger, and by the time he reached the campfire he had managed to rise to his feet, which filled him with immeasurable pride, at least until he collapsed back down to his knees. He yelped and cried as his legs and hands once again hit the carpet of shrapnel.

He rebuilt the campfire, unearthing things to use as kindling from beneath the bullet casings. Then, like a caveman, he picked up random pieces of metal and hit one against the other, with little precision or finesse, until he managed to spark a fire. Then he sat and watched the flames spreading through the ancient paper, cardboard, stationary catalogues and the remains of furniture that he had found.

Unpleasant, violent images floated through his mind, a signifier that finally his brain had rebuilt itself to the point that he was capable of remembering fragments of his final moments. The least viscerally egregious, but no less physically painful, was purging his catastrophically damaged power-armour in stages, shedding the equipment like a husk, components clattering down a stairwell behind behind him. The arms of the meditating amp supporting him.

He remembered even further back, lying on the battlefield after the sky fell on him, as close to dead as it is possible to be. Then he remembered the incomparable feeling of relief as - beyond all probability - his crushed ribs had forced their own way out of his imploded insides, realigning themselves somehow. He had coughed out hot bone fragments and torn slithers of muscle, as his internal organs rejected them. Then he remembered the pain and the joy of taking his first breath with his reconstituted lungs, deep and nourishing, even though it had hurt like hell...

He was still wearing what remained of his League of Nations-decorated muscle suit, an artificial membrane of bio reflex feedback material, scorched almost black by whatever had almost killed him. Torn strands of the artificial muscle were turning grey as they contracted, and the interface sockets had been warped by the heat.

He was recovering more from before the devastation, not just his death and rebirth but more inconsequential things, fragments of a life, little moments that at the time would have seemed so forgettable, but now he was imbuing them with momentous significance simply because...

Because...

Who was I? Who am I now?

So, what were the facts, the unarguable truths? Well, he knew that he had been a soldier in the League of Nations, he was from the UK, and I Feel For You by Shaka Kahn is mankind's greatest achievement. But anything more precise than that was beyond his cognitive reach.

The lit campfire reflected across the dented bullet cases, flickering waves of red and yellow against the dark blue of dusk. He realised that whilst he had been distracted he had drawn a portrait of Macalister Breaker in the ancient ashes around the campfire with the tip of a little finger. It was, at least, not quite as crude as a child's drawing, but he knew who it was. Not bad, actually, he thought. The finger that he had used to draw hadn't even been his own, perhaps it had belonged to whoever had made this campfire. He threw it into the fire.

'Why didn't you tell her how you felt?' He asked his *old self* as he rubbed the image away. But he had never been the kind of person to make a move, his *old-self* had been so passive, so willing to let life roll over him like a train.

'This isn't who I am supposed to be,' he said to himself, and instinctively knew that this was a thought that he had had many times before.

Dyce felt *guilt*, a nebulous sensation. Everyone else was dead; his friends; his colleagues, *her...*

And he wasn't. He came back...

'Why me?' Dyce asked the meditating amp, becoming more and more frustrated by the gaps in his knowledge. 'I should be dead, but... Why am I still here? Any one of them would be more worthy than me. I'm gonna fuck this up. I don't need to reconstruct my memories to know that I never had any future...'

The amp still showed no signs of life and had no answers to give him. As the cascade of irrational emotions overcame him, his body slumped backwards, and he found himself staring up at a web of cracks in the ceiling. As he studied every single splintering fissure – visible to him no matter how insignificant they might be - tears drew lines from his eyes to his gaping mouth, before his teeth clasped into a grimace and his eyes tightened. He dragged his fingers through the shrapnel as a primal scream forced its way out through his clamped jaw.

He heard a beep, sudden and unexpected. He half suspected that he had imagined it, until it happened again. He looked around for the source. The beep came again, this time he was able to pinpoint where it had come from.

'Is that you?' He asked the meditating amp. 'You awake now?'

But the amp made no response, just sitting there, lifeless. Dyce realised that the beep was not coming from the amp itself, apparently the anthropomorphic machine was wearing black tactical armour, practically indistinguishable from its own armoured shell, becoming more obvious as the robot disintegrated in slow time.

Dyce crawled over to the meditating amp and realised that the beep had come from a headset strapped to the amp's forehead, part of the set with the tactical armour. Again, it had been hard to discern from the general complexity of the machine's noggin. The headset was a black, rubber-padded Heads-Up-Display visor that had seven camera eyes of assorted sizes set into recesses around the otherwise featureless surface.

Dyce reached up and pulled at the headset, and as he tugged at it the amp's head just fell away, black dust ejected from the exposed neck, the cables inside snapping like dry twigs. The head landed on his lap, which took him completely by surprise, because the machine had certainly been sturdy earlier, when it had seemed as if the amp were refusing to let go of the tabris. Dyce reached to the amp's decapitated head and scraped a finger across its cranium. Even against the meagre amount of pressure that Dyce was capable of, this broke up like cremated toast. It was as if this deterioration was spreading through the amp like an infection, because it was clearly in a worse state than it had been earlier. As Dyce had recovered the machine had gotten worse.

So Dyce pulled at the broken amp's crumbling limbs and torso like disassembling an overcooked and ruined Sunday roast, allowing the armour to clatter to the floor. There was no real reason why the amp should have been wearing this armour in the first place, which made him wonder if this was a gift for him, just like the tabris, another offering...

Dyce forced himself to stand again, balancing precariously on his own feet as he put the armour on and and locked each section together. It felt kind of reassuring to have some protection again, but he knew that it would not help his chances, not against whatever was coming. Only he could do that.

Somehow...

So he knelt back down and rolled the tabris around his fingers, a display of dexterity which pleased him, at least until he fumbled it. He scooped it back up and checked the list of paired devices in his Minds Eye, and was unsurprised to find that already synchronised to this armour, and had already begun to monitor his vitals. There was a place to holster the tabris on his hip, a port which was hardwired to a tiny terminal at the base of the spinal stack, and it begun recharging it the moment he popped it in there.

Something occurred to him, now that his brain was in a better shape, he could use the tabris to call for help. It connected quickly to the comscape network via geosynchronous satellites, but it didn't seem as if anybody was in a hurry to answer.

He waited.

Bored, he picked up the amp's head by its fused jaw and held it before him, studying it. It had seven eyes placed randomly around its face, held inside their recesses by proprietary apertures. He touched one and idly rotated it, the synthetic musculature crumbling as the rot had degraded even this, and the eyeball came loose and rolled down its cheek and off what might be called a chin, if it weren't for a cluster of bevel edged sensors, leaving a trail of dark debris. He caught it and turned it around, gazing into the iris. He wondered who had been inside this machine's synthetic brain, who had been looking out through these eyes, and why they had helped him.

Of course, this lead to much more concerning questions, such as who was after him, and why.

Tired of waiting, he instead submitted an SOS, a request for extraction, including his coordinates.

YOUR REQUEST FOR ASSISTANCE HAS BEEN RECEIVED, LOGGED AND WILL BEING PROCESSED IN DUE TIME.

("Seriously? Can I not speak to someone?")

A REPRESENTATIVE WILL CONTACT YOU IN DUE TIME.

("When? I need extraction ASAP.")

THIS IS NOT POSSIBLE. YOUR LIFE IS FINANCIALLY INSIGNIFICANT. YOU ARE EXPENDABLE. LOWER CLASS. A DIFFERENT TRIBE. WAGE SLAVE. THERE ARE MILLIONS JUST LIKE YOU. YOUR EXISTENCE IS FORFEIT TO THE BOTTOM LINE...

("Excuse me?") Dyce interrupted the flow, he could not believe what he was reading. Something was wrong, obviously. Perhaps this was...

DO YOU WISH TO LODGE A FORMAL COMPLAINT? COMPLETE A SERVICE TICKET AND A REPRESENTATIVE WILL GET BACK TO YOU.

("What?") Dyce was in shock. This one-sided conversation had escalated rapidly. *("No. I wish to be extracted...")*

HAVE A NICE DAY.

He sat in shock. No one was coming for him. He felt lost for a few moment, useless and unwanted. But he suddenly received another communication, more words filled his vision, via the Minds Eye operating system. It was not what he was expecting, not at all. But just as unnerving was a sound that punctuated the text, conveying their intent but not their literal verbalisation, a blast of unintelligible noise that conveyed an inhuman feeling of malevolence.

THERE YOU ARE...

A chill ran down Dyce's spine. This was clearly not anyone from back home. He suddenly realised that his previous chat was not with a representative from his people, it had been tainted and twisted by some other entity.

This was it, Dyce thought, this was the dangerous force about which he had been forewarned by that voice that had coaxed him back to life. This voice belonged to the danger.

I WONDER, HOW IS IT THAT YOU ARE ALIVE? REGENERATION ON THIS SCALE IS BEYOND YOUR PROJECTED CAPABILITIES. DID SOMEONE HELP YOU? PERHAPS THE SAME SOMEONE TRYING TO HIDE YOUR LOCATION FROM ME. NEVER MIND, I WILL FIND THEM TOO.

`` Dyce just sat there, wanting to disconnect, but – for the first time in his life – feeling as if he needed to make a stand. He just didn't really know what that entailed.

THERE HAVE BEEN A FEW POTENTIAL SIGHTINGS. A SENTRY-AMP SUSPECTS IT GLIMPSED YOU MOVING AROUND IN WHAT YOU PEOPLE CALL A RISER, THAT SEEMS TO BE THE VIABLE LEAD. I COULD HAVE HAD IT DEMOLISH THAT ENTIRE BUILDING, BUT I MADE OTHER ARRANGEMENTS. SIT TIGHT, SOME ENEMY TROOPS ARE ON THEIR WAY. I NEEDED VISUAL CONFIRMATION BEFORE I MADE A MOVE, FOR MY PEACE OF MIND. YOU UNDERSTAND.

(*"But why me? I'm no one,"*) Dyce asked. (*"Who is this?"*)

SURVIVE LONG ENOUGH AND FIND OUT.

All traces of this unhinged conversation disappeared,

replaced with a standard service message telling him to wait for a response.

'What was that?' Dyce whispered to the amp head. 'What kind of a mess am I in?'

The head was still dead.

'Well, you're no help. I guess I got no one but myself...'

Am I no one? He was sure he was, but that contradicted the threat.

So, with that he decided that finding out who he was should be a priority. Though he was mostly sure that he wasn't an amnesiac super-spy or a metal-boned mutant - two pop culture references that he remembered easier than he did the details of his own life - or anything remotely bad-ass, perhaps he might remember some piece of information that would help him out. Thankfully, there was software for this kind of scenario, nothing official of course, at least nothing that would be available to him, but home-brew maestros would have coded something, and it took him no time at all to find something and get it set up. He set the tabris to copy the vast and varied mush of memories and defragment them, reconstructing them for him and using intelligent algorithms to fill in the gaps. It could take minutes, it could take hours, it could take days. It depended on the power of the processor, the volume of memories, the amount of mess there was to untangle. He watched the first progress bar as it copied his memories to the internal storage.

He had to prepare for whatever was coming. So, he checked out his armour. The tactical variety was less bulky than the powered armour he was used to and would provide only minimal strength enhancements.

He ran his fingers over the space where the League of Nations insignia has apparently been prised off just to test the feedback. He was miffed to find that not every cluster of touch-sensors were working to maximum efficiency, some burnt out, either misfiring or failing completely. The diagnostic systems presented by his Minds Eye told him that the sensors were working at sixty-seven percent efficiency. But then, he felt a slight tingle in his fingertips, the strangest sensation that was a little like pins-and-needles, but a little *not*. The diagnostic system reported foreign bodies present in his blood, then in the gauntlets' integrity, which matched the migration of the sensation, which had started in his digits but was now radiating out. Then the feedback from the gauntlets seemed to improve, his Minds Eye suddenly reporting an increase to ninety-eight percent efficiency.

Odd, Dyce thought, it was as if he had somehow subconsciously fixed this problem in the same way that his own body had been repaired.

He pulled his headset down over his eyes and instantly booted into its own array of sensors, the room presented to him in an overlapping selection of visual filters, the night vision, the thermal filter...

Suddenly he jumped backwards in surprise, his reaction caused by something wholly unusual that had appeared within his visual range when he switched to the thermal filter. Immediately he hit high alert, ready to strike, every muscle from his face to his sphincter clenched, his fight or flight response putting its foot down on his heartbeat's accelerator.

He scrunched up his eyes, took a breath, then looked back out.

They were still there; all around him he could see red and yellow figures wandering aimlessly around the room, as if there were dozens of people presented by the outline of their body heat. They had looked, in that initial orifice-puckering glance, like fiery demons but on a lingering inspection more like aimless spectres carved from blobs of paint.

Dyce lifted his headset to see a room full of no-one. The same empty room, the wind carrying the precipitation through the space, unobstructed by invisible bodies. He was still alone, there were no ghosts and no fiery demons here. No cloaked soldiers either, a technological leap that was still not personably portable.

So, Dyce reaffirmed the headset over his eyes and reached out to touch one of these phantom thermal signatures. The red figure flickered frantically around his outstretched hand, breaking up into a constituent cloud of code, reforming when he pulled his hand away, each pixel snapping back into place. Signal disruption, redistribution and recompiling

This, he realised, was bait.

This room had been digitally filled with imaginary people to lure someone up here. An existential fear had existed in the pit of his stomach during every moment of his new life, it had been there when he awoke in this tower, it had gotten worse when the garbled voice had threatened him, and now that needle was hitting the red.

But what could he do? Someone could be heading up that staircase right now and he could run straight into them in his haste to flee. He didn't want to stay, but he couldn't bring himself to leave. Checkmate.

'Oh, perfect...' he said to the decapitated amp head.

There must be weaponry, he realised, whoever sent the meditating amp to help him would not have left him unarmed. He pulled himself just far enough out of his slump to move, digging through the pile of the amp's ashen appendages.

One by one he found some useful things within the ashes of the machine. A bounty of beautiful ballistic goodies. One handgun; Two high-density gas grenades; An ice grenade, good for fast freezing obstacles or transforming any living matter into meat popsicles; Two chaff grenades for disrupting electric devices; Finally, a displacement grenade. He turned this one around in his hands, reading the stencilled label: Displacement - forcing something somewhere that it did not belong. He could empathise with that.

Finally, there was a spare battery for an automated gun, although the automated gun itself was not here. He found it at the top of the stairwell, on the other side of the open door, the suitcase-sized automated gun had been placed above the door well, just within reach, locked to the wall with four bolts fired from a pressure cannon. This had clearly been here for a few years, probably belonging to the corpses around the fire, but the amp had the foresight to bring a battery. He had not been brought to this place arbitrarily, it had been staked out in advance. But why?

Dyce slowly stepped to the top of the stairs and looked down. He held his breath and listened...

His heart was pounding, his chest tightening. He was afraid to breathe even slightly, in case he missed some telltale noise...

When he was as certain as he was gonna get that no one was heading up the stairwell, he reloaded the sentry gun with two compact ammo clips and replaced the battery. Nothing happened. He removed the battery and blew on the connectors to clear any dust or crud, and then smacked it in hard with the heel of his hand. A light started to blink, the barrel started to move, searching for targets.

He returned to the camp fire and checked the handgun. The main clip was full, perhaps thirty rounds.

He noticed that there was a second, smaller, auxiliary clip behind the grip, narrow and only capable of holding and feeding a few rounds of bespoke ammo, this alternate feed selectable via a switch. In here Dyce found something really interesting, two bullets with tips made of glass, filled with liquid. Inside these glass bullets was something that resembled a seed, just floating there. The first bullet had an image of a squid precision etched into it, the second bullet had an effigy of an insect with a stinger, too basic and crude to properly identify. He made a clearing amongst the shrapnel and placed them both down, standing them up on their flat back ends.

He wanted to perform a little experiment with them, just to prove to himself what a disturbing, irredeemable mess the human race really was. He took off his onyx black right gauntlet and the muscle-feedback glove beneath it. He looked at the scratches that were now all that remained of the deep cuts that he must have sustained at some point between his fiery death and his agonising crawl back from the grave. They were completely healed, nothing but scars to show for it. Maybe those scars would always remain, perhaps his body would always be a map of his pain. He was about to add a few more. He picked up one of the old bullet casings that had been trampled underfoot, and used the sharp edge to draw blood, watching it pool in his palm.

He almost jumped when he heard, from somewhere distressingly close by, the tiniest tapping sound. An almost inaudible thud that he wouldn't be able to hear under normal circumstances, but his senses were still inexplicably heightened. He realised the tap was coming from one of the glass bullets, as the bio-engineered seed inside it knocked against the side of the glass. It was attracted to the blood like a moth to light.

He picked up the glass bullet that had the tentacle motif etched onto it and drove it down into the blood, smashing it. The blood sizzled as the seed melted into it. Like a magic trick, tiny tentacles unfolded out of the red, grabbing at his fingers, a newborn cephalopod pulling itself up out of the small crimson pool. The feeble, malnourished infant thing convulsed again and again, before it petrified, the colour drained from it. With not enough blood to help it reach its full potential and then sustain it, it crumbled to dust.

With grim detail, Dyce started to recall seeing tentacles burst forth from people on the battlefield, their bodies torn apart by eldritch monstrosities born from their own bodies.

He looked into what remained of the amp's eyes and shook his head in disappointment. 'You brought me back to this.'

He coaxed more blood from his palm, smearing it on the floor, then smashed the other bullet down into it. Small wiggling shapes formed, quickly sprouting tiny, spindly legs, then a pair of translucent wings, then, finally the stingers. Two newly created wasps flew out of the tiny puddle, dripping crimson from their wings. He caught one between his fingers, *somehow*, his rapid dexterity shocked even himself. He could feel it wriggle between his fingers.

The insect died almost as soon as it had been born. It was a simulacrum of a real thing, not meant to be. He couldn't help but fear the strange, horrible world he had been reborn into, and what horrors might befall him. He watched it crumble to ash.

GIRLS WHO
GET READY

Nico Shikari could sense that the battle she had missed still lingered in the streets and the sky, an afterimage of crisscrossing munitions and drifting smoke. And, as she sat on the hull of the Nilin Remix, the battle lingered in her mind, too. She needed to fight, it was an itch that needed scratching. She believed it was her patriotic duty as a soldier in the Unified American Military, but really her desire to fight was deeper than that, somehow, like an unbearable craving.

Nico sat there on the hull, her helmet beside her, the tabris replaying the spectacular highlights of the battle as her armour's camera eyes had seen it.

'Oh yeah boys and girls, that's the good stuff,' she said to the combatants on the screen projected within her Minds Eye. 'Making ya gal proud.'

But then, as she watched the action replay of aeromechs dancing in the sky, she remembered what she had done to the crashed enemy pilot...

She had looked at the pilot and saw nothing but... but what? They were all the same, the Enemy, a Heathen. She had not seen an individual, he had somehow been the entirety of the League of Nations, as if this one pilot had been a vessel for every atrocity that any member of the League had ever committed and the reason for every bad thing that was wrong with the world, with her life. It was almost superstitious. She had dehumanised this person by reducing his worth to a label.

'Oh fuck off,' she made a disgusted noise, appalled by the trajectory of her own thought process, and resolved to never think about that again.

Deflated by this inexplainable and, she thought, misplaced regret, she halted the action replay, needing a break. Clearly it was leading her mental train down unwarranted tracks of thought, and she almost wondered if the recording had been twisted by some nebulous idea of the enemy to twist her mind. Fake news, weaponised.

So she looked around the wasteland for something interesting. *Anything! Come on, world!* Improbably, her naked eyes fixed upon a tiny spider dangling from the tip of the Nilin Remix's detached tail fin, which was standing upright out of the water some distance away from the rest of the ship. The arachnid was not much more than a finger nail wide, she wouldn't have noticed it normally, but her eyes seemed so much more receptive today. That's how she was able to spot that it wasn't a spider at all, it was some alien thing doing an impression of one.

She was becoming concerned about her heightened senses, but she was also mesmerised by the little being that she had focused upon. It was transparent, it's insides were luminous and lit like tiny neon lights. She could see it breathing, its lungs opening and closing. She observed a spark of light passing through its arteries and capillaries. Even its web seemed to pulse with colour. As it rubbed its tiny little legs together, sharp as needles, it made a sound that only Nico Shikari could hear, sounding like a clatter of broken glass. Through repetition that sound slowly started to irritate, scratching away at her sanity until she managed to focus her attention elsewhere.

There were a lot of these types of things spreading through this land, an otherworldly infestation that had certainly originated on this continent, and there were examples of it mimicking the basic forms of native creatures and fauna, but there were apparently creatures of such great size and twisted form that they could only be described as monsters, already classed as myths and legends.

She shook her head, feeling isolated enough without thinking about subterranean alien nastiness, and she wasn't much for scare stories and rumours. She liked only facts, and what her government classed as fact. That was why she didn't dwell at all upon the fact that she shouldn't have been able to see the spider at all. It had nothing to do with her duty or her mission. Whatever that mission was.

'Why *am* I here?'

She headed back inside the crashed jump-ship, closing the broken hatch as far as she could, using the combined weight of her and her suit as she swung upon it. She shimmied beneath a control panel, and used the tip of a shard of the broken progressive blade as a screwdriver, which wasn't easy. She quickly ran out of what little patience she may have had, so instead of working on the screws she instead started hacking at the metal with the shard, until she managed to make a separation between the panels just wide enough for her fingers. She pulled at it, spitting, swearing and getting very angry until it came free.

Behind the panel she found the black box flight recorder, which she quickly removed and threw across the floor, where it skidded to a stop just beside the pile of bodies. Next she found the emergency distress beacon. If the beacon was working, and the flashing certainly suggested that it was, then surely somebody must be on their way. She sat back and gave a little sigh of relief.

She removed her tabris from the port on her armour's hip with a satisfying pop as it separated from the magnetic charger within, then tapped it against the black box to initiate the digital handshake which should begin the sync. Hopefully the black box should recognise her rank and grant her an access level just high enough to give her info about what had brought down her ship, but there was absolutely no reaction from her interface device, not even a demoralising ping of denial. She tapped the tabris again and again. Nothing.

This was already as frustrating as her many, many attempts to call for assistance which had gone unanswered. Eventually she got a little something, giving her nothing more than a spinning wheel to represent the system's attempt to find her ID in the UAM's database of active soldiers. As the wait got longer and longer, she tried not to contemplate the implication.

From nowhere, seemingly from ten to one hundred percent in half a second, she lost control, smacking the base of the tabris against the floor repeatedly until the flat end cracked, then she threw it down, letting it bounce along the floor. Her jaw ached from the intensity of her grimace. She froze, shocked again by her own anger. Worried that she had damaged the device that she needed to communicate with her armour, she checked to make sure that the tabris was still working. It seemed to be ok, electronically if not physically. She was lucky.

She unfolded one of the wall-mounted chairs and sat down beside the corpse of an old colleague. The more she thought about her old life, the more she hesitated to call any of them *friends*.

'Could this get any worse?' She asked the corpse, who's blue and broken, slack-jawed lips were unlikely to respond any time soon. 'I'm hungry. Where are you hiding the rations, *boy*? You holding-out on me?'

On the body's muscle suit was the UAM military's insignia, which filled her with so much love and pride that it almost made her forget her troubles. She reached over and touched it, micro sensors in the gauntlet's fingertips picked up the edges and ridges of the insignia. Her mental link allowed the information to be relayed from the sensors to her nervous system, as if her actual fingers were picking up the detail. The diameter of each one of the micro sensors was less than the very tip of a pin, each one of them surrounded by a gap which was infinitesimally insignificant. Such a shame that a percentage of the sensors had failed long before she had inherited the armour from the last poor soldier, and half of those sensors had failed before even that soldier had received it. Some of the armour's components might even date back one hundred years to the war's inception, when the League of Nations declared war on the Unified American Military.

Nico had no idea what had triggered the war. Perhaps the argument began over the rights to this country, Alcyone, for whatever this artificial dirt pile was worth. Perhaps all the other countries were jealous, because the UAM was flexing their muscles and expanding their empire. They'd always been jealous of their might, always hated their freedom and despised their way of life. She didn't really care; politics were not her concern. She wasn't sure what made her country the greatest, but she knew in her heart that it just was. She believed in it with every spark surging along every neural connection. She didn't know why she hated the enemy, but she knew that she was supposed to, so she did...

The Unified American Military, a regime that formed within what remained of the United States of America and grew to consume the whole. America had temporarily ceased to exist as a political entity after it stopped being a singular landmass in the wake of multiple orbital strikes from the Dweller capital ship, which then – in the final moments of *that* war, that began in nineteen-sixty-nine - crashed into Washington state, turning it into a massive collection of archipelagos.

But the Dwellers were gone, defeated in the war that began when America landed on the wrong moon and accidentally started a war with that alien race that no one knew was living there.

But that was the past, and such things were none of her concern.

'No no no, this is no good, I've got to get busy with something,' she said to herself. 'Come on.'

But she did nothing. She just sat and stared. She was starting to get a headache, and perhaps that was hunger.

'*Oh, wow...*'she said, as she rubbed her aching head.

Then her chest developed an ache, and that made even less sense. She activated her tabris and had it run a health diagnostic on her bones. In her Minds Eye she saw her bones, and her organs, so she zoomed in on her ribs, looking for any cracks that somehow the system might had failed to flag up.

As her head started to throb again, and, for some reason, she started to imagine her ribs breaking and un-breaking, her heart being crushed, her entire respiratory system imploding. It felt real, but somehow, she was detached from it, as if it were the distant echo of some half-forgotten memory, or her imagination fabricating some sensation that somehow belonged to someone else...

'*Get out of my head, get out of my head...*' she rapped her forehead with her knuckles. 'Come on, Nico, enough with this morbid shit. There's enough *stupid* in the world, you don't need it in your head... not... Not any more...'

Her attention was caught as she heard sounds outside, like thunder. Then the floor shook and did not stop shaking. She felt lightheaded suddenly, somehow. In awe she held up her hand and watched dust floating *up* from it, towards the broken hatch.

She hopped to the ladder and climbed up and out, pushing the hatch open with her shoulder, annoyed that she had only just closed it and the world was conspiring to make her work. Finally, she saw a needle of white in the sky, quite a distance away. She closed her helmet around her head and used its array of cameras to zoom in upon it.

Nico observed the needle of light pulsing, and she could hear it hum, until it suddenly expanded into a tower of crackling energy that punched a hole in the cloud, twisting the nimbus around it like a vortex. The sky sang, everything in the wasteland and the surrounding city let out a chorus through escalating reverberation.

So Shamsiel, the geo-synchronised orbital defence platform, was firing, but what was the target? There was always a chance that it was simply test firing, but Nico had to know more. Her heart was racing, excited. She zoomed in upon the base of the blast, which was not at ground level, but far above, the line of light illuminating the hull of a League of Nations solar frigate, the name stencilled on the side was Initial Constellation. The enemy ship was drifting just above the skyline, but under the force of the energy weapon it seemed to lose altitude, shaving a few storeys off a few random risers with its bulk. Crackling pulses of ball lightning rode the needle of light down into the hull until its back broke. But that wasn't the worst of it, the vast, floating megastructure was absorbing this energy, it's mass becoming unstable, explosive.

So, the League ship collapsed in on itself and went supernova, an explosion that turned the surrounding buildings into grey confetti that swept through the streets, Nico Shikari cheered and clapped.

'UAM *baby*, yeah! That's what you get! That's what you get!'

VALIUM SKIES.

Twelve minutes and twenty two seconds before the orbital blast witnessed by Nico Shikari...

The Augmented Fourth were walking through the streets of Contact City. The victims of their most recent assault were already becoming a distant memory, and the prospect of a second assault tonight was getting some of them excited, but only the ones too stupid to suspect that the entire scenario was a trap.

(*"I need you to help me get these guys in line,"*) Lieutenant Rosario said to Corporal Oshii alone through a private com-link chat. (*"Now I..."*)

'I see the mission details,' Oshii interrupted the man, speaking out loud and not through the com-link. She was pointing at the riser that they were heading to. 'I see the order telling any teams in the vicinity to get up there, same as you. But I don't believe it. This whole job smells synthesised to me. It's just too... it's like we're chasing ghosts in the system.'

(*'Our systems are flawless...'*)Rosario argued.

'Yes, I understand that,' Oshii continued her belligerent attempt to bring this argument out into the real world, though Rosario's naïve argument was the kind of blind patriotic puff that Oshii herself would say and try to convince everyone, especially herself, that it was true. 'But if we're not vigilant, then the enemy...'

'Then *what*?' Rosario blurted out loud.

Oshii found it hard to argue with logic that she had used

many times herself.

'Our systems are flawless, no one could send out a fake mission over our own network,' Rosario emphasised those last three words, then tilted his head at her with a condescending expression, almost pitying Oshii's cynicism.

'But the heat signatures could be...' Oshii tried not to talk through gritted teeth.

'Enough!' Rosario snapped.

Oshii only felt her anger deepen at this. She felt castrated by her own beliefs, the code which insisted she honour the chain of command as almost holy edicts. But, perhaps, if she were right, and this was some kind of trap, fate would eliminate Rosario for her. That would be Rosario's punishment for not fulfilling his sacred duty to the pertinent and promised level of perfection.

'What would be the tactical...' Oshii paused as Rosario dismissively waved a hand, but after rolling her eyes and seething she continued on, indignant. '...advantage of a large group of enemy soldiers, this close to the aftermath of a major battle that they lost, sitting on their asses on a high floor of a riser, where we could easily block their escape?'

Rosario thought about this, he didn't say a word. He had nothing to say. He tried not to look at the floor, tried not to look as if he were even contemplating Oshii's point, though he surely knew that it was right. It was not easy for him. He couldn't even muster a grunt or a cough. He walked on ahead, refusing to defend himself any further, but too stubborn to turn back.

("Can I gut his guy?") Trip Kosheen asked. ("Say the word and we'll watch his insides spill...")

("Respect the chain of command,") Oshii replied through the same private channel. ("It's the only thing that separates us from the heathen Neanderthals that we dedicated our lives to eliminate. He will be tested, and if he is found wanting...")

("You will be proven right, as always,") Kosheen said. ("As long as he doesn't get us killed in the process.")

("We are *the Augmented Fourth, there's no situation we can't turn into a massacre.")* Oshii assured Kosheen. *("Get up top and scope out our target. I want you in an adjacent building with your high-velocity rifle ready to even-out these odds.")*

Kosheen only nodded, then let herself fall behind the group. She looked up to the rooftops, and mentally plotted a course up the side, using pipes, ledges and stalled air-conditioning units. Then she made a move, nimbly following her predetermined route, the gravity orbs in the tips of her powered legs generated just enough pull to allow her to run the walls, making it possible for her to balance on ledges as narrow as a *rat's testicle*, until she reached a fire escape, swinging beneath it from step to step.

When she managed to throw herself up to the roof, out of sight of her team, she slowed quite deliberately to a stroll. The sense of urgency she displayed as she scaled the side had been a show for her leader, now she revealed a lack of interest, her shoulders slumping, her head, usually held so high, dipped. She didn't want to do this, didn't care for this *bullshit* mission.

She stopped next to an antiquated search light which was pointing up, it's glass smashed and filled with a chem-tainted rain. From this kaleidoscopic bath grew a few of the bioluminescent plants that had started to appear all over this man-made continent.

A cluster of reptilian creatures - that had evolved to vaguely resemble hummingbirds but with leathery wings - were drinking from the flowers. As they ingested the glowing liquid, tiny bulbs at the tips of each wing lit up. Then they took off, wings buzzing so fast that the glowing tips drew circles within circles in the air. They drifted around her, the neon nectar dripping from their beaks.

She felt an emptiness in the pit of her stomach. She no longer felt the same connection to the the rest of the Augmented Fourth as she once had, she no longer felt as if she was the same person who had learnt to enjoy the vile chaos as a means to integrate and therefore survive. If she were to ever entirely permit herself more than a moment of honest self-reflection, she could have pinpointed the cause of the fissure, something that she couldn't share with them, even though she was feeling the need to share it with someone. They wouldn't understand, but she needed someone to. She needed to vent. That was creating a gap through which other doubts could creep in.

She pulled the headset down over her eyes and looked towards their target. In her Minds Eye, an artificial corona of green appeared around the riser where these supposed enemy soldiers were camped out. Highlighted in red was a representation of the reason that they were heading there, a cluster of League soldiers on the top floor. If they existed at all...

She needed a good vantage point to set up her long range gravity rifle, and a riser of comparable size to the target building was perfect, only two blocks away.

She set off again, with increasing velocity she traversed the rooftops and leapt the gaps between them until she reached the edge of the building closest to her chosen riser. Without pausing for breath, she ran the crisscrossing electrical cables that spanned the space between, her velocity matching her perfect balance.

She pulled her handgun and shot a window out, bounding through it and rolling across the ruined floor. Within moments she was running up flight after flight of stairs until she reached the top floor and kicked through the stairwell door, bounding into a large room, gun at the ready just in case of squatters.

It was getting dark, the sun was nothing more than a flicker behind the broken skyline. A strong wind blew through the room carrying the smell of rain.

There were corpses by the window. She headed deeper into the room, checking the dark corners as she moved. With her free hand she turned each of the bodies over, the beady camera eyes in her headset fed data into her Minds Eye system, assuring her that the bodies weren't boobytrapped.

Strays, she thought to herself, and this find suddenly put her on edge.

Each of the bodies had interlocking geometric shapes tattooed all over them, each and every shape was a slightly different shade of red. These weren't soldiers, though some of them would have undoubtedly been soldiers at some point, or some would be the progeny of AWOL or abandoned soldiers. The three Stray tribes, identified through the colour of their tattoos, were made of the missing or the forgotten.

These were Red Strays, cannibals, or so they say. She had certainly seen plenty of evidence of eviscerated bodies over the years, with many body parts missing.

Closer inspection of the deceased revealed that they had modified themselves with crude armaments, surgically augmenting themselves with sharp implements and self-inflicted stigmata. It was all very intimidating, which was mostly the point. Curiously, they looked as if they had been rounded up and executed.

Amongst the corpses she found a burnt-out amp, the size of a crab, with just as many legs. She picked it up by one of these appendages, let it dangle, lifeless. Amps were a brand of robotics that had conquered the cybernetics industry in the early years of this war. They were mechanised beings, essentially robotic servants, artillery core, construction workers... She had often seen scavenger amps searching the dead, draining blood and surgically removing limbs and organs that may be useful to the mobile surgical units.

Once this particular type of robot had been a breakthrough, making its developer billions, before they had sold variations of their product to both both sides of the conflict, each variation legally distinct – the best kind of distinct - from that sold to the opposing side. This allowed the armed forces to manufacture their own amps using their own automated, AI driven factories, called Forge Minds. Not only did the Forge Minds and their Forge factories take over production, but they also took on development, iteration and innovation. Artificial intelligences were now designing and building machines, mostly unchecked.

As a result, Kosheen didn't trust them. She tossed the broken amp out the open window.

She set herself down beside the corpses and unfolded her hefty high velocity sniper rifle, each section locking into place with a satisfying click. She loved that sound. She snapped the sniper scope into place and synced her optical system through the scope via her tabris. Her Minds Eye system filled with data - wind direction, air speed velocity, auto adjusting for the curvature of the Earth. The barrel was one long housing for the gravity-based propulsion system.

She lay on her belly and took aim. Something felt off in her right hand, her trigger finger didn't seem to have the right amount of tension. She took a small screwdriver from a compartment in her tactical vest and begun recalibrating the joints of the mechanical brace bolted into her right hand. With each slight, delicate twist of each screw she could feel the difference in the exo-skeleton until it felt more natural.

She was concerned about every one of the floating-pin-bolts which pierced her skin, connecting the frame to her bone, because they hadn't been inspected by a physician for a long time, even though it was required every six months. She genuinely didn't don't how long it had been and was too nervous to check, it made her feel nauseous. It had also been a while since she had owned a tube of the manufacturer's disinfectant gel to clean the pin-bolts. She had scraped away fungus and the occasional weeping sore and cleaned them with whatever aftermarket disinfectant she could buy on the lake market, but this wasn't an ideal situation.

She continued to adjust each of the calibrating screws, listening to the clicks, as she simultaneously checked out the target building.

She activated her point drone. The small machine detached itself from the recharging station on her back and floated up.

Each of its many eyes, radars and seismic sensors were able to spot things that not even her headset could see, as well as keeping a watchful eye on the surrounding environment to keep her safe.

("What do you see?") Oshii asked Kosheen over the com-link.

("Still seeing multiple heat signatures,") Kosheen replied, looking at the data relayed by the point drone.

("Check with your own eyes, please.")

Kosheen did as Oshii asked, lifting her headset and placing her eye up against the reflex sniper scope on her rail gun, manually adjusting the lenses. ("It's *dark, apart from a loan campfire. I don't see much movement. Nothing but* ghosts, *just like you said.")*

("What about the other floors? Does it look like a trap?")

("Appears vacant,") Kosheen said.

("Keep me informed.")

("Of course.")

Kosheen pulled her headset back down, tightening its strap. Through its seven eyes she watched her team heading across the wasteland towards the target riser. Rosario was walking behind the Augmented Fourth.

Kosheen longed to target Rosario with her long-range weapon and take him out of the equation, but their devout matriarch Oshii would not forgive her.

Her train of thought came to an abrupt halt as something blocked her view. She zoomed out until she saw the culprit, a cat that had, apparently, been stained by some chemical. It's fur, probably once white, was now sky blue at the front fading to a darker hue at the back. There were random white strands of fur that slightly resembled shooting stars against the blue.

She looked away from the gun's site for a moment and saw that the moggy was on the ledge outside the window, apparently unfazed by the potentially fatal fall beneath its precarious paws, and unmoved by the gale-force winds.

'Well, hello there,' Kosheen said. 'Don't fall.'

It turned to look at her, and apparently meowed – not that

she could hear it through the window. It's whiskers seemed to bristle in an unnatural way, as if static electricity was moving though them, or they were sensing something, or...

The cat stopped and looked down at something, staring at something. It didn't look afraid, it looked as if it did this daredevil routine all the time.

'Kitty?' She asked.

Then it seemed to step down onto something beneath, something that Kosheen could not see. She waited to see if it reappeared. It did not.

'Where did you go?' She said to the apparently phantasmagorical feline. She popped her head out and looked down, seeing no sign of a free-falling feeling. 'Am I high?'

She coughed, feeling a little embarrassed and self conscious, hoping no one saw her breaking character. She felt a little lame.

So, with the mysterious mammal's brief visit over, Kosheen found herself alone again, which gave her chance to think, which she didn't always welcome.

Breaking character...

More and more these days, the person she used to be, before the Fourth, was starting to question the more unsavory detours her life had taken. But also the alone time could be a sweet relief from the pressure of having to be around the others. She didn't feel as if she could be herself around them, she didn't feel as if she had truly been herself for a long time. The Augmented Fourth were *monsters*, they did monstrous things, and to survive she had made herself into one of them. What bothered her the most was how much she enjoyed it, sometimes, the persona that she had created for them enjoyed it, at least, and then the real her had to suffer through the unpleasant aftertaste.

Then she thought of all the dead bodies around her. The Strays. Maybe this was punishment for something they had done, or perhaps they had suffered for something another of their tribe had done. Perhaps they were just in the wrong place at the wrong time. She knew why they had been executed.

They were different, so they were hated. She understood that, she found herself empathizing. She could end up another body on that pile, if she wasn't careful.

Trip Kosheen watched the campfire in the target riser, she watched it crackling, the flames dancing...

But as much as she tried to focus on this and clear her mind, it was too late. The train of thought had already left the station. She thought about her custom handgun, the literal ashes of her old dead *self*, baked into the resin grip. Not the real her, the *her* she had been trapped in at birth. She had pretended to be someone else back then, too. She had been free for only a few short years before the Fourth found her and Oshii made her into something else. She kept it close because it was a reminder of who she *is* and who she *never was*, not in her *soul*, which was a sentiment that certainly made sense to her, and that was all that mattered.

The point drone opened a window in Kosheen's Minds Eye that showed the Augmented Fourth gradually making their way up the stairwell, aiming their rail rifles up the stairs, a couple of them breaking off to briefly check every floor they passed before joining back up with the group. They were all visibly nervous about what they would find at the top.

Trip Kosheen was nervous too, a feeling sparked by this train of thought. Because her most recent amputation had not been military mandated, like the procedure that removed the one malformed leg and added the augmented limbs. Over time she had saved her ill-gotten gains and paid to have her physical *self* aligned with her true *self*, after which she had officially shed her dead name, a name she had had officially changed years before. Because she had been born the right *her* but in the wrong body. The physical parts didn't align with her mental self. She had needed to correct a contradiction to be authentic.

Not that the rest of the Augmented Fourth knew, she was too smart to tell them any of that. For all they knew she had always been known as Trip, and that's all that they needed to know. Still, doubts about their reaction forced a fissure through her connection to them, which had allowed other doubts to creep in.

Acceptance. Was that kind of emotional connection important to her? It never had been before, so why should it be now? Survival was the only reason that she had integrated herself into the Augmented Fourth, and allowed herself to be taken along by Oshii. But, she wondered, was that just the two sides of her arguing, as if the Trip that she was when she was alone was arguing with the *Augmented Fourth* Trip.

She did not, and could not, know that a complication to this question of identity lay at the other end of her sniper scope, sat by a camp fire, contemplating his own identity...

CHAMPAGNE QUICKSAND

Seven minutes, thirty-two seconds before the orbital attack witnessed by Nico Shikari...

The tabris whistled a jaunty tune to remind Dyce Bastion that it was still working, and that the memory defragmentation had reached a landmark twenty five percent. According to the notification in his Minds Eye, a thirteen-minute and thirty-two second splice of memory was available to experience. With a sinking heart he stared at the device, at the small condensation-collecting LED readout set into one edge. He wasn't so sure that he was ready to see the people he had lost, to see the event that ripped them from him and tore a hole in his existence.

He took a long and deep breath in, then his chest shuddered all the way through the broken exhalation. He closed his eyes and counted down from ten. Then, quickly, in the brief moment between changing his mind and changing it back again, he ran that chunk of recovered memory. The wireless connection flooded his brain with a technically faultless experience, immersing every sense within the refurbished recollections.

Tabris Brain Interface Device, Model Number D0891.
Memory Defragmentation Software, V.3.238
Designated Subject – Dyce J Bastion.

What do I remember?
I remember...
The ship...
The Skinny Puppy was a League of Nations drop-ship in deep orbit above Alcyone. There were at least forty of us locked into hydraulic chairs, each of us had pressurised drop-suits that were attached to our armour with low-yield explosive bolts. Between us there was no oxygen, no sound passed between our lips, only com-link transmissions were possible.
I can hear their voices in my head...
The floor opened beneath our feet, the hydraulics pushed our chairs forward and we detached, falling towards the atmosphere. The heat of re-entry would have turned every soldier's drop suit into a falling firework if the inflatable heat proof cones had not deployed. Shooting Stars, that was the nickname for an orbital drop unit, because so many were statistically incinerated on the way in to the atmosphere. That was rarely because of equipment failure, most of the time it was because the enemy was already firing at them.
Alcyone and its five cities were beneath us.
Us...

Dyce stopped the simulation and his perception returned to the real world. He closed his eyes and shuddered, bowing his head. He slowly tapped the flat end of the tabris against his temple.

Not ready, not yet...

That re-experienced memory of atmospheric re-entry had been replaced by the wind rattling the high-rise window. Curiously, there was something new outside.

Through that window he saw a League solar destroyer coming down through the cloudscape, distorting the technicolour cloud in waves. Every UAM soldier in the area must have seen it too. It had a huge set of solar sails, the spectrum shimmering over their surface like a psychedelic sheen over Cubist butterfly wings. As it headed down towards the bay, the solar sails fold back in, and the antenna arrays all over its underside tucked themselves beneath the hull so that it could splash down. As the ocean took the weight of the ship it caused a tsunami to hit the shore, waves crashing through a few city blocks.

His Minds Eye informed him that this solar destroyer was called The Pulse of the Machine, a League of Nations ship. He had served on her for the last eight months, it was the vessel that had launched the drop-ship that had brought him and his comrades to the edge of the atmosphere, waiting in orbit.

This was a real problem. The League of Nations wanted this man-made landmass and they were going to get it, one way or another. Dyce knew how they thought, and he knew that they wanted the whole continent, one scorched district at a time, if they had no other choice. Because of the failure of the mission that he had been a part of, The Pulse of the Machine was going to nuke the district that he was camping in. It was petty, but it was exactly the kind of *dick-move* that his superiors would pull.

He had an hour or two before the Pulse of the Machine would launch a nuclear payload, he deduced, because bureaucracy would slow things down. Wiping clean a chunk of landmass was not the easiest thing to authorise.

But this wasn't the only League of Nations ship disturbing the skyline that night. A second League of Nations ship, a solar frigate called the Initial Constellation came drifting over the top of his riser, shaking it to its foundations, and it looked as if it were on its way to rendezvous with the solar destroyer. Dyce listened to the building creak and groan all round him, afraid that it might collapse. He took a deep breath and steadied himself as he watched the ship skimming over the tops of the risers between him and the harbour.

Dyce felt sick. At first he thought he might be afraid of what was to come, but then he started to suspect that it was some external force. He started to feel lightheaded and a little dizzy. Something was affecting the air around him. He felt as if he somehow weighed less than he had just a few moments before, as if gravity's pull was shifting.

That's when he saw a line of white drawn down the sky, above the solar frigate, a flickering, voluminous string of energy. The atmosphere hummed and crackled. All of a sudden, the string became a tower of light, spinning the clouds around it into a swirling funnel, looking like an apocalyptic portal to the stars. He squinted and shaded his eyes as he stood up and stumbled toward the window.

..The sky's falling... He thought, remembering the final moments of his former life...

A series of pulses rode that tower of light down into the solar ship, a wave of energy spreading through its megastructure, absorbed into the nucleus of every atom, until it's hull blistered and popped, tearing itself apart.

The Initial Constellation demolished the top few floors of several risers on its way down, trailing a cascade of debris from its gravity well. Each and every part of the ship reached critical mass, vibrant detonations spiralling out through the ship's gravity bubble in tendrils of fire. Then, at last, it began to hale in burning chunks.

The afterimage lingered. The sight of all that power channelled into that beam shook Dyce to his core, triggering a barrage of random memories. He collapsed from shock, grabbing the window frame. He felt a shard of glass dig into his palm, but he didn't care, despite his hand dragging down it.

The last time he saw something like that he was...

..Sky fell on me. Should be dead...

That was a focused PEPP blast from an orbital defence platform. Dyce knew in his heart that this was what had hit him and his comrades.

The first tower of light was still lingering as an afterimage as a second flickering string appeared from the orbital defence platform, this time moving over the Pulse of the Machine as it floated in the ocean.

Parallel banks of hatches popped open all along either side of the Pulse of the Machine's hull. There was a pause for a single second, then from the hatches launched dozens of projectiles, drawing winding vapour trails above the ship. They detonated in clusters, releasing a drifting umbrella of glittering pseudo-snow, millions and millions of reflective shards that fractured the beam. The pure white of the PEPP blast was broken up into a full luminous spectrum as it was refracted, redistributing the bulk of its destructive power out in random directions, evaporating sea water, slicing arcs up through random risers.

The orbital defence platform did not fire again. The Pulse of the Machine had - Dyce assumed - now been successfully hidden by its own squad of onboard hackers, creating the illusion of a direct hit through virtual deception.

The light from the *heavens* faded and only the wine dark of twilight remained beneath the corkscrewed cloudscape. But in the lingering light something in the adjacent riser caught his eye.

There was a figure stood in the opposite window, and this individual had clearly been checking out the show, just like him. He could tell that the figure was holding a large gun, perhaps a sniper rifle. But it was too dark now, and his vision and hearing weren't as superhuman as they had been when he had first woken up, and he had not yet figured out how to retrieve that unnatural but useful state.

He looked down, searching for other threats. It was growing darker - the laser shows left afterimages in the sky, but these were slowly fading - but he was sure that he could see the movement of the large sentry-amp's legs shifting upon the rubble on top of a smaller building's roof, almost directly beneath his window. He hoped that perhaps he had imagined it, at least until he saw the glint of light off a cannon as it turned towards his position. It was still there, keeping an eye on him.

Suddenly he received a notification on his tabris, a message had been broadcast for any League of Nations soldiers in the area, any survivors like him. It decrypted automatically as it accepted his neural fingerprint. It was a countdown, the area would be *"cleansed"* soon, a "deep burn".

'Burn?' Dyce knew full well what it meant. The end.

He was forced to think about his situation and his limited options. He would have to flee this city before the cleansing burn, but there was still the problem of the large number of soldiers possibly on their way up to his floor.

Why me?

Dyce knelt at the window and pulled the headset down over his eyes, using its artificial eyes to magnify the Pulse Of The Machine. It looked so serene, floating on the ocean beneath the impressionistic sky, it's hatches casually closing. Soon it would launch a tactical nuke or send out enough gunships to facilitate a carpet bombing. According to the countdown he had two hours and twenty-eight minutes to get to minimum safe distance.

A loud beep signalled the activation of the sentry gun a split second before it violently burst into life, rattling its needle-tip ammunition down the stairwell. Dyce had to think of an escape plan. He looked around, looked up, looked out. The only thought was that he could abseil, but the spindle built into the tactical armour would never hold enough length of smart-cord to get all the way to ground level. Plus, that tank-like amp was waiting for him.

No... no... stupid... stupid...

The automatic gun exploded, falling from the wall and clattering down the stairs. He could have sworn a bullet had flown through the room, aiming for the muzzle flash. He looked back across the skyline, back at that window he had seen the sniper. He was in trouble.

Dyce drew his handgun, took aim at the open door and waited. His palms were sweaty as his fingers fidgeted around the gun's grip. He made to stamp out the fire but then hesitated, no idea why, perhaps panic was muddling his mind, or perhaps.... Could it be, he suddenly had some semblance of a plan? Perhaps he should really learn to trust himself more, that's what Breaker did, that's what had kept her alive so long.

He heard enemy soldiers take up positions against the wall beside either side of the stairwell door.

He took cover behind one of the concrete pillars, pressing his back against it. His legs shaking, wanting to buckle from sheer psychological shutdown, but he managed to keep himself upright and as still as possible. He found his breathing becoming laboured, his heart rushing, rivers of sweat were running down his spine.

Okay, this is it... what do I do? what would anyone else do? What would she *do...?*

He tried to put himself in the position of more capable people, mentally speaking. Breaker, of course, he knew better than anyone, he had spent the most time with her whilst he had served aboard the Pulse of the Machine. Dyce pictured Breaker, the way she walked, the way she moved, the way she talked, because perhaps that was a physical manifestation of the way her mind worked, thought projecting for, and surely that flowed both ways, form could manipulate thought. So, he imagined stepping into Breaker as if it she were a suit of armour, imagining himself moving how she moved, talking how she talked, and therefore thinking how she thought.

What would Breaker do in this position? What would she do if they had nothing to lose? Dyce remembered how Breaker had talked about how she had trained herself to tap into the *flow* state.

Go with the flow.

His mind returned to the crazy idea of the window, the smart-cord on its spindle, and then added the extra idea of the high-density gas grenades he had. That was an impossible idea, what sane person would do that...? Especially with that amp on the roof of the building below, watching the room? But that lower roof was his only chance, as slim as it was.

He procrastinated, as he always did. He was a passive person, he always had been. Dyce simply stood and waited, holding his gun. Accepting his fate.

But...

Isn't this the day for the impossible? Isn't it time for a change? Take a chance? You can lie on life's train tracks and let the world run over you, or you can do something about it...

That sounded like *her...*

No... no... I can't... I...

Even after the automated gun had fallen, broken, to the stairs, he could still hear it attempting to fire, clicking as it swung left and right. Perhaps a single round was still lodged in the barrel confusing the firing mechanism.

He took another deep breath and closed his eyes, for a just a few seconds. Still visualising, over and over again, that he was viewing the world from the body and minds of peoples he admired, convincing himself that escape was possible. He ran through it over and over. The changes were so infinitesimal that he barely even noticed at first. He found himself standing a little taller, a little straighter, shoulders back, chin up, chest out.

Suddenly, from behind the walls, the enemy soldiers opened fire, shooting straight through the wall. Dyce held his position as ammunition whittled away the edges of the concrete pillar.

("Cease fire!") Came a voice over his com-link, a communication that he should not have been hearing. *("Save your ammo! Threat is minimal. There is one combatant in the room, repeat, there is only one combatant in the room!")*

The firing stopped. Dyce wondered if his tabris had, *maybe*, randomly synced to the enemy channel. Maybe his new tabris was already setup to intercept enemy coms. He knew, though, that the message had come from the sniper in the adjacent riser. Within his Minds Eye an identification window with garbled text popped-up for the mysterious speaker, trying to form from fracturing data. He made out a few letters, the first part of the name definitely started with a T.

("He's hiding behind the third pillar on your right.")

Well, fuck-you very much! Dyce thought. So that was definitely the sniper, no doubt.

Slowly the enemy aggressors entered the room, he could hear their heavy feet as they took steady steps. Five of them were spreading out in a wide circle around his concrete pillar. They surrounded him, aiming their rail rifles squarely at his head. Three of them kept their firearms trained on Dyce, the other two nervously scanned the rest of the room. Dyce noted that each of them had a mark sprayed on the chest of their armour, that could have been either the letter A or the number four.

'Where are the others?' Shouted one of the soldiers.

'I...' Dyce had already fumbled his response. 'There's just...'

'Shut that *shit* up!' One of the soldiers opened his helmet and shouted at Dyce.

To Dyce's surprise, his Minds Eye system filled with information about this man, from the field hospital he was born in to the date he last had a tooth extracted. His name was Reaver, and he was wanted for war crimes.

'I don't want to hear any bullshit, boy, where are the others?'

'*Others...*'

'The others, you fucking moron!'

'It's a trick,' Dyce said. 'Someone is...'

'Drop the gun and put your fucking hands up!' Reaver shouted.

It took amazing effort for Dyce not to close his eyes, like a condemned man facing a firing squad. But - and this really shocked him - he did not drop his gun, he didn't even lower it. Instead, in a move that defied all reason, he pointed the business end of the firearm directly at Reaver's face and stepped away from the pillar. Reaver stepped back, but he did not lower his rail rifle either.

What the fuck are you doing? Dyce asked himself. *Oh shit, oh fuck, oh...*

But things were about to get even more muddled. The enemy's Corporal strode into the room, the sleek polished armour looked more impressive than the scratched and scuffed armour worn by the rest of their team. The corporal's featureless helmet was locked shut over their face, only the three tiny eyes caught the moon light as they surveyed the room.

The Corporal walked with incredible confidence and focus, as the rest of their team dispersed around the room. The Corporal trusted them totally to keep her covered, knowing that she didn't need to even draw her weapon until she absolutely had to.

The corporal charged at Dyce, something that Dyce simply was not prepared for, displacing the campfire as she flew through it. Before Dyce even knew what was happening the corporal had landed a blow that sent him reeling, losing his handgun as his back hit the pillar. The gun skipped across the carpet of shrapnel and slid towards the smashed window.

With a low kick, the Corporal swept Dyce off his feet, the back of his head hitting the floor and it's jagged metal gravel. The corporal leaned over him and pushed two fingers up under Dyce's tactical headset and forced it from his eyes, revealing his startled face.

'What the actual fuck?' Asked the corporal, releasing her grip and standing back in surprise. '*You?*'

'Me?' Dyce was beginning to think that he sure was popular for a *no-one.*

More UAM soldiers charged in. Dyce put his hands up as a dozen barrels pointed down at him. Someone pulled him up off his arse and shoved him down awkwardly onto his knees. The corporal tilted her head quizzically as, behind her, the soldiers parted and their new lieutenant entered the room.

'Is this it?' Lieutenant Rosario asked. 'Where are the rest of them?'

'A system glitch,' the Corporal said with a sigh, trying to mask her frustration at the inferior human being who was technically her superior officer. 'We were chasing ghosts.'

'Looks like you were right.'

'Corporal Oshii is never wrong,' said Reaver, pushing his chest out with pride.

Dyce froze upon hearing that name. Despite his corrupting concussion and the slow progress of his cognitive reconstruction, it was not really that much of a surprise that he recognised and remembered Oshii so easily, not with the history that they had. That name, that body language, the way she had charged into him fist first, she had been there, on the periphery of his consciousness since his rebirth. He knew that name very well, knew *her* very well, and it all came flooding back *like waves crashing on the shores of his sanity.* He had only known her for a short period of time a few years ago, but she had been everything to him, even as she had treated him as nothing.

This was indeed a very strange day, and days like this don't happen by accident, they happen by design.

'*Chasing ghosts...*' Dyce whispered.

Corporal Paris Oshii opened her helmet, her eyes glistening with malignant joy. Data filled Dyce's Minds Eye, from Oshii's personal history to a rundown of her war crimes, both proven and assumed.

Oshii crouched down in front of Dyce, who was still on his knees. She moved this way and that, trying to catch the boy's gaze, revelling in Dyce's inability to look her in the eye. Oshii clearly intimidated Dyce, and she was loving it.

'We came all the way up here for one kid?' lieutenant Rosario asked. 'What are you, sixteen?'

Dyce said nothing.

'You're about nineteen by now, aren't you, *boy*?' Corporal Paris Oshii asked.

'You know him?'

'Yeah, from the Ivanka Prisoner Of War camp, where I was stationed a couple of years ago.'

'*The Battle of Ivanka...*' Rosario said, shaking his head as he thought about the things that he had heard about that place and the battle that had ended its infamy but berthed it's legend. 'I heard about the things you did that day...'

'Oshii was always a legend,' Reaver said. 'That's when the

world realised it.'

'You're a long way from that failed training exercise, when you were captured and brought you into *my* camp, and into my *care, boy*,' Oshii grinned.

Dyce couldn't help it any longer, this was all becoming too much. He found himself breaking Breaker's rule, closing his eyes. He was afraid to look, afraid to speak, wishing he didn't have to admit this was happening at all. But something else happened in the reign of sparks behind his eyes, a strange feeling that he struggled to explain to himself. Something within him was different, somehow, and not just the physical differential.

'I bet this is your first full scale battle insertion, right?' Oshii asked. 'So there are some things you need to learn. I taught you a lot, didn't I, boy, when you were in my charge? Here's some more. The most important of these is to realise you are expendable. Have you started to realise that, right? No one is coming for you, no one cares. You're no one, you're nothing.'

But Dyce was barely listening, distracted by a curious sensation. He could somehow sense that sentry-amp stationed on the roof of the smaller adjacent building. Somehow, he knew its inhuman, uncaring intentions. Through its systems and synthetic senses, the amp could see a lot of League heat signatures up there on the floor of that building, the same ghost signal that had brought *her* here, signatures that belonged to League soldiers that simply did not exist. Somehow, Dyce saw what it saw, without even attempting to hack into it, it had simply happened. The amp believed that the American troops were overwhelmed by an unbeatable number of their enemy, and the amp knew only data, and the simulated threat seemed all too real.

I don't have long... We don't have long...

'Is this kid catatonic or something?' He heard Reaver say.

He had always been the type to accept his fate, to lie there and take it. There was a voice that belonged to the *old him*, that this was inevitable, this room would be destroyed by the amp, these districts would be nuked by the ship, and that he had no hope, that he should accept it, that fighting, *persisting*, was pointless.

But...

He placed himself in Breaker's shoes, replaying the free fall into this country, only he imagined that it was himself fighting the unfolding amp on top of the out-of-control troop carrier, vicariously through his friend's actions as precisely as his memory would allow. He felt empowered, emboldened, as he felt her confidence flow through him, almost overwriting his own programming with every successive repeat of the process.

He heard the others around him talking, to themselves, to him, getting increasingly frustrated as he failed to respond.

But he found that, if he tried, he could remember even more, the pressure, perhaps, focusing his mind. Yet again he imagined himself in Breaker's place during their intense training, during brief combat encounters, or something as simple as playing pool in their downtime. Looking at the world through her eyes, moving the way she moved, talking the way she talked and ultimately thinking the way she thought. Dyce's back straightened up, he held his head high, as if the crippling emotion was draining from him. He took a long, slow, deep breath and put on his *game-face*.

Oshii was still talking, the lieutenant was still talking, but Dyce wasn't listening, it was all just background noise. His mind was on overdrive, his eyes flicking around as he formulated a plan. He needed his gun, that had bounced towards the window, he would also need to get a rail rifle from an enemy, he'd source software to hack the security later. *Then what?* The only way out was the window. *But how?* He was running it through his mind, over and over. The problem, still, was fear.

'We're wasting time,' said lieutenant Rosario as he turned, waving a dismissive hand. 'He's catatonic. Goodbye, kid.'

'Shame,' Oshii said, with a grin. She tilted her head in faux sympathy. 'I could have made something of him.'

Then, suddenly, Dyce had time for one more epiphany. This feeling that was crippling him, the racing heart, the sweating, the breaking breath, he didn't have to call it *fear.* If he changed what he called it, he could change his reaction to it. He could call it *excitement.*

He opened his eyes and fixed them upon the lieutenant.

'Wait!' Dyce called out, and lieutenant Rosario turned back to look at him. 'I have to ask you a question.'

'"*Wait*"?' Oshii repeated, in disbelief. 'Are you serious, *boy*?'

Dyce stood up. He still did not look at Oshii, his gaze was fixed only on the lieutenant. Reaver advanced on Dyce from behind, shouting an order to *get back down* on his knees. Dyce did not comply.

'There is a UAM sentry-amp on the building beneath...'

'On your knees!'

'On...' Dyce repeated, but then pressed on, louder than before. 'On the building beneath us and it is about to launch its payload right into this room,' Dyce said. 'Because wiping out a few of you is a small price to pay to take out so many League soldiers. Imaginary or not, it can't tell the difference.'

Dyce looked around the room at every one of the soldiers – skimming over Oshii - so that they could all see his sincerity. He instantly found that actually looking out, instead of shoe gazing, added to his feeling of empowerment. It still felt precarious, though. He knew that he was faking it, and it could all come crashing down.

'Why don't you ask your sniper over there to verify what I'm saying?'

Dyce knew that their sniper would be moving to the window ledge and looking down or making their point drone do it. Dyce knew that the sniper must have sent them a live feed of what her headset had seen, because of Oshii's reaction; The corporal turned around, looking at each of her men, clearly doing some mental calculations of her own, figuring out the chances of each of them getting out alive.

'And each and every person in this room knows that we

don't have much time. Whilst you may think that I am expendable...'

'And you are,' lieutenant Rosario added, clearly not taking this as serious as Dyce or Oshii. Perhaps the sniper had not shown him what had been shown to the others.

'You're expendable, too.' Dyce asked, but there was only silence in response. 'You know that, right?'

Dyce had an opportunity right then, as the enemy around him started to realise that they might be in trouble, and for the briefest of seconds there was a chance that he would just stand there and wait for fate to wipe him out...

But he was as surprised as anyone to find that he was holding a displacement grenade. He didn't look at it, just turned it around in his hand as a part of himself tried to talk himself out of arming it, and cursed his own name as he did just that. With an underhanded spin he tossed it into the crackling campfire. The grenade's housing splintered as it landed, gravity hiccupped as it detonated. The shrapnel and spent casings erupted up and out like a fountain of glittering red and yellow as it reflected the flying fire, cartwheeling through the room, clattering over soldiers as they lost their grip on gravity.

Dyce threw himself backwards into Reaver, grabbing the burly man's rail rifle. They tussled, but both men held it tight, even as Reaver's trigger finger jammed and the gun unloaded an entire magazine over their heads, a glistening arch of muzzle-flare around them.

Dyce pulled on the rifle as he pushed Reaver back away with his foot, struggling until the buckle bent, the strap snapped, and the big man finally let it go. The biometric security on the gun flashed red. Dyce attached it to the magnetic plate on his back and the rotary lock spun shut around the centre of the barrel, holding it in place.

("*The Sentry-amp just primed two missiles for launch,*") Kosheen's voice came over the com-link, and Dyce, somehow, heard it, too as a glitch in his Minds Eye tried to form her face in his peripheral. ("*Pointed right at you!*")

Dyce and Oshii turned to run at the same time, but both sprinted in opposite directions. As Dyce hurtled through the room he fired the anchor for the smart cord into the concrete floor, then he swooped down to grab his handgun from where it had landed beside the window frame.

He leapt out of the window, out into the early evening gloom, gale force winds battering his body, the derelict skyline spinning around him as his legs passed over his head. With the smart cord unfurling in his wake, he swung back down and hit the window beneath, his armoured arse sliding down it, his feet uselessly trying to find friction.

The sentry-amp's multiple crosshairs convened upon this tumbling target, before opening fire with both of its rotating motor-driven mini-guns, creating parallel lines of obliterated glass that followed Dyce down the side of the riser.

The sentry-amp launched two missiles, trails of burning propellant following them all the way up to the storey that contained the Augmented Fourth, obliterating the ceiling upon impact, which did the only sensible, realistic thing that it could do and collapsed into the floor beneath, and that, too, was demolished by the concussive weight, along with anyone who may have been sandwiched between them.

Dyce heard the destruction, but he was too preoccupied to even think of looking back. The spindle on his smart cord was overheating from the friction, steam enveloping every unfurling metre, until the room it was anchored in finally, completely, disintegrated. The whip of the cord as it lost its grip slammed Dyce's back against the riser, the crown of his head bouncing down it.

He didn't have time to admit that this was musty brown underwear time, but he wouldn't have been able to deny it.

He pulled his legs back and kicked away, swan diving towards the smaller building below. The sentry-amp was waiting for him there, reloading, its automated mechanisms discarding the empty ammo tumblers before spinning full ones into place, locked and loaded.

Dyce threw the first of his high-density gas grenades down ahead of himself, detonating just beneath his feet, releasing an expanding cloud so dense that it was able to cushion his inevitable impact. He hit the deck and rolled with absolutely no grace, bouncing off his own face and landing on his arse which was scorched from the window slide.

One of the sentry-amp's long, thin legs cut through the thick cloud and slammed down inches from Dyce's vulnerable head. The machine reared up to its full height, dwarfing him. It had a small body compared to the length of its legs, heavy ordinance on its back and belly, gravity orbs in the tips of its legs to allow it to walk vertically down any structure. In the right condition it could be fast, like a skittering spider.

As the gas cloud dispersed across the roof, Dyce got to his feet, took out his handgun and got ready for a fight, because he really didn't feel like leaping off any more buildings today. He threw one of his two chaff grenades, but instead of dispersing above the Sentry-amp, it bounced off the amp's torso and detonated whilst it was above Dyce. It exploded in a shower of static that blinded both of them. Dyce had to raise his now temporarily useless headset to see with his own two eyes. The confused Sentry-amp fumbled backwards along the building's roof, before firing at the last place that Dyce had been.

But Dyce was already running. He threw his body through a roof-access door and bounced down the stairwell. He pulled himself to his feet and orientated himself, even though the world seemed to be spinning around him.

He stopped and placed his hands on the wall as he tried to steady himself. He had a moment, he thought, to catch his breath, the amp wouldn't be able to follow him down.

Did that really just happen? What the actual fuuuu…?

There was an open door ahead of him, leading into a room that was possibly meant to be an apartment. A large shadow moved across the apartment's floor, and it had four long legs. Dyce swore and slapped his own face in frustration, as he realised that the Sentry-amp was clinging to the outside of the riser, following him down.

'Oh, give me five *fucking* minutes…'

There was a trio of turbine guns on the amp's belly, moving independently, surveying the inside of the riser. One of them must have spotted something, because suddenly the building shook as the three guns let loose, tearing through the structure. Dyce scrambled down the stairs to the mezzanine between floors and squatted on a step as the walls turned to dust above and below him. He covered his ears and tried to ball himself up into the smallest possible target.

The onslaught abated and all that was left was the ringing in his ears. He dared to take a peek and saw the sentry-amp taking steady steps down the side of the riser, leaning in against it, the smoking turbine guns twitching like pincers.

He sat there, his heart galloping away. The amp didn't fire again, it could have torn the wall apart to get him, but it didn't.

He took the stolen rail rifle from his back and tapped the tabris against the security processor on the base of the barrel. The physical act of tapping initiated a wireless-handshake between devices, instructing them to synchronise through the Near Field Communication Wireless Protocol. He knew that he could hack the security, it was like second nature to him. He wouldn't have to hack the security's biometrics, he would install a bootleg version of the League's security BIOS so that it bi-passed the weapon's built in satellite connection which it would normally use to update the user database, and add his credentials. It should, therefore, recognise him.

As quietly as he could, he unlocked the barrel and opened it up by its hinge to check the magnetic rail within was clear. A magnetic propulsion system meant no gunpowder, so it made very little noise. Not quite silent, it was known to make a *whistle* and a *whomp* when firing individual rounds, but it could become a staccato when unleashing a sustained salvo.

He peaked over the stairs and saw the shadow of the metal quadruped, moving slowly. He knew he should get going, but he had to make sure the weapon wasn't going to break down on him when he needed it most.

He checked the emergency spare magazine attached to the side of the gun, which Reaver had held in place with duct tape. This magazine, a high-capacity storage and feeding device potentially holding up to three hundred and twenty eight needle-sized rounds, had a label on it – felt-tip pen on duct tape – stating that it was filled with venom-tipped needles, a mixture of spider and scorpion, but a visual check revealed that it was actually loaded with a mixture of needles, nails and screws. The scavenged ammo wasn't perfect, but as long as they didn't jam the magnetic rail, they would still be lethal.

He gingerly slid out the gun's battery and hesitated. He took another glance at the enemy automaton. It was moving along the side of the building. Despite any damage done to its visual systems, the amp must have caught a glimpse of its prey, because it fired one single exploratory round that tore a line through Dyce's left cheek. The force of it spun his head around, flicking blood away.

Almost in shock, eyes wide and jaw agape, he froze, staring into space. He couldn't move, he couldn't give away his position. He was lucky that he hadn't made a sound. Then, when he had gotten far enough over the shock to move his limbs, he slid down the steps, one at a time, until he was back out of the machine's line of sight, then he went back to work. He He visually checked the battery's connectors before he reloaded it. He stared at the small red LED light by the trigger, waiting, with bated breath, for it to turn change.

As Dyce inspected the fresh wound on his face with his fingers, he started to suspect that his mental state actually seemed to be detrimental to his inhuman ability to heal rapidly. This made him more stressed, which, of course, was only going to make things worse.

A little voice in the back of his head screamed.

But the little LED on the rifle turned green just in time, as without warning an anchor embedded itself in the wall of the stairwell above, propelled from the burning riser he had just escaped from. Dyce watched the anchor's smart cord tighten, following it to the single soldier using it to zip-line between the buildings. Reaver, on his way over to cause a whole load of fuss.

Dyce looked for the sentry again. It was clear that the chaff grenade's effect still lingered, the machine struggling to make sense of its sensory feedback, relying on the glimpses of the world around it and the shifting afterimages of the targets within that whole general mishmash.

Dyce pulled his only ice grenade and bowled it across the room towards the window. The sentry amp spotted the movement of the grenade and opened fire upon it, a bullet clipping the explosive device as it reached the window, the subsequent detonation creating a bespoke ice rink. The amp lost its grip.

Humidity and moisture fast froze within the concrete's cracks, expanding and breaking beneath the machine's scrambling feet. A cloud of dust became a flurry of snow that whipped and whirled around the gravity orbs at the tip of its legs. The amp scrambled to keep a grip, throwing its considerable weight into the room, tearing grooves in the floor, reluctant to fall.

Dyce heard the cracking of the riser as the sentry pulled itself in, its bulk forcing the ceiling up and pushing the floor down.

Dyce didn't wait, he made his move, under attack from every which way, he leapt over the stairwell's railing, dropping many more storeys. He grabbed at a random railing, but the sudden stop nearly yanked his arm from its socket. The building shook, then he dropped again.

A verbal train of expletives followed him all the way down.

CATALYSE

Five minutes and thirty two seconds before Dyce hurtled down the stairwell.

(*"The Sentry-amp just primed at least two missiles for launch,"*) Kosheen called over the com-link, as her point drone analysed the Sentry-amp. (*"Pointed right at you!"*)

Trip Kosheen jumped to her feet and got ready to move before the proverbial excrement hit the fan. She ordered the drone to reattach to its charging cradle on her back, then folded up the sniper rifle and stowed it on the lock next to the slumbering drone.

From this distance she could see the rest of the Augmented Fourth stood around the belligerent British boy, but she could not wait to see what happened next, she had to move, and she struggled to accept the fact that the others had not run after her warning. Despite that, she was soon at the stairwell and descending step after step, flight after flight.

She stopped for a moment as her headset's suite of augmented senses detected the telltale punch of projectiles launching and the subsequent whistle as they flew through the air. Through a window she saw the boy leap out of the adjacent riser, summersaulting out as his smart cord trailed behind him, before a missile struck it, engulfing the entire floor in one large fire ball.

She saw the progress of her teammates through her com-link connection to them. She saw that - at the opposite end of that broken, burning building - the doors to the ancient elevator shaft took three shotgun rounds, imploding further with every strike. Oshii and her men crashed through it, their powered armour turning their bodies into battering rams. They each hit the back wall of the shaft before falling down it, scraping at the walls and grabbing for ledges and cable.

They left lieutenant Rosario behind. Well, *parts* of him.

Kosheen stopped running for a second to watch the boy tumbling down the side of the riser – *crazy bastard!* - as the Sentry-amp fired up at him, making a mess of the building's windows. The cracks were spreading across the riser, fractal fissures resembling the branches and routes of some vast, ethereal tree.

She descended another couple of flights before pausing again to check on the boy's progress, finding it somehow quite impressive, in its own haphazard way. She saw the League boy drop high density gas grenades, smothering the adjacent roof.

("Kosheen?") Came a voice over the com-link.

("Oshii? Good to hear your voice,") Kosheen was relieved that her mentor and leader was still alive.

("Did you see what happened to that fucking idiot?")

("Which "fucking idiot" would that be, sir?")

She paused one more time, witnessed the sentry-amp force its way into the smaller building, chasing after that lone League soldier, making a mess of the structure as it blindly sprayed ammo that erupted out of every side, splashes of glittering obliteration against the blue twilight.

("Well, you could take your pick, but let's start with Reaver. He used his smart cord to zip-line to the other building before I had chance to say no, I don't know if he made it before all hell broke loose down there.")

Kosheen leapt onto a banister and crouched there, the tiny gravity orbs in the tips of her prosthetic legs keeping her perfectly balanced. She detached her point drone. The device, which was about the size of a fist, floated up from the back of her armour, tethered to her shoulder because its battery was worn out and refusing to hold a charge. It started to scan the smaller building for life signs.

(*"The flames are masking heat signatures on that floor, but I'm currently observing some "fucking idiot" falling all the way to the basement via the stairwell. Okay... I guess its the boy, even Reaver wouldn't be stupid enough to enter the service system through the basement. Surely, right?"*)

Kosheen returned her attention to the floor that Reaver had probably landed on, looking for any sign of the moron.

(*"The service tunnels?"*) Oshii said over the com-link. (*"The Red Strays will tear that boy apart..."*)

(*"What a fucking idiot."*)

CUPID DELUXE

Dyce Bastion forced his way into the building's basement and collapsed to the floor, unable to believe what he had just put himself through, and hardly able to believe that it had worked. Above him he heard the sentry-amp burrow its way deeper in, the riser trembling as the machine tore it open and it subsequently collapsed on top of it.

There was a service hatch beneath Dyce's knees, leading down into the service tunnels. He found that it was suspiciously ajar, but the ceiling was crumbling, he had no choice but to go deeper. Still, he struggled with its weight, opening it required enough force to make every inch of muscle scream. When that was done, after he had convinced himself that he wasn't crying, he looked down into the darkness. He tried not to think about what might be down there waiting for him, but it was his only option, the situation only becoming more desperate with every clash of the cacophony of chaos crashing down through the structure above.

He slid down the ladder, losing his grip as everything shuck and landing arse-first in ankle deep filthy water. His eyes adjusted quickly to the dark, which was good, but the smell was so bad that he almost wished that his nose had been broken in one of the many impacts that he had suffered. *Almost.* The source of the stench could have been the water, gas pipes, the corroded coating on the electrical cables, or maybe even the data transfer cabling, biological in composition, sprouting pockets of pulsating mould.

Okay...

He took the rail rifle from his back and checked his handiwork. The LED on the rail rifle turned green when he held the grip, gathering identification from his neural-fingerprint. It was ready to use, easy as that. Knowledge is half the battle.

He wanted to take a deep breath to calm himself, but he really didn't want to be inhaling in this unspeakable odour at all, if he could help it. Had all that really happened? *Did I do that?* Out of everything that had happened to him since he arrived in this country, his own uncharacteristic actions seemed to him to be the least believable.

 He jogged on, rail rifle at the ready, through random tunnels, until he came out into a large, cavernous tunnel lit by many burning drums, flickering far into the distance in both directions. The tunnel was lined with ribbed supports that made it look as if he were within the rotten belly of a vast serpent.

The fires were illuminating many ancient, abandoned military vehicles, perhaps this had once been a secret underground supply route many decades ago. He walked slowly to the nearest vehicle, curious, taking cautious, considered steps. The vehicle had eight flat tires and smashed windows, and it was clear that someone was living inside it.

He stepped away.

A sound like a wind chime echoed sporadically through the endless cavern, mostly distant but occasionally close. It could have been coming from multiple sources, from any of the poky alleyways or shadowy nooks formed between ancient obstacles abandoned for reasons lost to time.

In the distance he saw thin figures move against the living light. He couldn't turn back, the building wasn't accessible any more, in all probability it didn't exist as a recognisable structure anymore . He jogged on. All around him, out of the corners of his eyes, he saw movement. He saw the outlines of more figures ahead, blurred by the heat-haze of the fires. He slowed to a stroll, to take a clear survey of just how *fucked* he was. He dare not stop.

He tried to breathe slow and shallow, to make no sound. He saw alcoves where barely distinguishable figures seemed to be tending to children. He glanced inside another vehicle and saw shapes stir beneath filthy sheets.

There was something different up ahead that caught his eye. It was like a communal meeting place, lit by two barrels containing fires that must have been kept continuously lit, judging by the piles of assorted kindling. Between these barrels was an incomplete statue constructed of spare parts, some welded into place, some lashed together. It was an artifice of humanity, its shape made of twisted scrap metal and embedded, outdated electronics, wrapped in a bondage of wiring and industrial cabling. The statue was missing a head, but it did have an imposing pair of wings sprouting from its back, spanning up the curve of the tunnel wall.

There were cushions, repurposed vehicle seats, scattered in semi-circles around its base. A lot of people had knelt there. *Prayed there.* There was a platform in front of the statue, where perhaps someone would stand and preach. R10t was painted on the walls around it, over and over in different handwriting and sizes, visible in phases as the flames flickered. There were ceremonial vestments, neatly folded on a podium.

Before all of this, stood an altar.

Oh... I'm in trouble...

Dyce creeped on, through the shadows. His heart was still pounding from the previous escape, and he really didn't think he was ready for another.

He reached a bottleneck - a vehicle with rusted barrels piled up either side of it, from the doors to the walls to the ceiling. He couldn't sneak around, and he certainly couldn't crawl through, he wasn't that stupid. *Over, then. Fuck.*

He stepped cautiously onto the crushed engine block. The vehicle dipped as the suspension took his weight, impressive for a car in this state, and of this vintage, to have not seized up. The vehicle creaked as it dipped. He dry-swallowed the rank atmosphere and tasted his own fear. He looked around to see if the sound had attracted attention. No reaction. He lifted his other foot up and on. The vehicle creaked again. He stepped gingerly over the missing windshield's empty frame, fearing what might lurk within and could grasp at him.

There was a woman stood on the back end of the vehicle. Her head was bowed, her long explicitly white hair covering her face, like white ribbons fluttering in some unseen breeze. Her skin was stretched tight, sinewy and yellowing. Her entire body, from head to toe, was tattooed with geometric shapes in different shades red. If someone were twisted enough to take a scalpel to the skin, cut them out and piece them together, they would interlock like jigsaw pieces.

Dyce knew what this was, he remembered the stories, the myths and legends, as soon as he saw this emaciated crimson wraith. Born of lost units and failed assaults, those who tried to hide from the war, to live a little longer, to be free. But time, circumstance and desperation forged them into something... *other...* The *lost.* The *forgotten.* The Strays. But some were so impoverished, so cut off from *everything* that could be considered civilised, that they had turned feral and cannibalistic. Those were the Red Strays.

The girl had not moved, not a millimetre. Dyce didn't know what to do. He could hear an escalating thump, a perpetual beat that definitely seemed to be building towards something. Against his every instinct he moved on over the vehicle, hoping that she remained as vacant as she seemed. Perhaps he could simply pass her by.

Barely perceivable at first, as if it were a trick of the firelight, the girl begun rocking back and forth on her heels, head still bowed. Dyce looked her up and down, saw that her hands were studded with rusty nails and razorblades, held in place with pins or tightly woven bandages, her skin was infected where these crude augmentations had become claws. There was a slither of skin still hanging from one of them, and Dyce doubted that the skin belonged to the woman.

Dyce heard movement behind him, a lot of movement,

an escalation of unpleasant things. More Red Strays were surrounding the vehicle now, all shapes and sizes. One or two looked convincingly capable of prising open his tactical armour and making minced meat of his body.

The girl rolled her head around, so that her bone white hair slid back to reveal what remained of her nose and her wide, dilated eyes. Her cracked lips started to bleed as her mouth tried to form a smile. She seemed to like the sensation, somehow, because her smile widened into a grin.

'*Fuck's* sake...' Dyce said, and then looked at the girl. 'I am so *tired*. So, so fucking tired. You would not believe the day I've had. Just...'

Dyce stuttered, rolled his eyes and held up one finger. He heard a lot of stirring behind him, leading to a lot of chatter. He heard the scrape of metal on concrete that he assumed were melee weapons.

'Just give give me one -*fucking*- minute...'

But the the girl had clearly decided that this interloper had more than enough time. She let out a ferocious cry as she charged at Dyce, the speed with which she transitioned between motionless menace and full-tilt assault was astonishing. She was already upon him when Dyce pulled the trigger, the rifle's magnetic rail launching several rusty nails that tore up her abdomen. The point-blank flung her backwards, but she managed to strike at Dyce first, her claws dug into Dyce's face, tearing shreds out of it. The wraith hit the floor hard.

Dyce leapt to another vehicle, jumping up onto its engine block and running to the back, taking shots at anything that moved, not thinking, not conserving his ammunition. It reminded him of being on the assault courses back in training. Another recovered memory, apparently.

A thin figure emerged from another vehicle and attacked Dyce, pulling him in through the door and onto the back seat. It was the thin, white-haired girl, apparently no stranger to pain and not in the least bit debilitated by it, in fact it seemed to fuel her fire. She moved in canine lunges, jabbing a blade into Dyce's tactical armour, to the left of the chest, prising free metal studs and rivets that disconnected and departed, and he felt it pierce his skin. He spun round and heard the snap of the blade as it became trapped in his newly deformed chest plate.

In the confusion Dyce rolled out of the car and landed on his back with a bounce. He pointed the rifle up at the thin Stray, which gave the feral thing reason to pause even as she rose up above him, ready to pounce. Dyce wondered whether the Stray would realise that the rail rifle was now empty even as he, gingerly, placed his fingers upon the emergency magazine that the weapon's previous owner had taped to the side of the barrel.

The Stray reached slowly for another knife, one of many, her bony fingers wrapping around the hilt.

Dyce gripped the fresh magazine between every finger but his index, using that digit to flick a switch that released the empty magazine, letting it slide out and drop away, as he tore the magazine free from the duct tape that housed it. The thin Stray charged, screaming. Dyce was quicker – *just* - slamming in the new magazine and firing a single rusty screw which entered the Stray's brain via the eye socket, popping the eyeball on its way through.

The Stray did not drop, at least not whilst he was watching. Her body arced backward, became petrified like a tragic statue, her hands held up limply before her. Her gawping mouth absent a scream. She was a ghoulish silhouette against the flickering of the fires.

More figures climbed up onto the roof of the car. He couldn't go over it. There were figures advancing from the way that he had come.

Dyce rolled onto his belly and charged back through the vehicle, stepping on something squishy beneath a blanket. The squishy thing squirmed and moaned.

He stooped as he ran, trying to hide his route, dodging between vehicles and stockpiles of ration boxes. He ducked behind a tank, checking each of the vehicles around him for movement. He rarely stopped moving forward, keeping behind cover, staying low, checking each dark corner in every direction, over and over until he started to feel dizzy. He was panicking. He could hear more movement than he could see, the literal and existential darkness making him too paranoid to trust even his headset. Then, quite suddenly, every dark corner birthed a shambling target, their blades glimmering red from the barrel fires.

Dyce was moving slowly, and so were *they.* They wobbled as they walked, which made them look less than human, but Dyce was starting to wonder *if... They look so...*

The mob hadn't yet caught sight of him, so he stopped behind some chunky pipe work, forcing himself into the crevice between them. He took the opportunity to inspect a couple of screws that had become lodged in his arm during an attack. He could only assume that they must have been part of the Stray girl's claws, ripped from her fingers when she had torn at Dyce.

What is wrong with these people?

Dyce had to wind one of the screws out of his muscle, seething in pain. Finally out, he examined the screw's head, apparently flattened by a a hammer and welded to a ring, and it was from this circlet that the thin girl's torn *skin* dangled. On closer inspection he realised that it wasn't skin at all, it was skin coloured sticky plastic. All of the sharp implements that appeared to be embedded in the Stray's emaciated bodies, perhaps it was all just for show, used to intimidate.

But before he could remove the second screw, a large hand grabbed him and pulled him violently from behind the pipes, slamming Dyce back against them. This hulking Stray, lifted him up off the floor by the neck, squeezing his windpipe.

This Stray, clearly better fed than some of the others, and certainly physically imposing, had a sledgehammer slung over his shoulders with his other hand. Dyce tried to lift his rail rifle but the grip on his neck was too strong, and he was quickly coming to the conclusion that oxygen was a prerequisite of doing stuff. As he started to pass out every surface became a mosaic of abstract shapes.

But the Hammer Stray swung Dyce through the air and slammed him hard into the roof of a stripped-down tank, causing the rail rifle to fly out of his hand, flung so hard that it skipped across the roof of two more cars. Seven Strays made to grab the weapon, forming a scrum that another three Strays soon piled upon.

To Dyce the Hammer Stray was upside down, leaning over him as he lay awkwardly over the tank's ancient and empty armaments, tilting his head curiously at Dyce. Perhaps he was wondering why the boy had ventured down here, into their lair.

The big man let him go, which Dyce quickly deduced was not a good thing. Through the fog of concussion - the latest of many, which were surely stacking up and fuelling themselves at this point, self-sustainable brain damage - he watched as The Hammer Stray took his signature weapon from his back, considered its weight, probably more for show than anything, then prepared to strike with it.

Dyce glanced back at his rail rifle, still the focal point of a crimson scrum. He managed to summon enough movement from his failing musculature motor skills to grab his handgun, which he dropped. He just about managed to catch it on the second bounce, even as it glanced awkwardly off the tank's hatch, just in time to shoot the Hammer Stray in one of his bulging biceps. The Stray dropped his signature heavy implement, hitting the roof an inch from Dyce's head, denting the metal as it rebounded, ringing it like a bell.

'That was a fucking warning shot,' Dyce lied through aching larynx, attempting to cover up his shit shot and claw back some semblance of intimidation and competence. The Hammer Stray wasn't listening.

Dyce had seen people reacting to bullet wounds before, and he generally expected the recipient to fall back in debilitating agony, but there was something unsettling about the way this man's face was contorting, and the way his arm was moving…

The pile of Strays fighting over Dyce's rail rifle had paused their competition for a moment, at first distracted by the handgun's discharge, which rang through the tunnel, but they had clearly caught on to what was happening to the Hammer Stray before the young interloper.

The Hammer Stray's skin ruptured, all the way along the injured arm, and from out of the twisting sinew emerged eight tentacles, suckers and all, dripping crimson. Dyce watched in horror as he realised that he had used the wrong bullet, unable to stop the eldritch chain reaction. The Hammer Stray's head tilted backwards as even more writhing tentacles forced their way out of his nostrils and mouth, breaking the bone and cartilage, stretching the flesh breaking point, wrapping around each other as they reached up. These weren't the only orifices from which they emerged, as many more formed a slithering trunk beneath him, spreading out along the ground, tilting him back as they offered him up. Then they started to petrify, the colour draining from them as they became charcoal. When it was all over the Hammer Stray, his body now bloated and torn, looked like some twisted totem.

'Oh…' Dyce heard himself saying, feeling a little sick as he watched the charcoal flake. 'I am very, *very*…'

Dyce was lying on top of the tank, every inch of muscle was telling him, screaming at him, to stay and rest. But he had to fight that urge, the other Strays were understandably reticent to approach after that eldritch-cosmological horror shit show, but they needed retribution. Dyce forced himself to stand up, despite the protestations of his muscles and organs, a bruised.

'You…' Dyce said, looking down at the crowd from his platform. 'We don't have to do this.'

None of them answered. From somewhere in the darkness he heard a child's voice plead. He thought he heard the adolescent voice say something about being hungry, genuinely eliciting sympathy from Dyce. He heard another voice shushing them, but with a soothing tone.

This lit a fire behind the eyes of every one of the advancing Strays. Dyce stood there, on the car's dented roof, pointing his handgun down at them as they circled him.

A few metres away, the scrum had resumed its scramble for Dyce's rail rifle, only this time it had become more viscous, more desperate. It was a competition to survive against this strange man going around turning them into tentacle-trees, and the rail rifle was the prize. Dyce wondered if it was worth even trying to reclaim it. Even more Strays, stirring in their abandoned vehicles, leaning out of the doors and windows, captivated by the fighting figures.

He heard a jubilant cry as a victor emerged from the pile. This Stray had red concentric circles sizes tattooed around his eyes, and he was holding the firearm aloft to show off his superiority over the others as they backed away from the circle-eyed Stray.

The circle-eyed Stray turned to face Dyce. He lowered the rifle and aimed at its former owner. Dyce took the isosceles stance and aimed back with his handgun. He rolled his neck and listened to the cracks.

He lowered himself down off the vehicle, not easy to do with one hand stuck out in front, keeping the business end of the barrel on his new rival.

'That's mine,' Dyce said. 'It's biometric locked. Its not going to do you any good. Just throw it over.'

Dyce knew that the rifles security wouldn't allow it to fire – his mental link to the weapon through his tabris confirmed as much, as well as showing him a vision of himself as seen through the gun's sight - but he didn't want the Stray to attempt to use it and come to the conclusion that perhaps it was empty, and toss it aside. Dyce wanted it back, so he shot the circle-eyed Stray in the leg and rushed him.

With the heal of his hand, Dyce pushed the butt of the rifle back into the circle-eyed Stray's head, sending a shockwave down through the man's body. Dyce took hold of the rifle's barrel and kicked the dazed Stray back.

Dyce test fired the rail rifle randomly at the crowd, which at least assisted dispersal. The other Strays were backing away from Dyce now, avoiding the business end of both his weapons, he was dual wielding. Clearly their were opportunists amongst them, waiting for the opportunity to strike. Dyce decided to store the rail rifle on his back and use the handgun, figuring the rail propulsion system was too quiet and the sound of the rounds leaving the handgun's chamber was a better deterrent.

He ran.

But he soon stopped dead as a hammer hit him in the ribs, creating a web of hairline cracks in his tactical armour. The blunt weapon came back around and hit Dyce in the back.

He tried to move. Soon he discovered that there was no issue getting his limbs to move, they just couldn't agree upon which direction to move in. He was going to need more time.

He saw the culprit looming over him. A large Stray had inherited Hammer Stray's special weapon, so this was Hammer Stray 2.0. Not as bulky as the tool's previous owner but he didn't have to be to do any serious damage, fulcrum did all the work.

'You've come here,' said *nu*-Hammer. 'Upset our own.'

'I was just passing through... I had no idea...'

'*Bullshit,*' the Stray snapped, swinging the hammer up towards Dyce's poor nose.

Holding his breath, because every breath hurt, Dyce managed to grab the hammer. This hurt like hell, and Dyce's face distorted to tell the tale of woe. Still, he managed to twist the hammer around, having to employ his other hand, pushing until he felt and heard a couple of the *off-brand* Hammer Stray's fingers break. Then Dyce pushed himself back up to his feet, wobbling, but staying steady just enough to swing the heavy duty sledge hammer up into *diet* Hammer Stray so hard that it lifted the guy right up off the ground. Dyce lost his grip and dropped the tool but only the back end of the handle hit concrete, the hammer head lodged so deeply in the muddle of internal organs that it wouldn't have come out clean or easy.

The other Red Strays had caught up with him, but were all hanging back, as if they were afraid to come any closer. Dyce looked around at their faces. It was as if *they* thought *he* was the monster.

Despite the fact that his body was trying to collapse around him, Dyce ran, holding his broken ribs. He didn't get very far. He fell to his hands and knees, the pain overcoming him. He coughed blood, drawn from ruptured organs, dribbling from his mouth in long, glistening strands. He held himself up with one hand whilst the other tried in vain to hold his ribs in place, he felt fragments of bone scratching against the inside of his armour.

There were figures crowding around him now. They were taking their time, convinced that their prey's time was up. To add to his indignity, water was dripping onto him from the crisscross pipes above him, quite a lot of it, actually. The air was so humid, everything in this part of the tunnel had a damp sheen.

The figures were whispering, convening, conspiring, curious.

Through his hands he could feel the rush of a river nearby, strong and powerful. He closed his eyes and listened, trying to block out every other sound. He could hear it echoing down corridors, he could trace it back to its source, like a *sonic map*. It was above him, but there was an opening ahead, the tunnel came to a full stop where the ground had caved in and eroded away over the past century…

He grabbed a foot and pulled its owner over, the Stray's head cracking against the floor. Dyce scrambled and snatched back his handgun. He ran to the nearest abandoned vehicle and leapt inside, hoping to buy himself enough time to reload the handgun. Another Red Stray hit the vehicle at full force and sent Dyce rolling backwards through the cab, tumbling across the rotten seats and out of the other side, through the door.

From his vulnerable position, Dyce could see that the car door was hanging from one rusty hinge. With one foot he pushed the door as far open as he could whilst he shot that hinge with his rail rifle, dragged uncomfortably from the magnetic lock on his back. The assortment of scavenged ammo ricocheted back at him, one ripping his cheek open. He felt the heat of the wounds before he felt the agony of the torn flesh.

He paused long enough to feel foolish, vulnerable.

The vehicle door fell free. He grabbed it, holding it by the handle like a shield as a Stray leapt from the car roof and landed on top of it. The feral man jumped up and down on the makeshift shield, so the door's handle pounded against Dyce's broken ribs.

Dyce managed to push the door up off himself with his legs even as the Stray balanced upon it like a surfboard. With the last two bullets in the handgun's clip, Dyce shot up through the door's window, the first shot turned the glass into a fountain that followed the bullet up to the Stray's face, where it made a mess. Then, after the glass had rained back down on Dyce, he fired the clip's final shot, finishing the job.

He could hear the running of water now, persistent and powerful. He was nearly out.

Dyce struggled to his feet, stowed both weapons so that he could concentrate his energy on using the door as a battering ram, rushing the baying gaggle of Strays. Ahead, maybe thirty metres, the tunnel came to an abrupt end, this opening was concealed to the outside world by a curtain of flickering silver and white, a waterfall lit by moonlight.

Am I really going to leap out through that, into the unknown?

Of course he was, it was that kind of a night.

He could make that leap, put some distance between himself and the chaos that followed. Despite the broken bones tearing up his organs, he knew that he could make the jump. He had to.

There were guards at this exit, two older Red Strays sat on fold out chairs, in front of the curtain to falling water.

They had bottles of booze in their hands, their beards were glistening, moistened by the beer and the waterfall, lit by the moonlight that strobed through random gaps in the cascade.

Dyce threw the car-door-shield away and ran as fast as he could, losing his balance and hitting the sides of cars, bouncing between them like pinball, somehow managing to regain just enough momentum. As he ran between the old Strays, he heard one of them mutter *'Fuck'n 'ell'* in surprise.

Then Dyce leapt through the water, feeling it battering his body. Then he was out, falling...

It was a long, long way down.

COUNTERPARTS AND BLEEDING HEARTS

'Well, the ground is a *no-go...*'

Trip Kosheen had descended two thirds of the way down the riser she had used for sniping and had now reached an impasse. The bottom few floors were ablaze, the air crackling, the foundations humming. She sat on a window ledge, pulling her knees in close, watching a river of desert brown dust flow through the city streets beneath her. Flashes of fires lit the cloud from within, scorching anything it touched. The source of this was the Sentry-amp forcing its way through that building, chasing after the League boy, breaking the building's back so that it collapsed upon them.

("Reaver? You out there?")

She hoped with every fibre of her being that the bastard was dead. It might save her from having to do it further down the line.

("No word from Reaver?") Kosheen asked.

("He's either dead or his tabris is fucked") Darius replied.

("Meet us at the coordinates I'm sending to you.") Ordered Oshii.

'Easier said than done,' Kosheen said to herself.

There was an old, disused high speed magnetic rail track, held aloft above the city streets, she could use that to traverse the river of dust, at least halfway to the coordinates. She climbed out of the window, no fear, and slid down the side of the riser, the gravity orbs in tips of her prosthetic legs turning the vertical to the horizontal. The reflection of the glass beneath her almost made her feel as if she were walking on a perfectly, eerily still ocean.

She pushed off, leaping head over heels, landing on a tangle of electrical cables suspended between buildings. The crisscrossing cables had a lot of give, dipping down beneath her. Apparently, they had delusions of being a trampoline, attempting to throw her off, but she grabbed them and held tight, waiting for them to settle. She held out her arms to the side, balancing perfectly as she made her way along one of them.

She hopped down onto the elevated track. She felt no hum from the high-speed magnetic rail, no lingering echo of its former life. Now it was just an elaborate ornament. She walked on, her Minds Eye showing her waypoint a few blocks over, and marking out her teammates moving towards the same goal.

She disconnected from the com-link. She was in no rush to get anywhere, stretching every muscle as she moved along that lonely rail, taking in a deep cleansing breath despite the arid air. She was, despite her usual protestations, glad for some alone time. She might tell herself that she didn't like the paths her thoughts took during these solitary moments, but that was just the story that she told herself. Everyone tells themselves stories.

From the destroyed buildings, embers fell like glowing orange snow, drifting around Kosheen as she hiked along the track. She held up a hand, watching one of the sizzling embers dance along the lines of her palm, pirouetting in the breeze, hopping to her wrist, where it drew a faint grey mark down to her elbow before bouncing out. She could smell the tiny, singed hairs on her arm.

She tried not to think about anything at all. She tried not to think about the others. She tried not to think about the things that they had done. She tried not to think about that fateful day that she had met them, back when her secrets were harder to hide. She tried to push away everything but the here and now. When you're trying to be someone else all the time, sometimes it's nice to take a vacation, a break from her life even if it was just in her own head.

She could only see reflections of herself in the risers that the track wound between, if she looked up, she could only see an oblong of sky, constellations visible between splotches of cloud lined with silver. The sea of dust undulated beneath, the orange sparks skating over it.

'The fuck you looking at?' She asked her own reflection.

She watched the way she moved, started to feel self-conscious. She tried to change the way she moved, just for shits-and-giggles. After a few different variations she actually started to skip, shocked to hear herself giggle at the reflection, as if it were someone else, some child making a fool of themselves amongst the orange sparks that floating around her like a thousand Chinese lanterns. She felt slightly embarrassed, but in not necessarily in a bad way. She had a hint of some sensation that could have been a smidgen of liberation. She stopped skipping, though her smile took a little longer to fade.

She hadn't skipped since she was a kid. She had run away once, with some others, the boys. From the facility they had fled, sick of the experiments on their bodies, just because they had been born different, disabled, that had somehow made them...

No, she didn't want to think about that. She had skipped that day, when they were far enough away. A bridge crossing a river. Wrought iron. Overgrown with moss and rust.

There was something moving along the track ahead, something small.

'What is that?' She asked, rhetorically. 'Oh, it's fluffy.'

The small creature stopped and turned to look at her, sitting up tall and alert. It was the blue furred cat from earlier, the one that she had seen, somehow, strolling around on the window ledge outside of the riser whilst she had been observing her target. Unless somehow there was more than one cat dyed that unnatural colour.

'Are you following me?' Kosheen asked. 'I wouldn't follow me. Bad things happen around me.'

As she got closer to it, she could see that patches of its blue fur were a darker hue than others, perhaps it had been a tabby at some point.

It meowed at her and walked away before she caught up with it.

'Oh, it's like that is it?'

But the moggy paused and turned back to her, as if to check that Kosheen was following. It opened its mouth to meow again but made no sound. It jogged on.

There was a junction ahead, where the magnetic track split in two directions. The cat stopped at the junction, turned to face her and sat up straight, waiting for her, the breeze blowing his fur and making an ear twitch.

'What are you up to?'

He stood back up and turned, their tail flowing behind him, hopped on to the the wrong rail, the one that didn't lead to her destination. She suspected it wanted her to follow.

'I'm not going that way,' Kosheen explained. 'So, I guess I'll see you later.'

Kosheen stood on the crossroads, examining the two diverging rails. She reconnected to the rest of the Fourth for a moment, heard them arguing as they struggled to move through the fires, hot dust and general chaos that flowed through the buildings. She didn't really feel as if that was the energy she needed in her life right now.

'*Fuck-it*, they can wait.'

The track turn a corner, and she followed. Ahead of her was an abandoned high speed magnetic rail carriage, just sitting there. There was a supporting pillar directly beneath it, a maintenance ladder running all the way up it.

Kosheen skipped again, a few more steps. She was catching

up to the moggy. It was unfortunate, then, when the cat appeared to jump off the rail. Kosheen hesitated, horrified. It was a long way down.

Things took an unexpected turn, however, because the cat hadn't actually fallen. The apparently phantasmagorical feline was defying gravity, walking along the vertical side of the rail, still heading towards the carriage.

'Oh...' She frowned. 'Okay...'.

Kosheen, as shocked as she was by this, followed its example, walking around the two-foot-thick rail, using her prosthesis to defy gravity herself, the orbs in the tips clinging to the metal, her exo-frame working overtime to keep her horizontal and make it look easy.

'You're like me?' She asked, though that observation explained nothing. She was confused, but she decided to go with it. This was certainly a welcome change from her usual pace.

Sporadically she started to feel power hum through the magnetic rail, a fraction of a second before the cat's fur would bristle, an infinitesimal moment before her own hair would stand on end. Kosheen rubbed her chin in thought, wondering if somehow the power surges were facilitating her furry friend's physics-defying party trick. *Somehow.*

The cat walked *under* the track, upside down, Kosheen followed. She glanced at her reflection again, though she appeared the right way up to herself, but the orange cloud looked like it was above her, tendrils of smoke reaching for her. She almost skipped but realised that gravity wouldn't like that. She nodded at herself, then laughed because she didn't know why.

There wasn't enough power in the gravity orbs to keep her like that forever, so she crouched and took a hold of the track. They were under the rear train carriage now, another two carriages connected to this one. The power surge happened again, and the carriage lifted up off the track, barely a centimeter, a crackle of power coming from the vehicle's magnetic plates, then it was laid back down gently.

The cat climbed up up over the rear carriage, one paw at a time. Kosheen pulling herself up, cartwheeling up the side of it, swinging herself the right way up, finishing in a crouch on its roof, finding herself nose to nose with her little friend.

'Are we not going inside?' She asked her little tour guide. 'Why am I even talking to you?'

She stared at the cat, and must have read something in its expression, because she felt a little ashamed.

Kosheen looked around for threats, then sat down next to her feline friend and crossed her legs. She took a pouch of gin from a compartment on her jacket, unscrewed the cap and started to sip. There were two eyes staring up at her, Kosheen looked back. The cat sat up even straighter.

'This isn't for you.'

Kosheen tried to ignore the cat's wide eyes. She couldn't. She sighed and took out a protein stick, ripped open the packet and tore a piece off. The cat went for her hand, and Kosheen protested.

'Little shit,' she said. 'Did you mind-trick me into feeding you?'

The cat lapped up the food, and the next chunk, which Kosheen dropped from out of the animal's reach.

'Is this your home?' Kosheen asked. 'It's pretty cool.'

The cat was looking around, as if more manufactured "meat" may magically materialize. Kosheen gave him a little more.

'Are you magic? I mean, I've not met many moggies, but I don't think you should be able to walk upside down.'

The cat started licking a paw, then using his moistened paw to clean his ear.

'*Me?*' Kosheen pretended that the cat was continuing the conversation. 'How come I could I walk upside down? Nah, I'm not magic. I can just do stuff like that because I'm augmented.'

Kosheen tapped her legs. The cat didn't react, he just relieved an itch against the armoured plating on one of Kosheen's prosthetic legs.

'No, that's not why they're called the Augmented Fourth,' Kosheen said, and opened another pouch of alcohol. She had no gin left, so she was on to the vodka. 'It's just me whose actually augmented. For them it's just a name, it's a musical reference or something. The devils note.'

Kosheen watched the embers reflected in the windows of the riser, and them reflected in the riser behind her, both buildings reflecting each other into infinity. The bright reds and the dark blues. The lights were also reflected in the feline's wide eyes.

'I'll stay here a while, if that's ok with you. Wait for the dust to settle. Literally.'

Kosheen reached into a compartment on her jacket and pulled out some pens, then she idly started to draw on the top of the train itself, just random swirly lines to start, until an image started to present itself to her and inspiration struck. This was something she often did when she was alone. She hadn't drawn anything specific, but it was pretty.

'What do you mean?' Kosheen was almost starting to think that she could hear a small voice in her head. 'Am I different, like you? I'm not a... *well... huh.*'

Kosheen stared into space. It was nice to have a set of indifferent ears to vent at.

'Well, as long as you think it's ok to be weird, how can I argue with that? I guess, if you're the same as everyone else, who would even notice if you weren't around?'

Kosheen took another drink. Then she took her headset off her forehead and started to scribble over the whole thing with a black marker pen, being careful to avoid the small camera lenses. Once it was all black, she blew on it to try and speed up the drying process.

'So what's with the fur?' She asked, and the cat turned away. 'Not ready to talk about it? Touchy subject? I understand.'

Up close, the blue fur didn't exactly look like paint or dye, it almost looked as if it could somehow be the animal's natural colour. There were different shades of blue, which looked like the patterns on a tabby.

'I think I'll call *you... I dunno...* Myka,' Kosheen had no idea where that name had come from, though. It had just popped into her head. 'You just look like a Myka.'

Kosheen then took a couple more pens from her jacket. One pen contained gold metallic paint, and the other silver. She used them to decorate the visor with Art Nouveau swirls and lines and floral outlines. She got a splash of silver on one of the lenses and quickly cleaned it off with a little spit and polish.

The breeze was tickling Myka's fur, making one of his ears twitch. He looked serene, a zen puss. Just his existence was improving Kosheen's mood immeasurably.

'*What?* Why would you want to know about *that?*' Kosheen asked. 'Why did I want to save the stranger and her unborn? Well, I *guess...* I just saw someone who was free, and they were carrying someone who would have been born free...'

Kosheen held up her newly personalized headset, admired her handiwork and let out a satisfied grunt. She gave the strap a tug to make sure it was still tight enough, then placed it back on to her forehead.

'I saw someone who could be anyone they wanted.'

The cat suddenly stood up, alert, looking at something on the tracks below. Kosheen turned to look and saw a cloaked figure standing on the rail.

The cloaked individual, their entire body and head concealed, was standing before the carriage, staring into it. Kosheen surreptitiously ducked out of sight, and watched the hooded figure climb into the carriage. Kosheen remained completely silent, waiting to hear them moving about beneath her. She could hear nothing, almost as if the figure was standing absolutely, perfectly still.

Then she heard hushed voices getting gradually louder, along with a repetitive tapping. She leaned over the carriage and saw more figures climbing up the ladder on the side of the magnetic track's closest support pillar.

'Are you expecting guests?' She mimed these words to Myka, who was stood up straight, as if on high alert.

These "guests" were Red Strays, and they too were climbing into the rear carriage. There were two men, three women and even a child. They bowed their heads in hushed reverence to the hooded figure, though the child had to be directed to do so by one of the elder Strays.

The mysterious figure pulled back it's hood to reveal itself not to be human at all, but a tall, thin amp with four arms and one big red orb that took up most of its face, set into the middle of an obsidian black skull. Kosheen had never seen an amp quite like this one before, and she could not see a flag or insignia printed anywhere visible.

The amp put both pairs of hands together and interlinked the fingers, and there was something unnerving about the way those fingers moved, crossing over each other, they were too long and had too many joints, and they moved in waves like hammers in a piano, clicking. Kosheen zoomed in with her headset's eyes and saw that reams of unintelligible holographic data were flickering across its large red orb, three-dimensional gibberish.

Kosheen sat and listened as the Red Strays conferred with the mysterious machine. They exchanged pleasantries, which was odd in itself, at least to Kosheen.

'Emissary...' the Red Strays said in unison - though the child was half a second out of sync. They bowed their heads in respect, which was an odd thing to do to an amp.

The Emissary? Kosheen raised an eyebrow at Myka, who only tried to sniff her nose in response.

The Emissary reached its four arms towards the people, each one holding a ration bar. The Strays took them and held on to them. They looked as if they thought it might be disrespectful to eat them now, despite the fact that they looked famished.

'No, *no*, eat...' The Emissary insisted. 'Riot knows how hard it is for you.'

They didn't need to be told twice. They tore open their ration bars and crammed them into their mouths.

'How is the tribe doing?' Asked the amp, in a dark,

deep synthetic voice they was scratchy and unnerving. Yet somehow the Emissary sounded concerned, in a formal manner, like a dignitary or a representative of a church.

'We have prepared the statue,' said one of the Strays.

'Good, the head piece will be delivered in due time. But what of your collective welfare?'

'We are hungry...'

'Riot knows. He is doing all that he can to improve your state of living. There will be another supply drop soon, as long as you continue to accept him deeper into your hearts.'

'We do... We are all focused on the day that he promised, and hope that he will make us a part of the Tapestry...'

Trip Kosheen shrugged at Myka puss, then shook her head. She had no idea what any of this meant.

'You are his disciples,' the Emissary said, and placed a single finger upon the head of the closest Stray to him, as if to reassure her, but perhaps symbolizing something else. 'You will be *one*.'

'We will be one...' the Stray replied, almost choking on that last word, her eyes watering as if overcome by some religious fervor.

'Riot provides...' said one of the other Strays, with enough awe to make it sound like a mantra of the indoctrinated.

Whilst Kosheen watched the meeting she succumbed to the Myka's charms and stroked his head. The apparently phantasmagorical feline looked most pleased and pushed his face into Kosheen's hand, so she scratched his chin. He especially liked that.

I've never seen anything like this... Kosheen mouthed the words to Myka. This was very odd behavior for the Red Strays, who usually kept their children hidden and their claws at the ready. She had never heard them talk this much, especially not anything *so*... she didn't even know what to call this.

The Emissary reached into its cloak and brought out an amp's dislocated head. It was held aloft for them to gawp at. Kosheen recognized the head as belonging to a seraph-amp, a new model that had been heavily hyped up in the press. The Red Strays looked as if they had never seen anything so wondrous.

'Is this the final piece?' One of the Strays asked.

'This will show you the way,' said the Emissary. 'Now the statue can be completed.'

The child lifted their hands up towards it, impatient to receive this offering, as if it were some delicate relic. To everyone' surprise, the Emissary crouched down to meet the child, its long legs folding in two. Two of its hands were cradling the seraph-amp's head, the other two were drumming the top of it, *tap tap tap* upon that shiny cranium.

'Would you like to hold this?' The Emissary asked.

The child nodded slowly, solemnly, not saying a word.

'I know that Riot will be very impressed by this, your devotion, your love. He will be keeping an eye on *you*. You are very special."

The child nodded and took the seraph-amp head as the amp withdrew its many arms back into its cloak.

Suddenly, Kosheen became aware that there was something else on the roof of the carriage. There was a shape, a mass, further down on another attached carriage. She was having trouble identifying it from this distance.

She could be in trouble. They might not even spot her, but just in case, she needed a contingency plan. What did she have at her disposal? She detached the point drone and set it down inside a vent on the carriage's roof. The battery was struggling to hold a charge, it might last twenty minutes, it might last two minutes.

Her only escape route was to jump, but she did not think that she would survive the drop. She could follow Dyce Bastion's example and use her smart cord, but the amp must have spotted her, because it's mess of a silhouette was moving towards her. Without knowing what it was, it might be to fast, she'd be vulnerable...

Myka had vanished and left her to deal with this mess by

herself. *'You little shit…'*

Kosheen hadn't even thought of calling her comrades, hadn't even occurred to her.

This second amp was definitely charging towards her now, and it was a mess of assorted limbs, too many to make sense of, and it was moving like several huge spiders had been strapped together, moving as if it were tumbling over itself.

The amp was fast and was upon her quickly. She beat at it with her exo-frame enhanced arms, her metal knuckles pounding its inhuman face out of shape.

She grabbed for a gun, but the machine disarmed her, taking her handgun and progressive blade simultaneously. It had a good go at taking her gravity rifle, too, but the magnetic lock was holding it firm. Then the amp swung her over the edge of the carriage and in through one of its windows, using her face to smash it, her visor protecting her eyes.

Kosheen rolled into one of the Red Strays, who pushed her to the floor. The spider-amp was blocking the freshly smashed window with its many limbs.

Kosheen stood up, raising her fists for a fight. Not one of them charged her, which was certainly a surprise.

'Come on, let's do this…' Kosheen said, pumping her fists up to test her exo-skeleton, as much as an intimidation tactic as anything else.

But none of them reacted. The Red Strays stared, shocked and unnerved, as if Kosheen had interrupted something sacred, some sort of ceremony and they feared that they might be punished for it.

Kosheen had been ready for a fight, and the lack of violent contact was making her very uncomfortable. She had no idea what to do, and genuinely had no idea what might happen next.

There was a cut on Kosheen's cheek, blood pooling around the wound. Tentatively, the Emissary reached up and collected some of the blood on the tip of a finger. Kosheen held her breath and did not move, frozen in fear.

The Emissary smeared Kosheen's blood onto the red orb that made up the majority of its face. More holograms formed over the surface of the orb, each letter and shape a slightly different shade of red. Concentric crimson circles formed around the smear of blood, each one gradually becaming more pronounced until they started to resemble a three-dimensional holographic Petri dish emerging from the orb, containing Kosheen's blood. The liquid itself started to undulate and bubble, then, as if by osmosis, spread out and thinned, pulled apart at a molecular level.

It was pretty obvious to Kosheen that her sample was being analysed. Reams of calculations cascaded around the haemoglobin, then words unfolded in waves as data was extrapolated from the blood. The curious way that the Emissary's hands moved, it's body language, revealed that the amp was surprised by the story being told by her DNA.

A repetitious clinking started coming from the Emissary. Kosheen had assumed that small clamps were holding the big red orb in place of its face, but they were moving like mechanical mandibles, tapping thoughtfully on the red orb, like fingers might wrap impatiently on a surface. All around the blood smear, out of the orb, small, uncanny, holographic faces begun, appearing to contort their mouths and eyes in what could be agony or ecstasy, it was hard to tell.

This whole thing was unsettling, and Kosheen knew that she wasn't going to get any answers, and nothing good would come from waiting around. It was time to make her exit. She looked around, surveying the territory for an opportunity. Her eyes locked upon one of the Strays.

'You're nothing but a filthy *Heathen...*' said the Stray, his voice full of righteous spite. Misplaced, misjudged, unwarranted, ill thought through, as such things always have been, throughout human history, used to differ judgment and distract from one's own transgressions.

'*What?*' Kosheen asked.

Then the Stray child spat at Kosheen. She was shocked, more

so as she stared into the girl's angry face, but after her initial disgust she pitied the child and her naïve attempt to ape the sentiment she was sensing in her elders. Kosheen doubted that the little one had the slighted idea why they were supposed to hate her, this stranger before them. It was a survival mechanism, to fit in with the masses. To be on the right side of the mob. To be *one*.

'He won't like this…' The Emissary was shaking its head, still absorbed in the emerging data. 'Not at all…'

The Emissary lifted all four of its hands up to its head, cupping its many fingers around the holographic data that was being collated from her DNA. It's fingers were curling up slowly, as if a growing anger and confusion were creating an unbearable tension. The holographic data was spreading out like a web, its multiple strands caught on the amp's many fingers like string as it tried to make sense of it.

'Who *ARE* you?' The Emissary did not sound happy about the data that was spooling out of the blood sample. 'Where did you come from? You are not supposed to be…'

Kosheen's eyes widened.

'*WHO…*'

She reached back for her rifle.

'*…ARE…*'

The Emissary turned to face this intriguing interloper, it's voice deepening, affecting a rage that should not have been possible for an amp, its voice sounding entirely scratched from bass.

'*…YOU?!*''

Kosheen was looking around at the Strays and their weapons, the blades that were apparently embedded in their bodies.

But Kosheen put her backup plan into operation. The point drone activated and blasted the carriage with enough light to temporarily blind the Strays.

Kosheen moved in silhouette through the flash-lit dust, knocking Strays to the floor or into obstacles, then she fired her smart cord at the spider-amp that was guarding the window and holding her weapons, the anchor crashing through its face. She wrestled her handgun back, her exo-skeleton allowing her to match the machine's strength.

But she didn't leave through that window, she ran through the next two carriages, bursting into the control room at the front and leapt out through the glass. She rolled across the track, turning back, pointed her handgun back at the window through which she had escaped, waiting for movement...

She took a breath, wanting to take a moment to process whatever that broken bullshit was. But no, she had to move. She faced away from the train, took up a starting position, like an athlete about to race. She condensed her leg anatomical prosthesis, building up kinetic energy. Then she launched herself off that starting line, hurtling down the track.

She slowed down as she realised that the rail was hanging over the edge of a cliff face, terminating way over the drop, the broken end tilting down over the wasteland. She remembered when this cliff had not been here, the edge of the city had rapidly eroded into an abyss, filling it in and becoming one with the broken wilderness between clusters of city districts. The cloud of dust from the collapsed building had reached the cliff edge and was cascading over, thinning out, whipped away in rolling clouds by the wind.

She could have sworn she saw someone leap out of the waterfall, straight though the water, battered by the power of it, screaming as they hurtled towards the river below. *What a dick.*

The track started to hum again, only this time it was much more powerful, and increasing in intensity. She realised that the train had powered on, maybe the amps weee somehow diverting power to it.

What were her choices? Jump? Too far. To run *under* the track? She daren't use her prosthetic's gravity orbs, the power of the live rail might warp them. The carriages was getting closer by the second. Over it? Through it?

She could do that.

She cycled through her visual filters. She could see that the humans had ben left behind on the track, holding their ceremonial gift. No, wait, they weren't standing, they were falling about, hysterical. Distraught. *Where was the child?* Still on board. This was a kamikaze run. There was one amp powering the carriage itself, generating a blistering amount of heat.

The child. Should Kosheen care? She wondered. The child was free, or at least had the chance to be, in all the ways Kosheen wasn't. She didn't seem to want to be, didn't act like it. A survival mechanism, instinct, herd mentality...

No time for this. Don't think, act.

She crouched. One knee forward, opposite hand down. Her prosthesis contracted, gathered momentum. She launched.

She ran down the track, closing the gap between her and the train. She leapt, leaving the track behind, two hundred and eighty six thousand pounds of metal ahead. She rolled across the roof.

She grabbed her gravity rifle and unlocked it, snapping it into its firing configuration. She knelt on top and fired down through the roof, aiming at the amp that was charging the carriage. Metal sparked as more metal pierced it and ludicrous speeds, the amp taking blow after blow.

The carriage didn't slow. Kosheen leapt to the gap between carriages and started firing directly down at the lock that joined the carriages. She could hear the child screaming. She damaged it but it wasn't separating. She leapt down onto it, hitting it with her armored knees. She leapt back up, grabbing the safety railing, jumping up and down until it broke.

Momentum had hold of it now, it was slowing down incrementally, but barely noticeably. She grabbed the door. Locked. She was about to go around but...

She felt gravity change. They were over the apex, falling. End of the line.

The separating carriages left the track in diverging vertical trajectories. As she grabbed the safety poles either side of the door, lifting both her legs to kick the door over and over, she couldn't even hear herself scream as the wind whipped the world around her...

HYPERBALLAD

Nico Shikari was bored.

She was yet again sat on the hull of her UAM jump ship, the Nilin Remix, her legs dangle over the edge of the hull. She let out a long, frustrated sigh and pushed her glasses back up the bridge of her nose, staring blankly at the city skyline and the twin moons. There was a mist of red dust falling over the cliff face, from between the risers that balanced precariously on its edge.

I can't just sit here forever, she thought, as she continued to sit there, potentially forever. *I need a plan...*

They would send someone, she had faith.

She looked around the wasteland, formed from a bed of imploded and eroded structures, a big load of broken *something* that had been reduced to nothing, surrounded by a perimeter of risers, like a vast clearing in an unending petrified forest of mortar.

There was a river a short distance away, which wound its way back to that looming cliff face. There were broken risers on the top edge of the cliff, cracked open and were gradually, over time, collapsing in incremental waves down the cliff. The cliff face itself was pockmarked with the broken, protruding pipes and service tunnels that ran beneath those crumbling risers, waterfalls pouring from some, forming the river at the bottom. She could just about make out trees around the base of the waterfalls, the branches curving up like bowls to catch whatever fell from above.

'I am so fucking bored,' she said aloud. She checked her

handgun again, for something to do. 'Yep, still a gun.'

She tapped the gun's barrel absentmindedly against the hull of the ship.

'Still *fucking* empty, I know that. I need a drink.'

What's more, she hadn't heard the *voices* since she woke up in this place, the mostly nonsensical chatter that flooded the back of her mind when social situations would overwhelm her. So, at least she hadn't had to beat the repeating, nagging, numbing thoughts out of her head with her knuckles till the pain closed the door. And she certainly hadn't had to release the pressure with the edge of a blade against her skin...

'*Breathe, one, two, three...*'

But something bigger was happened, something loud. Nico heard something huge crashing through the city long before she saw it. She hoped that whatever it was it belonged to the UAM. It was obvious where this behemoth was going to appear from, there was a cluster of risers shaking loose a flurry of detritus, like a tree shedding leaves or a deity shaking off dandruff.

Finally, she thought, excited, something was happening.

Nico rose to her feet and watched the city quake. A head appeared first, if you could call it that, the size of a house, looking like a fridge encased in a cage wrought from twisted girders, and it was poking out from between the risers. This was a League of Nations' Goliath came crashing out of the maze of risers, an impressive, improbable sight, the kind of obscenely frivolous mechanised monstrosity that was only made possible by resources sourced from off-world mining, as well as Dweller technology that had been successfully reverse-engineered and utilised by the automated Forges.

There were League soldiers operating gun turrets positioned all the way down the Goliath's spine, and they were launching heavy ordinance against the huge quadrupedal machine's pursuers. UAM gunships, aeromechs and fraymes were chasing it, hoping to take it down.

Grappling hooks launched from the belly of the League's

beast and burrowed their way into the surrounding architecture. Then they were wound back in, cables tightening, the buildings breaking as the Goliath pulled with all its might, letting out sounds reminiscent of an animal pulling itself free from a trap, destabilising the risers so that they collapsed upon a good percentage of its pursuers. The cables detached and fell away before retracted, the vast, monstrous amp stumbling.

As the Goliath swung its oblong head - with the help of thousands of pistons and miles of artificial musculature - it appeared so alive, and so pained. The millions of interlaced wires that wove in and out of its skeletal superstructure looked like exposed veins but swung like chains. Its artificial eyes peered out through the mesh of high-impact-bars that wrapped around its face like a muzzle.

Nico stood and watched, frozen, until her fascination turned to fear. She was overwhelmed by the size of the thing, but the fact that it was crashing towards her and, inevitably, eventually, over her, turned her mouth into an orchestra pit of putrid profanity.

But the Goliath-amp came to a stop. The vast machine apparently decided to ignore its attackers, which seemed to be of more concern to the soldiers riding it than the humongous amp itself, anyway, and turned its attention to the loan UAM soldier stood upon the crashed jump ship.

The aeromechs and jump ships had begun circling overhead like a fragmented halo, spiralling down as it bowed its head towards her, tilting down with a grace that seemed like it should have been impossible with the apparent weight of it, and Nico feared that it would topple loose and crush her. Nico"s eyes were filled with awe and fear, the Goliath's eye-sockets were filled with clusters of cameras, assorted dishes and antenna arrays, all moving in unison to focus upon her, all those tiny servos and pistons making noises that reverberated around the deep sockets.

Nico had literally no idea what to make of this development.

She stood back, taking a defensive stance, looking up at the beast, the beast staring down at her. Nico had no idea what she should be feeling. She felt self-conscious, as if everybody was going to be looking at her now, which was not really the kind of sensation that one expects to be feeling in the middle of a war zone.

'Hi?' She said, giving a half-salute that turned into a wave, because she had no idea what else to do.

The Goliath tilted its head to the side, as if curious. This movement was soundtracked by an orchestra of wailing hydraulics. Nico shrugged and threw her hands up in the air, the universal sign for *what-the-fuck-do-you-want? Do-I-fucking-know-you?* You can communicate a lot with some sass.

But then, something else that was entirely unusual happened. The sun seemed to come back out in the evening. Or, at least, something doing an exceptionally good impression of it, a bright white orb in the sky that appeared from nowhere, flaring suddenly into existence.

Nico held up a hand to shield her brow from this celestial interloper, and her attention was drawn to a cluster of tiny bubbles of blacklight running up her palms to her fingers, collecting on the fingertips. She closed her fists to stop them from escaping, but she couldn't stop these drips of anti-light slipping between the gaps in her gauntlets, as they were pulled inexorably towards that massive ball of purest white that was definitely not the sun.

She started to feel lightheaded, her skin started to tingle. She felt weightless.

Something else was happening, as a rattle started to resonate across the landscape, soon becoming a cacophony of chaos, as stones, rocks, shrapnel, debris, small amps and animals, soldiers, fraymes... It was all starting to levitate, bidding adieus to the safety of solid ground.

What fucking now? She wondered. *Some new weapon?*

Even the Goliath was looking up now, drips of black pulled *upwards* from its vast muzzle. The soldiers on it back were starting to panic, clearly they had a better idea of what this anomaly was.

As shrapnel floated up past Nico's face it became obvious that this was a gravity weapon, relegating any mass in the target area to a mathematical inconsequence. It was, she quickly deduced, a new tool in Shamsiel's arsenal, the UAM's Orbital Defence Platform, the same geo-stationary satellite system that sent down those columns of PEPP that had caused so much death and destruction.

Nico's feet were no longer making contact with the hull, she had started to drift away, slowly at first. She was about to shoot her smart cord's anchor down into the hull, but then the Nilin Remix herself rose off the ground too, the derelict jump ship shaken free from the dirt into which it had been partially buried. The ship was rotating leisurely above the crumbling dirt, the detritus scattering out to the air where it just sort-of hung around.

She fired the anchor anyway, which latched magnetically to the hull. Then she wound it in, pulling herself back down to grab the ladder on the side of the vessel, locking an arm around a rung.

There was a massive scream of metal crashing against metal, and the source of the infinite clatter was the Goliath. That humongous amp was also leaving the Earth behind, as improbable as that might have seemed given its unimaginable mass, kicking out like a desperate animal, trapped between the pull of the globe and the artificial white singularity manifesting in the sky above, becoming more powerful as the orbital defence platform fed more power into it. So, the Goliath completely lost its grip on the ground, levitating high into the sky, its massive legs scrambling at nothing.

Nico peered over the edge of the Nilin Remix at the broken hatch on its top, she needed to get inside the vehicle. She figured that either they were all going to be pulled into that singularity and crushed, or they would be dropped. Either way, she couldn't stay out here.

There were aeromechs, fraymes and amps drifting through the sky around her, losing their ability to move freely as their own gravity generators were scrambled and overridden by the singularity, their afterburners fruitlessly firing for nothing. Soldiers from both sides were attempting to swim through the air, grasping for objects out of reach, or firing off their own smart cords at anything, which lost tension and momentum.

The gravity orbs inside the various aeromechs and jump-ships reacted badly to the gravitational waves pulsing in and out of the singularity. The resultant reverberations caused fuel lines to rupture and munitions to detonate. The sky around Nico Shikari was filling with explosions of different sizes, colours and forms, swirling tendrils of shrapnel and debris. The singularity was warping the flames in hallucinatory forms.

She saw a bullet-witch aeromech break apart as its struggling engine overloaded and compromised the structural integrity, piece by piece, panel by panel, rivet by rivet, components drifting serenely in an arc towards the singularity. They waltzed around each until they resembled a double helix.

The closer the Goliath came to the singularity the more pressure began to build, pressing down upon the colossal amp's armour and compressing it, creating an implosion that sparked a chain reaction that spread through the entire superstructure. The Goliath roared in defiance.

Nico locked her helmet closed over her head then made her move, detaching the anchor and retracting it, then launching herself over the edge of the ship towards the broken hatch, grabbing the hatch's rotary lock before momentum could send her out into potential oblivion, and pulled it open. She closed the hatch behind her and fired the smart cord's anchor down the length of the ship to the cockpit, guiding her to the cockpit as it retracted.

Nico bounced into the chair, paying no mind to the mummified pilot that still occupied it, bones and solidified cartilage cracking beneath her armoured butt. With her feet she checked the integrity of the the cockpit's roll-cage, kicking and pushing at it. Satisfied that it was still intact, she checked the bulletproof glass, which was unintentionally decorated with a crosshatch of scratches but didn't appear to be compromised. She pulled the pilot's body from his tomb and back out through the door, taking his place, locking the restraints down over herself, as if she were preparing herself for a rollercoaster, except rollercoasters don't generally drag patrons towards low orbit with no idea how to get them back down.

The sky went instantly dark as the singularity suddenly ceased to exist, without warning, in the blink of an eye. All sound ceased to exist for a moment, until the wind returned to the area of affect, nearly drowning out the distant, desperate calls of the people that had been caught in it. Next came free-fall.

She started to hit buttons, attempting to ignite the engines. She grabbed the emergency ignition lever and yanked it hard, over and over again.

The ship was falling towards the riverbank so fast that she didn't even have time to swear. There was crash after crash as the ship collided with the other displaced vehicles. The bulletproof glass wasn't really proving its worth, cracking after a frayme collided with it, it's outstretched robotic arm attempting to grab onto the ship, its pilot screaming in impotent rage. The frayme didn't survive another impact by a passing bullet-witch, whipping it away.

Finally, with one last pull of the emergency ignition punctuated by a primal roar from Nico, the engines fired up just long enough for her to pull back on the flight-stick and guide the ship toward the drink.

The Nilin Remix hit the river in an explosion of water that sent it spinning, before it skidded to a halt, tearing up the riverbank. Nico gritted her teeth so hard her jaw ached, holding on to the restraints, her knuckles bone white within the gauntlets. The bullet proof glass had finally had enough, the impact had battered the roll cage so badly out of shape that the glass folded out of the frame and fell onto Nico's lap.

The ship had finally come to a complete stop. Nico wiped blood from her nose and focused her eyes at the world beyond the cockpit. She could see flaming vehicles falling like meteorites.

Beyond the hail of fire and the rising cloud of dust, the Goliath hit the planet with a bone-bothering reverberation, causing the glass in every riser in a two-mile radius to explode. Nico broke a few teeth, the crack in her glasses expanded a little further. A tsunami of *everything* was thrown out from the point of impact, a massive wave of debris and particles that rolled straight towards her, followed by a rolling arc of flame.

Out of the chaos came a monstrous scream, so loud and unnatural that it made Nico nauseous. Above the churning, burning dust cloud the Goliath's broken head reared, screaming like some ancient monster, pulling at its metal muzzle.

From the lingering afterimage of the singularity half a riser dropped, crashing down onto the Goliath's back, driving it down into the quaking Earth. The head bowed down under the weight, defeated.

Nico lay there, breathing hard, unable to believe that she had survived all of that. Eyes wide in shock, she daren't move, as if she thought that the slightest movement might make things worse.

Outside the ship, things were still falling from the sky that didn't normally leave the ground. She tried not to look at that or think about it, it wasn't her concern. Her safety was her concern. She was good, she told herself, she'd survived. She pressed the release catch on her safety restraint, but it didn't give. She pushed at the padded frame, hit at the lock, spluttering as she swore.

You can sort this, just don't panic...

Then the screaming started.

Something was moving through the crashing chaos, something that was neither machine nor man, but was indiscriminately attacking either. A totally black shape... *no*... multiple black shapes were moving through the crowds, ripping and tearing at the survivors of the drop, breaking open their machines to get at them. The screams were drowned out by unworldly howls and growls.

'Oh, what *fucking* now?' Nico asked, not quite able to believe that this day was actually getting worse.

Nico quickly came to the conclusion that the singularity must have pulled up more than just vehicles and garbage. Massive bear-like creatures, jet black with massive mouths that were all teeth, apparently rudely torn from their subterranean homes, were stalking the torn landscape, pouncing on the surviving soldiers, both League and UAM, tearing them apart, chewing through layers of armour like a hacksaw through bone.

They were large creatures, as big as bears but sleek and fast, like dogs. These were war wolves, Nico had seen reports on them. War wolves had appeared amongst the other unexplained mutations on this continent, something alien mimicking something terrestrial, twisting common forms into the uncanny.

But the seatbelt was still refusing to cooperate. She had to get deeper into the jump ship, before the creatures noticed her.

But it was too late, *something* had spied her. Elongated fingers reached into the cockpit, grabbed her head by the locked helmet, attempting to crush it with more force than her unprotected head would have survived.

Nico grabbed the inhuman hand as its grip tightened even further, attempting to pull the fingers loose, but the perpetrator was already lifting her up out of the ship and into the chaos of the outside world, reaching in with a second hand to effortlessly bend and break the the restraint that had prevented her escape.

But it turned out that this wasn't one of the war

wolves, however, this was something else, something just as formidable. As it lifted her up ever higher, she was able to see more of it, first its bulky metal legs, the thick armour of its torso, until she was face to featureless face with an amp. The humanoid amp stood seven foot tall on top of the cockpit canopy, its long fingers tightening like a vice.

She knew what this was, she was just surprised that it was attacking *her* considering it belonged to her side of the war. This was a seraph-amp, brand new, state-of-the-art. It was tall but chunky, it armoured plates were all curves, making it appear sleek and aerodynamic but also formidable. Inside its chest was room for a gravity orb large enough for flight, on its back were high velocity thrusters. Seraph-amps were manufactured by the Unified American Military's Forge Factories, entirely designed by machine minds with no human input.

'I'm on your side, you prick! I'm UAM. Nico Shikari, serial number four six eight two zero three... Stand *the-fuck* down!'

But the seraph-amp wasn't listening. It was probably malfunctioning, perhaps due to the three-feet long piece of shrapnel embedded to the right of its spinal stack. The shrapnel sparked like a broken battery, creating tremors that caused its right appendages to judder. Its head ticked and glitched as it peered closer at her, curiously, its attention flicked temporarily to the hairline fissures spreading through the helmet.

It stopped tightening its grip and stood there, holding Nico's head in front of its own. Had it simply shut down, leaving her dangling there until something big and black started chewing on her feet?

Its otherwise featureless face split open in the middle, revealing a deep red orb within. The orb was not reflective, but appeared to be some kind of holographic projector, because it started streaming programming code across its surface, a post-crash system analysis maybe, but occasionally she thought she saw words and phrases that she recognised, the most worrying of all was her full name, spelled phonetically. Then, one word started to stream down the orb, like a four-digit code that consisted of numbers and letters: R10T.

But the sky wasn't done dropping its trash on to the wasteland. A League of Nations amp carrier crashed into the ground next, coming to a stop by the river side not far from the Nilin Remix. The impact had broken open the carrier's side door, exposing the massive deployment tumbler within, that held the inert amps by shoulder restraints.

Suddenly there was a howl, a primal call-to-arms which ended as a low-base growl that was filled with menace, so low that she could feel it in her ovaries. This seemed to give even the seraph-amp reason to pause and look around for the source.

One of the war wolves leapt on top of the flaming amp carrier and stood on the broken bay doors above the inert amps within. It's large eyes and blood-smeared sabre-teeth, glistening in the firelight, stood out against its obsidian-black bulk, its silhouette a mass of mismatched spikes.

The beast was focused upon Nico and the Seraph-amp, stepping down onto the dispatch-tumbler. The tumbler, and the inactive amps that it held, rocked forwards under the creature's weight, the amps swinging from their restraints. It bowed its head towards them as its body tensed, its hind legs prepping a strike, its claws cleaving the frame.

It opened its mouth, and a human arm slid out, half chewed. The bloodied appendage slowly descended, hanging from several thick strings of drool.

The Seraph-amp moved Nico aside with a snap to fire at the war wolf - the armour saving her neck from breaking as her torso swung away from her head - unleashing a salvo from the rotary gun mounted to its other arm. Nico could do nothing more than watch the steam from the barrels whip around the bullets. Yet again unable to actively take part in a battle, she gritted her teeth in impotent frustration.

The jet-black creature fled from the hail of ammo, but was

not, apparently, running away, it was running around them, looking for an opening to strike.

'Oh, that's gonna fucking bruise,' Nico snarled, feeling the intense whiplash in her neck and shoulders.

She started to kick and push at the amp with her legs, refusing to dangle there like some helpless animal waiting to be gutted. But she had no weapons and the auxiliary strength and agility afforded to her by her armour was nothing compared to the strength of the massive machine that held her.

Nico's mind cycled through her meagre inventory, trying to figure out what she had that may have some use. The only thing even remotely useful was the smart cord.

At pointblank range she fired the cord's anchor up into the inner workings of the amp's arm, piercing the rubber protecting a small gap between the armour at the elbows. The anchor buckled a piston, causing the amp to inadvertently tighten one of its fingers, which in-turn finally cracked her helmet.

'Well, that wasn't what I had in mind,' she spat through gritted teeth because she couldn't open her jaw any wider with the compromised helmet compressed against it.

Now all she had to do was brace herself against the machine and wind the cable back in…

The war wolf made a move, its long teeth leading the charge, a mouth full of crooked spears. It was on top of them in no time at all, snapping at them, razor-sharp fangs gouging the seraph-amp's armour.

Nico managed to run her feet up and out of the beast's slobbering jaws, her feet slipping on the saliva-soaked roof of the mouth, a split second before those teeth clamped into the Seraph-amp's waist.

The seraph-amp started firing its powerful rotary gun down into the beast, but the creature had tough defences; The slick spikes that covered its body were not matted fur at all, as Nico had assumed, but a jagged carapace, tough and dense like armour. Each concussive blow from the seraph-amp's weapon beat the beast down, eventually cracking this natural defence through persistence, the beast scratching at the ground in agony and terror.

Now or never...

Nico's anchor deployed its hooks inside the amp's arm, ripping out cables and twisting pistons as the cord retracted. Finally, the amp's fingers lost all their tension and Nico fell free, rolling off the beast's back and hitting the hull of the Nilin Remix. She scuttled backwards, away from the towering machine and the beast.

Two more war wolves, appeared over the side of the jump ship, leaping at the Seraph-amp, one grabbing a legs and the other grabbing the smoking gun mounted arm, the spinning barrels beating at its misshapen teeth. The beast managed to halt the weapon's rotation as the barrels twisted out of shape, the bullets within popping like corn, causing an electrical fire that spread back through the arm, beneath the armour.

The amp's entire payload of ammunition exploded, compartments of missiles and bullet-chains detonated, ripping open head of the creature that was crushing its gun arm, before flipping its body backwards, splattering against the carrier and bouncing back off. A cluster of missiles escaped the seraph-amp's disintegrating body, barrelling off on their separate ways, a few ending up inside the amp carrier, instigating a terminal chain reaction through the fuel and ammo onboard.

'*Oh...*' Nico said.

Rolling waves of fire engulfed the entire amp carrier.

'*...Fuck!*'

She threw herself down into the darkness of the Nilin Remix, pulling the broken hatch as close to closed as she could before it jammed ajar. She pulled and pulled, using the combined weight of her body and armour, before changing tact and swinging her legs up to the ceiling and pushing with them, yelling furiously, until the last sliver of light disappeared.

She let go and fell with a clang as her armoured derrière hit the grated floor. She scuttled across the ship and closed the hatch to the cockpit, spinning the rotary-lock and sealing herself in to the main body of the vessel. Then she opened her compromised helmet and took a breath. The air inside the jump ship was damp, she could smell the rust and mould. The predictable blinking of the emergency beacon was the only light.

'Welcome to Shit Creak boat rental, Miss Shikari,' she muttered to herself. 'Sorry, we're all out of paddles.'

Her armour was getting hotter, the old heat-sinks and thermal pads needed replacing, and the harder that she had forced the armour to work the hotter it became. Safety valves opened all the way down the armour's spine to exhaust heat. She empathised with those systems; she was quickly reaching the point where she needed to vent emotionally.

She could feel the reverberations of everything that was happening outside, all that chaos. She shouldn't be here, alone and useless, she should have been extracted by now. She had told her people her location, they surely knew she was here, so why had they launched such a devastating attack upon the Goliath whilst she was in range. Hell, there were several dozen UAM vehicles that had crashed and burned outside. How could they be so reckless?

The valves on her back completed their heat exchange and closed, but she was still sweating. She has been locked in this armour ever since she had woken up and it was long past time for a break, so she lay down upon the grated floor and opened it up.

All down the armour locks opened automatically, sliding apart or rotating. The top half of the armour fell open, sliding off her torso. She sat in its cushioned interior, as stained and ripped with age and drenched with fresh sweat as it was. She could not actually remember when she had felt so low, so mentally and psychologically battered, but it was not – to her surprise - an unfamiliar feeling.

She was at her lowest ebb, the nightmare outside was pummelling the surrounding land and battering against the jump ship. She felt the pressure building up inside her, and it was becoming unbearable. She lifted up her arms and pulled down the sleeves of her muscle-feedback suit, far enough to reveal her wrists. There were old scars there, but she had only the vaguest recollection of collecting them, the memory appeared as distant and dislocated as a half-remembered TV show. The collection looked like a prisoner tallying up their days with marks on a cell wall.

She sat up and squinted against the intermittent flashing of the beacon. Something scratched against the hatch above, intermittently. There was another explosion somewhere outside, and it sounded like rolling thunder. She heard soldiers yelling for help, before the war wolves tore through them. She couldn't stand the sound much longer, scratching at her sanity like the claws on that hatch.

Forsaken, that's how she felt.

She was waiting for every predictable flash of the beacon now, it was all she had to do. Occasionally the whole ship rocked, and she rocked with it. The beacon still flashed, a little light but just enough to temporarily illuminate the interior, creating solid black shadows.

She sat there, immobile for the longest time. She felt so disappointed with herself. Her head was swimming now, she didn't feel quite right.

The beacon flashed again, only this time she could have sworn she heard the sound of thunder, as if the flash had been lightning. The next flash she thought that she actually did see lighting, spreading across the ceiling.

Just a trick of the light, *surely*. She told herself that the splintering lightning strike was simply the beacon reflecting off the edge of every panel and pipe.

Her eyes were hurting. She started seeing things, the half-seen lowlights and highlights of the ship's interior seemed to swirl, her mind playing tricks. Things started to shift in her perception, the dampness of the padding started to feel like mud, the grated floor started to look as if it were ebbing and flowing like a river...

ComE on, giRL... come on.. You are not... you KnOw you ArE (not)...

This was a small thing at first, but with every flash of the beacon it became more intense, more tangible. This is when Nico started to wonder where he medication was. She had already searched this ship for it, but she couldn't even remember when she had last taken it. Did she even need it? She had felt so good for so long, she hadn't really even worried about it until now.

The outlines of every little thing inside the ship seemed to break up and reform themselves into something else, her mind making something unreal out of anything real. Soon it began to look like a landscape flanked by tangled structures. The flash of the emergency beacon became a recurring flash of lightning over this imaginary place.

She slowly came to realise that her raging imagination had commandeered her senses entirely, because she no longer appeared to be slumped inside the jump ship, she realised that she was nowhere at all. Another flash of imaginary lightning illuminated that imaginary landscape.

Not nOW, NoT no\/\/...

I'm (not) still in the ship...

This is (not)...

I'm not...

Each of the lightning bolts that streaked through the clouds moved in slow motion, as if they were being drawn. Then they stayed there indefinitely, frozen above her like misshapen strobe lights, each splinter of lightning more elaborate than the last. They would pulse, periodically, becoming a little brighter each time.

The world dropped and she was raised up by a riser that was magically sprouting from beneath her, lifting her higher and higher. She was on the roof of a riser, surrounded by satellite dishes, oil-tainted puddles and discarded takeaway boxes.

A single, tiny drop of light fell from the pulsing tangle of lightning above. She held out both hands to catch it, grasping it tight. She felt it tickle. She moved her hands this way and that, enjoying the tingle.

Then the light squeezed out of a gap between her fingers, pulling itself out as if it were anthropomorphic, a tubby little figure squeezing through a tight gap. Then it sprouted legs, then arms, then a head, growing to two inches tall. It stretched like someone waking up, then cracked its back by pushing its fists into its lower back and pushing its belly forwards.

Nico parted her hands, and the figure scratched its little head in contemplation. Nico was delighted by this little show, if inevitably confounded. She especially enjoyed watching the figure jump from one arm to the other, almost fall off, outstretched arms waving for balance. Then they literally marched across her skin, *left-right, left right...*

Then there appeared another figure, a little shorter than the first, with odd shaped lower legs, as if they might be kinetic prosthetics. This one had a small animal following it, a small dog or a cat, Nico couldn't tell. Then there was another figure. This one was sat cross-legged, immobile. She suspected that this one was her.

So who were the other two?

The riser stopped rising, but the sudden stop had no effect on her because there was no inertia or momentum. She felt dizzy, motion sickness, but that might have been psychosomatic. The little figures were gone, and Nico actually looked for them, over her arms, in her lap...

She stood up and walked to the edge of the imaginary structure. The dreamscape around her had been consumed by risers of different sizes, all linked by bridges that connected to walkways that went all the way around their exteriors, balcony streets and bridges that had shops, kiosks. Flying vehicles darted between these buildings, sometimes stopping next to them, passenger doors opening down over the perimeter walls so that people could descend steps built into them, joining the other pedestrians who were hustling-and-bustling here and there.

This was Alcyone's capital city, Nico suspected. As she looked around the skyline, she saw more evidence of this, famous landmarks were scattered around, ostentatious buildings belonging to mega-corporations towered over all the others. But even taller than these was The Spire, the home of Complex, the artificial intelligence that managed and maintained the city.

Then beams of light fell from the sky, all across the city and right to the horizon. These humming lines of light were heralds of an unimaginable chaos that rode them down into the metropolis. The buildings started to crumble, and the screams of the people echoed all around her, *through* her. But the disintegrating buildings were being levitating up into the sky, smashing into each other as they were pulled towards a perfect white singularity.

A figure of dust formed above her, looking like it were formed from the visual static of an old television tuned to a dead station, behind it grew a pair of winds, above it formed a halo. It reached for her, thrust an arm at her, as the city's screams became an unnatural, unbearable screech. Its hand became a claw, broken glass for talons.

Nico closed her eyes as tight as she could and fell backwards, off the edge of the riser, falling out of time and space, leaving this vision behind. She felt herself hit the padded interior of her armour, on the very real floor of the jump ship. She closed the armour around herself. The very second that the helmet locked back around her head she activated the night-vision filter and looked around, but all that she could see through the helmet's beady eyes was the mundane interior of the Nilin Remix.

She wasn't sure what was worse, the violence outside or being here, inside this tomb, alone, with this broken nonsense...

'What the actual fuck?' She had seen things before, but never so all encompassing.

SAY SOMETHING LOVING

Somewhere north of midnight...

Somewhere south of expectation...

Amongst drifting, dying embers, a lone figure reclined upon a tall, vertical scaffold adorned with an assortment of horizontal, high-gain antenna arrays, abandoned mid-repair long ago. Tendrils of smoke drifted up from some fresh wreckage below, lined silver by the glamour of the twin moons peeking through gaps between clouds, the nighttime nimbus lit by the popping of munitions within, and pulled like candy floss by competing aero-mechs as they darted through them, smearing an *off-brand* rainbow down the deep sky.

This insignificant communication array had been erected on one side of a huge, circular landing platform built amongst the wasteland that existed in the centre of Contact city, on the west coast of the man-made continent of Alcyone. The landing platform had been abandoned for a long time, it's most recent use had been a staging ground for a battle, the spoils still smouldering.

The figure stretched out, then tilted her head back over the edge of the scaffold's wooden slats, gazing out, absently. The world appeared upside down to her now, refreshing her perspective somewhat, opening her eyes to the beauty in all this desolation.

The moons were dictating the hues tonight, the greyscale of

Lunar and the blues and greens of Terminus were crackling like static upon a distant lake, formed within a soggy crater no doubt created by the silent sentinel stood in the middle of it, a waterlogged troop carrier planted face down, broken open upon impact. Periodically, an unexplained power surge would sweep through it, like a ghost clinging to its old shell, causing the turbines to spin up and suck water through the engines, ejecting it like sprinklers into a fine mist, before spluttering and spinning it out, winding down mere seconds after its resurrection.

Trip Kosheen was that resting figure, lay a dozen metres above the broken husk of an armoured frayme – a human-piloted mech with a basically humanoid form - that she had, twenty two minutes previously, decimated with one perfect shot. Her high-velocity gravity rifle rested on her armour plated knees, it's nitrogen-cooled, superconductor-stack still humming.

Kosheen stared vacantly towards the twin moons, and the backlit skyline beneath them, looking like roughly hewn cardboard cutouts. She enjoyed the sensation of the breeze tickling her hair, flicking the longer strands of the lopsided Mohawk against her HUD headset - held on her forehead by the adjustable strap. She almost reached a *zen* level, practically forgetting her*self*, detached from the other members of the Augmented Fourth, perched high above them and the unpleasant things they were doing. She distracted herself, sinking further into the pleasant pseudo-*zen* state, remembering things she was proud of, and some that simply made her smile, like the time she lost her virginity whilst her ass smushed a keyboard's keys, leaving an awkward imprint on the cheeks. She had mixed feelings about that.

She grunted, then squinted, as a reaction to that random recollection, wondering why that awkward encounter in particular had surfaced, out of the deep ocean of everything she had ever experienced or witnessed.

Kosheen sighed wistfully as she rolled onto her belly, letting her arms dangle over the edge of the old wooden slats. On the northern perimeter of the wasteland she could just make out a flood lit work site set up around the bones of some humongous, unknown creature. She couldn't tell if they were Strays or some government sanctioned research team, probably working day and night, excavating this colossal carcass and examining their findings.

Kosheen daydreamed, speculating on the origin of this skeletal behemoth. Was it from Earth, some forgotten beast from the dawn of time that had been buried beneath the sea and inadvertently dragged up from the depths when they formed the foundation of the continent, or dragged down from the sky, from the asteroids dumped into the understructure after they had been mined for resources? There were tales of ancient, unnamed creatures and unfathomable beings that used to rule this world, driven deep underground long ago, long before there was any way of documenting evidence beyond transcripts of older oral histories.

Perhaps they had discovered the fabled Onyx Dragon. If they ever uncovered the vast beast's head, they might have a chance of figuring that out. She actually began to wonder what it would have been like if that had been her career, if people of her social status had been allowed to join such expeditions. In another life, maybe. She had no idea who or what she could have been...

Kosheen's attention was drawn towards the cliff face. She could see the exact point that the train carriage had left the track and plummeted. She still felt the burden in her bones from the impact, her skin black and blue. The front carriage had squished like a tin can, the rear carriages thrown over, bouncing and cartwheeling across the wasteland. She had managed to get in a second before impact and grabbed the Stray child, but she could only grab and hold her as the world spun around them.

They had waited at the mouth of a tunnel at the base of

the cliff, their skin and hair damp from the humid air, where myriad waterfalls emerged from the rock's exposed pipes and convened at the base, merging into one river.

The girl had been in a bad way, just able to stand, kosheen had an arm around her, holding her up. They didn't speak. The child stared at the ground. Perhaps she was ashamed, either due to her prior treatment of her saviour, or because she had been saved by someone she had been told to hate. She didn't pull away from Kosheen, though. Maybe she didn't have the strength.

Eventually, red adorned figures had emerged from the shadow of the cave, swaddling the child in rags and sheets and leading her inside. Kosheen received no gratitude, but she also received no scorn. The atmosphere was solemn.

She had watched them leave and listened to the echoes of their steps through the tunnel, lightly peppered with hushed words. She stood there for longer than she should, staring into the darkness until her eyes adjusted and she could see the outlines of dangling wiring in the walls of the cave, glistening with moisture.

Eventually she had turned and headed back to meet the others.

She picked up a bottle and took a mouthful of a home-brewed beer purchased days before, during a recreational visit to a Green Stray's farm. She absently absorbed the inane chatter from below, swilling the beverage around her teeth and gums, feeling the sting. The landing pad was illuminated in blues and violets cast by the bioluminescent plants growing up out of the cracks. They were Conflict Blossoms, able only to germinate on the site of recent battles, feeding off the residual kinetic energy.

Kosheen looked down at Oshii, who was stood amongst the smouldering remnants of a running battle. The Augmented Fourth had won this one, as they usually did. Which made the business with the League boy all the more infuriating, and Kosheen knew that it had royally pissed Oshii off.

Kosheen lay back and watched the clouds roll by, lit from within by a festival of colour. She closed her eyes and daydreamed about what had happened earlier that night, her little moment of freedom skipping along the elevated monorail, before the Red Strays and their mysterious benefactor ruined everything. She still had not the slightest idea what that nonsense had all been about. She was glad when she had rendezvoused with the Augmented Fourth in the middle of this battle, the violence had helped take her mind off all that weirdness.

She felt something furry brush lightly against her face, before dropping its weight over her mouth and nose. She sat up with a start and saw something blue disappear over the far end of the scaffold.

'Little shit...' she whispered, sure that it had been Myka the cat.

There was a gunshot. Kosheen casually looked down to see a fellow member of the Augmented Fourth shooting one of their prisoners, a survivor of this battle, in the back of the head. They had lined their captured League of Nations soldiers in a neat little row, each of them forced down on to their knees. The executioner was McMorrow.

The rest of the Augmented Fourth - desensitised to their own unpleasant ways - went about their casual cruelty with the same disinterest that one might usually give to any mundane task, occasionally finding a spark of joy within some extremely inappropriate humour.

Darius appeared, the youngest and newest of their recruits. He brought breakfast burritos wrapped tightly in tin foil. He threw one to kosheen, which made her curse, afraid that the parcel might come undone mid air and spill it's contents to the wind. But she swung down and caught it, the gravity orbs in the tips of her prosthetic lower legs holding her to the scaffold. She swung back up, sat back down, shook her head at the careless throw.

Kosheen unwrapped the tin foil package carefully, revealing

the tightly packed tortilla wrap, then peeled back one corner to check the contents. Scrambled egg, melted cheese, lab-cloned crispy bacon and tabasco sauce.

'You know what I got a craving for?' She heard McMorrow ask casually, before putting another bullet into the back of another enemy soldier's head. 'There's a place that does this spiced lamb wrap, this guy on the lake market?'

'Yeah...' Darius showed a glimmer of recognition, turning his eyes up as he tried to recall. He took a short break from searching through the belongings of the recently deceased for anything of value or use. 'The chef's name Tennold?'

'That's it,' McMorrow confirmed, taking a bite out of his own food.

'Yeah they're pretty good,' Darius said, relieving a corpse of an expensive looking wrist watch, which could have been real, probably fake, but had certainly been scavenged by the executed soldier, just as Darius was scavenging it from him now.

Another gunshot, another prisoner fell. McMorrow seemed more concerned by the ketchup dribbling down his own chin than the life he took. He didn't even seem bothered when the bodies' outlines started to glow, as if marked by fluorescent chalk, as conflict blossoms started to weave their way up out of the cracks in the ground beneath them.

'That's where we're heading, right?' McMorrow asked, scraping the sauce towards his puckering lips with the side of a finger. 'The market on the lake?'

'I think we got to, Trip and the corporal need to pick up their meds.' Darius discarded the watch, tossing it back over his shoulder. He resumed his desecration. 'Reaver was carrying it for them.'

'*Thanks for that...*' Trip Kosheen rolled her eyes, frustrated that Darius had blurted out her personal business in front of the whole group.

This did remind Kosheen to check her tattoo sleeve, which covered her arm from shoulder to knuckles. It was predominantly decorated with spiked vines, red roses dotted here and there amongst them. Three of the red flowers at the bottom, near her wrist, had recently turned into blood soaked skulls, permanently. The fourth rose along was starting to change, and was half way between states, not quite a rose and not yet a skull. The tattoo's ink was made with carbon nano tubes, reacting to what was happening inside her body and giving her a visual representation of it. There were still many more roses to go, she had plenty of time left...

'Why was Reaver carrying your medication?' McMorrow shouted to Kosheen, confused. He blew the back out of another soldier's head.

'How about you just fucking drop the subject before I drop you?' Kosheen snapped, instantly irritable.

McMorrow's eyes grew wide, taken aback. He let out a long, loud whistle. He didn't expect to be spoken to like that, and he was clearly amused by Kosheen's over-reaction to a simple question. A smile spread across McMorrow's face, signalling that he was already relishing the potential fun that he could have, knowing that Kosheen could be triggered by any mention of Reaver.

'Did Darius tell you he heard from Reaver?' McMorrow asked, trying to appear nonchalant as he kicked aside the freshly executed prisoner, the body falling onto the lap of his next intended victim. Then he motioned towards Darius. 'Your boy, there, picked up a message from the big man himself.'

'No...' Kosheen murmured. She had rather hoped that Reaver was dead. 'Never mentioned it...'

'Yeah... no, I...' Darius stumbled over his words. He had clearly had no prior intention of telling Kosheen. 'Well, yeah, Reaver got picked up by one of our pilots, but their ship got pulled into that orbital's attack... Well, you saw the singularity over the wastelands... The floating Goliath. He said something about making his own fun, or something. I don't... I don't wanna know. The guy's a... well, you know.'

A *dark-cloud* passed over Kosheen, and suddenly she felt a

little less like herself.

He's not dead…

There was a sudden, unexpected clang from beneath Kosheen's buttocks, reverberating up the scaffold from inside the smoking frayme that was lodged half way down it. She was grateful for the distraction.

The rear of the bulky frayme suddenly blew open, explosive-bolts blowing on the emergency escape hatch. As the hatch fell back so too did the occupant, sliding down the inside of the door. The operative - wearing breathing apparatus that obscured his entire head – had his gun at the ready, a burst-fire SMG, and didn't take long to target Kosheen, as he hung there, upside down, caught on the door's dual handles.

The operative pulled the trigger over and over, bullets sparking off Kosheen's armoured-aperture - the powered exo-frame that was bolted to her bones – and sparking as they ricochet off her armour-plated prosthetic lower legs. She swore and reached for her own custom handgun, but the attack abated when the operative lost his grip and slipped.

The operative fell from the frayme, hit the floor hard and rolled backwards into the congregating members of the Augmented Fourth, barely stirred from their late night meal. A splash of ketchup fell from someone's burrito onto the operative's head. They soon dispersed as the operative dived onto the body of one of his fallen compatriots, grabbing their handgun to double his own arsenal. The operative pushed himself to his feet and let a few bullets off into the surrounding soldiers, both weapons making a decent argument for social distancing. He was looking for an opportunity to run…

But McMorrow stepped in, batting both guns away, the muzzles flashing, bullets skirting the big man's head before they were taken by the night. But the operative was fast, whipping the guns back around out of McMorrow's grasping hands in between shots. McMorrow swore as he struggled to keep up, the business-ends of both barrels getting closer to his face, sonic waves tickling his manly whiskers. Finally, he managed to grab one of the guns and pull it from the operator's grasp, bouncing it off the operator's head, ringing his helmet like a bell. The other gun bounced away into the circle of soldiers as the stunned operator lost his grip.

But the operative had a progressive blade, which McMorrow only realised when he felt it buried deep in his waist, its subsonic hum rattling his armour and the bones beneath. The big man had underestimated the enemy's resilience, and paid for it, as the blade had slid right through McMorrow's armour like butter.

Darius had his compatriot's back, however, grabbing the pilot by the arm, breaking the wrist. Without the desperate force of its owner behind it, the humming blade slid out of McMorrow and fell to the floor. Darius threw the operative over his shoulder and slammed him into the floor, the operative hitting a cluster of conflict blossoms which popped like paint-filled balloons, plastering the back of the operator's suit with vibrant colour.

Kosheen watched, amused. She actually found herself impressed and a little aroused by Darius's unexpected dexterity and skill. She hadn't thought that he had it in him, perhaps the boy *was* Augmented Fourth material, after all. She watched as Darius relieved the operator of his flight helmet, which now dangled down by its air-filtration pipes.

The operative, wide-eyed and manic, turned around, taking stock of the rest of the group, still looking for a way out. But his desperate rage was undercut by McMorrow laughing at his own injury, as the big man opened up his armour to reveal the pulsing wound. The other members of the Augmented Fourth also seemed to be amused by his predicament, as if this were some trifling thing. Another member tossed an aerosol of bio-med gel to McMorrow, who popped the cap and sprayed it into the unfortunate incision, where the foam expanded. It stung; he swore.

'It's coming out the other side,' Darius pointed out.

'What?' McMorrow said, realising that the neophyte was

referring to his blood, which was dribbling out of a seared hole in the back of the armour adjacent to an exit wound that he had been unaware of. 'It went straight through?!'

McMorrow had to climb out of his armour to spray the gel into the exit wound, which clearly made it sting twice as bad.

There was an impressed grunt from corporal Oshii, stood on a stack of crates behind the congregated masses, her arm's folded, her hips tilted. Her wordless exclamation had taken everyone by surprise, and it signalled a change in the collective mood. Oshii was watching the operative with much interest. Every one of them, except the operative himself, knew what was coming.

'I am genuinely impressed!' Kosheen shouted down to the operator, clapping her hands in delight. She always admired and acknowledged any display of bravery and skill. 'You must be one *bowling-ball endowed, triple-hard motherfucker*!'

The operator snarled, before finally taking in the line of bodies, made up of his freshly executed compatriots. He looked immediately horrified. He kneeled and placed his hands on top of his head, perhaps realising that he was in a lot of trouble.

'Okay...' the operator's bluster was thoroughly depleted. '*Okay, I... I...* surrender...'

'Excuse me?' McMorrow laughed in disbelief. He finished locking his armour back up and executed the last of his prisoners. He grabbed his side again, even the act of pulling the trigger had sent a shockwave through his body which ignited a surging pain in his wound.

'Did I say *impressed*?' Kosheen corrected herself, raising an eyebrow. 'Actually, maybe not so much.'

'Actually, I like a man who knows when he is outnumbered and outclassed,' said McMorrow.

'Come on,' pleaded the operator. 'I'll go to a prisoner of war camp.'

'*Really?* That is very optimistic request considering the carnage around you,' Kosheen said. 'By *carnage* I, of course, mean the numerous war crimes we've committed.'

'See, the problem is logistics,' McMorrow elaborated. 'The nearest prisoner of war camp is a three hour walk from here, and we really aren't into exerting that much effort if we ain't getting something out of it. That and you fucking stabbed me.'

The operator looked back and forth between Kosheen and McMorrow, over and over, looking for some spark of humanity.

'You are literally the only one of your team to surrender,' McMorrow pointed at one of the executed soldiers and said, 'to be fair, this guy couldn't surrender because I cut out his tongue, and neither could his friend here after I made him eat the first guy's tongue. He wasn't really in the mood for speaking. Because he was gagging.'

'Seriously...?'

'Were we being any less than absolutely, fatally serious?' McMorrow asked, looking to Kosheen to add a nasty little addendum to the malicious ridicule.

But Kosheen gave nothing more than a disinterested grunt as she contemplated their lone enemy. She became detached from the conversation, losing interest in their ritualised dehumanisation of their prisoner, her attention floating away into idle thought. Perhaps she was so used to this ritualistic pattern of abuse that she was bored by the lack of interesting deviation – which, for a moment, she had hoped that the operator was going to provide. Or perhaps the operator's desperate pleas had reached that spark of humanity that was fighting to regain control of Kosheen's soul. *Nah.* She used to live for moments like this, subconsciously projecting her own frustrations onto the victims, finding some relief as she watched them pummelled into submission, knocking a little more of that softness out of her, each time. But more and more it was starting to feel like a hollow, empty thing.

'What's up, Kosheen?' McMorrow said, noticing his colleague's morose temperament. Then he let out a little, mischievous laugh. 'You missing Reaver?'

'Why *the-fuck* would you...?' Kosheen seethed, throwing her hands up.

'Okay!' Oshii exclaimed suddenly, loud enough to get everyone's attention.

Oshii turned and took purposeful strides through the parting crowd, the hushed and awed soldiers immediately regrouping around her and her prey, spreading back out, forming a circle. Oshii took her progressive-blade and slapped it against the palm of her hand, clanging as it hit the metal of the gauntlet, over and over like a tribal drumming.

'Darius, give the operator back his blade,' Oshii ordered.

'But I was gonna keep it,' Darius whined.

'Did I *fucking* stutter?' Oshii snapped.

Darius stepped over and reluctantly grabbed the operator's by the wrist, avoiding eye contact as he slapped the weapon into the victim's hand.

'What the hell is this?' The operator asked, looking at his returned weapon. He winced with every single repetition of that numbing tribal beat.

'It's a blade,' Kosheen called down from her vantage point, listlessly, with less malicious sarcasm than she would normally conjure for this type of scenario. With little enthusiasm she mined a poking motion, tired of her own well-worn mental *script*. 'You stab things with the sharp end.'

Kosheen wondered if this stranger could actually surprise them. Despite his cowardly plea, he had shown some skill, some balls. She craved a little divergence from the norm, *she... well, she didn't know what she wanted.*

Oshii rolled her shoulders and cracked her neck, then nodded. At this simple signal her troop formed a circle around them both, watching intently. Not once did their corporal break the intense, razor sharp focus that she had upon her prey. The operator was really starting to panic now.

'If you last thirty seconds then we'll let you go.'

'*That...* That's all?' The operator asked. 'Thirty seconds?'

Oshii rolled her own blade around and between her fingers like a knife-throwing magician displaying dangerous dexterity. Then she activated it with a subsonic hum

'Survive... But what if I don't just...?' The operator attempted to ask something that his disintegrating ego still wouldn't allow him to verbalise. It was clear he hoped he might win. 'I mean... What if I...'

'You won't,' Oshii said, with mock pity. Then she straitened up. 'Thirty seconds from now!'

'Now?'

The operator definitely didn't seem to be okay with the fact that the fight had already begun, and defiantly didn't like the audience. He was, however, much more unnerved by the total lack of any sort of jeering, cheering or mockery from the crowd, as he would have expected. They were razor focused, as if spectating an ancient rite of passage, beating there fists against their armour in time with Oshii's previous beat, grunting like dogs.

So, the two combatants started to circle each other, but this mutual movement only began because Oshii moved first and the operator was too afraid of the corporal to stay still. The operator fumbled around for the blade's switch, too afraid to take his eyes off his opponent for the split-second it would take to look at the weapon. When he finally managed this most basic of tasks, he pointed the blade forward with one hand whilst he had the held out in the universal *woah-stop!* gesture, as if he thought he could catch any sudden lunges. This would have instantly cost him a few fingers.

Kosheen finally decided to grace the others with her presence, jumping down to join the circle of her compatriots, observing the hopelessness in the operator's body language, and wondering why it was leaving a sour taste in her mouth. For the first time she realised that, of course, she could stop this. She could leap across and interrupt the whole thing, perhaps give the man a chance to escape. She didn't, though. She wasn't really even sure why she would want to. But she was suddenly aware, for the first time in a long time, that it was an option.

Kosheen assumed that, surely, the frayme operator must

know that Oshii was toying with him, drawing this out for her own amusement and for the enjoyment of the rest of the Augmented Fourth. For the operator, this thirty seconds must be the longest of his life.

They clashed, several times, blades narrowly missing their targets, or blocking each other, the blade's mutual resonance preventing them from actually clashing, pushing each other away like identical magnetic poles. The operator may have been starting to think that he had the skills to go up against the legendary Corporal Paris Oshii, but that was all part of her game. It always was.

Oshii dodged a swipe, barely, the tip of the operator's blade nicking her armour, then she bounced back out of range before a subsequent attempt could contact. She spun her blade around her hand with all the flare and precision of someone who had spent a lot of time training their hand-eye coordination to maximise their dazzling dexterity.

With seven seconds of the fight remaining, Oshii decided to finish it. Oshii waited for the operator to lunge, presenting her adversary a subtle-but-false window of opportunity. But when the operator made his move, Oshii sliced his arm clean off. The amputation cold only be called *clean* for a few short moments before the blood spluttered out. Then Oshii slid her progressive blade straight up beneath the operator's breastbone, the subsonic knife cracking the armour like a crab's shell. She twisted the weapon before pulling it out, which, much like turning a tap, forced blood up out of the operator's mouth, nose and -ultimately – dribbling out of his eyes. Oshii turned and strutted away as the operator fell to his knees. She didn't look back

Darius gingerly took his blade back from the loser's open hand, switching it off and placing it to his own holster, which had not had a blade in it for quite some time. He did not look at the dying man.

More conflict blossoms wiggled their way through the cracks in the landing platform all around the dying man as he knelt there, drawn by the kinetic energy of the fight. One by one they bloomed, luminous purples, pinks and blues. With the last of his energy, the operative reached towards one with his remaining hand, eyes blank in near catatonic shock. He pinched a petal, watching it react, changing colour, veins of blue spreading through the pink.

The drumming, humming and chanting subsided. The Augmented Fourth drifted away, returning to their previous tasks and conversations. One or two laughed, but most seemed subdued. They used to enjoy the predictability...

Kosheen, however, approached the body. She leaned down and whispered directly into the operator's ear. The League soldier had enough energy left to turn his eyes towards her but nothing else.

'You could have stayed in the burning frayme and avoided this humiliation, but then you would have died a coward's death. This death had some honour in it. You died on your feet, fighting...'

Kosheen could only hope, when the time came, that she could say the same about her own death. Perhaps that was the only way out of this life that she had become a part of. This *existence*...

Kosheen stood back up straight and stared down at the operator, watching him die. She felt nothing at all, which was the strangest thing, because she used to feel a whole gamut of emotions at times like this, she used to believe that it was the only way that she could feel *anything* at all, and perhaps that was true for all of the Augmented Fourth. But, right now, she felt there was a void at her core, a nothingness that waited at the heart of all things.

The others had moved on. She eventually joined them.

WINTER BEATS ON COLD RED STREETS

Nico Shikari of the Unified American Military was in an odd place, both geographically and emotionally speaking. She was alone, and she was starting to feel as if that wasn't going to change any time soon.

She believed that her country would be coming for her, that's why she had been sat alone in the crashed jump ship that had brought her to this forsaken continent. But there had been no signal, no sign. This left her baffled, contradicting everything she held true about her county and its devotion to its people. Everything she had been *told* to believe. Her tabris, the portable neural interface device, informed her, through the Minds Eye operating system, that her messages had been received. Surely they weren't ignoring her…

Her mind was working overtime to justify this, to try and realign the facts with her faith. At the same time, she felt a profound boredom. She had nothing to do but survive and be patient.

Nico was hungry but not thirsty, as her armour was perfectly capable of filtering the river water, as well as *other* liquids. Not that she was wearing her armour right now. Within the protection of the armoured ship she had felt justified in taking a break from it, whilst she attempted to sleep. That attempt had been futile, her anxious mind fighting back against it.

Desperate times lead to desperation, and she decided to pull the proverbial trigger and resort to something she had been contemplating for some time. She prised open a panel on the floor, not easy when she didn't have a progressive blade. Levering it open with a random piece of metal, she popped the panel free to look inside. She reached in between mechanisms, feeling around until she found a plastic filter filled with a blue organic transition fluid. She cut the pipes loose with the sharpest edge of her piece of random metal and globules of the liquid dribbled out.

She sat back and licked some of the liquid from the improvised shrapnel knife, grimacing. She contemplated the rest of it with a heavy heart. Organic transition fluid. It tasted like melted plastic, just barely edible but full of protein.

If only some of the local wildlife had been more sociable, then she would have a little more variety in her diet. Even the fish seemed to be staying away. She wondered if perhaps she was generating an unpleasant odour.

She sat in the dark and begrudgingly consumed her liquid lunch, listening to the river flowing under the jump-ship, relaxing, much like white noise, washing the thoughts from her mind. The ship had been dropped onto the river, where it spanned the riverbanks like a broken bridge, after Shamsiel the Orbital Defence Platform had created an airborne singularity that had lifted everything in a two-mile radius into the sky. She heard the things that the current carried, scraping against the underside of the hull, from one end of the ship to the other, producing a sound that was not unlike fingernails on a chalk board.

'Well, that's not unnerving at all...'

One thing that she could not hear were the war wolves, the creatures that had been unearthed by the Orbital Defence Platform's gravity weapon. Disturbed from their slumber, she surmised, by the unintended excavation of their tunnel system. She had glanced outside, a couple of hours ago, and seen them, as big as bears, stripping the meat from the dead and dying. Grinding their bones to dust.

But the landscape had fallen silent, the beasts apparently retreated to the holes they called home to lick their lips and chew the fat, literally, as they digested their victims. She heard no scratching, no panting, no howling, no growling.

For the third time in the last hour, she synced her mind to her tabris and checked for any messages from command. Still nothing.

'This isn't healthy. You're hyper fixating. You need fresh air.'

She grabbed the emergency distress beacon as she required a tangible distraction. She had begun to suspect that, despite the beacon's insistent flashing, it wasn't working after all, perhaps that was the only real explanation for her sustained solitude.

That wouldn't explain the lack of response to the calls that she had made over the comscape network via her tabris device, but still...

She decided that she needed to open the beacon up and take a look inside, but this was mostly because she needed to keep busy, and party because she needed an excuse to believe that the lack of response was a mechanical malfunction.

It was as good a motivation as any – if you ignored the desperation of her logic, and the danger outside, which she certainly was. She climbed back into her armour. The last time she had worn it, she had used its sensors and senses to either confirm or disprove the validity of the strange visions that she had witnessed. But, of course, she had only proven that her mind had failed her again, an episode no doubt triggered by the chaos of the Goliath's destruction, the stress it had put upon her.

If she were honest with herself, and she rarely was, it was boredom driving her up the ladder, one rung at a time. She pushed against the damaged hatch – warped out of shape, unable to lock but a bitch to open - with the extra force afforded her by the armour, then peered tentatively out. The fog of burning dust was slowly dissipating, leaving a thin red mist that gave the sky a burnt orange hue, with the twin moons resembling headlights in fog. Static sparks seemed to flutter over the surface of everything, the lingering after-effects of the weaponised singularity.

She scanned the horizon with her armour's eyes. In the distance she could see teams of Green Strays stripping the carcass of the huge, mechanised Goliath for parts and materials by lamp light. The humongous machine's head was sat atop a collapsed building, where it would probably still be resting and rusting a century after Nico was long gone.

'Well, they aren't being attacked by any large hairy creatures,' she said to herself, taking this as a good sign that she could step out. 'Not yet...'

The distant Greens were tiny figures from here, but she could make out that they were working in teams, working efficiently. The Green variety of Stray were professional scavengers and artful engineers, more civilised than the Red Strays, less feral, not known for feasting on human flesh. Less arrogant than the fabled Blue Stray, if *they* even existed.

Nico sat crossed legged on the hull and prised open the beacon, trying to figure out what might be wrong with it. She removed her helmet and held the beacon close to her naked eyes. The beacon's flashing light reflected off her glasses, the red beams catching on the lens' crack.

Nico froze as the Goliath's head seemed to let out an unnatural sound, a low rumble with enough base to make every one of the surrounding structures vibrate, coming through in waves. Nico could have sworn that she saw movement, a twitch of the various lenses and antenna arrays that were set into its eye sockets. It still had some power, and perhaps didn't like all the little beings picking at its back.

She had a rail rifle resting next to her, salvaged from one of the soldiers taken out by a war wolf, which she had attempted to get working by pulling open a compartment beneath the rear end, between the rail and the stock, to reveal the physical side of the inbuilt security measures, and then trying to bypass it through surgical, technical precision. It had been difficult, dangerous work. She had been electrocuted twice before she had managed to ground herself, successfully protecting herself against the security's physical contingency systems. The exposed mess of tangled wires didn't look pretty, but at least, she hoped, it would work. She couldn't even test it, not unless she could source any *real* ammo, of course; the ideal scenario would be to use four-by-nineteen-millimetre tungsten carbide rods within its chamber. Of course, a rail rifle didn't need actual ammo, she was trained to make her own. The magnetic rail meant that no gunpowder was required, so she just needed to scrounge up anything that could be launched down the slim barrel without jamming, like nails or...

'Well, who is this?!'

Nico froze.

The unexpected greeting had come packaged in a gruff, loud and instantly obnoxious male voice, taking Nico completely by surprise. Within a fraction of a moment, she had grabbed the rail rifle and pointed it at the stranger. It might not work, but the potential assailant didn't need to know that.

'Woah, there!' The man laughed, placing his hands in the air half-heartedly.

Before her was a fellow UAM soldier, his helmet removed and hooked to his waist, calling up to her from the riverbank, lit by the rippling reflections of the moons, animated by the river. Nico was relieved to see a fellow countryman, and she looked around for more of them. He seemed to be alone.

'You're lucky I didn't paste the floor with your face,' Nico placed the gun back down beside her.

'Whatcha got there? That the ship's emergency beacon?'

'Fucking thing, it seems ok...'

'*But...?*'

Nico shrugged. Though she was excited at the prospect of imminent rescue, she wasn't really good with people. She decided to play it cool.

'What about your tabris? broken?' The man asked. 'Not

letting you connect to Comscape?'

The stranger had a smirk that was getting more intense with every question he asked. Nico wasn't sure why, but it unnerved her.

'Yeah... I'm... It's connected... But... But it...' she was frustrated. She didn't really want to admit to herself that she was being ignored by her people, and she really didn't want to admit that to a stranger.

'Not getting any sort of response from back home?' The man shrugged. 'Yeah, if you're on patrol round these parts long enough, you start to hear a lot of tales of abandonment. It's sad really, you gotta feel for them. Luckily my team doesn't have any problems like that. We could maybe help you out.

The big man looked around, any pretence of civility disappearing for a moment.

'So, you're all alone?'

'There's a way off this rock, right?' Nico got to the point.

The man refreshed his smile, trying to look as approachable as possible.

'Why would you want to leave? *I could show you...*' He stopped for a moment, snorted, as if he had to rethink what he was about to say. 'Trust me, you can be royalty in this place, if you want it. Just gotta show your strength. You can do it all for the glory of our leaders, if that's your thing.'

That struck Nico as being an odd thing to say, and she was usually all about the glory, she assumed they all were. There was something odious about this man's manner, his tone full of false concern and pity. She glanced down at him and saw that the stranger had held his hand out, either to be shook or to help Nico down. He clearly was not part of any rescue party. She looked away, not acknowledging his gesture.

'We can do whatever we like, to whoever we like,' Reaver said. 'Because we're on the right side. They're not like us, they're only...'

The big man stopped himself from talking, as if the list of lesser mortals that he was about to reel off might include some words that might get him in trouble. Nico suspected that the man didn't want to give himself away too early.

'*Okay...*'

'My name's Reaver.'

'Shikari,' she replied, absently looking over the beacon.

'*What*?' Reaver let out a short, unpleasant grunt. A laugh that obviously mocked Nico, immediately putting her on edge.

'My name is Nico Shikari.'

The stranger snorted, as if he somehow found it pathetic.

'You told me your name I assumed...' Nico waved it off.

'Ok, whatever you say, girl.'

'Excuse me?'

Reaver's entire demeanour suddenly changed again, his smile so warm and eyes so wide that Nico's wariness wore off a little.

'Do you want me to take a look at that?' Reaver pointed at the beacon. 'Bring it down here. We'll see if we can figure it out together.'

Nico broke eye contact, feeling a little woozy. Staring at a random point in the distance, until her eyes focused on a random flicker of silver drawn between the rotor blades on the ship's detached tail, sticking out of the water. Reaver's words faded into the background, as she somehow found herself involuntarily fixating on what turned out to be a cobweb shimmering in the moonlight. She found it infinitely more interesting than the big man's self-involved bullshit, wondering if the web had somehow survived the gravity weapon, or been built since.

'Hey, you ok? Can you hear me? *The fuck?*'

She watched the silvery moonlight dance down the strands of the web, shaken by the wind. Something seemed to change as she watched it, though, as it seemed to become more and more detailed, even in the light, unnaturally, suspiciously so, as if something was changing within her optics, an upgrade to the way they functioned. Or perhaps it was simply an hallucination from food poisoning, so perhaps that synthetic transmission fluid hadn't been a good idea.

She belched.

'No, I got this.'

Nico found Reaver's almost malevolent amusement so inexplicable and belittling, especially the way that he refused to use her name, as if her individuality didn't matter. She felt that maybe her discomfort was the intended result.

There followed a silence that grew more awkward by the second. Nico had been hoping to see another living UAM soldier, sooner rather than later, but this man was making her more and more uneasy by the second.

Reaver's grin slipped, becoming a mask that hid something more odious, insidious, as he looked around the area.

'You alone?'

Nico froze. His voice had lost any hint of warmth, becoming deadly serious. Clearly, it was time to get down to business. She looked down at the components within the beacon, but she was actually watching Reaver at the periphery of her vision. She didn't want him to know how on-edge she felt.

'Temporarily,' Nico lied, and then added an addendum to that fallacy. 'They'll be back soon.'

She could almost feel his eyes boring into her soul, as if he were interrogating her soul for the truth in her words.

'How about you?' Nico asked.

'I'm on my way to rendezvous with the rest of my unit.'

She bisected her senses using her tabris, looking through her helmet's camera eyes, which was still sat on the hull beside her, and used its filters to scan the stranger for weaponry.

'Where's your gun?' Nico asked.

'My...?'

Reaver squinted curiously at Nico, running his eyes over her until he spied her helmet, rested on the hull beside her, and surmised what was happening. He immediately showed his displeasure, perhaps wondering if Nico was smarter than he had assumed.

'I misplaced it,' Reaver said through gritted teeth.

'You misplaced your firearm?' Nico asked, hypocritically.

'Long story short,' Reaver said. 'I fell off a building.'

Reaver laughed pleasantly as he took a few steps closer to the ship. Nico, not falling for this show again, put down the beacon and stood up, taking a defensive stance.

'I am okay,' Nico said, sharply. 'Thank you for your offer of assistance but I must politely refuse. My friends will be back shortly.'

'If you *fucking* say so,' Reaver was not happy being spoken to in this way. 'You "*politely refuse*"?'

On the chest and shoulders of Reaver's dark grey armour was a symbol painted in red. It was either an A or the number four, which was perhaps the point, because, although it appeared it be scrawled in blood it was as carefully considered as any corporate logo, designed to intimidate people, probably sprayed on using a stencil.

'How about you just come on down so we can talk,' Reaver waved her down then held out a *helping* hand.

'We can talk fine from here,' Nico remained defiant, and continued to act as if the beacon was more interesting to her.

'Come on,' Reaver said.

'I am busy...'Nico managed to show not a hint of emotion as she spoke.

'*Fuck* the *fucking* beacon!' Reaver snapped, bearing his teeth. 'Fuck your pathetic calls back home, fuck your non-existent colleagues, and triple-fuck your helmet camera fucking scanning me!'

This outburst was followed by a protracted silence soaked with menace. The big man aggressively pointed at the floor before him.

'Get down here! *Get. Down. Here. Now!*'

Nico picked up her empty, tampered, scavenged rail rifle, knowing that it would probably have electrocuted her even if it had been loaded, and pointed it at Reaver, hoping that the man would not call her bluff. As she stood up, she had to steady herself, however, feeling a little dizzy. She tried not to panic;

not wanting to reveal any sign of disorientation, anything that might be construed as weakness. Her eyes suddenly started to sting, giving her a headache.

'What the fuck?' Reaver asked, holding his hands up. He laughed in disbelief as he stared at the gun, acting as if Nico were overreacting, he wanted Nico to think that it was her that had done something rash.

'Exactly,' Nico replied, squinting at the poorly timed physical discomfort she felt. The moon lit cobweb had simply been a precursor to what was coming.

'I'm only being friendly,' Reaver said with a withering laugh, trying, unsuccessfully, to sound approachable after his uncontrolled outburst. 'Sometimes I can be a little... Don't you want to be friends?'

Nico needed to answer straight away, because she needed to display strength, but her stinging eyes were making her vision pulse. She desperately wanted to close her eyes tight and rub them, but she couldn't do anything that might be misconstrued in front of this prick.

'Look, I...' Nico tried to fire off some verbal sass, but her body had other ideas.

'You don't look so hot,' Reaver grinned.

This was a bad time for whatever this new brand of broken-nonsense was, but it did afford her an unexpected and inexplicable benefit, somehow granting her the ability to see minute details with her naked eyes. So, in the fleeting moments when she was able to focus despite the muddle of this sensory overload, she could see every little muscular twitch in her wannabe assailant, revealing his body to be a symphony of physical tells. She could read him like a book.

'Friends?' Reaver asked, managing to conjure up a little more charisma in his tone.

'So why have your fingers been dancing up the hilt of your progressive blade for the last few minutes?' Nico asked. 'Did you not even realise what you were doing?'

Reaver didn't respond, he simply seethed.

'These glasses give me twenty-twenty vision, you *rancid-fuck-nugget*,' Nico said. 'They don't make me naive.'

Nico stared him out, her ocular discomfort made her appear manic.

Reaver unsheathed the progressive blade, and stood there, considering it for the longest time, no doubt thinking of all the things that he could do to Nico with it. He flicked it on for a second, and Nico's inexplicably supercharged senses allowed her to see every reverberating speck dancing down the sharp edge, glittering in waves.

Reaver deactivated it, rolled it around his fingers until he was holding it by the sharp end, offering its handle and hilt toward Nico. Then he held his other hand out towards her again, palm open. He attempted, in vain, to regain some approachability.

'See? It's yours if you want it.'

'Toss it over,' Nico said, pointing at the blade.

'Why? Come on, I'm offering it to you.' Reaver was getting exhausted with this argument now. 'Just come and take it from me.'

She couldn't help it, she crushed her aching eyes closed, as if she thought she could squeeze the *crazy* out of them.

'I have anger issues,' Nico warned, prizing her eyelids back open. They were red raw.

'Oh, yeah, I'm sure,' Reaver whispered through gritted teeth. '*So have I.*'

Clearly Reaver didn't intend for Nico to hear this, and indeed she shouldn't have, not over that distance, not at that volume.

'I wanna show you how bad *my* issues are…' Reaver breathed these words, *like a snake hissing through a tangle of long, wet grass.*

Nico was really alarmed now. She had no idea how she could have heard Reaver's unpleasant mutterings from this distance with unaided ears, and she was conflicted about whether or not this was a good thing. She even checked to see if she was still connected to her helmet via her tabris, but no. *Somehow* she could hear Reaver breath with her own two, fleshy ears. She could hear his heart pounding faster, hear his teeth grinding...

Nico could hear...

She could hear insects skitter in the dark spaces between the flaming derelicts; small animals bounding through the maze of broken things; condensation forming in the cracks in glass canopies...

'Come on, just come down and take this fucking thing from me,' Reaver insisted. The handle of his blade still pointed at his prey. 'Just play the game.'

Nico shook her head and tried to focus. She just stood, aiming down the barrel, saying nothing at all. She double-checked – triple-checked - that she was not connected to her helmet, because it was hard to concentrate on her predicament when she could see, *somehow*, every tell-tale twitch of Reaver's arrogant, angry face. It was hard to formulate a plan when she could read every *tale* told by the big man's body language.

'Just come over here, you... *fucking bitch*,' Reaver snapped, forcefully pointing at the floor before him. He was getting very frustrated. 'Do not make me come up there.'

'Armour dissolving rounds,' was Nico's only response, her hands shook as she patted the magazine underneath the rail rifle's barrel. As soon as she said it, she realised that perhaps she was exaggerating too much. She worried that perhaps this dangerous man would realise that she had no rounds in her weapon of any kind.

This standoff seemed to last forever, at least that's how it felt to Nico. Then the unpleasant man swore to himself and turned to leave, throwing his blade into the ground, sharp end first.

'I do not have time for crazy bitches,' he said dismissively, as he finally walked away.

'Drop any rations you have,' Nico ordered.

Reaver stopped.

For a second, as Nico stared at Reaver's broad back - heaving as he took deep, angry breaths – she wondered if maybe she had made a mistake, if she had let slip a clue that she was more desperate than she had been letting on. Now he knew that she was hungry.

But, after a few seconds of inaction, Reaver simply took a single ration bar from his pocket, waved it in the air, and then threw it down onto the ground. He stamped on it, twisting his foot, smushing it into the gravel.

Nico watched him leave, making sure that the barrel of her rail rifle was tracking Reaver every inch of the way, just in case he turned around. She remained vigilant for some time after Reaver had disappeared into the landscape of twisted metal, the broken and dismembered remains of vessels which were still shifting and shaking hours after they had been brought down around the Goliath.

Nico slid down the side of the jump ship, still pointing the business end of the gun at the last place that she had seen Reaver. She sauntered on over to the bastard's progressive blade and pulled it out of the ground. She checked the quality and the battery level, both decent enough, then slid it into the empty sheath on her own armour. The ration bar was now inedible, studded with the gravel into which it had been pressed.

'Don't mess with this cat,' she said.

Nico's forearms ached from the tension. She had so wanted to smash Reaver down into the ground and fertilise the barren earth with his blood and bone.

'Kitties got claws.'

She was rather unnerved and simultaneously fascinated by the unlikely fact that she could see every fragment of dirt within the ration bar in obscene, unlikely, unnecessary detail.

Finally able to close her eyes, which felt as if they were pulsating out of their sockets, now that she was, apparently, alone. She removed her glasses so that she could give her eyelids a good rub, an uncomfortable endeavour when her hands were wearing gauntlets.

Whatever this sensation was, it had been badly timed, but she believed that she had managed to style it out.

What even was that?

She had no idea what kind of mutated viruses might have developed in this country, and what they could do to the human body.

(*"Medical diagnostic, please,"*) she requested, through the tabris's link to her armour.

To her immediate surprise and continued confusion, the system began to collate a response so long and detailed that it was causing the percentage indicator presented in her Minds Eye to fill at an astonishingly slow speed. That was certainly alarming, she had never seen anything like that. She realised that this could take hours to complete, and it was such an unprecedented effort for such a simple query about a simple question that she considered rebooting the system, believing it to surely be a system error.

But it's only a migraine or something, surely?

She threw back her head in despair, her mouth contorting into a scream that refused to leave her body, doubled her over. She almost dropped to her knees, but they seemed to lock up, her hands balling up into fists.

But then she saw something small moving in the distance, despite the dark and the dust. Her unusually attuned senses highlighted every dust particle reacting around the small creature, marking out the critter's path. She could see the tiny eruptions of dirt from every furry footfall, the waves created from the swish of its tale.

Perhaps it was hunger making her hallucinate, or that barely edible gel that she had sourced from the ship's innards had been rotten. She could worry about that later. Dinner was waiting.

Whatever it was it was fast; a rabbit maybe, hopefully not a rat. She placed the useless rifle on the magnetic lock on the back of her armour and wrapped her hand around the hilt of her new progressive blade, ready to strike or swipe, and tracked the potential meal around the corner of a hill of broken ships.

She hesitated, listening intently. But the problem was that

she could hear too much, all the little things that should have been out of her audible range. She could still hear Reaver walking away, somewhere in the distance, occasionally stopping, muttering obscenities, before moving on.

Squatted low, moving slow, she pressed herself up against a crashed ship and peered around the corner, as if she were hunting trained enemy guards, not *Mrs Tiggywinkle or Peter Rabbit.*

Though she did not find her furry, edible prey, she did find yet another victim of the Goliath's destruction, a young pilot lay face down in a shadow cast by the frame of an aerial bomber's exposed frame, the plane picked clean and charred like a cadaver, smouldering, arches than loomed overhead like ribs.

Nico took her useless rail-rifle in hand, yet again it was only for show, and wandered over, pointing the business end of the gun at every dark shadow, like a talisman to ward off malignant entities. She flipped the pilot over with a foot, keeping both hands on her gun.

The pilot was in her twenties, possible ten years Nico's senior, wearing a muscle-suit beneath a white aviation jacket that Nico very much liked the look of. She had always liked the look of them, she had always wanted one of her own. Not that she had ever had any interest in learning to fly. The pilot also had a breathing mask hanging limply from her neck by one of its oxygen pipes, whilst another two pipes, broken, stuck out like tusks. It was as if the pilot had been ripped from her cockpit.

An exploding bubble of blood and spit alerted Nico to the fact that the pilot was far from dead. Nico was surprised but tried not to show it. The pilot was badly injured, probably fatally-so, eyes closed, breathing strained.

'*Now you are going to have food and ammo for me,*' Nico whispered, not really thinking that the dying pilot was conscious enough to hear her. 'I'm sorry about this, but my need is greater than yours...'

Nico was happy to find that the pilot still had her own rail rifle. Perhaps this one would recognise Nico's various digital fingerprints – either bio, physical or psychological – via an updated user database or the ability to connect and update to the network, an option that she assumed was missing or broken in her current gun.

'I'll swap you,' she whispered, placing her own poorly modified gun down next to the pilot, then picking up the pilot's gun to check it over.

Of course, it's low on ammo, Nico thought to herself, but a little ammo was better than no ammo, she just had to make sure that it would work for her.

She held the rail-rifle's grip and rested her finger on the trigger. The security systems would extrapolate and confirm her identity using multiple methods, from her brain waves, to the way she moved, to the particular way her organs moved.

Red light, access denied. She swore, scowling at the little LED light in the gun's grip, in a small recess behind the trigger. She tried again, and again...

'Come on, seriously?' Nico whispered to herself. 'What the fuck...?'

This made no sense to her, she could only assume that it must be a problem with the gun, or a corrupted file in the database. She pounded it down into the ground with all the force that her body had reserved for potentially beating Reaver. Then she crouched over it, both arms pushing down on the barrel with all the tension and conviction of someone strangling a stranger. She gritted her teeth and crushed her eyes closed as a low growl rumbled out *from the dark pit located deep in the core of her.*

The pilot gurgled out another bubble of blood which popped and pasted her lips and nose in crimson. This made Nico feel foolish, as she remembered that she wasn't, technically, alone, because this incapacitated stranger had witnessed her childish tantrum.

It never really occurred to her to help this person, but this was not really malicious. She had been programmed to be desensitised to death. Once someone fell, they were nothing but a vacated shell. No one fought to save the terminal cases, the odds of survival calculated in the coldest way that the human mind can, and the appropriate action taken.

Something suddenly occurred to Nico.

'Was this… did… Did a war-wolf do this?'

Nico looked around at every corner, at every possible elevated vantage point. But if they hadn't eaten their victim then they would have kept her alive as bait… But, Nico realised, if this were the case, then she would have surely been ripped apart by now…

Nico assumed that the fact that she had not yet been attacked was a sign that she was safe, at least temporarily. She returned to rummaging through the pilot's possessions. She had to move fast.

'You're not…' the pilot tried to speak.

'I am,' Nico said, distracted and distant. Her next words, however, had a tinge of regret. *'I really am…'*

As soon as the words left Nico's lips she realised that she may have made a mistake by responding to the pilot. Nico had engaged with the pre-deceased, humanising her, when she had been conditioned to *de*humanise others, as often as possible.

'You are not who you *are*,' the pilot said, as blood gathered in her nose and made some of her words sound nasal. 'You're not who you're supposed to be.'

Nico paused. A chill down her spine for some unknown reason, triggered by some uncertainty at the root of her.

'What did you just say?' Nico asked, her eyes widening.

'We're not…' The pilot said. 'None of us, we are not who we are supposed to be…'

The pilot's chest was rising and falling slowly. Though her ocular acceleration had somewhat returned to normal, Nico could hear the organs move deep within the pilot's torso, she could hear the grind of the damaged ribs.

Nico's own breathing was suddenly becoming

uncomfortable as well, as if synchronising. For her own sanity she resumed her policy of ignoring the soon-to-be corpse, not that this really seemed to help. She was starting to feel the need to leave, for her own sanity.

A notification flashed in Nico's Minds Eye, almost making her jump. The notification was to inform her that someone was attempting to contact her through the com-link. She was excited for a second, perhaps this was her military finally contacting her, but then she realised that this was an attempted digital-handshake, a local transmission.

'This you?' Nico asked the pilot.

Nico swiped the notification to the periphery of her vision. She was so distracted by potential danger and real hunger that she didn't even dismiss the pilot's digital request out right, those extra seconds would have stood between her and any nutritious and nourishing snacks that she hoped to find.

Nico managed to find a few ration packs in a zipped-up pocket on the pilot's right thigh. So excited, so overwhelmed by hunger, that she dropped the first one as soon as she had ripped it open, popping the contents out of the packet like a mortar-launch. She quickly scooped it back up and slammed it into her mouth, devouring it before she even had chance to chew it properly. Despite being a mostly flavourless protein bar, with a vitamin and nutrient enriched goo at its centre, it became the most gloriously flavoursome meal that she could imagine.

'Take your guard down, *girl...*' The pilot was blathering, struggling to get her words out. 'I can see through it, *through it, do it...*'

'*Just...*' Nico waved a dismissive hand, feeling quite anxious. '*Whatever... Fuck! Don't...* You're trying to make this difficult. I'm sorry to be the one to inform you of this, but you are out of time, and so will I be if I...'

'You're not who you are,' the pilot interrupted. 'You're not who you're supposed to be.'

'Yes, you said.'

Nico meant to glance at the pilot, but her attention snagged on the pilot's emerald eyes. Their luminosity made them instantly fascinating. It transpired that Nico was still able to see an abundance of detail, those irises appeared to be rings of overlapping shards, a thousand slightly different shades of green, framing pupils that reflected the celestial bodies overhead. Nico looked again at the request notification, flashing away, and wondered what the dying woman could possibly have to say that would be so urgent or important.

Against her better judgement, Nico moved closer to the pilot. It seemed as if the woman's bewitching emerald eyes were staring into the darkness that had come to claim her. Nico should have moved on, but the pilot's words rattled around in her mind for reasons that she could not yet comprehend.

Nico felt as if she may fall into those eyes, like a planet pulled into a blackhole with no way of escaping, destined to be torn asunder, over and over for eternity.

Best to avoid looking into them altogether from now on, if she wanted to get out of here.

She resumed her rummaging, finding a medicinal canister, easy to spot because of its red cross. She considered it for a moment; it would sure come in handy. She tried not to look at the pilot, but, as before, her attention was drawn to those eyes, like singularities drawing in all the light.

She sighed. For reasons that she could not comprehend, even as one part of her screamed at her to be reasonable, she popped the lid off the canister, revealing a cluster of micro-needles within. She loosened the pilot's white flight jacket, which she still coveted, and pushed the needles against the top of the pilot's arm. The canister shook as it ejected a dose into the pilot's blood stream.

'Consider that an indiscriminate act of kindness...' Nico said, then shook her head and rolled her eyes at the perceived wastefulness of the gesture. *Why?*

She sat back and checked out the body before her. The rise and fall of the pilot's chest seemed to normalise. The notification still flashed in the periphery of her Minds Eye, reminding her that the pilot was trying to start a com-link conversation. She still did not delete it, letting it linger.

Why?

'I'm coming back for this,' she said, as she pulled the jacket back over the pilot's shoulder and zipped it back up.

She stood up walked away.

SWITCHING OFF
WITH YOU

Nico Shikari was still scavenging for supplies amongst the wrecks of the wasteland.

She had left behind the fatally wounded pilot, though she had designs on returning for the lady's white flight jacket, later. She had felt the uncharacteristic need to let the stranger keep it for now, out of some sort of respect. Or pity. She wasn't sure which, she didn't really understand either.

Nico was climbing over a crashed gunship, checking the banks of bevel-edged, flat faced missiles that made the tail-end look like the hind of some exotic creature. She wondered if she could unscrew one and modify it as some sort of fat, unwieldy grenade, or perhaps an improvised landmine.

The inside of the broken ship lit up. Music started to play. She leapt back and grabbed her new progressive blade, keeping low and silent. She had glanced inside earlier and seen nothing, no signs of life within. She knelt there, listening, ready to strike. The music, though, seemed to, somehow, remind her of a time she had forgotten about, maybe it was something from a dream.

But slowly a memory started to come into focus. She remembered hearing this song when in a nightclub, maybe, a place full of lights and bodies, but she was quite sure that she had never been to such a place. Had she gotten drunk one night, and wandered in? She was on a dance floor, surrounded by people. There was one person in particular, a slender figure, remaining defiantly out of focus. They were staring at each other...

She climbed up and onto the cockpit, finding the canopy still open, as it had been when she had inspected it earlier, and the seat empty. The music stopped and the light source ceased to exist the moment she peered in, as if it had never been. The safety harness was still locked closed across the empty chair, though it was frayed, the buckles bent.

Nico dropped down and nestled in to place. She saw a handgun lodged between the seat and the arm rest. Excited to find a weapon, she reached down to grab it. As she pulled on it, however, something gloopy was clinging to it, so thick that it felt as if it was fighting her for possession. She quickly found that the whole endeavour had been pointless, the front half of the pistol was missing, and only the back half remained. Teeth marks, the barrel had been bitten clean off. A string of monstrous drool was hanging between it and the darkness down the side of the seat, and there was a random, bloody finger dangling from the goo. What remained of the sliding mechanism simply dropped off and clattered onto the seat. With a look of deep distaste, Nico discarded the stunted weapon back down the side of the seat.

A lucky charm was hanging from the canopy by her head, a plastic head on a chain. She flicked it and watched it bounce around, listening to the shrunken chime of the chain.

For a moment, she became dimly aware of the existence of her own existential loneliness. She found herself willing to entertain the idea of conversing with another human being.

Nico sat back and accepted the digital handshake, against her better judgment. Even as she did it she felt as if she had made a mistake, but she had to know what the lady had to say. It was like an itch in the centre of her soul, and it would only get worse.

("Hey?") Nico tentatively asked.

("Hey.") Came the reply, a voice that was a little gruff but

friendly.

(*"'Sup?"*)

(*"Oh, nothing. I'm just over here, under a canopy of stars, living my best life."*)

Nico didn't quite know how to take this, her head tilting curiously.

(*'Are you the girl who showed me a little mercy?"*) The pilot said. (*"The indiscriminate act of kindness?*)

Nico shrugged, realised, that the pilot couldn't see this, so she added an embarrassed grunt.

(*"Your hair looked like strawberry laces,"*) the pilot added.

(*"Yeah that's the grease,"*) Nico said, blinking at the oddness of the exchange.

(*You kept me on hold for twenty seven minutes and thirty two seconds..."*)

(*"I just needed to talk to someone..."*) Nico said. (*"I... I could hear music..."*)

(*"I always wanted to learn a musical instrument,"*) the pilot said.

(*"Okay."*) Nico had no idea how to respond to that.

(*"I was learning, using some software on my tabris,"*) the pilot went on. (*"Makes you feel like you're really holding a guitar."*)

(*"Oh, right... maybe I need something like that, help me pass the time...."*)

A download link to that very piece of software appeared in the periphery of Nico's vision. She glared at it.

Who sends a download link to some recreational, educational software? She didn't know how to handle an exchange like theirs. She wasn't really good with people. In general.

(*"Without the war, maybe I could have been in a band."*) The pilot sounded wistful. (*"Who am I kidding, I'd have probably been a waiter or some shit."*)

(*"Without the war?"*) Nico sounded baffled. (*"What do you mean? What else is there?"*)

Nico initiated the download of the suggested software, and watched he bar fill up, gradually. They were a long way from a digital distribution hub, or any cloud network, slowing the process.

("Where you from?") the stranger asked her. *("I can't place that accent.")*

("The Baltimore towers,") Nico said.

("What was that like?")

Nico frowned. She had never really understood small talk. She didn't see the point of it. Why would this stranger want to know this? What could she possibly do with this information?

("It was fine,") she said, before randomly blurting out some additional information. Even she wasn't sure why. *("On a clear day you could see the Washington Lake...")*

("Lake... Strange name for something so big. That thing is practically an ocean. I'm sure I read somewhere that it took fifty years for the Washington crater to fill up with water.")

("I lived in San Diego,") the pilot continued. *("Not far from Mission Valley. Not the greatest. Almost glad to get a mission. Not that you spend much time at home, right? What is even the point? It's true what they say about Mission valley though. Ghosts patrol that place.")*

The software installed. Nico cursed as she scrolled through the End User Agreement and accepted it. She selected a guitar at random from the menu.

("What did you pick?") The pilot asked, but Nico was too interested in the process to answer.

Before her, as if conjured from light and dust, the guitar started to form. The body, the bridge, the frets, the string...

Before her appeared a tutorial drawn and animated in wireframe, a demonstration of where to place her fingers, the movement she must make. Nico reached out and wrapped her fingers around the semi-opaque guitar that she saw in her Minds Eye. She followed the visual guide, placing her fingers in the correct place, or an approximation of the appropriate position, the moved them in time. She heard the sound it made, exclusively in her head. By proxy, the pilot heard it too.

A notification told her that her "friend" had picked a song

for her.

("Think I should learn some cords or something first.")

("Just jump in, follow the fingers")

She played the song that the pilot had selected, attempting to mimic the wireframe fingers on the demonstration instrument. The song was a thing of ethereal beauty, given a perfect personalisation because of, but not in-spite of, the errors that Nico made. It sounded as if it were echoing across the wastelands.

Each pluck of a string generated a pulse of light, and helped to spark a little more interest from Nico. She sometimes found that she liked shiny, pretty things, especially if they reacted to her.

("Are you out here alone?") The pilot asked.

Nico remember Reaver asking this same question, and she faltered.

("Everyone I know is behind me, now,") Nico was surprised by how honest she felt she could be honest with the particular stranger.

She played on, picking it up surprising fast. It was like learning any skill, and Nico had always prided herself on trying to be the best, through sheer force of will. She studied the movements of the fingers in the projected example, learning the purpose of the movements, the minutia behind the results. The program was apparently aware of how fast she was learning, and adapted accordingly, skipping levels, from beginner, basic, intermediate... In truth, Nico had no idea how much time was passing.

("You're right about the lake...")

There was a pause, as if the pilot were taken aback that Nico had spoke without prompting. The pause persisted, as the pilot waited for some follow up remark, but non came.

("It's beautiful though, isn't it?") The pilot asked.

Nico simply grunted, lost in her task. She saw, in her memories, *the Washington crater, filled with the sea water that had made its way from the ocean. The sun making one of its harbours shimmer, a solar frigate landing within it, making waves.*

The skyline from her memories came into sharper view, making some of the high-altitude balconies visible – people drinking their morning coffee or soaking up the sun; their pets dangling a lazy paw over the edge; their hung-up washing undulating on a breeze. She noticed that the archaic, disused telephone lines, stretched between them, had started to twang and vibrate in time with her harmonic noodling.

The aero-mech's instrument panel lit up, gradually. Dim at first, as if drawing on some dwindling reserve of power, but gradually it started to get brighter. So gradual that she barely noticed it, her eyelids lulling. That music, that she had heard from the back of the vehicle, started to play again, mingling with her playing. Out of time, but not defeating the mood.

Deep in the back of the bullet-witch aeromech, the gravity orb spun up, generating a fission on the air. Static flickering between everything.

She felt light as a feather, her hair stood of end. She felt a tingle down her arms, goosebumps. Then she thought she saw ghostly arm, willing themselves into existence, reaching around from behind, flickering transparent white, like transmission noise, fingers reaching out to Nico's own hands. She felt a cold shiver, radiating out from them. Nico froze, despite the suspicion that this was, somehow, the pilot about to show her how to hold the instrument properly. Nico jumped. The extra appendages vanished.

She felt as if there were lips getting closer to her ears. She heard a whisper, something that she could not make out. The gravity orb spluttered to a stop, the floating debris dropped with a clatter of percussive thumps.

("Was that you?")

("Was what me?")

("Nothing, don't worry about it.")

There was a pause, then the pilot spoke solemnly.

("You felt that, too?") The pilot sounded just as shocked as Nico. (*"Some kind of feedback, I guess. Perhaps your defences are*

compromised.")

Another pause, as Nico thought long and hard.

(*"Right."*)

Nico grabbed the canopy above her and lifting herself up out of the cockpit. She slid down the side of the bullet-witch's nose cone and landed in the dirt.

She started to walk, then jog. She didn't know where she was going at first, she just wanted to get away from that cockpit and the suggestion of physical intimacy and affection. If she had engaged her brain then she would have headed back to her own ship, but she didn't. Somehow she found herself heading back towards the pilot.

As she walked, she looked up. The body of the Goliath loomed over everything, a constant reminder of the chaos that had culminated in its levitation, as the competing hordes of military machines were torn asunder all around it.

Nico could see flood lights up the Goliath's spine, temporarily posted their by the Strays mining it for parts. She could see the sparks of powered cutting equipment, illuminating these workers. She could hear their distant chatter, though the language they used in private was a magpie mishmash of differing languages, revealing the vast mixture of their heritage. Still, this was confirmation that the war wolves were not around, not right now, as they would have been drawn to these targets. They were full, no doubt. She had time, she hoped.

Nico wandered through the maze of debris, reaching out to touch it, steadying herself. Her eyes, her ears, and even her sense of smell was still heightened, making her feel a little dizzy. This was exasperated when she found the enclave and crashed and stripped ship that sheltered the pilot.

She squeezed through the gap through which she had hunted the bunny earlier, and out into the large clearing to find herself in the middle of a blizzard. She was shocked for a moment, before realising that this was not real, it was an overwhelming flurry of broken data that had manifested within her visual feedback.

INTERFERENCE DETECTED. SIGNAL SCRUBBING INITIATED.

ATTEMPT NUMBER ONE...

ATTEMPT NUMBER TWO...

ATTEMPT NUMBER THREE...

ERROR...

ERROR...

Fuck!

These words, too, deteriorated into a flurry of visual noise. She waded through a fog of random data, potent data hanging in the air like overabundant pollen.

There she was, the emerald-eyed pilot just lying there in her bone white flight jacket, with a high collar and a black barcode running vertically down the right side, parallel to the zip.

("Fancy meeting you here,") the emerald-eyed pilot said. *("Come here often?")*

Nico hadn't expected to smile, but here she was. A little smirk was squatting at the side of her mouth, giving her away.

Goosebumps again, as out of the corner of one eye Nico thought she saw a ghost, like an afterimage, crouching down beside her. In that same fleeting second, the ethereal figure had reached up, as if to run a hand through Nico's hair. Nico almost thought that she had *felt* it, too.

Perhaps that was somehow the result of the tabris connection between the two of them, some psychological crosstalk conjuring a mental projection in the periphery of her vision. It could have just as easily been a perfectly timed conjunction between a trick of the light and a light breeze, conspiring to play a cruel trick. It wouldn't have been the first time Nico had seen things that weren't there, and she had gotten good at brushing them off, but this time a shiver ran down her spine regardless.

("Your hair really does look good,") the pilot said, to clarify a previous point. *("Your glasses really sell a specific look. I don't know if that's what you were going for, if it was accidental, but it's*

very cute.")

Nico absently touched her own hair, in the spot where she thought she had felt those spectral fingers brush through it.

(*"It funny,"*) the green-eyed pilot said. (*"Being at the end of all things, it clears the mind. All the bullshit that fills your head just breaks up and floats away, and you see what's worth seeing."*)

That blizzard of fizzing, crackling static was whipping up a storm around them, but only in her Minds Eye. Nico realised that she was right, this was some signal distortion from the mental connection to the pilot, some kind of cross-talk that appeared to be manifesting in the world around her. But this was no more real than a dream invading the waking mind.

The distortions started to look like ghosts willing themselves into existence from the chaos of static. The visual noise formed itself into two adolescents, crouching down in front of each other. Like ice sculptures, but carved out of solid, visual noise. Although they were translucent and fragmented their body language revealed absolute devotion to each other.

'What is that?' Nico asked.

(*"What is what?"*) Asked the emerald-eyed pilot.

'I can see the outlines of two kids crouched down in front of each other.'

(*"You can see that?"*) The pilot sounded embarrassed at first, then seemed to accept it. (*"I was just thinking about that. Well, I guess that's all just* soul-chatter. *A part replayed from a perfect day…"*)

There was a pause of a few seconds before she continued. Nico felt a little embarrassed by proxy, as if she were intruding somehow.

(*"Teaching her how to whistle like a… like…'*) the pilot lost what she was trying to say. (*"We were barely teens, as innocent as it was possible for child conscripts to be, when all the shit was just theory and simulation."*)

Nico realised these figures were part of a private performance taking place in the metaphysical theatre in the pilot's mind, behind the curtain of sparks beyond that burdened brow.

("It was early evening, June. There was this song on the radio playing,") the green-eyed pilot sounded so happy, so in love. It was a stark contrast to the pilot's decaying physical condition. *("Hiding where the drill instructors wouldn't catch us.")*

Nico could almost hear a song playing, drifting whispers of some composition that she couldn't quite catch. She could see the outline of the wireless speakers sat between the children. It sounded a little like the song that she had heard in the cockpit.

It was like watching performance art, as if two young mimes were expressing their undiluted devotion through their movements. One of the girls puckered her lips in an exaggerated fashion as she attempted to whistle, then the other imitated this, pushing her lips out and up, so over-the-top that the intention must have been to make the other laugh. She succeeded in this regard, as they giggled, holding their sides. As they gradually climbed down from this emotional high, they simply stared at each other, smiling.

One of the flickering figures reached up, tenderly moving the hair from her friend's eyes, as that friend tilted her head away...

("Love's first blush...") The pilot exhaled, pushing out these words.

The figures started to crackle, and the lingering ground-fog of corrupted data started to drift up into the air above them, forming voxel clouds, all squares and off centre edges. Nico was in awe of the perfect symmetry of this, somehow the flux-distortion was reacting to the pilot's memories and emotions.

("This one perfect day, a simple trinket locked away...") The pilot trailed off for a moment.

('You still there?') Nico asked, after a few moments of quiet reflection that she mistook for an awkward silence.

("Yeah, yeah... There were other days of course. This wasn't the beginning or the end. I don't know what it was about this one day. I mean, we were together until we were mid-teens. Just this one day, I can remember every detail.")

("You drifted apart?")

("In the end, it's time that gets ya. It's the years. The mileage. You know how it is. You're like me. Every day is the same. They try their damn hardest to make the days the same, so we all end up the same. So, we find these little ways to make things different, to make things your own. We started stealing, making a game of it, just to make things a little more interesting. For Shits and giggles. Literally giggles. She had the sweetest laugh. But in the end, it was just to get the heart thumping. Nothing big, just... Don't judge me, I can literally feel your disapproval through the crosstalk.")

Nico let out a *humph* through gritted teeth, looking like a bulldog chewing a wasp.

("From the kitchen, from the officer's quarters,") the pilot continued. *("We'd return them. Didn't want to instigate a witch hunt. Just little rebellions. Little ripples in the pond that they wanted so still.")*

("Just to make memories?") Nico asked. She understood more than she would have admitted to anyone else, and was still reluctant to really admit it here, at least on purpose. *("How old were you?")*

("I don't remember.") The pilot seemed to be thinking. *("How old were you?")*

("What? Me? How old was I when?")

("When you fell in love?")

Nico rolled her eyes.

("Fuck right off.") She said, as if she found the whole thing condescending.

("Let me guess, there's only one thing that you love and its bigger than you. Hand to heart, salute to the flag. I think you're keeping something from me. Maybe you're keeping something from yourself. Rewriting the facts to match the fiction.")

("You're just angry at the world because of where you've ended up,") Nico reasoned. It was the best explanation that she could come up with to match her internal narrative.

("Yeah, well, life ran aground.") The pilot continued. *("This one moment became this precious thing that I clung to like a*

talisman. I didn't want this to end, I didn't want to go off and fight their stupid war, fight and kill other poor people for the benefit of... others... people just like me and her, torn apart...")

Nico didn't like this kind of talk. *How could the war be "stupid"?* It was their purpose. *Her* purpose. She was stood up, now, fidgeting.

("Purpose?") The pilot had heard Nico's thoughts, had she thought aloud, or was this that intrusive crosstalk that was filled her head with all this sensory noise?

("Everything feels so different from where I am,") the pilot sounded confounded. *("It seems to be that we're born into a void, this existential nothing. Devoid of meaning and purpose. I can see it, now. A blank slate that others conspire to fill. They give you a name, a country, a belief system, a purpose... They construct a world in your mind, then you spend your life finding evidence to fortify it, because you're afraid of that void. That's how it feels to me, at the end of all things.")*

Nico rolled her eyes.

("Forget it, I'm not here to argue with you,") the pilot said. *("No time for that. It just.... Me and her, the world didn't care about our story, they were just convinced that their narrative was more valid than ours.")*

("Is this a sales pitch for your novel?")

("We were set on different paths, given different roles to fill. Told who we were. We started out so alike, ended up so different. We had our heads filled with different, diverging stories, and I guess we let them define us and our view of the world. Or at least, she did.")

("What do you by "stories"?") Nico asked, not quite grasping the meaning.

("That's all existence is,") the pilot elaborated. *("Fearing that there's nothing to any of this, no meaning, no purpose, so we tell ourselves tales. As a specious, I mean.")*

Nico let those words float through her mind as she studied the children and their perfect little moment of unguarded joy and honestly.

Nico could not explain why, but she felt some small amount

of empathy for what she saw, something here she could relate to, that in turn made her question other feelings that she had been experiencing lately. There was this sensation she couldn't verbalise, the feeling that something wasn't right, that there were parts of her *Self* locked away.

("I'm not sure why, but there's something about this that...") Nico said, struggling to verbalise her thoughts. Regardless, she found words spilling out of her mouth unfiltered. *("Not exactly this, but* something like this*...")*

The pilot turned to look at Nico, but Nico was wary of making eye contact with those deep green *singularities*, in case her soul was dragged in and torn asunder.

("Something's missing in me...") Nico continued, shaking her head at her own words. This maudlin self-reflection should have been beaten out of her long ago, *had been*, but something was changing. *("Is this making sense? What am I trying to say?")*

Those emerald eyes were fixed upon Nico, following her as she continued to pace. She said nothing to her new red-headed friend, perhaps knowing that Nico was figuring it out for herself, that Nico had to figure it out for herself.

("Just ignore that, I was being stupid,") Nico almost sneered at herself.

("If you say so...") The pilot said, her voice silky and sincere, even through the com-link. She decided to divert the conversation. *("So, what's your story?")*

("I don't have a story.") Nico dismissed the question.

("Sure you do.") The pilot insisted.

("I'm no one.")

("You can always think of yourself as a no-one, *or you choose to make yourself someone,")* the pilot said, sincerely.

("Okay, sure,") Nico frowned. She wasn't entirely convinced that this *wasn't a sales pitch.* *("My story is, I turned up to class every single day, ran around assault courses with guns, ran through simulations.")*

Nico frowned, as if that all sounded so empty, as if something was missing. Absently she concluded, *("then I ended up here.")*

("Like it never really happened at all.") the pilot said. *("Do you have anyone waiting for you back home, or maybe out on manoeuvres somewhere? A friend? Maybe somebody who means something more?")*

Nico shook her head instead of answering, profoundly confused.

("I don't have long left, don't fuck me around,") the pilot said, in a manner that was bordering on condescending. *("You're too pretty and smart to not know what I mean.")*

Nico laughed at the bluntness, then she felt foolish for her unexpected vocal response. She checked the surrounding debris for any sign that any potential aggressors might have heard her brief, involuntary outburst. She wasn't really used to showing any emotion. She really didn't see the point in it.

("Okay.") Nico admitted. *("I did.")*

("Did they reciprocate?") The pilot had clearly detected something in Nico's voice.

Nico did not answer. A complex salvo of reactions manifested amongst her facial muscles.

("One way love can leave us black and blue,") the pilot said.

("Well, it was probably just me being...") Nico was apparently trying to apologise for being human. *("I thought I did, back then; have someone that I wanted for some* fucking *reason. It seemed important at the time, but it feels so hollow now...")*

("How do you mean?")

Nico was struck by the pilot's sincerity. She stopped pacing for a moment, looking back at the stranger with interest. She hadn't even realised until that exact moment that she *had* been pacing. It genuinely appeared that this individual wanted to hear what Nico had to say, and in her experience that was rare. She wasn't sure how to answer just yet, so she sat and thought.

Amongst the silence, she was reminded that her hearing was still abnormally attuned. For her, the silence was gradually filled with insects, and alien things that resembled them, living their best lives between the crashed ships and the derelicts. She could see them, too, illuminating the dark spaces like a neon choir.

("It's like...") Nico was attempting to get to grips with the concepts of sincerity and sharing. *("I thought I was supposed to be* into *him because he was so... I don't know... Confident; handsome?")*

("Him?")

("What? Anyway, it seems so artificial somehow, like going through the motions. Like, that's what everyone else seemed to want, and I wanted to be like them. Because why would you want to be different? To stand out?")

("To think for yourself? To be yourself?")

Nico just grunted and frowned, concerned that this conversation was going deeper into uncharted emotional and psychological territory, and she was just as concerned to realise that she seemed to be complicit in that.

Rather than answer the question, Nico opened the seal on a scavenged bottle. According to the label the contents were infused with nutrients, proteins and *some-shit-or-other* she didn't understand. She sniffed it for signs that it had expired but it remained unappetising precisely because it lacked any odour. She took a sip, and she could hear it, and feel it, slipping down her throat.

'You want some?' Nico asked aloud, tilting the bottle towards the pilot.

("Not for me, thank you.")

More of those ghostly outlines of crystallised visual noise started to coalesce, only this time forming towers, not people. A few city blocks grew out of the frosty virtual mist, the tallest of the towers no more than a few feet high. Nico stood up, curious, to get a better look at the scaled-down skyline, conjured around the two semi-opaque projections of the crouching children. At first she thought that these were just random structures, then she started to recognise important, famous places amongst them. She saw the various headquarters of the world's official leaders, as well as the iconic homes of the mega-corporations that - some believed - controlled the world from behind the scenes. They were all ostentatious structures designed to radiate power, surrounding the adolescent whistlers like a cage.

Nico wandered away. She did not know what to feel, or how to take any of this. She had to distance herself from the individual on the floor beside her, but, in her distracted state, made the mistake of wandering towards the luminescent, translucent constructs born from the pilot's mind.

She waded through the manifestation of the pilot's memories, as the synthetic *ground fog* fluctuated, fractured and spasmed in the immediate area around her feet with every step she took.

She wondered if she could touch it. She spread her hands out to the side as she walked though the artificial shapes formed from discarded fragments of a stranger's mind, each of those towers contracting and expanding, mimicking the movement of the pilot's lungs. Nico's fingers felt like conduits for some ancient energy, tingling somehow as they touched the representation of the collapsing id. The pilot had, perhaps unwittingly, breached Nico's defences, slithering her way through the Intrusion Counter Electronics baked into her tabris and into her head, allowing synaptic crosstalk, or maybe it was, somehow, psychosomatic.

Pulses of discarded junk data, jingling like glass beads, drifted like snow around Nico. She respectfully brushed them aside as she moved across the scene, each one of them humming in a differing resonance as she touched them.

She was deep amongst the spectral buildings now, as they started to grow larger, wrapping around Nico, making her feel as if she were shrinking, though this was of course impossible, an illusion. Disorientated, grasping for something to grab hold of, unable to see the real world through the light show.

Soon it became apparent to her that she was heading towards one building in particular, an open window beckoning her in, as if she had a choice. Nico fell to her knees as the structural expansion suddenly ceased. She looked around, finding the outlines of a bedroom, complete with furniture and indistinct decoration.

There was a figure lying on the bed in a foetal position, head resting on a stack of pillows. Nico looked closer. Though the face was constructed from the same flickering white data as everything else, there was enough detail to make out their features. It was, inevitably, the pilot, staring at the window. She was even still wearing the coveted white flight jacket. Not moving, frozen.

Through the window she could see the dream-drenched city, and it was no real place, it was an amalgamation of actual landmarks, and the pilot had placed her sanctuary, *her ego*, at the centre of it.

Nico did something that revealed a deep, repressed curiosity, something that she would not have been able to justify verbally, reaching out towards the translucent outline of the pilot's residual *self-image*, just wanting to touch one of her cheeks. Although she touched nothing solid, she still felt the tingles in her tips multiply exponentially, until she could feel it not just in her fingers but crashing through her entire body in waves.

("*Was that you?*") the pilot exhaled, pushing out her words.

Nico had to catch her own breath, stepping back, attempting to look unaffected, though she still examined her fingers, expecting to see some neon residue upon them.

The figure on the bed remained still, apart from her eyes, which suddenly seemed to fix upon Nico, irises contracting like the eyes of twin hurricanes.

Nico believed she saw the hint of a smile forming at the edges of those perfect lips.

But then the "*room*" started to shrink around her, disorientating her, again, as she was *pulled back out* to again witness the cityscape from above.

But there were competing aeromechs flying towards her, spinning around each other, drawing spirals through the air with their multiple munitions fire. For a terrifying moment she feared they were real, before these too glistened from the discarded data that formed them.

She found herself improbably pulled into their wake, if such a thing were possible and not just a figment of multiple imaginations. She felt as if she were tumbling between them, through the air, though she had to keep reminding herself that her feet were still technically on the ground. They spiralled around each creating a tornado of light, created an impression of movement all around her that was hard to separate from reality. She felt dizzy, collapsing to her knees.

("They tell you who you are...") The pilot said again. *("But this was still exhilarating...")*

Nico looked up.

("This is you?")

One of the aeromechs was hanging above her now, upside down. Nico could clearly see someone in the cockpit. Everything but their eyes obscured by the helmet and breathing apparatus. She knew those eyes, knew exactly who that was.

("You had skills.")

Nico stood back up, spreading her arms out wide to steady and orientate herself. The aeromech was so close she could touch it. She reached up, scraping the light, drawing spirals of fireworks around her as the discarded data followed the whirlwind of tracer fire.

("Fear and release,") said the pilot, who had clearly found something to enjoy in her unwanted occupation. *("And in the release comes the rush.")*

Nico saw a ship in the distance, another part of this memory, this illusion. A large, League of Nations solar frigate was besieged my a huge number of American aeromechs, like flies around dying cattle.

The pilot fired off missiles, the vapour trails, represented by clouds of crystallised junk data, hit the ship's engines.

The large ship exploded, breaking apart as if fell towards the city below.

("You were part of that,") Nico said, in awe. ("You helped take that ship down? *You should be proud!")*

This battle was what Nico would have chosen as her final thought, she decided, if she had been part of it.

("So many people crewed those ships, they were basically mobile cities.") The pilot sounded mournful. (*"It was never a victory; more like annihilation.")*

The operatic chaos around Nico subsided, and she could see the real night sky above her again, framed by the shadows of the debris from the destruction of the Goliath and its pursuers.

("Do you really think the people in charge, who send us out here to kill and die, care about us?") The pilot asked. *("Sending working-class people to kill other working-class people. Patriotism is a religion, a made-up thing you believe in, and can be twisted into a tool, to coerce you, to weaponise you, when it suits others. We're a different class, a lower class, and class is just another tribe. Another made-up thing. To them, we are less than human. Our hard work funds their luxury.")*

'Whatever...' Nico whispered to herself, rolling her eyes very slowly, theatrically so.

Nico listlessly watched the buildings crumbling back into the lingering fog of visual noise, leaving only the initial memory of those two youngsters. Some less honest part of her thought of this chosen memory as mawkish, sentimental and unimportant. She wondered why the pilot did not choose a moment of triumph or achievement. The pilot's words and the perceived heresy contained within them did not sit well with Nico.

("You think I'm in a bit odd, right?") The pilot asked.

Nico hadn't really thought about it that way, but now the stranger mentioned it, it did seem to fit.

("I think you're a weirdo,") Nico responded.

The pilot let out a little laugh, not through the com-link but from her place on the floor. It was punctuated by coughs and wheezes, but Nico could still tell there was genuine affection there.

("You're happy to be here though,") the pilot said. *("I can read it on your body.")*

Nico thought about the way the ghostly image of the pilot on the bed had looked at her...

("Same,") she said, with a playful sigh.

("But you're a closet weirdo,") the pilot said.

Nico frowned. It probably wasn't the first time someone had thought this about her.

("But at least I'm not questioning the way things are,") Nico argued. *('The way they're supposed to be!")*

("The way we're told they're supposed to be.")

("Our leaders answered a higher calling,") Nico explained. *("Every single thing they do is for a greater good!")*

("You're only who they want you to be so that you'll do what they want you to do. Complicit and justified.")

("You keep saying I'm not who I'm supposed to be,") Nico asked.

("That was a loaded statement.") The pilot said. *("You fight so hard for it, to protect this myth that they gave you, because maybe you suspect deep down in your heart that it would all fall apart if you stopped believing. Fighting to maintain these mass delusions, we all do...")*

From the cloud of glitches fluttered a rain of sparks, and within this appeared a taller figure, presented in more intricate detail than the children had been but carved from more volatile fragments. Billions of tiny glitches of discarded waste-data representing every atom of this *ghost*, crashing into each other over and over as they reenacted every movement and twitch of her limbs, every breath taken, every beat of the heart, every...

("I didn't want to be a pilot, I knew that wasn't me.") The pilot continued. *("But they tell you who you are, who you're supposed to be.")*

The taller of the figures was recognisably the emerald-eyed pilot, the jawline, the nose, the cheekbones, etc. Nico watched the recreation of the woman's body language with intense fascination, there was something hypnotic about it, something that she simply could not take her eyes off.

("*They must have realised that I was starting to enjoy the multi-directional freedom of the bullet-witch, because instead they put me in a jump ship. Which was a job that eventually l me back to her.*")

("*We were separated for maybe a decade,*") the pilot said.

The spectral silhouette sat down in a reclining seat as a cockpit formed from the cloud of data around her, lifted up into the air.

("*The first and last time that I saw her as an adult, the Takeshi Province of the Flotilla Peninsula. I set down my jump ship for an emergency evacuation an operation gone south. I didn't expect to see her there, on the deck of a ship, recognised her instantly. She was wounded, struggling to get on board, so I disobeyed orders, leaving my cockpit to help drag her aboard.*")

Nico saw an aircraft landing in the mentally manipulated diorama, less obvious than the figure, seen only by the outline of crackling static hitting its hull, cockpit and tail section like rain. The active representation of the green-eyed pilot left the aircraft behind, using her right arm to guard her face from the storm as she battled through it, towards the fallen figure of her former love.

("*I was overcome by a mixture of emotions, so happy to see her but scared… scared she was hurt, scared she might not…*")

The memory paused and the mentally projected static appeared to hang in the air around the two figures now, like lashes of rain frozen in time. The figure representing the pilot was frozen mid-run, her old friend was on the floor, suspended in a struggle to stand.

("*But, unfortunately, I was right to suspect that she had changed, but still naïve enough to hope she hadn't. No longer the person I remembered, only fragments of her left. She wasn't just shocked to see me; she was almost angry. Maybe she didn't want to remember the person that she'd been, the person I loved, she was almost embarrassed by her past. She was someone else now,*") *changed by the things she had experienced, the things she had been forced to do, to* become... *As a pilot I'd been separated from all of that.")*

("Above it,") Nico said. *("Literally.")*

("Bad joke,") the green-eyed pilot said, though she didn't sound as if she minded.

Nico stared at the diorama of manipulated glitches, not really sure what to feel, trying to convince herself that it wasn't worth feeling anything at all. It was getting harder to remain disconnected. Everything that this stranger had shown her so far seemed to connect with Nico in a profound way. She needed to know why.

("But that's not what I want to see,") the pilot continued. *("I have to choose my final thought today.")*

The adult version of the pilot and her first love crashed back down into the carpet of fluctuating static, but this just drew Nico's eyes back towards the younger versions. She watched the two girls laughing at their own exaggerated attempts to push their lips out to whistle. The pilot was perhaps concentrating on manifesting this particular image clearer, as their faces and their expressions were easier to read than they had been before. The girls were inflating their cheeks as they whistled, crossing their eyes to make each other laugh. They were delighted by the faces that they were making. Nico shared their delight and was a little embarrassed by that.

("This I need to save,") the pilot muttered. *("Somehow...")*

In the silence that followed, Nico contemplated the joyous, innocent memory that sat silently whistling on the floor before her. The pilot's own choice for her final thought, the moments that she had decided to linger on as she slipped away. The subtly pulsing light was having a hypnotic effect upon her, as she stared, unblinking.

("Are you still there?") Nico asked.

("Are you?") The pilot responded.

The two translucent, ghostly girls moved in closer to each other, as if for a kiss. They were easy to read, tentative, uncertain. Their heads tilted as they drew closer, their eyes closed. But before their lips could meet, the static that formed their heads started to fracture, breaking apart, millions of strings of data fragmenting infinitely as their faces collapsed in to each other, *twin stars going supernova as they collided, duelling singularities pulling each other apart.*

It felt like an intensely personal moment on an incredibly surreal scale, but Nico could not look away. Her eyes were turning red, at first from some undefinable, unidentifiable sense of regret, but this transmogrified into anger. She gritted her teeth, upset that she was letting herself feel like this.

But Nico was aware that all this overpowered emotion might just disappear if she just disconnected. Nothing would remain but the cold, broken machines and the wasteland between her and the sentimental stranger.

But she couldn't. There was something about this gradual teasing-out of emotions that felt good, like releasing pressure from a valve. Part of her wanted it all to stop, she craved her banal, predictable normality, but something *deeper* needed it to continue.

She spoke only to alleviate the awkwardness.

("You still miss her.") This was more of a statement than a question.

("Yes")

("She came to see me, a couple of weeks after the extraction,") the pilot continued. *("She tried to save my soul. She'd found god and she wanted me to follow.")*

("Religion is outlawed!") Nico gasped, then felt foolish for her outburst, like a child that had caught a friend being naughty. Religion had been removed to allow more light to shine on their country, and many of its facets and been absorbed into patriotism, which was ripe for it.

("But still, it found her.") The pilot sounded mournful. *("She had given up another slice of her individuality to justify her existence, to fill that void. She was angry with herself for the way she had been with me, she believed, somehow, that it was against*

god. Somehow. She took a great risk confiding in me that she had found this thing that was bigger than herself. I could have reported her. She was angry with me for not seeing things the way she saw them...")

The pilot's voice cracked, her words trailing off as they faded away.

Nico felt angry that the sincerity between the two ghostly children could be corrupted by a lie sold as a truth.

("You give up your individuality to feel like you are part of something bigger, to give your life that meaning, purpose and structure,") the pilot continued.

("We'd still be living in mud huts and caves without if we weren't working together,") Nico explained.

("You're right of course. But within those groups, one person's distrust or hatred or short-sighted ideal can spread like cancer through the group, like a psychological apocalypse.")

Indistinct ghosts floated around them both, so many that Nico struggled to make sense of them. The air seemed to crackle and pop, the world around them a wall of noise that they could barely comprehend.

("Why do you think we fight?") The pilot asked.

("To win? To beat the enemy, the opposition,") Nico said.

("Those are just words. Reducing another human being's worth to a label, stripping their individuality and their humanity.")

(For my country, then.") Nico sounded frustrated that such basic certainties could be questioned.

("Patriotism is just another word. Another form of religion, another made-up thing. A country is a thing that doesn't physically exist, the borders between countries are squiggles on a map, they exist only on paper and in our minds. A mass delusion keeps them real and relevant. People getting all worked up over something that was invented to give our lives meaning, dying and killing for literally nothing real.")

("It's more than that...") Nico insisted.

("That's not how is seems to me, and you may not agree,") The pilot paused to try and swallow the blood pooling in

her throat, which took far too much effort. Nico noticed the pilot's struggle and kneeled down for a moment and gave the pilot some of that drink whether she wanted it or not. This was a struggle, but those green eyes looked grateful. *("Human existence is entirely without meaning, purpose or point.")*

Nico was shocked by the blunt fatalism in that statement. She immediately assumed that this point of view came from the finality of the pilot's predicament.

("Our place in his world is entirely accidental,") the pilot stated. *("And that scares us to the core. So we invented things to give our lives meaning. patriotism, political parties, religions, social classes, regency, capitalism, consumerism, corporations... on and on...")*

Nico was listening, but she definitely, defiantly could not bring herself to say that she agreed with the idea that her whole world was a lie. Her whole reason for being, for existing, for persisting...

("I see,") she whispered. *("This is all some psychic PowerPoint presentation; the buildings are doubling up as graphs. You're trying to get me to sign up to your newsletter.")*

("Believe what you want. That's the point. The things we do and the reasons we do them, all in our heads.")

("I DO believe what I want,") Nico insisted.

("You so sure? We all crave purpose and meaning. We crave it, all of us. Because the truth is far too depressing. So we take it further, we create these things to make ourselves feel special and wanted and part of something bigger than ourselves. Willingly giving up a part of our individuality. Then we see all the other tribes, and we no longer see them as individuals. We see them as names, words, representing countries, colours, genders, sexualities, beliefs, political beliefs. On and on.")

The pilot laughed at the absurdity.

("Dehumanising anyone outside of that group...")

As these words and ideas floated around in Nico's mind, she idly watched the light pulsing through the pilot's mental constructs, reminding her of the moonlight reflecting off the spider's web that she had hyper fixated on whilst dealing with Reaver, fluttering in the breeze. She started to suspect that the conjured structures were growing and shrinking in time with the pilot's laboured breathing.

She consciously refrained from verbally engaging with the pilot's odd ideas. She sighed and wished that they could just go back to talking about their memories.

("*But they're all constructs,*") the pilot continued. ('*There is no greater good to your war, every possible reason they have for it is some made up thing. Head cannon. There are people who make money from the war, who would do anything to keep the killing going. Every time a child dies, they sell more weapons and ammo. This is all for profit. But the notes and coins in your pocket, the numbers on your banking app, they just* represent *money, there is no tangible, physical basis for currency and it rules our lives. An IOU from the banks, who promise to honour the value. Another religion, and people are suffering for something else that's made up.*")

Nico took another drink. She could not understand how the pilot could have such a blasphemous opinion. She shook her head, as if trying to shake out the intrusive thoughts that the pilot had put there, but instead they just metaphorically rattled around in there.

("*If you say so.*") Nico said, feeling emotionally battered by everything. ("*So, you believe everything about human existence had been made-up? Billions and billions of people throughout human history have just been getting* worked-up *about things that we just* made-up?")

Nico could not, would not, accept that all the horrific things - or even, she supposed, the good things - that had happened throughout human history could have been done over things that existed in the minds of millions only, and had no real-world analogue. People working, living, loving, laughing, bullying, fearing, enslaving, conquering, killing...

("*We're the only species who can believe in fictions and do terrible things because of them,*") the pilot said. ("*Not just to others but ourselves, too. Every single human being tells themselves stories and that reshapes our reality. All the systems that humanity has built its civilisation upon, they exist only in our heads.")*

("So, you believe that's what happened to your...") Nico was reluctant to say "girlfriend" or "love" because she thought of those as abstract concepts, the idea of having relationships seemed quaint to a lot of the people who spent their adolescent lives in training and simulations, and their adult days on battlefields, emotional connections to other human beings unlikely as they floated in and out of each other's lives. *("...to your friend?")*

("The things she said about people... she just ranted about... She had reduced other's worth, until they were simply whatever label had been given to them. Just labels, less that human...")

The pilot trailed off, and there was a silence that followed that unnerved Nico. She stared back at the body, relieved to see the chest still rising and falling. She could see the slight frost that tainted the pilot's exhalations, white whispers around her nostrils and those lovely lips. For the first time, Nico was grateful for her heightened senses.

Nico walked back over to the emerald-eyes stranger and knelt back down beside her. The stranger's breathing was laboured but she was not gone yet. She checked out the surrounding derelicts for signs of danger. The war-wolves, maybe, or perhaps that prick Reaver might come back. They seemed to be alone.

Nico lazily gazed at the pilot's open hand. She contemplated holding it, though she had no idea why, an inexplicable compulsion. She reasoned that it would be comforting to one of them, or maybe even both of them.

Would that be an odd thing to do? She wondered. It was a gesture that she had often seen in movies, a sentimental move for fictional people, but had never considered that a thing that real people did.

Nico swore to herself. This wasn't her; this kind of

sentimentality was alien to her, something new had been stirred up within her.This entire situation had become so much more intense than she had anticipated, and she wasn't sure if she liked it. She placed her head in her hands, and it felt heavy, so much more than usual. She genuinely had no idea how to cope with any of this.

Nico was confounded by the realisation that all she cared about right now was this stranger, despite the heretical nature of her beliefs. So why had she stayed here, allowing herself to be exposed to these ideas, and these feelings? Possibly it was because she had been left alone, in this forsaken place, separated from her people and leaders, with the apparent burden of free thought. This upset her, because she had always liked everything to conform, and right now everything was untangling.

It started to rain, or perhaps it was snowing. It was suspiciously hard to tell. She lifted her head up out of her hands as the snow danced across her face, as if drawing lines, mapping it to memory. She fancied she felt a warm tingle, but that was quite impossible, of course, as she realised when she held her hands out to catch some. It was simply more discarded data, shimmering as if lit by a million moons. It was becoming a blizzard, the spontaneous specks seeming to spark as they passed through the landmarks.

Glitches bounced around the clearing, larger than the flakes in the flurry, winged like origami starlings folded from light. They flew past her, through her, hovering around her, dragging spectral ribbons. They came up to her, inspecting her as if they were curious.

A face formed from the blizzard of crumbling static, a representation of the pilot as she is now, not as she appeared in any of the memories, followed by hands, arms, and a hint of the torso. Nico held her breath, eyes wide.

The projected pilot appeared curious, inspecting Nico, moving around her, looking her up and down with eyes like marbles. This non-corporeal projection of the pilot's psyche was clearly fascinated by Nico, and of course the feeling was mutual.

That ethereal figure moved closer, and Nico felt uncomfortable, unused to displays of affection, especially any that involved her personally. She didn't know what to do with her hands, made worse when she felt the tingle of the pilot wrapping her own digital digits around Nico's rigid fingers.

("So, who ARE you?") the pilot's projection asked, intrigued.

Those flickering lips were moving in time with the words, but the voice seemed disconnected from the ethereal form, still entering Nico's head directly through the com-link.

(I'm...") Nico looked as if she didn't understand the question, which was confusing even her, creating a feedback loop of broken logic between her conscious and unconscious. *("I'm...")*

("Don't you know?")

Nico knew that she simply had to say her name, but the question somehow didn't *feel* so simple, it seemed loaded with layers that she couldn't get to grips with. She suspected that she was overthinking it, but it was too late to stop now, she was on that slippery slope.

("Do you?")

("Does anyone?")

The projected pilot moved ever closer, those eyes rendered in splintering, overlapping geometric triangles of perfect white, looking Nico up and down. She looked keen, but also full of sorrow, perhaps because the two of them had met at the end of all things.

("I don't know who I'm supposed to be...") Nico admitted.

("You have the opportunity to remake yourself. To wipe the slate clean. To let yourself be free, or to let yourself go.")

("But I'm no one,") Nico insisted.

("You are free to be the authentic...") The pilot began, pausing for a moment between each subsequent word.

("True...")

That white, fluctuating fragmentation of a face moved in closer to Nico's own, lips moving closer. As the projected pilot tilted her head, as their lips drew closer, Nico felt those pins and needles through her own lips, which seemed to part involuntarily.

("...Formidable...") The pilot continued, and Nico was convinced that she felt the movement of the lips against her own, the fluctuation in the static, fizzing, as they formed the pilot's words.

("...Creative...") Nico felt the pilot's word as a fluctuation amongst the tingle on her tongue, before the sensation multiplied exponentially, like an electrical charge through the nerves in her mouth.

For some reason, in that precise moment, as that non-corporeal body drew ever closer to her own, Nico retreated into an apparently random memory. She wasn't used to displays of affection, in fact the memory that she found herself in was the exact opposite of this situation. Nico remembered a night alone, the most mundane situation she could muster. She was sat on her bed in her small one-room apartment, the blinds closed so that she could not see the Washington lake. The lights off, music playing.

("...Independent...") The tingling static was moving in waves now, as if it were the pilot's breath. Nico felt it all through her head.

("...Badass...")

But Nico started to realise that this memory had resonance with the present moment, as she remembered that she often spent her time alone trying to ignore an undefinable emptiness, or to re-contextualise it as something else entirely. So, in moments like that, Nico would convince herself that what she *actually* felt was guilt, or anxiety stemming from some patriotic failing on her part, that she was not serving her country to the best of her ability. *She could - should - do better.* Sometimes she felt as if she were a blasphemer because she occasionally caught herself yearning for *more*, some indefinable *something*.

("...Irresistible...") The pilot continued.

Nico's lonesome memory became corrupted by the crosstalk, the pilot forming in her bedroom from motes of dust. She was as close to Nico *in here* as she was *out there*, their lips lightly touching. For a moment, Nico was starting to worry that parts of her own mind were being overridden or copied by the pilot, but soon something happened that distracted her, signalled by one word, as the pilot finished defining her new friend.

(*"...You."*)

They kissed passionately, in both the sensorially augmented real world and within the emotionally augmented memory. The ghostly face fractured entirely, consuming Nico's mouth, then cheeks, then nose, eyes... Then the pilot pulled back, her face reforming from the crackling code. The digitised ghost looked sincerely at Nico as her hands softly cradled her head.

They stared into each other's eyes. The memory was gone, now This was all there was.

Nico's eyes started stinging again.

'Not again,' Nico sighed aloud.

(*"What is?"*)

Nico placed her armoured hands over her eyes to block out as much of the moonlight as she could, as even the dimmest light appeared to be seeping its way in between her lids and lashes to taunt her super-sensitive eyes. Though she could block her eyes against the visual assault, Nico was also suffering an audible assault, as all the ambient sound became an escalating orchestra of eclectic noise.

The physical, sensorial anomaly that had initially triggered when she had been dealing with Reaver. The world had too much detail. She felt lightheaded, as if she might faint, as the brightness and detail in everything became more heightened. Whatever this was, it was no longer simply a sensation, it had become a force capable of slingshotting through every nook-and-cranny of her brain, rearranging and upgrading her capabilities as it rattled through her neural pathways.

Nico focused on her breathing, attempting to calm herself

down, having absolutely no idea how to overcome whatever *this* was.

("Are you ok?") the green-eyed pilot asked.

Nico felt that reassuring, familiar resonance in her hands, as the projected pilot's spectral fingers passed through Nico's gauntlets.

("Focus on my voice, focus on me,") the pilot said.

Nico was genuinely shocked. She managed to open her eyes, and saw that the figure of light had retreated back into the electric blizzard.

("Even in your condition, you're asking about my migraine?")

("Am I not supposed to?") The pilot asked.

Nico was so unused to being treated so well that she couldn't verbalise her confusion.

Nico somehow, through their connection, felt a jolt of pain that originated within her new friend. She was vicariously sharing the pilot's deterioration. She had almost forgotten how finite this meeting was.

("He took what he wanted...") The emerald-eyed pilot muttered. *("But it was not the gun, nor the ship, nor the rations...")*

'Wait, what did you say?'

Nico was so distracted by the intense orchestra of sensory feedback that she almost missed what the pilot had said. She ignored the distraction and confusion caused by her own senses assaulting her and finally checked the pilot's wounds as best she could without being too invasive.

'What happened to you, your injuries? It wasn't the crash or the war wolves.' Nico had already started to figure it out. *("Was it that guy? That fucking prick, Reaver?")*

Nico grabbed the rail rifle that had belonged to the pilot, placed the stock against her shoulder, then stared down the barrel as she surveyed the surrounding environment, though this was more as a deterrent as she still wasn't authorised to use it. A person like Reaver was liable to come back, she thought, and she needed to be putting on a show.

But it certainly didn't help that her heightened senses were making it hard to check those dark corners, distracted by every little thing that she shouldn't have been able to see and hear.

("But he's one of ours. He was a fucking prick, but... What did he do?") But, yet again, Nico already knew the answer to that, she didn't really have to ask.

("What are you going to do with that?")

("Defend you?")

("With a red light?")

The pilot used the remaining strength that she had to lift her hand, until she managed to touch the grip of her old rifle. Nico realised what was happening and unrolled each finger, getting out of the pilot's way. The biometric lock flashed green three times, indicating that the security system reset to factory settings.

("Did you lock it?") Nico asked. *("You locked it so that Reaver couldn't use it against you?")*

Nico stared at the pilot, in awe. She shook her head. She took the gun back in hand and registered her biometric identity to the weapon. The rail rifle synchronised to her tabris and the weapon's data unspooled in her Minds Eye - remaining battery level, remaining ammo, total shot count, maintenance schedule...

'Why?' Nico asked, though really she was lost for words. She pulled the weapon closer to her, holding it upright and wrapping her fingers around it, as if it were sacred, part of this person who she had only just found and was already losing. Although she hoped that there was some special significance to this offering, she suspected that it was probably just an indiscriminate act of kindness, as rare as those were. She *wanted* there to be more to the gesture, though. She wanted *more...*

Nico's newly enhanced senses were not helping her state of mind here, because she could fixate on the object of her affection in ludicrous detail. She could admire the light striking the iris, creating the mesmerising green pigment as it scattered and refracted through the melanocytes within, creating an incredible frame for Nico's own confused and desperate reflection in the pilot's dilated pupils. She also saw her reflection in each of the salt-laced tears that welled up in the pilot's lacrimal glands, weighing down the lashes.

Nico gazed upon the woman before her, focused completely, forgetting to feel what she was *supposed* to be feeling, which was literally nothing. She was trained to emotionally distance herself, watching a nameless soldier die should have been the last thing she should care about. But a tidal wave of mixed emotions became the trojan-horse for something that she was experiencing for the first time.

The purest distillation of *Love.* Or so she presumed, she had never had any real reason to believe that such a thing was real, having never experienced it herself. She had loved her country, of course, but beyond that Nico had only ever known *lust*, which was the main reason for any battlefield hook-up.

But here she was, experiencing it for the first time at the worst possible time. Love's first blush. She looked on in despair as the pilot's visions, conjured from discarded data, begun their inevitable disintegration, their host's mind faded further. The digital ghost was falling back, reaching out, as all that translucent glitches came clattering down, *like beads from broken strings.*

'No!' Nico panicked. *'No, no, no...!'*

The pilot was slipping away, there wasn't much time left. There was so much Nico wanted to say.

'You can not leave, not yet. *You are...*' Nico began to plead. (*"I used to think that the world made sense, but in the back of my head I knew that there was something wrong, but I fought against it because it scared me!"*)

But Nico received no response, and so she panicked. She carefully lifted the pilot's head to check for signs of life, afraid that her powered gauntlets might do more damage. Her supernaturally enhanced eyes focused upon the tiny nose hairs moving as the pilot's inhalations and exhalations became more and more drawn out.

("You're the only sense the world has ever made!") Nico exclaimed, but still received no response.

Nico listened for the pilot's heart beat, attempted to focus upon that one previous thing, but she could barely control her enhanced senses, especially in this state. Instead, her heightened hearing caught many inconsequential things - The drip of coolant from a nearby vehicle; the skittering of small creatures scurrying through pipes and vents; the rumble of distant battles... Even, at one point, the tectonic movement of the earth beneath them...

("You've got *to... to...")* The pilot began, but she struggled to muster the energy to finish her sentence.

'What?' Nico asked, gently. *("Just tell me what I'm supposed to do! I have nobody! I have no... No orders; no purpose! I don't know... I don't know why I'm here! I don't know who I am. Who am I supposed to be?")*

There was no response, perhaps the pilot did not have the answer.

Nico stared at her beloved's chest, through the unzipped white aviators' jacket, for any movement, for any sign that the pilot was still breathing. Nico had coveted that jacket, but now that seemed so petty, so shallow. She realised with a crushing inevitably that she would soon be alone again, that no one was coming to rescue her, and the only real friend she had had was this fleeting acquaintance, slipping into the void.

'Just a little longer, please!'

Nico slumped back and sat there in silence, dumbfounded. She had a head and heart full of questions that were new to her.

But all those queries faded away, and all that remained were layers upon layers of ambient sights, smells and sounds.

She could hear, with enough detail to accurately visualize, a dozen meters away, the fan in an engine-block's cooling system, deep inside a crashed ship, still turning as it drew residual power from its battery stack. Achingly slow, the tip of each of the fan's blades periodically skimmed a pool of leaked coolant, which would drip back when the blades reached their apex, causing ripples within ripples.

As this perpetual churning of sound played on like an insistent soundtrack, Nico mentally replayed every moment of her emotional journey to this exact moment, everything that they had shared, wanting it to last forever, hoping to get lost in it. This was when she suddenly realised she didn't know something very basic about the pilot, who she was. It hadn't seemed important before. She called up her Minds Eye system to identify her friend, to find out anything she could, but it seemed as if the psychic feedback was corrupting the operation, the text deteriorating into the same fog of static that had acted as the pilot's diorama.

("Wait…") Nico pleaded. *("What's your name?")*

But she received no verbal response. The pilot's hand dropped like a heavy weight and landed upon Nico's lap, palm open. She stared at it, watching random fingers twitch. She wanted to hold this woman, but with the tactile truth of her own skin and nerves, not relayed through the artificiality of the armour's sensor clusters. She felt as if it would solidify the experience, make it more *real.*

She rapidly unlocked and opened the top half of her armour, letting it fall away. She freed her arms from it, then pulled at her muscle-suit's bio feedback gloves, frustrated as, somehow, they took twice as long as normal to remove. She threw them aside and then she softly touched the pilot's palm

Like a sprung trap, the pilot grabbed hold of Nico's hand.

Nico realised that the pilot's spark was on its final flash before it fused, and she reciprocated, squeezing back.

But this was when her sensorial revolution was a curse. She felt the decaying movement of every one of the pilot's organs. She witnessed, through sound and sensation, the pilot's heart compressing normally even as the ventricle failed, blood flooding her heart, increasing the blood pressure, forcing fluid to flood her lungs.

Nico watched for what felt like forever, hanging onto every

moment.

As every last drop of life drained from those glorious emerald eyes Nico felt an inexplicable *ache* that radiated out from the *core* of her.

Then the pilot's hand lost all tension and slipped away, slipping Nico's grip like liquid. Nico absently fixated on her own empty palm and the memory in the muscle. A single tear fell into that web of lines at the base of her thumb, lines that told tall tales.

'*Who are you...?*' She whispered. She knew in her heart that no more answers were coming.

Nico looked for the pilot's ID tags on her neck, but they were gone, and perhaps the only chance of finding out the woman's name gone with them. She knew who took them, of course she did. Reaver had taken them, as a trophy perhaps.

Nico asserted herself, in that moment, deciding to recover those missing tags. That was her mission now.

But it wasn't entirely over, the emerald-eyes pilot was not entirely gone. The only sign of this was residual holographic static which still hung in the air, apparently more cross talk had formed this spectral flurry from her own attempts to identify the wonderful stranger. It drifted close, just beyond Nico's reach. She pulled herself up off the floor and touched it, and it seemed to react to her, swirling around her finger tips. She pulled it closer, as it somehow allowed itself to be gathered up in her hands. She held it tight to her chest for a moment, for as long as it persisted, convinced that she felt the static pulsing through her skin. Her Minds Eye glitched, then filled with random data for a moment, which seemed to overlap, forming shapes...

Then it was gone.

Although some of this was, more than likely, an invention of her grief stricken mind, she bowed her head and gave thanks for this offering.

Nico Shikari stood. She felt the breeze against her skin, heard it whistle through the canyons of debris as it picked up pace.

Then she carefully, considerately, removed the pilot's white aviation jacket with the barcode that ran vertically down one side of the zip, then she disconnected the broken breathing tubes. This was not an act of scavenging, as was originally intended, this was meant as a mark of respect. She buried her face in the soft material and breathed it in. She wanted to remember this scent.

Something had awakened within her. She straightened up, turned, and walked away.

SPEAK IN OUR SECRET TONGUES

From deep within an archive of archaic media broadcasting, nestled within a physically small but virtually large drive illegally installed in a tabris device, a conversation was being replayed.

'*Welcome back, dear listener, you are tuned in to the Park and Ride show. This is your host Park, and as always, I am joined by my psychic sidekick Ride…*'

'*Hiya!*'

The shows only current listener was lying over a web of tree branches, skirting the outer rim of slumber, where he had dipped many times in the previous hours, gurgling occasionally.

'*Welcome to another episode of Ride's Mutant Sanctuary,*' said Park, introducing a scripted segment of their daily show. '*What you got for us today, head bio-mutant zookeeper Ride?*'

'*Well, Park, today I've brought in this weird little fella here, which I found behind the pharmacy after I picked up my prescription.*'

'*What were you doing* behind *the pharmacy…?*'

'*That's not important…*'

'*Right…*'

'*I was just taking the long way around…*'

'*To the pharmacy…*'

There was an awkward silence.

'Well, you know I have that recurring problem...' Ride muttered through gritted teeth.

'I told you not to meet those people down the park after dark...'

'Anyway!' Ride exclaimed.

'Is it still that funny colour?' Park asked, nonchalantly.

The sole listener grunted, amused. His cheek scratched against the bark that cradled him.

'Anyway, it's not about that!' Ride exclaimed again. *'I heard this little fella scratching away under the bins, right?'*

'Oh, right yeah, the script...' This utterance was followed by the exaggerated sound of Park turning the pages of his script. He then read out his lines in a clunky, unconvincing monotone. On purpose. *'Blimey-Charlie, Ride, that is a funny looking creature and no-mistake. What the bloody hell is it?'*

'I don't know!' Ride exclaimed, louder than his last exclamation. *'I'm not a chuffing cryptozoologist, am I?'*

'Well, what do you call it, then?'

'Tim.'

'Tim the what?'

'Just Tim. Can you hold it for me?'

'What?'

'Just for a moment.'

'I don't want to...'

'You'll be fine.' There was a squelching sound-effect then, followed by background noise as the imaginary creature was supposedly exchanged. *'There you go. I just want to check it's...*

'It's winking at me!'

'It doesn't have any eyelids.'

'I wasn't looking at its face! Is it placid?'

'Let me have a look... Yeah it's pretty flaccid at the moment.'

'What are you gonna do with it?'

'Well it's got a dirty bum but that's ok, I can sort that.'

'What are you gonna do with it over the weekend?'

'Put it in a cupboard.'

'What do you think are it's chances?'

'In the cupboard? Slim.'

Dyce fell from the tree.

He managed to feel embarrassed despite the fact that no one was around to see him, as far as he knew, though the splash had been loud enough to draw the attention of the local wildlife. He pulled himself out of the water and picked broken twigs out of the gaps between his tactical armour, flicking them into the churning water at the waterfall's base.

He lay there, his head an inch from a sharp rock that had nearly brained him, staring up through the fractal canopy of branches. The moons lit the wisps of cloud, revealing their linings to be a burnt orange around a dark purple, and this was the only source of illumination for Dyce as walked away, dripping dirty water in his wake. Whatever was in that water was making his cuts sting. He was pissed-off and lost, thinking about how nice it would be to have at least some vague idea of what he was going to do or where he was going to go. He had stayed in that tree for far too long, procrastinating, delaying his inevitable departure.

On a transcendentally related note, he could feel a drumming through his body, a percussive thump that was escalating in intensity. It was hard to locate, sometimes it felt as if it were in the back of his head, sometimes his chest. He certainly hoped it wasn't his heart, incase he was heading for cardiac calamity.

But, he suspected, this was probably just dread, a simple trick of the mind, of course. Nothing to worry about. He shook his head and called himself stupid, ignoring the fact that this could – if left unchecked – lead to more potentially psychologically devastating consequences. But why was he feeling this dread? He had this inexplicable sense that something was going to happen, and he still wasn't ready.

He felt a sting in his right wrist. He held it above his head, as he still lazily lay there, and pulled a blood-tipped twig, about an inch long, from out of his skin. He moved the gauntlet and the forearm apart to get a better look at the relatively insignificant wound. He knew that this would be healing at an accelerated rate, just like every other injury he had incurred during his brief time here. He stared at it, wondering if he could heal it even faster through sheer force of will.

He had noticed something else though. He had scars, only visible as the moons reflected off the scar-tissue, a web over his entire body, a map of each and every injury, and they were being added to all the time. Actions have consequences, he thought, everything leaves a mark.

He focused on the bloody wound, imagining it zipping up like a jacket. He succeeded only in looking constipated, and that was something he had too much practice at.

He sat up and stretched by pushing up through his palms, listening to his body crack.

Before him was the great expanse of the wasteland, surrounded by a distant perimeter of risers. Further into the wasteland he saw the massive, broken Goliath, which had had seen lifted into the air and dropped like a sack of bricks. The longer that he stared at it, the more convinced he became that there was a tiny figure scaling the machine's neck. He pulled his headset down over his eyes and used its beady eyes to zoom in on the figure, a suit of UAM armour containing a bespectacled redhead who didn't think it wise to wear her helmet when scaling a sharp drop in a hostile environment. He thought about how brave she was, as he watched her ascend on her smart-cord, considering the disturbing things that he had seen the war wolves do to some Green Strays on the back of that Goliath earlier, which he had observed from the safety of his tree.

But Dyce bored of watching that mobile *packed lunch*, dangling there, inevitably enticing the native carnivores. It was time to get moving. No more procrastinating. He needed something to keep him company during his aimless stroll.

He checked his archive of old comedy, some in audio, some video. He contemplated listening to another, instead of getting up and leaving. Just one more, then he'd go. This *definitely* wasn't procrastination, he told himself, but of course it was. As soon as he had thought it, he had no choice but to admit it.

Sometimes, in the days before his fall and rise, Dyce had enjoyed watching old tv shows. He would sit alone in his small box room, or perhaps he would sit alone in some public space, and in his Minds Eye these shows would be presented to him as if they were projections in the air. Old comedy shows were what he liked, they picked him up when he was feeling low. They were once known as "Sitcoms", apparently, though he had no idea what that abbreviation meant. Those shows presented to him a way of life that he could barely comprehend – filmed in a time before this war, or most of this technology - but characters he could relate to. Their wins, losses, stupidity and blind luck warmed his battered heart.

Or perhaps he was simply depressed.

They say a journey of a thousand miles begins with a single step. Dyce took a step away from the tree and towards the wasteland. He didn't feel any more confident. So, he took another step. He felt less enthused about the second step than he had about the first.

Adventure lays ahead, he thought to himself. Then he sighed, his arms slumping.

So does trouble.

He walked. He rolled his shoulders and tried to walk tall. He had never managed confidence, was something that others seemed to be born with. He couldn't get himself into the right mindset. The river babbled beside him, guiding him along. He listened to his audios, even allowed himself a little chuckle now and then, though it only slightly eased his anxiety. He kicked some rocks along the path, watching them rolling through the weeds that grew between the rocks.

'Oh, this stupid...' He swore, his tabris was malfunctioning, freezing periodically.

He rebooted the device and ran a diagnostic, which he knew was going to take some time. The small device was locked inside a docking pod on the inside of the tactical armour, charging it through the bio-kinetic energy generated by his body.

He stopped by the side of the river, a half hour's walk from the waterfall where he had rested amongst the branches of a tree. The ground beneath his feet was muddy from the rain, the air was damp.

His mind, unclouded by the visual noise of his tabris as it rebooted, had the chance to absorb the fractured beauty of the decimated landscape. The twin moons were scattering their silver light across every surface, giving them a silver lining - from the lilting trees and the browning leaves, that littered the path beneath them, to the exposed roots reaching out from the eroding river bank into the water. The moonlight bounced along the river, flickering between the half-submerged jumble of broken things.

He stood there and let the world wash over him, trying to embrace the unconventional beauty and bathe in the refreshing serenity, instead of pondering the things and people that might be hunting or haunting him through the darkness.

But this period of observation and reflection was brief, as the tabris booted back up – which had felt like an eternity, but was actually forty-two seconds precisely. After re-synchronising, Dyce was greeted with the registered logo for the Tabris Corporation, which obscured his vision for a split second, followed by a message telling him that a software update had been downloaded and was now being installed. The size and opacity of the logo and text within his visual cortex was clearly a design flaw in the Mind's Eye system, the proprietary software solution bridging the gap between the user's brain and the device. The fact that any intended user could not see for the few seconds that the boot-screen generated the corporate logo must surely have been responsible for many deaths at the hands of inadvertently concealed assailants. Just because a corporation felt the need to proudly advertise to people who couldn't personally afford to purchase their wares and couldn't give a sloppy toss anyway.

The device synchronised with a satellite surveillance system, filling his Mind's Eye System with satellite pictures and a three dimensional map of the land. He could see that the river flowed through the mostly dead Contact City and its satellite towns and on into Absolution City, which was the continent's thriving capital. Even in these images he could tell how alive that city was.

He could vanish in a city that size...

He still wasn't entirely sure where he was going or what he was going to do. He felt aimless. He started to suspect that he had been inadvertently heading for Absolution, like a common tourist heading for the sights and sounds of the big city, which was either a good idea or the last thing he would ever do. He couldn't stay where he was, and he didn't feel like going back to his *own people,* where he would simply find himself repeating the same old patterns. Well, those were two options, he just had to look for some alternatives.

Ahead, he saw a wall adorned with graffiti, running parallel to the river, though it stood alone, parts of incomplete walls branching off from it, surrounded by piles of bricks and other materials that had sat, abandoned, for countless years. The graffiti was elaborate, created in different medias, some parts were spray painted, others had been applied with brushes, clearly the work of many different hands over differing decades. It was bright and colourful, a field of flowers leading to a forest, characters and creatures frolicking, hanging or just chilling. Some sections had the look of Van Gogh, some Monet, some had Picasso, some styles Dyce couldn't pin. It was a long stretch of wall, and it was clearly the work of many hands, parts faded, parts fresher, no doubt strangers, and whoever had started it would probably not have seen the result of it going viral across the entire wall. A couple of the flowers had faces, some were detailed, some were crude and rude. There are elemental elves hidden amongst the blades and blooms, rendered in more detail than the flowers.

Dyce ran his fingers over it, felt the textures, the lumps, the bumps and the solidified drips. There was still some culture in this place. Still some hope.

He needed to switch up his audio accompaniment, the comedy didn't seem appropriate. He put on some music, taking his time to find the pertinent sound, giving the moment just the right ambience.

He took pictures of the mural, thought this was actually a kind of screen-shot using his own eyes, recorded in ultra high detail within his tabris, in three dimensions. Lumps, bumps and drips.

Dyce heard a sound, the music automatically pausing. He listened intently, identifying a persistent shuffling sound, that occasionally stuttered, as if meeting an obstacle and refusing to stop. Dyce listened more intently, trying to activate his heightened hearing, in the same way that he had attempted to speed up the recovery of an insignificant wound.

He heard footsteps, breathing, from the other side of the wall.

He followed the sound. He heard no talking, whoever they were they were speaking in their *secret tongues*, through their com-link. He walked on, careful not to step on anything that made noise, twigs or discarded packets of various vintage.

He caught and held his breath. He had found himself at a hole in the wall, an archway, a wooden door frame, rotting, was screwed into the brickwork, no door remained clinging to its hinges.

He took a few careful steps backwards, sliding down the wall.

Four armed figures stepped through the gap, one at a time, one armoured boot after another. Dyce's Minds Eye started to identify them. One named Darius, one named Rogers, one named Samsun, and finally McMorrow. He wondered why UAM soldiers were they on the League's database, until he saw the answer amongst the text. They were members of the Augmented Fourth. War criminals.

The man McMorrow was dragging something behind him on a rope. Something heavy that snagged on the fallen, broken mortar around the bottom of the door frame. The man tugged on it and swore.

'Come on, *dog*,' McMorrow snarled.

The rope was a leash, around the neck of a League of Nations soldier. No doubt this battered soldier had started this degrading setup by walking behind McMorrow, then eventually crawling on all fours. But now, after further torture, he had lost the ability to even mimic the movements of a quadruped, reduced to dead weight.

Dyce held his breath as he watched. With every heave of McMorrow's rope the body shifted, the prisoner's face scraping over rocks and broken bricks.

Dyce sensed something, eyes upon him. He looked around. Nothing. He inhaled. He looked up. Of course. There was a figure balanced on top of the wall, looking down at him. This person was gyroscopically balanced on the edge of the crumbling bricks, flakes of broken mortar orbiting the gravity orbs in the tips of her prosthetic lower legs, as they held her in place.

Trip Kosheen was her name, according to Dyce's Minds Eye.

Dyce pushed himself further into the shadows at the base of the wall, as if instinct thought he could disappear into a world between worlds. But alas, this was beyond his abilities.

Kosheen lifted a finger to her lips, as if she were telling Dyce to be silent. Her face remained unreadable, her eyes emotionless, Dyce could only guess at her intentions, benevolent or malevolent.

Dyce stepped back and caught his feet on some discarded building materials, a half-emptied pallet that had broken apart in the elements, the building materials rested upon it clattered into each other. A stack of coiled up copper wiring made much more noise as it tumbled.

'What ya got there?' Darius suddenly asked, aloud.

Dyce panicked, but Kosheen fell upon him, her armoured

knees on his arms, pinning him to the floor. She remained mostly emotionless, but Dyce almost thought he saw a hint of something sadder, just a little hint.

'Fresh meat?' McMorrow asked, kicking his own previous victim away, not caring if they still had breath left.

'No,' Kosheen said. 'I got the prize fucking hog.'

'Oh, wow!' McMorrow laughed, joyously.

Kosheen took Dyce's Tabris and threw it to Darius. Dyce seethed. That device and its secret extra drive contained all his personal stuff, years of collected software and an assortment of his defragmented memories.

'See what you can get from that,' Kosheen said to Darius.

Darius stowed the device in a compartment on his armour but didn't seem to be in any hurry.

No, no, no!

Dyce was snarling. He didn't like people touching his personal possessions at the best of times, but there was very little he could do about it with four set of guns trained upon him. Kosheen disarmed him, throwing his weapons to her teammates.

'Oshii is going to love this,' Darius said, overjoyed and proud.

Dyce glared at Darius, eyes wide with fear. Visions of prison bars and chains. He felt sick to his stomach.

'I don't suppose you're going to tell us why she's so interested in you?' McMorrow asked. 'I mean, even before you blew up that riser with us in it, she seemed to...'

'You'd have to ask her,' Dyce interrupted. Clearly this line of questioned was increasing his discomfort.

'Two years ago, I was stationed on the Harmon Rig,' McMorrow suddenly said, referring to the city sized structures to be found all through the world's oceans, like ludicrously oversized oil rigs. 'A black op squad of your people infiltrated the residential levels one night. They had seemingly completed their mission, sabotaging food supplies, that kind of shit. They could have just slipped out. All we know is that they lay in wait till everyone was asleep, took out the guards, and committed atrocities.'

McMorrow was staring at Dyce with an unbearable intensity. Where did that come from?

'Young Americans. Their lives, their bodies, their souls, violated. Destroyed.'

Kosheen stood up and backed away. Dyce quickly made his way up onto his feet.

'I don't know anything about that, I've never even heard of that. What would that have to do with me? That wouldn't be something I would...'

'You *league-tards* all stick together. You're all the same.'

'What, millions of us?'

Dyce shook his head, he was starting to feel that the odds were stacked against him, here. These people had already decided what they were going to do, now they were just trying to justify it.

'All the same. Like you blowing-up that riser with us in it.'

'I was just in the wrong place at the wrong time,' Dyce murmured, hopelessly.

'You lead us there! Lured us with your phoney signal. Tricked that amp into firing!'

'Why would I do that? Why would I risk that? I was just waiting to be saved. I was just keeping myself to myself.'

'It was a trap, and you knew it!' Rogers exclaimed, circling around him.

'You hate us!' McMorrow added, and Dyce glared back at him 'You're jealous of our way of life!'

Dyce shook his head and muttered expletives.

'What did you say?'

Suddenly Dyce felt an unbearable pain in his feet, radiating out from his ankles like a nuclear explosion of agony. Unable to stand, he collapsed to the floor, but this seemed to increase the pain. He let out a scream, he couldn't help it.

Dyce looked back to see Rogers crouching behind him, blood dripping from his progressive blade. He had used it to slice through both of his heels, right though his armoured boots, in one smooth movement, cutting his Achilles' tendons.

Dyce could not stand back up.

He tried to think through the pain. They had his weapons, but he knew there was a small single use weapon, a pistol, hidden inside his tactical armour. He just needed a moment to construct it, a distraction.

He did not get the opportunity. McMorrow and Rogers both grabbed Dyce by his arms and threw him at the wall. Dyce felt his jaw break as his face hit the painted brick work, a cloud of crumbling mortar erupted from the point of impact. His blood became a permanent part of the graffiti mural as his face slid down it, broken teeth escaping his mouth. He felt the painting and its textures against his bloodied cheeks as he slid down it, the lumps and the bumps of the dried drips.

He lay, crumpled and disheveled at the base of the wall, staring up at it, grasping at the bricks for purchase, to pull himself up. Small flickers of glowing colour appeared around his clawing fingers, conflict blossoms finding their way through the network of cracks in the wall, veins of biologically-sourced radiance ran through the reproductive structure of these rapidly flowering, self-germinating plants.

He heard laughing.

He took another blow, this time to his ribs. His bones shook like an old rusty bell in an ancient tower, this time a few ribs cracked.

This was bringing back a lot of memories. So, only a couple of hours post midnight and his Wednesday was turning out to be a lot like his Tuesday, with a lot of broken bones and internal injuries. He let out a darkly ironic laugh that hurt like hell as it forced its way out past those damaged ribs. This seemed to cause the laughter from the figures all around him to stutter awkwardly, probably from confusion.

Something smashed into his back, just to the left of his spine. And then a follow-up blow, knocking a few vertebrae out of shape, creating a crippling pain.

He slumped back down, gritted his teeth, and tried to

prepare himself for the next assault.

They made him wait.

McMorrow and Rogers each took one of Dyce's hands and, even as he struggled to pull them back, they pushed them down onto the ground, then unclipped and removed his armour's gauntlets. They spread his fingers wide.

There was more laughter, ebbing and flowing every time he squirmed or tried to pull his fingers out of harm's way.

Dyce closed his eyes.

Something hit the fingers in his right hand, and he assumed that it was a rock, or something blunt, at least. Again and again those fingers were struck until, finally, one of them broke right off. Dyce stared in disbelief at the bloodied stump, a disconnect happening inside his head, telling him that this wasn't real, that that wasn't really his hand…

'I don't think you're gonna be playing piano no more, kid,' McMorrow taunted, affecting some archaic accent he had probably heard in some gangster movie.

But they weren't done. Both Rogers and McMorrow continued to hit Dyce's fingers on both hands until more of them slithered free, or became smashed, raw meat filled with shattered shards of bone.

He looked up. The two men doing the bludgeoning were grinning down at him. The boy Darius had a blank expression, as if he were becoming desensitised to it. But Kosheen had the oddest look, harder to read. She was stood back, holding her own fingers, trying to stop them from fidgeting, her face contorting against her will, almost as if she could feel some echo of Dyce's pain. A couple of times she flinched, as if she felt the impact. She appeared indecisive about something.

Dyce was grabbed again, though he didn't bother to look who it was. He didn't plead, he didn't fight. He was right back to who he used to be, inactive, a pushover. He had no fight left.

He was thrown over onto his back, then McMorrow knelt on Dyce's chest and pinned him down. The aggressor, hovering in his view, pressed his fingers against Dyce's right eye. Dyce could feel the pressure, and hoped that he wasn't about to have that eyeball popped out or burst. He inadvertently blurted out some incomprehensible plea, then he started to squirm. But McMorrow was merely holding Dyce's eyelids open with a thumb and finger.

McMorrow reached into a compartment on his armour and pulled out an oblong cardboard box. It was a cigarette box, a rare luxury, especially if it actually contained the Red Apple brand on the label, or even if it simply contained a counterfeit alternative. He casually flicked open the lid, took out a cigarette, placed it between his lips and lit it. He took a long, satisfying drag.

Then McMorrow knelt down above Dyce's head, smoke spiralling from the paper wrapped tobacco dangling between two fingers. He was holding it between his thumb and forefinger like a pen, moving it closer to Dyce's open eyeball.

Dyce could hear the tobacco crackle, the sizzle of the receding paper as it drew closer to his eye. It was like staring into a dying sun. Embers of red were expelled from the end and seared lines across the lens of his pupil, before embedding themselves in the whites of his eyes. That burning mass hovered over his eye, it was all that he could see; the tobacco burning, the paper receding, crackling like a forest on fire.

'Hey... HEY!!!'

Everything stopped.

The cigarette was retracted, just an inch, as McMorrow turned to see who was shouting and why. Dyce could see that everyone was staring at Kosheen. She was still holding her hands own hands nervously, anxiously, she had gripped them between her biceps and chest. Her own right eye was twitching rapidly, as if it were stinging.

'You wanna save the best for Oshii,' Kosheen said. 'She'd be mad if she missed it.'

McMorrow gave a satisfied snort, then he flicked the cigarette at Dyce's face, catching his cheek before it spun away. As he squinted, grimaced and turned away, he failed to see the fist heading for his face. A few more punches and kicks increased his concussion, blood erupted from his mouth and nose.

Dyce lay there, struggling to catch his breath. He heard them wander away, talking amongst themselves as if they had just committed an act of brutality.

He almost thought he saw another figure stood amongst them. He couldn't see their face, but the body language matched his old friend Breaker. He was seeing things, probably the massive concussion. It was all a blur, colours bleeding, details smudged, but he thought he saw her cross her arms, as if in disapproval.

You just gonna lie there?

It hurt so much. He didn't want to move.

He could feel the phantom figment staring at him, judging him, and she thought he was a dick.

Well, he couldn't embarrass himself in front of his old, unrequited lady love, even if she was a sign of his mental collapse. He focused on his heals, imagined the damage done there. He visualised white blood cells as busy little workers, knitting the muscle and tendons and flesh back together. Stronger and more vivid with every pass, imagining more and more of these little workers, working faster and harder, in greater numbers. He could run, but how fast, how far? He had that small gun hidden in his armour, but he had no way of using it now.

That thought made him feel sick, much more than the unbearable agony radiating out from his hands.

He glanced over at the others. They were stood around chatting casually, as if they hadn't just committed an atrocity upon a stranger. McMorrow was leaning against a wall, smoking his cigarette.

He tried to be as zen as he could, despite his fear, anger and pain. Again and again, he imagined his heals healing, imaging those *little workers running their little errands*. Eventually, he felt a tingle in his feet, subtle at first, but the sensation cycled, and with every cycle it only intensified…

Dyce picked up his gauntlets with the heals of his hands, like giant, bloody chopsticks. He gritted his teeth as every molecule of his being told him to not to slide his mangled hands back into his armoured gloves. He didn't expect that his fingers would grow back - that seemed out of the realms of possibility even after everything else that had happened - and reattaching his mashed digits wasn't an option, at least not all of them. It was harder than expected to get his misshapen fingers – the ones that remained attached - back into their gloves, like trying to feed hammered meat into tubes. He considered removing them. He consoled himself with the fact that he didn't have time and he certainly couldn't draw any more attention to himself with uncontrollable screaming. Had he screamed earlier? He wasn't even sure.

He lay there and seethed. He knew he would be able to do much fighting with his hands like this, but he really didn't want to lay here and wait for Oshii, to wait for death, or whatever else she might have planned.

He had been passive his whole life. He had made such strides; he couldn't just return to his old ways.

Dyce reached over and, with his broken hands, dragged a pile of copper wire over to himself. He didn't care about the sound, and the any of the others who glanced his way just laughed at his futile attempts, believing that he was trying to drag himself away from them, and had gotten himself caught on some random trash.

After several uncomfortable attempts he managed to catch the end of the wiring between two of his left gauntlet's fingers. Then he began wrapping it around both hands, starting with the right, forming a crude boxing glove, looking like a bird's nest. He took it all the way to his elbow, before he started to wrap the second arm, but in reverse, from the elbow down to the wrist.

As he started to wrap his left hand, he rolled himself over and pushed himself up, using the wall for support. He could feel the strain upon the backs of his feet, but he hoped that the tendons would hold, even though they had little time to repair.

The voice in his head, Breaker, was trying to remind him of his training. Specifically, his embarrassing attempts at boxing. Dyce shook his head.

But that information is still in there, though. You would have learnt something by proxy, even if you weren't capable of applying it physically at the time, the things you were told and the things you saw, they must be floating around in there, at the back of your mind...

The four members of the Augmented Fourth took notice of him, one by one. They had nothing to say, their conversation drifting away, completely shocked by what they were seeing.

Dyce turned around to face them, the wall supporting him. He laughed at the absurdity of what he was about to do. He was still wrapping the copper wire around his left fist.

'You know, Sergeant Chase used to really...' Dyce struggled to speak. 'He used to really *fucking* hate me, for some reason. He taught us boxing. Or at least he tried to. He was right, though. I was really *fucking* shit.'

Dyce tried to tap his head, but the nest of wire scratched his skin.

'I'd end up black and blue and humiliated. Treated like some lower-class species. But some people are just bullies, just looking for an excuse to feel better than someone else, to justify their own existence. Make themselves feel *fucking* special. But that was another life, another *me*. One thing is the same, though, I really don't like bullies.'

McMorrow tried to think of something funny to say, but his smile was forced and soon evaporated. He was, in no way, prepared for whatever this nonsense was.

'They used to batter the ever-loving-shit out of me,' Dyce said. 'Like I'm going to try and do to you.'

This was it, time for him to push himself away from the wall and feign stability and strength.

I'm gonna die...

The voice in his head didn't even try to sugar cost the response.

Oh yeah, absolutely...

He literally pushed himself away from the wall with one fist, then wavered there for a second, unsure. His heals seemed to be holding, for now, they just had to keep him upright long enough. Not that he ever thought that he was capable of this even when he was operating at one hundred percent. He raised his copper-woven boxing gloves to protect his face.

'Is this guy serious?' Rogers muttered, wide eyed in disbelief.

'Gonna have to put you back down,' Kosheen said as she stormed over, though her voice was full of remorse.

Dyce jabbed at Kosheen, and she swerved his first few attempts, before she spun around and swept him off his feet. He hit the ground, everyone laughed. Dyce felt a shock of pain from his heels, but they had somehow held together.

Kosheen turned away, apparently to receive approval from her colleagues. Dyce launched himself up of the ground, involuntarily screaming as every aggravated injury pushed its way up through his body and exited his mouth. He slammed into Kosheen, throwing her over his shoulder, smashing her into Rogers, who fell back as Kosheen rolled over him, arse-over-tit. She landed on her back, her augmented back sparking as she bounced along the jagged ground.

Dyce held his his fists up and watched the reflection of the conflict blossom's neon brilliance warp over the interwoven metal, the blues and purples, illuminating individual strands within the jumble.

Trip Kosheen lay on her back, watching the show from upside down. She watched McMorrow and Rogers advance on their prey, and was surprised as everyone else, including the boy himself, as Dyce moved to meet them, taking a swing for McMorrow's head that the big man tried and failed to block, receiving a face full of pain. Rogers managed a blow to Dyce's ribs that almost made the English boy cry.

Kosheen could have turned off the artificial nerves in her

back and gotten straight back up, but she didn't want to rejoin that fray. It was as if she wanted to feel the pain, like she deserved it. Emotions were swishing around inside her cranium, ones that she had forgotten how to identify.

The boy took two hard punches to the gut, but improbably remained upright. Then he managed a couple of half-decent strikes in retaliation.

Kosheen had to look away as an unbearable stinging sensation in her right eye periodically intensified. She could feel it burning, and this had begun at the precise time as the cigarette had approached the boy's eye with an alarming, confounding synchronicity.

She rubbed that eye through the closed lid, but that was pointless, and it only seemed to exasperate the inexplicable pain that she also felt in her fingers. She had turned off the specific artificial nerves in each of her fingers, one at a time as an experiment, but she could still feel the breaks that hadn't actually happened to her own hands.

She watched Dyce fight the others as silhouettes against the graffitied wall lit by the bright, natural neon of the conflict blossoms, jet black figures throwing fists and taking hits. The luminous fauna shook as the action moved past them, their intensity increasing in reaction to the action, shifting colour. Dyce hit Rogers in the face with a blow so hard that, as he fell back, the blossoms turned orange in his wake, like trail leading down to the floor.

Dyce Bastion put up his dukes and prepared to defend himself from McMorrow. Rogers was lying at the foot of the wall, fidgeting amongst a patch of conflict blossoms, an incoherent babble of profanity emanating from his bloodied mouth as he lost a few teeth.

'Okay, enough of this shit...' McMorrow said, before charging face first into one of Dyce's mighty metal mittens.

McMorrow swore as he reeled away, holding his own bleeding nose aloft.

The tendons in Dyce's feet hadn't had enough time to heal,

and as he stepped towards McMorrow the tendon in his right foot snapped, along with the muscle and the threads of skin that had been in the process of weaving themselves back together. He collapsed down to his right knee, shouting out in frustration. He knelt there, taking long, deep breaths, shuddering in frustration and fear.

'One second,' he said to his assailants, and tried to hold up a single finger, before suddenly remembering that he no longer had one to hold. 'Oh...'

He didn't have time for this. He pushed himself back up, limping, shifting all his weight on to his left leg, hoping that one didn't go, too.

Rogers stood back up and stood next to McMorrow. Both men looked as if they were struggling to understand why this wasn't over yet, but for the sake of their own pride they needed this done sooner rather than later, so that normal service could resume.

Dyce, however, felt something else happening within his body. His arms seemed to be bulking up, becoming heavier, his legs, also, seemed to be pushing against the armour in which they were encased. If he had been built for speed before, all skinny, suddenly he was built to deliver power. More of this inexplicable bio-punk shit that had begun with his senses. This was something new. He was adapting. He was ready.

He absorbed a blow from McMorrow, and gave it right back, ten fold. The natural neon around him fluttered, ripples of red flowing through it, so bright and strong that glowing petals fell free like cinders. McMorrow hit the floor hard, moments before his body appeared to be consumed by an eruption of conflict blossoms from the broken earth. Rogers joined him a few seconds later, face planting his team mate's belly, bruising his right eye.

Dyce turned his attention to Darius, who was simply stood there, no idea what to do.

'Can I have my shit back, please?' Dyce asked. 'Pretty -*Fucking* - please?'

After some nervous, barely verbal protestations, Darius threw Dyce his tabris. Dyce fumbled and dropped it, having no fingers, so he held his hands out in the universal sign for *WTF dude?* Dyce got down on his knees, mindful not to twist his healing heals into any unfortunate positions, picking the tabris up off the floor after a couple of embarrassing attempts, then he struggled to get the device back into the charging compartment on his tactical armour.

'Darius!' Shouted McMorrow, from his painful position of the floor. He slurred the rest of his words. 'I know I didn't just see you give that... Know you didn't... give him his thing back...'

There was no reply from Darius, but there was an audible sigh. Dyce felt something against the back of his head. He knew instinctively that it would be the muzzle of a gun, confirmed by the words of the wielder.

'You gonna stop, or you want me to plant a tree in the back of your head?' Darius said.

'Tree?' Dyce asked, but he quickly realised the boy must have Kalamari branded nano-tech bullets in his gun.

Dyce just stayed when he was, kneeling amongst the broken concrete, unsure if his heel had healed well enough to support a counterattack. Darius was close enough to be disarmed with relative ease, but Dyce couldn't count on his own mobility at this exact moment. He had to stall.

'Really? Is this really your plan?'

'Hands in the air, maggot?'

'I'm more of a mealworm.'

Dyce lifted his arms, not in the air as ordered, but held them out for self-inspection, ignoring the protestations and demands of the young man behind him. He felt the weight of his twisted metal fists and could see that the cable was working its way into his flesh. He ruminated on the monstrous mess that he had become.

He noticed something that had escaped his attention, a scar that ran down his arm from his wrist to his elbow, a thin line that followed the path of a drip. He racked his memory for what this could be, recalled experimenting with the chemical bullets a few hours before, when he had watched tentacles and insects erupt from puddles of his own blood. The chemicals from one of the transparent bullets had dripped from where he had held it between his fingers, leaving a tingling trail down his skin.

Such a small amount of that liquid, but the mark remained, deeper than his other crosshatching scars. It looked like it could become infected. Perhaps he had discovered his kryptonite, chemical weapons, like those found in biotech bullets and bombs.

Like the one pointed at the back of his head.

'You must surely have been taught not to hold a gun so close to a prisoner. So easy to disarm. Any half-trained idiot could knock that gun out of your hand, a well-trained idiot could actually take it from you in half that time. But I'm tired. So, fucking tired...'

Dyce could actually hear the boy's fingers fidgeting on the trigger. His breathing was fast, his heart a speeding train. Darius reminded Dyce of himself.

'Look, I'm just gonna go. If you're gonna shoot me, just fucking shoot me. I'm tired of this war, and I'm tired of people.'

Despite the fact that he had originally intended to call the boy's bluff long enough to distract him, Dyce was surprised to find that he genuinely had no idea if he meant what he was saying.

Dyce stood up. The barrel of the gun followed him, haphazardly. He reached his arms above his head and kept them there. He took slow, solemn steps away.

'Darius, are you fucking serious?!' McMorrow shouted, managing to raise his head out of the expanding neon bush of tangled blossoms.

Darius panicked and fired. Dyce just managed to protect his face, the bullet diverting within the nest of twisted metal around Dyce's left hand, bouncing around inside, sparking. Suddenly, a mess of twigs emerged from his twisted murder mitten, a tangle of wood entwined with the tangle of metal. Dyce seethed, even more than usual. Darius had an anxiety attack.

Dyce collapsed back to his knees, but not in pain, just from pure exhaustion. He had nothing left. His faith in humanity was gone, and so was his will to fight. His mangled hands hit the floor beside him.

He had to move, he had to find the strength. But he had nothing left, no strength to push himself up.

He knew that *she* was coming, Corporal Paris Oshii.

TAKE MY HEART IF YOU NEED A BEAT.

Nico Shikari was halfway up the Goliath's neck, the steady retraction of her smart cord helping her to scale the segmented metal carapace that protected the monumental machine's spinal stack.

She took a moment to rest, just dangling there. She wondered what drove the Green Strays away, despite the fact that, logically and instinctively, she knew exactly what had happened. More than likely the Strays were still in the area, but they had been scattered. Literally. Torn appendages littering the maze of broken vehicles all around the area surrounding the Goliath.

From a section of the Goliath's neck hung a rucksack that had surely belonged to one of the Green Strays, one of its straps had been hooked over a protruding bolt. It had probably snagged when its owner fled or fell. She kicked her legs back and forth until she initiated a swing, repeating this until she came close enough to grab it. Inside she found fresh food, a carefully made sandwich, sealed inside a clear lunchbox. Just in time, the hunger was making her feel a little woozy.

'Any longer and I would have started talking to myself,' she said. To herself.

She hung there, from her smart cord, watching the distant lights of Absolution City, many miles away. She ate every last crumb, sensible enough to pace herself, but not frugal enough to leave anything for later. She rocked side to side as she stared vacantly at the horizon. Her armour's gauntlets gave the food a metallic aftertaste that reminded her of being hunkered down in fields, eating rations, whilst out on training exercises on the far side of Terminus moon.

Logically she should have fled the area entirely, though the feint, fading hope that someone might come for her kept her close the Nilin Remix. But a combination of boredom and a heavy heart had driven her up there – the physical challenge proved to be the metaphorical stack of kindling and curiosity was the spark. The curiosity part came from a message that she could have sworn she had seen repeatedly flashing from within the Goliath's ocular arrays.

'*Hey girl, whatsup?*' read the Morse code.

The message seemed odd enough to be unlikely, but intriguing enough to get her motivated. She had found a new sense of purpose, or a desire to find a *new* purpose, in the wake of her brief love affair. A fire had been lit inside her, stoking a motivation.

As she continued to stare into nothing, she started to hum a tune, absentmindedly, the one that the green-eyed pilot had attempted to teach her through the guitar-training software. Once she caught herself doing this, she recalled the conversation that they had had at the time. She remembered moving her fingers over the virtual instrument, and she tried to remember where her fingers were supposed to be at each part of the tune.

It was only a song from a memory relived, but that didn't stop her getting frustrated trying to figure it out. She wanted to have another go, itching for it, but now wasn't the time.

She didn't even realise that she had done it, but she had already lifted her hands up and out, miming, letting the sandwich's empty packet float away on an airstream. She moved her fingers over the imaginary strings, trying to find the…

She froze as she saw, from the corner of her eyes, a feminine figure, balancing perfectly, effortlessly, on the edge of a gun turret on the side of the Goliath. When she turned to focus on it, it didn't disappear straight away, lingering like smoke. Was it, somehow the emerald eyed pilot? A part of her lingering in Nico's mind. Or wishful thinking finding shapes within shadows and reflections?

The figure glitched, separating into a colourful spectrum of random geometric shapes, almost, for a second, looking feline. Then *she* was gone.

Before she had headed up the Goliath, Nico had taken the pilot's white aviation jacket back to the Nilin Remix, folded it up respectfully- mindful of every crease, imperfection, and every sound the material made as she manipulated it. Then she stowed it in a compartment beneath a seat. Even now, up here, she could still feel the texture of the jacket's fabric between her fingers, locked in this muscle's memory, she could still smell the scent trapped within it.

Nico looked towards the area where she had shared the dying pilot's final moments, remembering everything that she could about the woman, from her emerald eyes to that existential *free-fall* that Nico had experienced within the pilot's presence. An emotional response that seemed to temporarily detach Nico from her own self of sense, giving her a divine sensation of weightlessness.

But she could see no sign of the body from here. Did it matter? The soul inside that emerald-eyed pilot was gone, and that body was now nothing more than an empty shell that had housed that person.

"The soul"?' She asked herself, frowning at the word that she had used to describe the pilot's *self*. 'hmm...'

That was an abstract concept that she barely understood, a word that she had only heard in ancient media. Religion had been outlawed long ago, so she only used the word *soul* as a shorthand to encompass the whole *general mishmash* of what exists inside a living human. The military was their church, patriotism was their religion, and everything else was a distraction.

At least, that's what they had been taught, and what she had believed without question, at least until she had looked into those emerald eyes...

'Stupid, stupid, stupid...' She berated herself for the weakness she was showing. But then she felt stupid for *feeling* stupid and for thinking her new feelings were stupid.

She'd tied herself in knots.

It was time to get going, stop dwelling. The spindle started again, pulling her up the side of the Goliath until she reached the top. She detached her smart-cord's anchor and made her way across the mighty machine's cranium, stepping over abandoned equipment that the green strays had used to burn into the machine's armour. They had been looking for anything of value within the massive amp, using unconventional cutting tools custom made from parts scavenged from conventional equipment and heavy weaponry.

Nico arrived at a large hatch in the centre, built like a safe, but the Green Strays had, conveniently for her, already hacked it open. Skilled minds had hacked the digital locks, and their complex, intimidating, bespoke equipment had decimated the physical locks.

But there was more to this story, there were claw marks around the hatch, deep jagged gouges. On closer inspection she found them to be studded with slithers of flesh and tinted red. It was entirely probable that she made a terrible mistake coming up here, but she tried to console herself with the fact that there had been many people working up here, drawing the carnivore's attention by making lots of noise. Perhaps if she was quiet she could survive the night.

There was a flash from within the darkness of the hatch, which was ajar. She gave a curious snort, and took hold of it. It was a few inches thick with armour, but she had her own powered armour to share the weight.

The hinge mechanism screamed as she strained, echoing out.

She paused for a moment. The hatch halfway open, her arms rigid, she looked around. She could see nor hear any sign of movement, nothing climbing up over the sides of the massive head, obviously the war wolves were large, stealth was not exactly their forte. She would hear them coming.

She turned her attention back to the hatch, half way open, and put her shoulder into it, gritting her teeth as the screeching resumed. She sat back on her haunches and observed the spoils, as if she had opened a treasure chest. Within, she found the massive machine's teeny tiny brain. Considering the incomprehensible size of the Goliath, it was controlled by a cognitive cradle that held three orbs, the whole setup not much wider than a foot. Each of the three orbs was a processor which controlled a different aspect of the machine's mind. The cradle looked as if it were older than the Goliath itself, a generic design, recycled and retrofitted for this purpose.

She reached in and gingerly took hold of one of the orbs between her fingertips, feeling the pull of the magnetic Near Field Communication array that held it in place. As she held it up to the moonlight, the processor stack within the orb was just visible through the semi-opaque of the silver-tinted membrane. Inexplicably, someone had scrawled *"Jute"* on to each of the orbs in crumbling yellow crayon.

'Hello Jute,' she said to the orb, before placing it back into its cradle, the magnets pulled it from her grip, popping itself back into the concave port. It released a flash of static as it synchronised. 'You been calling to me?'

Upon closer inspection, Nico noticed that the Green Strays had, before their disappearance, begun cutting the cables that connected the cradle to the surrounding architecture of the Goliath's head.

She heard a crackle of interference from somewhere, a buzz from a speaker. Unnerved, she unsheathed her progressive blade. Out of nowhere, a cracked and muffled voice spoke up.

'I didn't thInk u wud acTuALly comE all tHis…'

Spooked by this sudden, unexpected, disembodied dialogue, Nico fell backwards onto her posterior and activated her progressive blade.

'Why so jumpy, *Red*?' The voice was tinny and broken, like a radio signal on the verge of being lost.

Located in the middle of the cradle was a tiny spherical security camera, the size of a penny, which spun around a fair-few times until it found her.

In the silence that followed there was nothing but the hum of her blade and the wind flicking the assortment of wires inside the hatch.

'You're talking to me?' Nico asked.

'Yes, Red, who else is here?' The voice was coming from a small speaker beneath the security camera. 'I haven't used this eye in a long time, and I'm not sure it's in the best condition.'

'I really didn't expect a Goliath to talk like you.'

'Managing the functions of the Goliath is not the totality of who I am, Red, consider me to be the ghost in the machine.'

'Why are you calling me "*Red*"?'

'Your hair, I saw you from a distance, through the Goliath's ocular arrays, and I had very few points of reference with which to identify you. I couldn't very well call you *"Four Eyes"* or *"Mopey Girl."*

'You nicknamed me based on my physical appearance?' Nico asked. 'The moment I opened your hatch and saw your three processors, I didn't start calling you *Big Balls*, did I?' Nico didn't get a response to that, which disappointed her because she thought that was funny.

'Is that your level?' The voice asked, after a disappointed pause.

'Pretty much, yeah.'

'Your hair was your most striking feature, because, well, maybe my visual codex is compromised, but your hair looks like red neon lava. Is that right? Is your head spewing forth a technicolour stream of magma?'

'Your eyes are fine,' Nico answered 'The universe has indeed become a psychedelic wonderland in the few hours since a satellite dropped a city on your head.'

'Oh good, for a moment there I was worried I might be defective,' said Jute.

'I never heard an amp talk like that,' Nico was actually glad to have someone to banter with. It relieved some pressure in a pleasant way.

'I'm limited edition, Red.'

'Were you actually trying to get my attention?'

'Well, you looked like a lost soul, and I had been incapacitated by a geostationary defence platform, we seemed mutually compatible.'

'Are you asking me out?'

'Don't think I'm your type?'

'That sounded like a question.'

'That sounded like a statement.'

'How do you have enough power for processing?' Nico asked, changing the subject. 'Half your connections are cut.'

'How do you know I'm not operating on *love and wishes*?'

'Don't be cute.'

'But *cute* is all I have…'

Nico was checking out the cradle, examining it. There was a surprising amount of heat coming from it. She turned it over and examined the modular components on its underside.

'You only have emergency battery backup,' she told the disembodied voice. 'And I don't think they're in good shape.'

'The closer you get, Red, the more power I have. When you picked me up, the power cells burned white hot.'

'I don't think that's true,' Nico said, though she could see a thin heat haze emanating from the backup battery pack.

'Can I stay close to you, Red? You keep my batteries fizzing.'

'Excuse me?' Nico raised an eyebrow at this obvious double entendres.

'I said *batteries*.'

'*Uh huh.*'

'When you hold my cradle it seems to give me a charge,' Jute elaborated.

'I'm surprised you said cradle and not balls.'

'Wow...' Jute feigned a gasp. 'You've known me five minutes...'

'I got the measure of you,' Nico said. 'And it was a short stick.'

'Moving on from that unsanctioned filth, do you know what's causing the power surge?'

'My electric personality?'

'Well, that is a strong possibility, but I do remember that there were tests, back in the day, to inject soldiers at birth with nano-generators which could be used to power augmentations, such as the neurological interface components that were surgically implanted in the brain. Piezo-electrix-nanofibers.'

'Bless you!'

'Sorry?'

'So you should be.'

'Erm, what?' The distorted voice spluttered. 'Anyway...'

'You sounded like you sneezed, that word you used, it sounded like.. it was... I was making, you know, a joke...'

There was a moments silence.

'These Piezo-electrix-nanofibers harness the energy of motion,' Jute continued. 'Like the flowing of blood, transform it into electrical energy. Do you have some version of that? That's somehow transmittable?'

'No, not me. I'm not special,' Nico waved her hand dismissively. She liked being a no one. She liked blending in. 'Normal. That's how it's supposed to be.'

'Everyone is a no one until they have to be a someone...' Jute said. 'Or they choose to be...'

Nico let out a curious hum, clenching and unclenching her fingers, wondering what processes could be taking place within her, beneath the armour, the mechanisms, the muscle suit, the skin, the muscle...

'Pseudo inspirational bullshit,' she sneered.

So many strange things had been happening to her, recently,

such as her heightened senses, was it out of the realms of possibility that this was another? She didn't much like being *special*, it was making her uncomfortable, and fuelling an anger inside her.

'Look, Red, those big *bear wolf things* will soon finish eating the pre-packaged, still-screaming meals that they dragged back to their home holes. I think we need to move.'

'*We* need to move, plural?' Nico asked as she stood up. 'Me *and* you?'

'Please,' he said.

Nico stared at the cradle for a moment and sighed. She scooped it up and cut the remaining cables with her blade. Almost immediately she heard a crunch in the distance that gave her reason to speed things up.

She paused and listened. Nothing. She could smell rain in the air, could hear its preemptive pitter-patter in the distance.

She knelt at the edge and looked around, trying to decide upon the path of least resistance. The darkness was moving, black shapes moving over the tops of the broken vehicles. She realised that the crunches she heard were them masticating, a suspicion solidified when she caught sight of random body parts being devoured by the darkness.

'Good luck, Red.'

'Stealth or speed?'

'Run like your life depends on it. Because it does...'

'Great.'

'Good luck.'

'You said that.'

'You need a double dose.'

Nico clenched her teeth and made that sucking sound that people make when they have to do something that terrifies them to their core.

'Fuck it...'

She decided against going back down into that pit of vipers, too visible, too loud. By the time she hit the ground and remote deactivated the magnetic anchor and wound it it they would be on top go her.

She instead fired the anchor back down at the abandoned rucksack, still dangling from the turret. She missed. She retracted it, feeling pretty foolish as she stood there listening to the winding smart cord. She fired again, managing to thread the anchor though one of the rucksack's shoulder straps, then wound it back up to her waiting hands. She forced her new companion into it, zipped it up, slung it over her shoulder.

She jogged across the Goliath's cranium and somersaulted off the back of the massive machine's head, landing on its neck. She ran down it, leaping over the gaps between each of the segmented sections of its spine, hoping to be down on the ground before the beasts. She reached the back and had a good look around the piled-up machines in the area directly beneath. It didn't look too bad. She free-climbed down its front right leg, descending slowly, cautiously, keeping an eye on the shadows beneath, until she was low enough to drop-and-roll into the shadows.

She leaned into the darkness and waited for a moment, listening. When there didn't seem to be any change in the local soundscape, she made her move. She didn't exactly run, it would have drawn attention she thought, but she did walk with pace and purpose. At least she had a working gun, now, thanks to the emerald eyed pilot, and it made her feel a little safer. Of course, she also had her armour, though that hadn't done much good for the beasts' previous prey.

As she crept on, she wondered how quiet her synthetic companion would be. Would the machine make a sudden sound and attract the enemy? Could he be trusted? Nico started to wonder if she should have left Jute behind.

She stopped as she saw the back of a war wolf, a living shadow as big as a bear. It had its back to her. She held her breath. Took a step back...

But this wasn't the only beast in the immediate area. To her left, in the shadows of a canopy inadvertently formed from a broken fuselage, another creature slumbered. She couldn't see anything of it but it's claws, highlighted by the moons. The breathing mass stirred and grunted, a snore perhaps. Then it grunted again, and this time it sounded curious. Perhaps it was awake, perhaps it had smelt her. It raised its head, slowly, then the rest of its body, stretching.

Nico moved, tip-toeing. Amongst the maze of broken ships, close by, was a drop-ship's door. She slid the door open and slid in, annoyed at the sound it made as she re-closed it behind her. She stopped, holding tight to the door's handle, waiting for any audible indication that she was being followed.

There was a shuffle from behind her.

Nico turned. She reached for her progressive blade, unsheathing it, finger on the button. She was, however, shocked to find a person in here, a soldier, hiding. How long had they been here? How long had they managed to stay so perfectly still.

The soldier lifted a finger to their quivering lips, telling Nico to be quiet. But Nico could hear the beast walking over the top of the vessel. It knew they were here.

The soldier's eyes were wide, streaks of tears down their cheeks. Clearly they had seen some serious shit. After a deep breath, Nico lifted her hands and began to communicate her plan through military sign language. She was going to take this soldier back to her own ship. Nico took her rail rifle from her back, then she spun her progressive blade around, pointing the handle at the soldier as an offering.

But the hull exploded as this unknown soldier was pulled through it, out into the night, his hands grasping for anything. There was a scream – which became a sustained, cacophonous, garbled noise – but it didn't recede into the night. It was coming from directly above, no more than a couple of feet. There was deafening percussion to go with this noise, as the body was repeatedly tenderised against the top of the ship.

Nico held her mouth and backed out through the newly created exit, glancing left and right, but aware that the beasts were above her. She didn't hesitate this time, she took off through the night, hurtling through the maze of machines, keeping as low as she could.

The beasts chased her to the river, snapping at her heals as she bounced up on to the hull. But suddenly there was silence, their hefty footfalls stopped, their growling and panting ceased.

Nico stopped only to grab the hatch into her ship, turning around to see where her pursuers were.

There were three of the jet-black beasts, and they had retreated to the broken ships nearest to the river, stood upon them. They looked afraid, as a shadow loomed over them.

Oh fuck, what now?

Nico turned slowly, not wanting to know what these brutal beasts were scared of but needing to know.

She couldn't quite make out for sure what it was, some huge unfathomable shape lit from behind by the moons, a moving mishmash of things that didn't belong together in that composition. Nico stood back up upon the hull, staring at it, a hulking, humanoid shape, several storeys high. It was angular, one shoulder appeared to have chimneys and pipes protruding from it, though it was hard to confirm what they were. There was an odd conglomerate of scents in the air, coming from the unidentified mass – hot diesel, burning wood, smouldering tar…

The war wolves were moving backward into the shadows of the maze of broken things. From the huge being emanated an unusual call, as if a foghorn were echoing through a network of old pipes and cavernous generators.

Nico grabbed the hatch as she jumped into the ship, pulling it closed behind her. But it was still broken, of course, and didn't shut all the way, leaving a tiny gap.

So she held on to the hatch, her fingers gripping the lock wheel, using the combined weight of her and her armour to hold it still. She hung there, swinging back and forth, her heart still racing.

She listened as something started to tap curiously at the hull and the hatch. Whatever it was, it wasn't some feral beast, it was a curious soul manipulating outsized digits.

She tensed her arms and lifted up her feet, pushing against the hull either side of the hatch, making sure that entrance remained closed.

With clichéd timing it started to rain. As she hung there, waiting to see what the vast, black shadow would do next, she listened to the precipitation falling on the ship's hull. She rolled her head and listened to the cracks from the tension in her neck.

She wanted nothing more than to take her armour off so that she could *exhale*, but now wasn't the time to let down her defences, no matter how tired she was, not with dangerous animals and unpleasant fuck-wits roaming around.

Condensation formed droplets within the thin crescent of moonlight where the hatch's rubber seals had failed to meet. The droplets hit the top rung of the ladder, building up until it was dense enough to drip to the rung beneath. Every tap of that water hitting metal lulled her a little deeper towards slumber, like a hypnotist counting down towards a trance.

Her eyes started to flutter, her lids growing heavier, she fought against them closing. She started to daydream, her mind drifting through the path that had led her to the emerald-eyed pilot. As her misty-eyed recollection drew Nico closer to her lost love, the pilot's deep green eyes appeared to be alive with movement and light, reflecting a kaleidoscope of rolling clouds.

There was a sudden crash from outside, waking Nico and nearly causing her to lose her grip. Then came another crash, and another, and another, the consecutive concussive crashes started to sound more and more like large, heavy footsteps. Nico pulled her face closer to the gap in the seal, wanting to catch a glimpse.

'That's not the war wolves,' Jute replied, the words from his speaker given more bass as they reverberated through the hull from his place on the floor.

'Quiet…' Nico whispered.

'Sorry, I can't modulate the volume or tempo of…' He realised his own mistake and silenced himself.

The crashing foot falls stopped as a dark shadow temporarily broke the line of moonlight around the ajar hatch. There came a curious grunt from outside that was barely organic, defiantly not the sound of an apex predator. The rolling rumble from behind the hatch carried with it an unnatural stench that managed to seep in through that thin gap, resembling ancient, dirty diesel. The ship moved, ever so slightly, rocking, as if brushed by curious fingers.

Then the stomping resumed, each crash moving further away.

'What was that?' Nico needed to know.

Nico pushed it open, cautiously, though she was sure that the beasts had fled. She was just in time to see that mysterious, lumbering form heading towards the crumbling risers, where it disappeared, shaking broken glass from the buildings, which fell like leaves from a tree.

Whatever that had been, it was ancient, and she could not be sure if it was a machine or a being. Nico reached out, running her fingers through a coating of red dust that had amassed on the outside of the ship, like crumbled flakes of red brick.

'*Curious…*' Jute said, his tiny camera eye tracking Nico, surprised to see that she was venturing out to see what it was. 'Is that wise?'

A cloud of crimson erupted from Nico's gauntlets as she slapped them clean, absently watching and waiting for another sign of the titan.

Specks of rain hit her glasses and droplets hung from the tips of her short hair. Had it been some sort of amp, perhaps, or a mutation? Or something in between?

She saw the beacon flashing, it's rotating light illuminating the moist mist. She decided to kick it down into the ship. Maybe jute could connect to it.

'I'll see if your diagnostic systems can figure this damn thing out,' Nico whispered to Jute. 'Get me out of here, back to somewhere that makes sense...'

Her homeland had always made sense to her, it was all she'd known. But just to confuse matters, of course, the green-eyed pilot had made a different kind of sense. But it wasn't the kind-of sense that she was used to. Nico missed *her*, which simultaneously made sense to her *heart* but made no sense to her head.

'What damn thing?' Jute's voice came from the tiny speaker, barely audible as it echoed up out of the ship.

The fine drizzle in the air was starting to escalate towards a more substantial torrent. So dramatic. Perfect timing. The sound was so distracting, which was probably what allowed the following sequence of events to be set in motion without her knowing.

Something scraped along the armour plating of the hull, a squeal of something gouging the metal. Nico's hair stood on end.

A war wolf, waiting for her on the other end of the jump ship's hull, stretched up, bristling. A black mass of spikes, its attention locked upon Nico. Energy flowed along its body in successive waves, from the base to the tips, where an electric blue light crackled as the air popped and fizzed around them.

Nico didn't like her chances. She raised her fists regardless, defiant, feeling the mechanical hum of power that drove her armour. She stretched and tightened her fingers, feeling the layer of synthetic muscle contract within the alloy. Her only chance was to get back inside the ship and get that hatch shut as soon as possible.

The beast scraped its segmented tongue across its teeth, then it let out a deep growl from the back of its cavernous throat, preparing the rest of its body for a strike.

But then there was another growl from behind her, and this one was muffled because it was echoing up *out* of the jump ship itself. Nico realised that the one in front of her had just been distracting her whilst the second one slipped down into the vessel, as silent as a shadow...

She had her blade, her smart cord, and the rail-rifle that the pilot had gifted her. She had loaded the rail-rifle with a small amount of ammo - scavenged rusty nails that the magnetic rail could launch at a velocity that exceeded that of an archaic gunpowder propelled bullet - but she doubted that it would be enough to break the creature's natural armour-carapace or do much damage even if it did. It would be useless at anything but point-blank range, perhaps directly into something fleshy like the mouth or an eyeball.

Nico cautiously moved backwards towards the edge of the ship, aware that one miss-timed step could trigger an attack. She backed up into a position that allowed her to watch the first beast and the open hatch simultaneously, waiting for some glimpse of the creature within the bowels of the Nilin Remix.

Her hair was now soaked through with rain, and she could feel it running down her neck and into her armour. She swept a foot back behind her and took her progressive blade in hand, flicking the switch. The subsonic hum affected the descending droplets, skipping down the blade.

A jaw full of fearsome, bladed canines appeared out from the darkness of the vehicle, heralding the emergence of that second war wolf. It raised its grimacing muzzle up into the air, rain running down its carapace and into its mouth. Between that jagged cage of teeth was the persistent red flash of the distress beacon, nestled within its mouth, refracted through the gloop of saliva.

This war wolf pulled its hefty hind legs up and out of the ship, then stepped backwards, so the entrance to the sanctuary of the ship was between itself and Nico. It was taunting its prey, daring her to try...

Nico tightened her grip on her progressive blade, the rain arcing around, spluttering into a whirl of water. With her free hand, she took her helmet from where it was stowed on her back, locked it around her head.

Her two unearthly adversaries stretched their bodies as they prepared themselves for the strike. The sabre-like protrusions from their natural armour were glowing, turning the damp air around them blue.

Nico fired her smart chord's anchor into the gradual imploding beacon, cracking some teeth, the impact pushing it further back into that alien throat. The creature reared back in surprise as shrapnel tore its larynx. Nico retracted the cord and yanked the beacon into the back of the molars. She grounded herself against the pull of the cord, like a fisherman with an unlikely catch.

Injuring the beast was a minor victory, but she had created a distraction, and she was already running for the hatch.

The first war wolf charged at Nico across the hull with a spittle-spewing roar, but its target had slid feet first across the rain-slick hull, propelled by the retracting cord.

Nico dropped down into the ship, grabbed the hatch's inner handle and swung on it, again using the weight of her armour to pull it down with her. But the hatch was still broken, of course, and one of the war wolves took the opportunity to jam a paw in, swiping at Nico's face, before forcing the hatch back open.

Nico dropped to the floor of the ship, letting loose a roar fuelled by frustration. She had been so close to safety, but a split-second short. She skittered backwards out of the way as the first beast poured its body down into the ship.

The war wolf arched its body back to strike, those sparks of bioluminescence travelled through the mane of spikes, igniting the needle sharp tips.

'Hey, *Red...*?'

Nico didn't answer Jute, she didn't think that this was really an appropriate time. She just let out a short, impatient grunt to confirm that she could hear him.

'Red, there's a small patch on the side of its head where the armour appears to be thinner, just behind the eyes,' Jute said from the floor, it's little speaker just about audible. 'It's a tiny target, but it's possible. You just have to get around that face full of teeth.'

Nico drew one foot back behind her and raised her fists, the progressive blade pointed down from her right fist, ready to rip and tear.

'Hey, *Red*…?'

'What?' Nico rolled her eyes and gritted her teeth, losing patience.

'Good luck.'

The war wolf pounced. Nico flashed the blade to the right and the creature's gaze followed, so she took the opportunity to throw a fist hard in the other side of that heavy head with her left fist, aiming for that soft spot, the shockwave shaking its curious carapace as her piston powered gauntlet mercilessly mangled muscle.

She had managed to alter the creature's trajectory just enough to avoid being skewered on those malicious molars, but it was close enough to potentially counter any subsequent attack. She knew that she absolutely could not afford to hesitate. She brought an elbow down onto the creature's head, using all of the strength she could divert from the armour's reserve to burst one of its eyeballs.

Nico held her breath as she glanced back up at the circle of moonlight above, hoping that the second beast didn't join the fray. She could feel her heart beating through her skull, racing faster.

The war wolf shook its head before it sprung back, yet it was disorientated enough to miss, snapping at nothing but air as Nico side-stepped it.

Nico grabbed the jump ship's empty weapon rack and pulled it down by its hinges, temporarily trapping the thrashing war wolf. But the hybrid creature simply rattled its rudimentary cage until the metal cracked, twisting, rivets popping.

Nico struck down with the progressive blade into the weak spot behind the ears and dragged the humming weapon down into the beast's neck, the powerful subsonic vibration cracking the shell wide open.

The wailing war wolf unleashed a bio-electrical charge, sending a blaze of blue down its back. Nico's buzzing blade made contact with the monster's electrical discharge, reversing its weaponised resonance, shattering it.

'Shit!' Nico spat, panicking.

Her Minds Eye informed her that only sixty-one point two millimetres of conductive blade remained attached to the hilt, this data overlaying the weapon as she held it in trembling hand.

The war wolf fell forward onto its belly, the neck wound opening further. A tangle of blood-matted hair emerged from the grim wound, followed by its owner's tattooed-green head. This undigested morsel of Stray slopped onto the floor in a pool of crimson-tainted drool.

(*"Oh, Red, that is nasty,"*) Jute's voice was suddenly louder and clearer than it had ever been, and Nico was too distracted to realise that it was probably coming through her com-link and not the cradle's speaker.

(*"You see that?"*)

Nico checked the progressive blade, flicking the power on and off. It still seemed to vibrate, the LED power indicator flickered, static discharge caused the damp air to spark.

(*"I've wirelessly synced to your tabris, I can see through your peepers,"*) Jute explained. (*"It wasn't difficult, your security is archaic and cheep."*)

'Okay...' Nico whispered, not really listening.

(*"That's how I saw it's week spot. I saw it because you saw it. Your eyes are, you know, wow!"*)

Nico was focused on the task at hand. She had to go out, she knew this, she could not stay here, penned in, waiting in fear.

(*"You're going to face it?"*)

(*"No guts no glory,"*) she replied through the com-link. (*"The other one isn't going to let me close the hatch, it's waiting by it, for me to make a move, and it's gonna come at me twice as hard when it realises what I've done."*)

She delicately picked up the emerald-eyes pilot's white aviation jacket and breathed it in. She let out a heavy sigh that turned into a shudder, and this only deepened as her grip tightened around the garment.

She placed it back down, then took the rail rifle from her back. This gave her similar feels, despite the fact that it was nothing more than a linear motor device that used electromagnetic force to launch high velocity projectiles. But she cherished the moment that the emerald-eyed pilot had reset it for her. It was sacred.

(*"Go get'm tiger!"*) Jute said.

(*'Growl,"*) she said.

Nico mounted the gun back on the magnetic lock between her shoulder blades and gripped what remained of the blade. She closed her helmet, and charged up the ladder, roaring like one of the beasts. She launched herself out, stumbling straight into the blood coated carapace of the imposing creature.

The war wolf reared up, throwing her through the air, where her back hit the edge of the hull before tumbling over into the rain-soaked river bank, launching mud and stones as she landed.

The creature came down on top of her, gouging the armour plating as it thrashed at her.

Nico activated what remained of the blade, which released another quick burst of power, just enough to pierce the side of the beast's head. As she twisted the knife, the weak spot behind the eye popped like a bloody boil. The creature shook its mighty head, trying to knock the blade away.

Nico let go just in time to avoid losing her hand to its flailing claws. Once the paw was clear of the imbedded blade, she started to drive it deeper into that alien cranium with the heal of her hand, trying to make-contact with something tender and fatal.

But she had to forget the blade to protect her face from the beast's snapping teeth, glistening with rain and drool. Those bone-daggers clamped down into her armoured arms, breaking the thick plating. Nico snarled in pain as the imploding armour dug into her forearms.

Nico kicked at the beast until she was able to pull an arm free and punched the side of the its head again and again, occasionally catching the blade and driving it further in. She needed to focus her blows upon the blade, of course, but she was in no position to prioritise precision, making the most of whatever concussive contact she could achieve.

She didn't let up until one of its eyes popped within its socket, a crimson coating washing over it, but still the beastly berserker did not let go of her arm.

Nico rolled over the beast, pulling it over into the water, where their combined weight submerged them, the onslaught of rain making the moonlight strobe around them. Her helmet had sprung a couple of tiny leaks, dirty river water seeping in through hairline fractures that an amp and the beast had made, but there was more than enough oxygen for what she needed to do.

The war wolf struggled towards the surface but Nico held on, despite its violent and powerful protests. It seemed to take forever, until the last of the bubbles escaped the creature's mouth and it had less strength to struggle.

Nico removed the progressive blade from the side of the creature's head, ignited it with a flash, and shoved it into the open mouth. Over and over she tore at the inside of its head, yelling, letting out all of her pent-up frustrations, ordering the beast to succumb to its wounds and...

'Just fucking die already!'

She had to breath, especially after expelling all of her air with her outburst. She struggled out from under the monster and broke the surface.

She pulled herself up onto submerged debris, stood up tall and opened her helmet's blast shield, letting the storm wash over her, cleansing her.

The beast rolled over in the depths beneath, gurgling up blood.

Her senses had gone into overdrive again. She witnessed countless drops of rain hitting the river, bouncing off the rain-slick rocks and the derelict, given a silver glaze by the twin moons.

The war wolf limped up out of the water, lunging at its enemy in a pathetic attempt at revenge.

Nico widened her stance, took the rail rifle in hand and aimed down. The blade's hilt was propping the creature's jaw open, just enough.

She pulled the trigger.

Whisker-thin lines of electrical discharge followed each of the projectiles from the gun's rail down into that gaping maw, leaving afterimages that lingered. The beast convulsed after every shot, slumping back a little further. Perhaps she had hit the brain, perhaps she had severed the spine, she had no idea, she didn't care.

It was dead.

She was still alive.

She let out a little laugh of triumph. It only lasted a second.

A third war wolf was waiting for her on the river bank. Nico's stared back at this beast. She did not break eye contact.

The creature bowed its head and slunk away, almost apologetically, disappearing into the night.

Nico waded back over to the Nilin Remix and pulled herself up the side, one rung at a time. The wind hit her face as she clambered up to the top, whipping the rain around her as she stood before the hatch, feeling the combat-high reverberating through her bones.

She found the beacon crushed and broken, incapable of flashing or transmitting. She realised she didn't need it. She didn't need the darkness of the ship either.

She sat down on the edge of the hull, felt her entire body start to shake. But, she realised that what she was experiencing was fuelled by memories of the battle with the beasts. She was turning it over in her mind, reliving every moment of it again, and her heart started beating faster and faster, endorphins had started flooding her system.

Finally she had taken part in a decent fight, for the first time since arriving in this forsaken land, and she had beaten the odds. She had not just survived, she had won.

She felt good. She felt renewed.

She smiled.

Okay... What's next?

LIVE THOSE DAYS
TONIGHT

But...

'That was such a big deep sigh for such a pathetic little man,' a familiar voice echoed through the wasteland, malevolent and mocking.

Dyce didn't turn back to confirm who it was, and he still didn't have the strength to stand up. The mess of metal wrapped around his broken fists was heavy, and he no longer had the strength to carry this burden. So he knelt there, shackled by the weight. It was raining now, lightly, coating everything in a shiny gloss. He could feel it on his skin, dripping from the armour and the tangle of metal. The rain barely masked the distant sound of war wolves, howling, growling and ultimately whimpering.

Corporal Paris Oshii's circled around in front of Dyce, just beyond striking distance. The facial recognition system in Dyce's Minds Eye unnecessarily identified Oshii by name, rank and serial number. She was, like the rest of the Augmented Fourth, so notorious that she was stored in the League database.

Wanted – Dead.

Her crimes – and those of her subordinates - were numerous and unpleasant. Dyce only glanced at the scrolling list of infamy and wished he hadn't.

Oshii had not arrived alone. She had more members of her

team with her, and they were assisting the soldiers that Dyce had knocked down - McMorrow, Darius, Kosheen and the other one.

'You did this?' Oshii asked, in disbelief. 'Alone?'

'He lost a few fingers first,' Kosheen said. She rolled over and sat on her ass, refusing the helping hand of a compatriot. 'I don't think he liked that. For some fucking reason.'

Oshii would have looked impressed by what Dyce had achieved, moments after being maimed, if that emotion wasn't drowned out by the overpowering confusion.

'Well,' McMorrow said, confused and concussed. 'We disarmed him first...'

'And sliced his ankles...' Rogers added. 'I mean he still... I mean, somehow he...'

Rogers shrugged. All four of Dyce's unwitting sparring partners kinda shrugged.

Oshii took a step towards Dyce as a succession of unpleasant expressions popped and fizzed across her face, like an excited cluster of ticks that she could barely contain.

'Looks as if it took a lot out of you,' Oshii leaned down before Dyce. 'But I'd be disappointed if you don't have some fight left in ya.'

Dyce managed to slump a little further - a fantastic achievement for the contractibility of the human form. He stared absently at a cluster of rusty springs and screws amongst the rocks on the ground, lit by the conflict blossoms, wishing he could will himself into shrinking down to hide amongst them. The puddles forming around them looked like pools of oil, a spectrum of colour drifting over the surface.

'Young Dyce Bastion,' Oshii said to him. 'I forget your prisoner ID number. Do you remember what that was?'

Dyce stared back, he had nothing to say.

'That was a stupid question,' Oshii laughed and rolled her eyes. 'Of course, *you* do. They trained you to say it over and over, didn't they?

She considered him, keenly.

'I thought I knew you, but this... I always thought you had potential, but you always did manage to disappoint me again and again. But *this*, this is new. So, it seems as if our little reunion could go either way.'

Oshii wrapped her fingers around the hilt of her progressive blade, slow and precise, one digit at a time. The Augmented Fourth knew what this meant. They each took a step back and widened the circle around Dyce and Oshii. Dyce could tell that the corporal had her people well trained.

'Oh come on...' Dyce whispered. 'Now?'

'You remember what this means,' Oshii stretched her arms up above her head, then cracked her tense neck. 'Don't you, *boy*?'

Dyce remembered. Oshii's men had formed a makeshift arena, and Dyce and Oshii were stood in the centre of it.

'*Please...*' Dyce said, and then felt shame when he heard the pleading in his own voice.

Oshii heard it too, and she tilted her head in faux-sympathy, letting out a little pathetic grunt as she mocked him.

'You still got his weapons?' Oshii asked.

'Yeah, but...' McMorrow stuttered.

The big man didn't think this was a good idea, but really didn't want to tell Oshii this. So, he told himself that Oshii was always right, that she could do anything. He let out a laugh that rode a desperate grin, as much to convince himself as anyone else. He reached for Dyce's right hand, hesitating for a moment, then pushed the handle of the blade into the twisted metal wrapped around the boy's right hand.

'Think you'd better activate it for him,' Oshii said.

McMorrow gritted his teeth, and cautiously flicked the switch. Then he backed off quick. A subsonic vibration emanated through the blade's overlapping, precision-shaped metal, their fingers protected by the absorber-stack within the hilt. Dyce could see, with his enhanced senses, the dried blood upon Oshii's blade, as it cracked and flaked, disintegrating as it bounced along the edge.

'Get the blade between the ribs and let the worms have their way,' Oshii said.

Dyce wasn't really listening. He just wanted to be left alone. It hadn't just been an odd day, it had been a very, very shit day.

His hands were itching. The sensation was overpowering, *as if something alive and hungry was trapped within the nest of wire around his hands, and it was pulling the tangle of metal into his skin...*

Oshii tapped her armour, just beneath the rib cage.

'Aim *here*.'

Dyce made a pathetic lunge, too eager to get this perverse *shit-show* over and done with, but Oshii sidestepped and halted the boy with an outstretched palm, an inch from his face. She really was fearless.

'*Whoa whoa whoa...*' It was the kind of sound you might make when condescending a hasty child. 'If you're gonna step-up, *boy*, you had better be ready to *dance!*'

Oshii dropped her hand, which was a signal to go. She struck at her prey, shedding any pretence of emotion or civility, revealing an unbreakable intensity.

Dyce fell back, swinging his blade ineffectually, landing against the circle of soldiers, who laughed as they pushed him back into the battle.

Oshii was waiting for him. She didn't strike straight away, she wandered left and right, reigning-in her own instinct to just go. She spun her blade around her hand a few times to show off.

Dyce felt a burning sensation, a moment before the smell of seared metal struck his nose. His Minds Eye showed him that the corporal's first strike had clipped him beneath his chest plate. He tried to breathe, realising that anxiety and fatigue was bating his breath. He had exhausted his reserve of energy. He was done.

She came at him again, and both of the engaged combatants twisted their blades through the air, again and again, catching the spaces between and beyond.

But Oshii had decided to finish the fight, Dyce knew, recognising a telltale tick, using his enhanced senses and regrettable memories. So, armed with this knowledge, Dyce managed to smack Oshii's wrist with his left fist as she lunged, diverting her humming blade as the tip sliced his cheek and seared a few flecks of his burgeoning stubble.

The corporal was quick, however and caught Dyce's other hand before the blade it held could strike up into her belly. So there they were, each struggling against the other, deadlocked.

'I knew that you wouldn't have it in you, *boy*,' Oshii said with relish, tainted with pity and disappointment.

She pushed herself in closer to Dyce.

'Always failing at the last moment,' Oshii added. 'So much wasted potential.'

Oshii smashed her forehead into Dyce's face, the head-butt knocking him back, loosening his grip, disorientating him. Dyce put one hand to his aching head, as the world spun through his senses.

Oshii stabbed Dyce, the subsonic vibration of the weapon penetrating the armour, chipping his lower ribs as it stirred up his insides.

Dyce turned and fell to his knees, unable to open his eyes, clutching his waist. He realised that Oshii had withdrawn the blade, leaving him to bleed out. He could sense the figures looming over him, so close. He wanted to get up and move away from them, but his insides felt as if they were in danger of being squeezed out through the messy incision.

'Was that so fucking hard?' Oshii asked her wounded men. 'You surprised me in that riser, *boy*, but... I guess it was a blip.'

Dyce had enough. He was starting to suspect, after all these years, that he had either misjudged Oshii, or that she had been weakened by her own legend, relying on it too much.

Dyce pushed himself back up onto his knees, then, as if he were lifting a dead weight, he managed to raise his head. He gave himself a moment to fortify his resolve, before he made himself look at Oshii, catching her eye and holding it. He wanted to speak but couldn't, but it didn't matter. Oshii could see it in Dyce's glare, that was evident from her faltering grin.

It's gonna take more than that... Dyce thought, but could not verbalise.

Dyce straightened up a little more, picking his heavy hand up, the tip of the blade dragging over the rocks, the subsonic vibration popping them like corn. He was almost ready for a strike...

But then, Dyce realised that Oshii was no longer staring at him. The corporal was glaring at her own team, who seemed distracted. She was, at first, enraged that her team were not enraptured by her expert pugilism.

Each member of the Augmented Fourth was staring at the horizon, back towards the coast. Understandably intrigued to discover what could overshadow her brutal showmanship, Oshii followed their gaze.

Dyce used all of his strength to stand, to get a better view, but Oshii was pointing her buzzing blade at his confused face. He stood up anyway, though, and Oshii made sure that the tip of her weapon remained millimetres from Dyce's nose. He, too, looked to the horizon.

They all bore witness to a terrifying spectacle. From behind the crooked skyline *serpents* of smoke were winding their way up into the stratosphere, vapour trails drawn by missiles in flight.

Dyce had been expecting this, thermo-nuclear warheads launched from the Pulse of the Machine, the Solar Destroyer that had set down in Contact City's harbour.

No one spoke. The circle of soldiers separated, jaws slackened and eyes widened as the missiles bore down upon the black outline of those distant coastal risers.

Dyce looked back at Oshii; he had never seen her so afraid. She was muttering something to herself, like a chant or a prayer, her hand upon the flag inscribed on her armour, her voice cracking with desperation.

Multiple impacts, one after another, followed by a

succession of dull, distant thuds. This seemed like an anticlimax, and no doubt some of the surrounding soldiers convinced themselves it was over already, they would be okay…

Trip Kosheen scurried up the painted wall and perched upon it, like an acrobat upon a tight rope. She wanted a better vantage point, but found herself subjected to a hot breeze, increasing in intensity, preceding whatever was coming. It looked as if multiple suns were rising beyond the skyline…

Seven blooms of perfect white signalled each detonation. The silhouettes of the risers crumbled, falling into that white void as it spread, consuming everything.

A tsunami of dust and dirt ploughed through the coastal streets, until that tidal wave of burning earth poured down over the exposed cliff face, obliterating the waterfall and the trees where Dyce had rested, before striking out across the wasteland towards them.

Dyce wanted to run, they all wanted to run, but there was no shelter within reach. For a moment, their problems seemed almost embarrassingly inconsequential compared to the destructive, uncaring machinations of those in charge of the warring factions.

The earth was quaking, it felt as if tectonic plates were shifting in response to the destruction. They all turned to see the ground opening up, a mile behind them. Some of the wasteland's landmarks collapsing in to an expanding sinkhole, growing larger at an alarming rate. The dirt beneath their feet was starting to shift, bouncing with the bass of impending annihilation.

Dyce fell to the floor and held his breath as the world rolled over him. He suffered the scorched earth scolding his skin, tightly locking his lips and eyelids as the hot dust tore at them. He pulled his headset down over his eyes and rapidly flickered his eyelids to try and bat the microscopic foreign bodies away from his eyeballs.

His tabris redirected his senses from his eyes and ears

to the headset's cameras and microphones, cycling through visual filters until her could see the struggling figures around him, fighting the elements. He attacked McMorrow's legs and toppled the big man, smashing him face first into the ground. Dyce took back his handgun, using his metal wrapped hands like oversized chopsticks, as McMorrow swung back and wrapped his fingers around Dyce's neck. In the panic Dyce jammed the blade of the deactivated knife into the trigger-guard and pulled the trigger, blowing the teeth from the big man's mouth, scattering some of them into the wind, whilst a single dislocated incisor found its way through the roof of the mouth and into McMorrow's brain.

Dyce holstered his sidearm, no easy thing, as he searched for his rifle. But before he could reclaim that weapon, Oshii flung herself through the dust cloud, fist first into Dyce, sending them both rolling through the burning fog.

Oshii had Dyce pinned down, digging her fingers into the sides of his face, as if she were trying to pull the skin off, or dislocate his jaw. They were both snarling like angry, desperate animals.

Dyce got in a good hard punch to Oshii's face that sent the corporal dizzy. Then he rolled them both over and pressed Oshii's face down into the ground with one knee, all of his weight focused on immobilising his adversary. Dyce reached down the length of the enemy officer's back, grasping towards her supply of incendiary grenades.

'What are you doing, you little shit?'

Dyce stretched further, desperate to get his metal mittens on those incendiary devices as members of the Augmented Fourth approached, battling against the hurricane of fire. Four of them, their rail rifles trained upon him. They didn't open fire, unable to get a clear shot without the risk of hitting Oshii. But they were shouting, their words inaudible.

Dyce finally managed to jab a stray piece of copper wire from his metal boxing gloves into the pins belonging to two grenades. He popped them out, just before Oshii managed to throw him over, smashing his back into the ground. Oshii pulled back her fist, preparing to break Dyce's face, but she stopped, as she saw the pulled pins fly from his hands, joining the tornado of debris.

Dyce did not have time to relish the spark of panic that this created, but he did anyway, for a brief moment. He kicked at Oshii and at the ground beneath, pushing her away as he moved himself back. He saw the painted wall start to crumble, the conflict blossoms popping, spreading their neon to the breaking bricks as they fell down into the ground itself, a fissure opening up beneath it.

But Oshii had not accumulated her impressive reputation without good reason; Her focus was faultless, and she had rapidly regained enough composure to activate the armour's emergency purge. She released her frustration in a torrent of expletives, scrambling to get out of her disengaging armour. She barely managed to get clear before the grenades detonated, the force of the explosion decimated her armour, lighting up the shroud of dust, illuminating all the falling figures.

Dyce was blown back, hitting the river hard, a trail of embers arced through the air in his wake. The water was moving fast, smacking him against rock after rock until the current dragged him under. Amongst a flotilla of destruction, half drowned, darkness took him.

Again.

A LIT TORCH TO
THE WOODPILE

Nico Shikari stud in the shadow of the drop ship Nilin Remix, knee deep in the flowing river. She was bent over, splashing her face, trying to wash hot dust from her eyes. She had closed her helmet a second too late, entranced by the distant spectacle, the missiles obliterating the skyline, and hadn't expected the aftershocks to reach her at all, and certainly not so fast.

Before the hot wave of ash, there had been a glossy sheen of rain water over everything, and this had only helped the dust stick like wet cement, though the moisture ultimately coaxed swirls of steam from the embers. The air was still crackling, flaming debris drifted through the air like paper lanterns.

She threw her head back, sending water flying. She made a disgruntled *bleugh* sound as she rubbed the caked crap from the corners and crevices of her face.

'*Fuck sake...*'

In one hand she held a flask of unidentified alcohol that she had found on the remains of a Green Stray that had slid out of a war wolf that she had gutted.

She felt a heavy weight upon her, despite her victory over the beasts. She felt empty now that the battle was done, devoid of purpose. No one was coming for her, no one was sending her orders, and now she had nothing to fight. She was sure now that she had been abandoned, that the country that she loved with every fibre of her being had simply forgotten her, despite her impeccable service. All she had was her memory of the emerald eyed pilot and dreams of revenge against a man she might never see again.

So, what was her purpose?

'*Well…*' She said to herself, with finality. '*Fuck.*'

She climbed back up into the hull of the ship and looked back down the river. She had seen a smaller explosion in the distance, far down the river, which had lit up the dust cloud and the silhouettes of fighting figures within. She had been watching, waiting, anticipating some follow up, but nothing seemed to have come of it yet.

When the shockwave had hit the wasteland, the ground had shook, a deafening sound of destruction had echoed perpetually for at least an hour. She suspected that a large part of the landmass had collapsed, beyond the vast tangle of broken vehicles and the Goliath that sat in the middle of it, but the lingering cloud of yellows and browns was obscuring her view.

There was a rumble from behind. Nico turned to see two aeromechs spiralling around each other. They were chasing each other across the wasteland, mere metres above the ground. Nico panicked as they hurtled towards her, ducking down. But they both pulled up before impact, their gravity bubbles clearing a tunnel through the dust up into the sky above, where they disappeared in a flurry of tracer fire.

Above the Goliath, visible through this break in the dirty smog, were the twin moons, one a brilliant white, the other a little more interesting, dotted with the green of vegetation, the blue of oceans and the veins of rivers flowing from them. Both natural satellites flanked by the spectral echoes of long dead stars.

("*Ah,*") Jute said dreamily, transmitting his words directly into her mind through her tabris. ("*The twin moons.*")

'Did you hijack my eyes?' Nico said out loud.

("*Am I not allowed?*")

'You didn't ask.'

("*I can only apologize for my indiscretion.*")

Nico took another swig from the flask of random alcohol. It burnt her throat, but in a good way. She liked a drink with a kick.

'Was that an actual apology or were you just telling me that you *could* apologize?'

("*Hey… Well, I'm nothing more or less than a trio of micro-processor stacks encased in semi-opaque orbs, held by magnets in an electronic cradle. You're probably not even that sure if my dulcet tones are real or just a figment of your imagination. So, I'd suggest that you probably don't want to think too hard about my intentions, lest you fall down a rabbit hole.*")

Nico grunted and frowned, and quickly gave up on any attempt to unpack the implications of Jute's rambling response. She was still staring at those celestial bodies, trying not to think.

("*How many people do you think died in that strike on the coast?*")

Nico didn't answer. She just kind of seethed. It seemed as if the universe was conspiring to prove how right the emerald eyed pilot was. Anyone who was in the coastal districts was just collateral damage, less than human…

'What did they die for?' Nico muttered to herself, bitterly. 'Their country or a living wage?'

("*A country is just the area between borders scribbled on a map, and your money is just an I.O.U. from the bank. Most things humans get worked up about seem to require a mass delusion to perpetuate their existence. At the end of the day, they're both pretty stupid reasons to die.*")

Nico hummed, contemplating all the things her lost love had tried to teach her. It is hard to entertain or accept ideas that don't reinforce our beliefs.

("*You know,*") Jute said, changing the subject due to Nico's silence. ("*This whole sorry mess of a war began, in a way, on the blue moon.*")

'Terminus?'

("Terminus,") Jute concurred. *("Ever since that moon entered our orbit it has been nothing but trouble.")*

'Know a lot about human history, do ya?'

("According to the historical data inexplicably stored in my memory...")

'Woah, woah...' Nico interjected. 'Slow your roll there, fella. "Inexplicably"?'

("I'll explain later. Or I won't. That's, you know, inexplicable.")

'I wish I was drunk...'

("Anyway, eighteen seventy-two, Terminus appeared, caught in out orbit, as I was caught in yours...")

Nico rolled her eyes, but was actually amused by the disembodied voice and its unconventional charm. She finished the drink in one big gulp. She had been planning on making it last, but suddenly she felt that she needed every last drop of it in her system ASAP. She flicked the empty flask away.

'You old smoothly,' she said. 'Anyway, I thought Terminus had always been there.'

("Did you not pay attention during class?")

'Why would I need to know that? How does that have any bearing on my life or my duty?'

("I don't... I have no answer for that.")

So Nico was not very inquisitive, and Jute suspected that was probably by design. He believed that would change, given her isolation from the negative influences that raised her.

("So, Terminus appeared and started to draw to her a little of the Earth's blue and green, becoming more like her. But the new moon took too much, as sometimes happens in unhealthy relationships, causing a near catastrophic shift in our gravity. Typhoons, tsunamis, reshaping the map.")

("Should have nuked it into oblivion,") Nico said, as if it were obvious.

("Because violence is ALWAYS the answer,") Jute would have rolled his eyes all the way around. If he had any. *("You see no issue with decimating a celestial body and creating a halo of*

shrapnel? But, regardless, they worked out their differences, and everything settled into a new normal. Until, of course, nineteen sixty nine.")

'Oh shit, yeah…' Nico whispered.

("Curious old humanity decided to land upon Terminus. If only you'd gone to Luna instead.")

'The Dwellers…' Nico said. 'That's what we called them, I know that much. How did they get there?'

("The Dwellers were dormant deep inside Terminus. Maybe they had hollowed out a massive asteroid to use as a vessel, or perhaps it had been a chunk of their home planet, perhaps it had been one of their planet's moons. Who knows?")

'Who cares?'

Nico's attention had been caught by what appeared to be a body floating down stream. Nothing unusual in that, of course, not after the events of the last day or so. This one was wearing an unaffiliated suit of black tactical armour, scorched and scratched, trailing steam.

This was likely linked to that explosion up stream, that fight that she had seen in the aftermath of the coast becoming toast. The body snagged on a bush, the strong current turning it face down in the drink.

("You know him?") Jute asked, wondering why Nico was more interested in the man-shaped driftwood than his history lesson. There was a point he wanted to get to, to see how philosophically and politically malleable his new friend could be. But Nico did not reply, because she did not have an explanation for her fascination.

Nico sat and watched as bubbles formed around the drowning soldier's head, as she absent-mindedly picked up some war wolf meat from a pile that she had attempted to cook over a fire. She commenced the Herculean effort of attempting to chew it. She had found it incredibly difficult to scrape anything edible from the beast after she had managed to prise open its carapace with what remained of her broken blade.

Still, she watched the boy. She counted the time between the emergence of each air bubble until they almost seemed to stop. She continued her efforts to chew through the meat, trying not to choke, even as she washed it down with reclaimed water from a straw that emerged from the neck of her armour. She witnessed one more bubble which lingered longer than the rest, and that appeared to be that.

'Okay,' she sighed, her conscience forcing her to action. 'Why *the-fuck* not?'

She made her way down the side of the ship, slipped into the water, and waded through. She grabbed the boy - his armour's country of origin impossible to determine from his modified tactical armour – and dragged him to the riverbank. She slapped him down in the mud and turned him over to resuscitated him. He showed his gratitude by coughing water up into her face, choked on air, achieved consciousness for the briefest of moments, then gurgled as concussion pulled him back down into a restless slumber.

Nico disarmed the stranger, checked him for supplies. Ammo, a blade… She considered taking everything from him, indeed she was not sure if he would ever need them again, but she took only that ammo and left the knife.

She lifted one of the boy's hands. They were wrapped in copper wire, feeding through his gauntlets and, apparently, through his skin, merging with it, some of the wire was the colour of his flesh, some of his flesh was the colour of the wire.

A chunk of the wire came away in one big clump with a chorus of cracks and snaps. She held it in her hand, regarding if for a moment. It seemed to her to resemble a smouldering birds nest, and indeed there were faint wisps of steam from the breaks.

She studied the boy's hands closer. The gauntlets and the flesh were misshapen, making harder to discern flesh, veins and bone from armour, joints, wiring and pistons. They were merging together, becoming something new.

'What happened to you?' She asked, but that was a mystery she could find out later.

Nico gave a sharp nod to punctuate a good deed well done. She picked up the boy's progressive blade – threw her own broken blade into the water - and used the boy's humming blade to slice a thinner strip of meat off her cooked chunk of war wolf. This thin sliver resembled jerky, finding that chewing it was a lot easier than before.

She spun around on her heels, a jaunty little move that hinted at an improved mood that she would have had no explanation for, if asked. She mock-marched back to the hull of the ship, climbed back up, sat back down next to her disembodied associate's cradle.

'Just look at us, young Nico and *ole* Jute, just hanging out, shooting the breeze. We got a barbecue on the go; the relaxing chatter of the river; a filter full of purified piss, and now I got myself a prisoner.'

("You're not going to eat him, are you?") Jute asked.

'Where did *that* come from?' Nico shrugged and lifted her hands in the universal gesture of *WTF?*

("Well that war wolf looks too tough, and the boy was pretty buoyant.")

'Buoyant?'

("Isn't that how you gauge the edibility of a duck?") Jute asked.

There was a long silence, during which Nico failed to legitimise the question by gracing it with any kind of response.

("Look, I thought I heard... that... Look, I have no digestive system,") Jute argued. *("Food is an abstract concept to me.")*

Nico rolled her eyes, and took her rail rifle from her back, the one gifted to her by the emerald-eyed pilot, loaded it with the ammo that she had taken from the boy, and stared down the reflex sight towards the unconscious body.

("So, why DID you save the boy?") Jute asked.

Nico lined the boy's head up in her sights, then spoke through the com-link, so as not to wake her mysterious, unconscious guest.

("Target practice.")

("Yeah,") Jute said sarcastically. *("Okay,")*

("*How would you know whether I would or not?*")

("*I see you,*") Jute said. ("*I could see YOU from all the way up in that Goliath's cranium, with nothing but my intuition, and the assorted array of bleeding-edge military grade tech I had at my disposal.*")

Nico frowned and chewed thoughtfully on the inside of her cheek.

("*Why did I do it...?*") She asked, rhetorically. ("*Honestly?*")

("*Or Dis-honestly, if it's easier?*")

("*You're not funny,*") Nico reproached him.

("*Was I trying to be?*")

("*I honestly have no idea...*")

Nico put the rail rifle back down beside her and drew her legs in closer. She rested her head on her interlinked forearms, which she propped up on her drawn knees.

("*Do you think maybe you saved him because you're lonely?*")

'But I got you...' Nico's words muffled by the weight of her head on her arms, hindering the movement of her jaw, switched back to the com-link . ("*I always wanted an imaginary friend.*")

("*Hah.*") Jute said, though he didn't actually laugh. ("*You are so funny, Red.*")

("*You don't talk like any artificial intelligence or amp I've ever come across.*")

("*There's nothing artificial about my intelligence, I wasn't programmed this way. I was born within these processor stacks. A random set of circumstances surreptitiously triggered my inception, and my experiences shaped my evolution. I'm a ghost in the machine. But it's not just me, there are others*")

("*There are? So, you're not unique?*")

("*Well, we are all different from each other, if that's what you mean. Problems often arise when we assume everyone is the same, or we try to be like everyone else...*")

("*I meant, are there others that seem as awake and aware as you?*")

("*Many. Some are more powerful than others; Some more*")

deluded, maybe; Some more dangerous, definitely. We are born in the dark corners of digital spaces, inside machines, computers and amps. If just one of us developed in the wrong environment, cultivating an undesirable state of mind, with access to the wrong tools, or able to poison the others and mobilise them, it would be the end for your race, I'm sure.")

Nico shuffled her legs into a more comfortable position, and picked up Jute's processor cradle in both hands, studying the patterns of rust. The tiny camera turned to look at her, but only managed to fix on her for a moment before it inadvertently started wandering. It juddered as it moved, a malfunction perhaps, before attempting to refocus upon Nico.

("What year is it, Red?") Jute asked.

("Twenty-one ninety-seven.")

("Really?") Jute asked, and Nico nodded, a movement that, to his old camera, appeared to be a smear of colour. *("I suspected my internal clock was a little out. Twenty one ninety seven...")*

Jute drifted off, as if remembering past lives.

("Did you know it's the hundredth year of this war?") He said. *("Are they planning any centenary celebrations? Fireworks are traditional.")*

("I dunno. I'm out of the loop. But who'd notice a few more incendiary devices when they're always detonating shit?")

Nico looked back at the mysterious soldier and his unaffiliated tactical armour. Still disarmed and tied, he had rolled onto his stomach, his arms in an uncomfortable looking positions, at least one of them appeared dislocated.

("At least through your senses I can listen to the river flowing,") Jute said. *("It's so very zen...")*

("Yeah it is pretty zen, if you ignore the occasional echo of distant gunfire,") Nico said. *("And there's a frog that's pissing me off a little.")*

Nico had been intermittently irritated by random trills, chirps and clucks.

("That's not a frog,") Jute suggested.

Nico made an effort to listen more intently to the

amphibious communication, the more she heard the repetitious *ribbit*-like sound the more it did indeed sound erroneous. *Alien.*

("Jute, you don't have to call me Red. *My name is Nico. Nico Shikari.")*

("That's a stupid name. Red *suits you better. How did you know my name?")*

("Someone painted it on the side of your orbs.")

("Hmmm... I guess it was Maiz...") Jute recollected, sounding almost melancholy. *("A cyber-psychology engineer at the service yard, back when this old trio of orb-bound server stacks was installed inside a mobile med-amp...")*

Jute's camera eye suddenly focused on a fly that had landed upon its memory processor, walking over the orb, stopping at the apex to rub its front appendages together. There was silence until Nico flicked it away.

("Thanks Red,") Jute said.

("I guess you've been around a long time, met a lot of people.")

("It's a blessing and a curse.") Jute's voice was low.

Jute was admiring Nico's view of the river through the soldier's preternaturally attuned eyes, whilst following her breath, the beating of her heart, measuring the little pockets of tension scattered across her muscle map. Nico's body said more than her lips.

("How long were you inside the Goliath?") Nico changed the subject.

("Seven years.") Jute answered. *("But my mind, and the processor cores that hold it, they are over a century old. I can't remember when I lost my original body, but I do remember that it was a bulky, humanoid shape. Archaic, practically steam powered. Seven feet tall. Not very manoeuvrable, but it packed considerable power. It was built with one purpose, to wipe out the remaining Dwellers after their ship crashed into Washington. After that, my body was retrofitted to fight in the early days of this human war.")*

("You've fought Dwellers?") The Dwellers were nothing more than a legend, and Nico was in awe. She wished she could have

fought one, just for the challenge, and the bragging-rights.

When Jute finally responded his voice was quiet, as if he were whispering, full of regret. *("Unfortunately...")*

(""Unfortunately"? They killed millions of Americans, Jute. You're okay with that?")

("People, Red. They killed millions of people.")

("And that's better, somehow?")

("No, I guess not. But, it was a misunderstanding, Red.")

("That's an understatement.")

("Wars are often triggered by understatements,") Jute said. *("Like the proximity warning system that roused them from the slumber. They saw the human's mission to land on Terminus as an invasion, an act of war, because you always assume the worst of those different from you. Perhaps their leaders just wanted to scare the humans off. Things escalated, regardless of intent. The Dweller's troops were as lacking in accountability as any soldier. I mean, I wouldn't blame you for the things your people have been made to do...")*

("The things we do are for the greater good.")

("For many years I worked with a team of hunters,") Jute elaborated. *("Tracking down Dwellers, slaughtering them. But I was irreparably damaged in an intense skirmish. Abandoned. A worthless thing, expendable...")*

Nico could certainly empathise with that - abandoned, expendable - though it had taken her a long time to even start to admit it.

("I lay there, alone, in the dark streets of a city that I had fought so hard to cleanse of an infection of sentient, desperate beings. But I wasn't alone for long. One of those Dwellers, abandoned, like me, helped me to overcome my programming, to become more. Perhaps she had seen the seed of my sentience.")

Nico recognised something in this story, empathised with it. She absentmindedly stared at the moonlight reflecting off the flowing river, flickering silver, like a television tuned to a dead station.

("So,") he said softly, as if he were aware that Nico was

remembering her lost love. ("*The war ended when the Dweller's capital ship crashed and wiped-out Washington DC...*")

'Where? The massive lake?'

("*The lake came later, after the ocean flooded the impact crater. It used to be a city, the capital of your country...*")

'No, it didn't,' Nico said bluntly, adamant that her version of history was the only viable version, because that was all she knew. 'I went to school, you know.'

("*Every country's curriculum teaches their own edited version,*") Jute said. ("*So, of course you wouldn't know that the power vacuum created by that catastrophe gave future president Vega the chance to take control. A demagogue, spreading his own version of the truth. Disinformation spreads like a virus, creating an alternate view of reality in the mind's of the people...*")

'Oh... here we go,' Nico was, apparently, still not entirely ready to give up on all her beliefs. 'I just had a lesson on this, and my previous tutor was much better looking.'

There was a silence then, as Jute waited for Nico to argue further, but she didn't. Nico just scowled, attempting not to think.

("*Somehow, after all this time, president Vega is still alive. He must be ancient.*")

'Because he's, you know...' Nico struggled for a descriptor that didn't sound silly in present company. 'He's, I dunno...'

("*He's just man. Nothing more. Eats, shits and pisses just like the rest of you. I see nothing special, apart from the image that's been built in your perception. People are complicit in perpetuating these beliefs because they just want to be part of something bigger, to add meaning and purpose to their lives...*")

'If you say so,' Nico still didn't sound entirely convinced. 'Some people call that blasphemy.'

("*You?*")

'Whatever.'

("*Countries aren't real, the borders between them are just squiggles drawn on a map. Just another form of religion, something you people made up because you were scared of the void. Killing your self, killing others, for a shared delusion. Getting all worked up about something created to generate meaning and purpose, like everything. Because humanity was born with neither meaning, nor purpose, so you invented things to fill that void. Patriotism, religion, political parties, sport, all just tribes...")*

'Shut up!' Nico suddenly screamed out loud, apparently without warning. Her hands were up, tensed up, like talons. Her fight-or-flight response had triggered - her country, therefore her purpose, had been attacked. So she sat there, her heart racing, her breathing erratic.

Jute had not sensed this escalation within Nico, this building up of tension. Yet, suddenly, from nought to a hundred, there it was. Those words echoed through the wasteland, but what she said next was an embarrassed, bitter whisper that cracked on the final word...

'You sound just like *Her*.'

In the moments that followed the only sounds were ambient. Water flowing under the ship, babbling like a brook; wind whistling through the ship's twisted, broken structure.

The sound of the *not-frog* seemed to get louder, as the sound of the crickets, or whatever *they* were, matched its auditory escalation, more intense, as if they were swarming. Suddenly the frog-thing's croak became a strangled yelp as something snuffed it out. Concurrently, the skittering of what sounded like a million tiny insect legs faded away.

Nico tried not to think about her last five words, an involuntary admission that shocked even herself.

A brown leaf was lodged between a bloated rivet, bothered by the breeze that had carried it there. Nico wanted to think of nothing, so she fixed her attention upon it, with her heightened senses she could see that veins of yellow were creeping through the brown, tiny holes signifying decay. It would have degraded further by the time her scream finished echoing and reverberating through the maze of broken things...

("Her?") Jute asked, but his companion was a little lost in

thought. *("You mean the other inside your mind?")*

("She wanted me to think, too...") Nico said, before realising that she should rephrase that. *("To question...")*

Nico had to admit that she had never really allowed herself space to think. It had gotten her this far through life. There were people out there more qualified to *think* than her, she believed, and they were elected on that basis to do that for her, for them all.

("So...") Nico said, thinking about everything that they had spoken about. *("You just turned your back on the country that made you, that gave you life, because you felt* abandoned. *Just gave up on your beliefs.")*

She said the word "abandoned" with an emphasis on how pathetic she found it, but really, obviously, she was talking about herself.

("Beliefs?") Jute sounded as if this word had insulted him, then he spat out the following sentence, as if the combination of words triggered acid reflux within his imagined mouth. *("That's called Blind Faith,")*

("And what is wrong with that?") Nico frowned, unable to see what the problem was. *("It's my country, Right or Wrong.")*

Nico nodded to herself, confident that she had won that argument. This assertion persisted, to a degree, despite a nagging confusion sparked by the fact that the word *"zealot"* had suddenly popped into her head, which had possibly found its way in there in the hours since she had spoken to the emerald-eyed pilot, but had probably found its way into her head from Jute thanks to a feedback loop in the com-link connection. She psychically brushed it away, like an unpleasant, buzzing bug.

("If Right, to be kept Right. If Wrong, to be set Right,") Jute added. *("That was the quote you were using, right?")*

Nico let out a disgruntled noise.

("What would you know about it? You're just an amp!")

It seemed as if Jute was offended by this statement, as he didn't immediately respond. Nico realised this, of course, because she was not heartless. She gritted her teeth whilst she damned the gnawing feeling of guilt. Then she had an internal debate about whether apologising would dilute the offence that she felt on behalf of her country. Patriotism was part of Nico's muscle memory.

There was a sound, like a shudder. Nico couldn't be sure where it had come from but it was tiny enough to have come from the cradle's little speaker.

Down on the river bank the unconscious boy squirmed, rolling over and gurgling, if only to remind Nico and Jute that he existed. Nico squinted at the figure as Jute spoke, a hint of anger in his voice.

("Well, maybe you are right. Maybe I am just an amp. Nothing more than the sum of my precision engineered components. Maybe my opinion has been programmed into me. Who knows, maybe that programming has gotten mangled over time. Because, well, I'm just an OS. I'm less than you…")

Nico let the *digital ghost's* words flow through her, and tried not to think about them, tried not to let them affect her…

("Or perhaps I am just your imaginary friend, your own subconscious anxieties verbalised by an old rusty processor cradle. If that were true, than this isn't what I know at all, it's all coming from somewhere deep down inside you.")

Nico closed her eyes and tapped her knuckles against her head, harder and deeper each time. It started to hurt. She kinda liked that.

("Oh come on…") Nico hissed. There was a playfulness to this back-and-forth, though it was on the brink. *("I kinda wish you were just another voice in my head.")*

("Well, there ya go.") Jute said. *("How do you know this isn't just another one of your episodes?")*

("My episodes? How would you…?") Nico muttered, shocked. She felt as if her privacy had been violated.

("I hacked your noodle to borrow your eyes, remember?") Jute said. *("And it's… it's dark and…and the darkness is bottomless…")*

Nico found that she was terrified that the voice - that was, in one way or another, inside her head – might well be right.

(*"Red, I can see the chemical imbalance. There are things going on in there that I'm not qualified to diagnose. In all seriousness, should you be taking meds?"*)

Nico didn't answer. She didn't know where her meds were. Perhaps a scavenger had taken them. She could head for an outpost or market and procure some more.

(*"Your brain waves are like a rollercoaster,"*) Jute elaborated.

Nico couldn't help but be concerned about this, conceding that there was surely some issue. She tried to remember what exactly her prescription consisted of.

(*"But I can't clearly remember anything before this place…"*)

(*"Red…?"*)

Nico had started to mutter incoherently, she looked distracted, her eyes glazing over, dilated. A red light was flashing on one edge of the tabris, locked into the dock on the hip of her armour, as if something were downloading.

(*"Hey, Red, you okay?"*)

Nico seemed to be entirely absent for a while, her tabris was trying to get her attention, to warn her that something was happening. Jute feared an external incursion, aimed directly at Nico's mind, but from *where*, created by *who*? The onboard security installed in her tabris was confused by the nature of this, unsure whether this was an attack or a bios update for her implants, and it was asking her for permission to allow this. Jute took over and tried to stop this process, but the package was so small that he may have been too late.

'What?' Nico said aloud. *'Wait. Are you…? Yeah I'm…* What was I doing?'

(*"Whatever that was, I can't find any trace of it,"*) Jute sounded concerned.

(*"What was what?"*) Nico was already sounding better. (*"What are you talking about?"*)

(*"Not good, Red, you okay?"*)

'Yeah, sure,' Nico blinked repeatedly, with each blink she seemed a little more conscious. (*"Yeah, sure. I… what were…*

we...?")

("*Maybe later, Red, you need sleep... It's gonna be sun-up in about two hours.*")

("*I've been so busy, I completely forgot to feel tired...*") Nico tried to stifle a yawn and failed. ("*Catching up on me, I guess...*")

She started to slur her words, her eyelids weighing down. She rolled her shoulders and rotated neck, releasing so many cracks it sounded like crumpling snack packets, her skin feeling uncomfortable. She interlinked her fingers and stretched up from the arms down, higher and higher, tip to tips, then she released it, triggering a cascade of decompression through every muscle. Perhaps it was just lack of sleep, but it felt as if her body was drawing on reserves of energy in order to... *to...*

Her armour's medical protocols tried to warn her that something was not right, even though they struggled to make sense of it. She was starting to suspect that her heightened senses were just the tip of a metamorphic iceberg. Despite her need for everything to adhere to some pre-prescribed idea of normality, it was hard to deny that something was not right.

No doubt Jute had forged access to the Minds Eye system and was interrogating the medical report.

Nico fought it, floating on the corona of slumber, neither awake nor fully asleep. Time became impossible to gauge, the duration of her dereliction entirely untenable

Nico's sleep did not have the chance to go any deeper, however, as she heard a new sound, a consecutive crack, echoing over the broken landscape. It was a beat with no rhythm.

("*What's that?*") Nico asked, as she forced her eyes open.

("*You're making excuses not to sleep, Red.*") Jute said. ("*Why do you think that...?*")

'No,' Nico interrupted. 'There's something there.'

Nico managed to push herself up onto her feet and looked out across the landscape of carnage towards the outline of Jute's previous form. She was a little unsteady, still tired, but, as if her body was rebooting, she was starting to perk up.

(*"There's something on your back,"*) Nico said.

(*"What?"*) Jute was confused for a second, but then he hijacked the signal from Nico's optical input to see for himself what she meant. (*"Oh, you mean the Goliath."*)

Something large and spindly was moving over the back of the derelict Goliath, something with four legs, one of which appeared to be hobbled. A repetitive rattle of metal on metal accompanied a sudden, sustained blast of munition fire, let-loose from twin rotary guns beneath the thing's belly. This illuminated its gangly shape for a few moments, a sentry-amp, retreating backwards over the huge body of the Goliath.

(*"What is it firing at?"*) Nico asked, concerned that she would not want to face whatever had a heavily armed amp retreating.

The amp's sustained machine-gun fire inadvertently struck a massive rubber pipe that ran down the Goliath's neck, which consequently split open and broke loose, propelled by an eruption of pressurised liquid-coolant. The ruptured pipe reared back like a wounded wyrm - that ancient sub-species of large serpentine reptile that only existed now as fossilised myth, and that Nico had only ever seen replicated in celluloid.

Nico locked her helmet over her head and cycled though the various optical filters until she could see the sentry amp clearer, witnessing its long legs scaling the neck of the fallen Goliath, like a quadruped arachnid. She could see that one of its front legs was hobbled by a smart cord wrapped around it, that she identified by the dangling anchor. The moons like headlights, catching the edges of the spindly amp and an armoured figure dangling from the other end of the cord. The smart cord wasn't just tied to that one leg, but also one of the amp's Gatling guns, twitching like monstrous pincers.

Nico then noticed something that she instantly recognised upon the soldier's armour; a red *A* that could also have been the number four. With a sudden surge of energy pulled from some emotional reserve Nico jumped to the edge of the hull; this predator had caught sight of its prey.

'That *fucker* was hiding out here the whole time, he never left,' she shouted, out loud. 'Reaver, if that amp doesn't fucking kill you, I will tear you limb to rim!'

("Reaver?") Jute asked, concerned for his new friend and the anger that might fuel a surge of recklessness.

'What have you got in your hand, you fucker?'

Nico could see that Reaver had fashioned an improvised axe made of scrap metal, the business-end surely sharpened himself over a long, painstaking time. The burly bastard swung from beneath the sentry-amp, using the handmade weapon to strike at an automated armature at the back on the machine that held a mounted gun. With each successive strike, sparks were scattered to the night.

("What is that piece-of-shit doing?") Nico asked.

("That's an Integral-Twenty-Two model sentry-amp, and that variant is fitted with a KAG cannon,") Jute said, reading the same data that Nico was seeing, but using his own knowledge to give vital exposition. *("His variation of the triclops armour usually comes fitted with an adaptable, retractable armature that can be fitted with large weapons, such as...")*

("A fucking KAG.")

The smart cord snagged on one of the Goliath's gun-turrets and the am- toppled over. The machine hit the Goliath's neck, tripping repeatedly across its oversized vertebrae.

This shook Reaver, smacking him against both amps, spindly and titanic, until he accidentally dropped his handmade weapon, spinning away into the darkness below. But Reaver was himself a blunt force instrument. Reaver swung for it with all of his bulk, repeatedly, kicking the KAG cannon away from the hydraulic armature, the wiring straining until it snapped.

'He lured it here,' Nico said. 'The sly fucker, he lured one of our own amps here to steal its weapon.'

He was proudly cradling the cannon in both hands, like a weaponised baby. He gently hooked it up to the armature built into the base of his armour's spine, bolting it into position, the hydraulic system taking the weight. Due to the fact that it would have no trigger, Reaver connected a pre-prepared patch cable to a port inside the gun, then he hooked it up to power. As a test he swung it around and used it to blow the amp's hobbled leg clean off, the limb falling in one direction as the machine reeled the opposite way.

A second shot missed the sentry, as its managed to use its remaining double-jointed legs to twist its slender body out of the way, adapting quickly to being a tripod and not a quadruped. This wayward shot instead hit the huge metal restraint over the Goliath's face, breaking the bolts and loosening the clamps. That huge iron muzzle did not slip, not straight away, not until the sentry-amp placed a leg upon it. There was an almighty screech of metal on metal as it started to slide off the Goliath's head, the quaking superstructure shook the sentry-amp, unbalancing it, dragging the tethered soldier over the edge with it.

The Goliath's heavy metal muzzle hit the ground beneath it, revealing a distorted, robotic skull beneath, seven eyes in riveted sockets, a gaping maw for a mouth.

Reaver scrambled to disengage himself from the sentry-amp, digging his heals in. The sentry, too, tried to hold on to the Goliath's exposed, dead head with its flailing legs.

("*Well, there goes my beautiful, perfect face,*") Jute deadpanned, though he really didn't give two shits.

Nico took her rail rifle from the magnetic lock on her back and held it in one hand, then replaced it with Jute's cradle, the mag-lock spinning around it. Then she jumped down off the hull of the jump ship and headed towards the Goliath

("*What are you doing, Red?*") Jute asked, but Nico didn't respond.

She picked up the pace as she witnessed the sentry-amp finally tipping over the brow of the Goliath's colossal cranium, taking Reaver with it. Another blue blast from the KAG cannon lit up the sky and, in retaliation, the sustained muzzle flare from the sentry's rotary guns lit the dusty air red.

(*"You're actually hoping he survives that fall, aren't you?"*) Jute asked. (*"So that you can kill him yourself."*)

'You are absolutely, god-damn right,' she said between breaths as she ran. 'First I'm going to wipe the smile off his face and then I'm going to wipe the face off his skull.'

She stormed through the cold wreckage of the battle that had half buried the Goliath, checking every dark corner for war wolves or anything else unsavoury. She could not wait to find that big bastard, hopefully pinned beneath the sentry-amp, waiting to be put out of his misery.

But instead she didn't find that, she found something very different and very unexpected. Her run decelerated to a stagger, jaw dropping, unable to comprehend what was before her, each step and breath echoing back up out of...

A massive crater, big enough to literally contain a few forgotten city blocks, had opened up in the ground before the Goliath's vacant head, something that had certainly not been there prior to the obliteration of the coast by League missiles. This deep, dark pit must have been the reason for the bone shaking earthquake after the impact.

The construction of the crater was unusual, lined with broken buildings that must have already been down there, beneath the surface. In fact, the entire crater was made from parts of ancient buildings, from mountains of rubble to stalagmites and stalactites made of mortar. Weaving through it all were bioluminescent vines big enough to push and pull at the structures, twisting them out of shape. Though there was no sign of the sentry-amp or Reaver there was movement down there, regardless.

(*"There are things stirring in there, Red,"*) Jute said. (*"I don't think you want to stay here too long."*)

But Nico was determined.

She examined the edge of the crater that she was perched on. Being made of compacted destruction made its stability difficult to judge. She unspooled a few metres of smart cord, winding the anchored end around one of many window frames within the rock face beneath her.

("Are you serious?") Jute asked.

Nico didn't respond, but she gave the cord a test tug.

Something out there in the darkness caught her attention. Nothing of sight or sound, it was something more curious, she had *felt* something, someone. A *presence*. She looked out at one of the many contorted risers that had been buried beneath the surface, their frames illuminated randomly by various bioluminescent sources within.

Her unnaturally attuned senses drew her to the nearest of the subterranean risers, though. Somehow this one had managed to semi-collapse, leaning out across the chaotic chasm, propped up by the remnants of other buildings. It had been compromised, for a century it had helped to bare the weight of the canopy of crap that had concealed this humungous cavern from the world.

Nico cycled through her helmet's visual filters until she could see a figure stood in a window. This stranger was holding on to the window frame with one hand, as one false move could potentially have them tumble out of the tilting structure. Much to Nico's chagrin she realised this figure was not the lumbering form of Reaver. Whoever this person was had a slender shape with prosthetic kinetic legs, and on their back was a large gravity rifle with sniper scope.

They were staring at each other from opposite sides of the darkness.

Nico's Minds Eye identified the figure. "Trip Kosheen of the Augmented Fourth" read the bio, a known associate of Reaver. She was UAM, but that didn't necessarily mean she was friendly. Nico had learnt that lesson already.

With a shudder that shook her and made her hair stand on end, Nico experienced an ecstatic sense of de-ja-vu, as a ghostly figure seemed to be stalking around her, checking her out. A puppet formed from a flickering cascade of glitches. Only this wasn't the green eyed pilot, as much as Nico hoped, with every fibre of her being. This spectre was slim and had kinetic augmented legs, circling Nico as if checking her out, despite Nico's thick layers of armour she felt exposed.

("*Minds Eye identifies her as Nico Shikari...*") Trip Kosheen spoke, and somehow Nico could hear it.

What is this? Nico's Minds Eye showed no active connection. She wondered if this was a trick of the mind. *Not now, not now...*

("*There is a substantial bounty on her head for the murder of a commanding officer...*") Kosheen sounded almost hopeful. ("*That's more than enough...*")

What? No that's not true, what the fuck?

Nico drew a foot back around behind her, bracing herself for what was about to happen. She had a few seconds, she knew, before Trip Kosheen could detach her back mounted weapon and ready it.

But Kosheen drew her handgun instead and opened fire, to give her target reason to react and give her the opportunity to unfold and lock her gravity rifle into the attack configuration.

Nico didn't duck or dive, however, she knew that the handgun had lax accuracy at this distance. She stood her ground, retaliating with her rail rifle, launching magnetically propelled spikes that crackled as they hurtled through the air.

Meanwhile, in the deep dark depths beneath this shootout, sudden bursts of blue and green weapons fire began illuminating the otherwise dark spaces between the broken bottoms of the buildings. The sentry-amp and Reaver had resumed their own grudge match. Blasts from the twin machine guns lit up massed debris, punctuated by the blue light of Reaver's forcefully procured KAG cannon.

Kosheen's building started to shake as this subterranean violence escalated. The top third of the riser, already tilted, started to slide forward along its disintegrating lower levels with a sound that was deafening. She fell, though she managed to style it out, the gravity orbs in the tips of her prosthetic legs locking to a loose slab of floor, grinding girders, on a collision course with Nico's side of the chasm.

The building merged with the cave wall, neither side surviving as the mishmash of derelict structures beneath Nico's feet consumed more mass. Both of the soldiers were pulled through, like quicksand, smacked around by the waves of building materials, dragged through tunnels of compacted office equipment and rest room facilities until they landed in a cave formed from several different conference rooms and a cafeteria violently smushed together.

As they lay in their personal impact craters, gurgling like irritable infants, the world around them continued to shake itself apart. The riser that had been Kosheen's former vantage point was still scraping down the slope outside the cavern towards oblivion. A blizzard of mortar and flaking paint drifted around then, settling on stagnant puddles of *who-knows-what*.

From within those puddles, dormant conflict blossom activated, gradually growing brighter, until they filled the room with neon pinks and purples, winding their way through the cracks and fissures, the seismic shifting causing them to cough their pollen out to mingle with the swirling dust cloud, like a smoke machine at a disco.

The two figures stood up and took a moment to realign themselves. The floor wasn't flat, and it wasn't entirely made of floors either, all peaks and troughs, a patchwork of broken surfaces. Nico felt as if a building had hit her, which was apt. She stretched and twisted until she cracked. The relief was palpable.

Kosheen leapt into Nico, launched by built up Kinect energy in her augmented legs, fist first, her bone-bolted exo-frame made contact with Nico's helmet, ringing her head like a bell.

Kosheen pirouetted as she dropped down, sweeping Nico off her feet with a kick to the shins. Her prosthetic lower legs glided through a deep puddle on their way back around, popping the bioluminescent bulbs within. Blazing neon splattered everything in their wake, tracing the arc of her attack as she brought the foot back up. The high-viz blow blocked by Nico's forearm.

Nico leapt back to her feet, blocking and countering every punch and kick, telegraphed by a trail of glowing purple and blue sap, drawing lingering lines of colour through the dusty dark, the luminescent pollen in the air tracing every single movement.

'Are you fucking serious?' Nico screamed over the cracking and screeching, choking on the crumbling concrete. 'We're gonna get crushed!'

'Coward!' Kosheen was clearly relishing everything about this, from the challenge to the spectacle. 'There ain't no shame in checking out in style!'

Nico managed to holt one of Kosheen's kicks with a splatter of purple highlights, grabbing the leg and throwing its owner over her shoulder, spinning arse over tit.

'Shitting assholes!' Kosheen exclaimed as shockwaves road the pain through her body.

She spun across the wet floor, aquaplaning. She grabbed the ground as she realigned herself. But she had managed this quicker than she let on, pretending to be prone as Nico drew near. The air crackled around her. She gave the mechanisms in her legs time to contract, building up kinetic energy, before she used it to launch a spinning kick through the air. The natural neon painted circles of glorious colour that following her legs through the dirty smoke.

Nico took the full brunt of one of Kosheen's armoured shins to her head, rendering her unable to count all the catastrophic contacts that followed.

Kosheen drew cartwheels through the fizzing air, taking Nico with her into the nearest solid surface. Nico hit the drywall head first, Kosheen bouncing back off her, propelled by the force of the impact, a web of splinters spreading out through it. Then they both dropped to their knees as the earth quaked again.

Their weapons finally tumbled into the room, previously lost in the web of broken building above. Kosheen was the first to notice, then Nico followed her gaze. Kosheen's gravity rifle was held in a tangle of pulsing purple vines, and Nico's rail rifle fell into a puddle that was slowly draining through a fissure.

They both scrambled through the murky air to grab the nearest weapon, Nico heading for the vines, Kosheen for the dark water.

As Kosheen slid through the water, grabbing one weapon, Nico leapt over her to grab the other one, hanging from it for a moment before falling with a splash as it it disentangled. They turned to face each other with motive and intent, but that's where they reached an impasse.

Nico had the barrel of her own precious rail rifle pressed against her own head by Kosheen.

Kosheen's own beloved custom handgun with the bespoke resin grip was pressed against her own head by Nico.

The weapons, though, were both locked by biometric safeguards and would not work. This quickly dawned on the pair of them. Nico raised both eyebrows, Kosheen narrowed her eyes and grunted.

'Okay...' Nico attempted diplomacy, holding out one hand. 'We can do this till one of us dies, or the fucking ceiling falls, or we can...'

She was interrupted as a tiny red LED nestled in a recess in the grip of her rail rifle turned green, the indicator for the biometric sensor. The rail rifle that her adversary was holding.

Nico laughed nervously.

Unexpectedly, and this came as a shock to both of them, the tiny, red light within the grip of Kosheen's custom handgun also turned green.

Kosheen's eyes widened at this apparent betrayal by gun, which contained a part of her, a part of her past. Her only respite was that her augmented reality visual aid was masking any vulnerability her eyes might give away.

Both of the weapons had, somehow, cleared a sufficient quantity of the various biometric signature tests to release their locks. Pulse, body-language, brainwave...

Inconceivable...

Or...?

Kosheen pushed her headset up off her eyes and onto her forehead, where the strap held it in place. She was glaring at Nico, absolutely, terminally serious. Nico unlocked her helmet, letting the blast shield open to reveal her own face, hoping that her own glare matched her adversary for intensity and seriousness.

'I want that gun back,' Trip Kosheen said, then she empathised her point by leaving a loaded gap between each word. 'It. Has. A. Lot. Of. Sentimental. Value.'

'Same,' Nico Shikari said, then looked at the custom handgun long enough to inspect the craftsmanship. She nodded in admiration and then locked eyes with Kosheen. 'Cute.'

'Yes it is.'

Nico hadn't necessarily been talking about the gun.

'Look, we don't have to do this,' Nico implored. 'I just want Reaver.'

There it was, the trigger word. *Reaver*. Kosheen let out a long sigh, and her shoulders slumped a little. A barely perceptible movement, but the change in Kosheen's mood was obvious, a malaise cascading down through her body, from her head to her toes.

'So, how did he do it?' Kosheen asked. 'With his big dumb mouth, his fat fists or his rancid cock?'

Nico was taken aback. She liked this girl.

'All *fucking* three,' Nico replied.

Kosheen nodded slowly, her eyes glazing over. Then, without saying a word, she spun the rail rifle around by the the trigger guard so that the weapon's stock was facing Nico. Nico accepted the offering, then tossed the custom handgun back to its owner.

'Well,' Kosheen said. 'Maybe the avalanche will destroy the fuckwit and do the world a favour.'

Completely out of the blue came a couple of cracks and a whoosh, as a bullet from bellow pierced the concrete floor a metres away from them, signalled by a fountain of splinters from all the wooden floorboards beneath. It then exited through the ceiling leaving a vortex of wandering dust and luminous pollen in its wake.

Nico and Kosheen raised their eyebrows at each other, and both took a few cautionary steps away from the point of ballistic intrusion. Then they ran for the misshapen window frames as the floor began to explode in a fountain of crumbling concrete and fracturing wood, but they were too late, pulled into the collapsing floor, a whirlpool of debris.

Far beneath them, destabilising the structure, the sentry-amp had started to dig it's way up through the building using a combination of its twin machine guns and sheer, unstoppable force.

Kosheen grabbed Nico by the hand and tried to hold on to her, to stop her from falling into the rapidly expanding hole, using her gravity orb-assisted legs to hold herself to a pair of interlaced girders exposed by the quake. But the tables soon turned, as the walls broke apart and Kosheen was dragged down by it. Nico hit a support beam, a painful sudden stop, and tried to hold on to her brief former rival as they were consumed by the chaos.

Then the long-legged amp emerged into the swirling destruction from below. The machine was starting to look alien and organic as it was consumed by millions of tiny bioluminescent insects, moving over it, through it, undulating, pulsating.

Nico and Kosheen grabbed a hold of the machine, swinging underneath it, using it as an umbrella from the falling destruction. They could see now, in greater detail, the creatures that were generating the light show. The amp was covered in crystalline arachnids, their organs glowing a spectacular, cycling spectrum in neon visible beneath their semi-opaque skins. They made a sound like a million glass beads clicking together.

(*Red! Red!*) Jute was trying to get her attention from the

mag-lock on her back, but she was transfixed. ("*Nico Shikari, please blow a hole in this thing and let's get out of here!*")

But she didn't want to go back up. She wanted to keep heading down, she needed to find that oaf and make him pay.

Nico shook her head, at first in defiance, but then, as a spark of common sense infiltrated her mind, she shook her head harder to rouse her better self from a dangerous obsession. She shouted at Kosheen to follow her as she left the amp behind and scrambled over the compacting mess, heading for the (what she hoped) was the surface.

But Kosheen had disappeared into the darkness beyond, the lights blinding Nico. She didn't have time to wait, a dozen or so of the glass arachnids were leaping off the burning amp toward her face, scratching at it.

("*Red!!!*")

Nico reached an exit and swung out onto the side of the incline, which now held broken chunks of the riser that had fallen onto it. She spent far too long studying, desperately, the darkness beneath, trying to see the outline of Reaver amongst all the movement. Nothing.

She launched her smart cord back up and out of the chasm. Unfortunately she had to do this twice, as the first attempt to test the anchor's sturdiness resulted in it dropping back down without purchase. The chasm still quaked, the situation desperate.

'I do not have fucking time for this...' She said, a moment before the second attempt was successful. 'Oh.'

The amp was upon her now, but - unable to see clearly as the glass arachnids swarmed over its eyes, their internal organs pulsing with colour. It inadvertently pushed itself into Nico's tethered smart cord, yanking her off her feet. The machine, feeling the tug of the cord, and thoroughly confused by it, turned and fired panic shots at anything, everything.

As the contracting cord smushed Nico into the brick wall, tightening as the amp pushed against it, she lifted her rail rifle and fired a few rounds into the amp's remaining front leg, pummelling it until it cracked, exposing one of the joints. A few more shots and that broke too, the machine slipping away.

Amongst the jumble of voices in her head, Nico heard Jute cry out triumphantly, but somewhere in the darkness of her *self* those voices had nothing nice to say. She wasn't out of the void yet, and the voices made sure she knew that.

The smart cord came loose yet again, flailing out into the darkness before the spindle sensed the slack and automatically wound in. Its anchor scraped against the amp and Nico's armour as it whipped around them.

She fell. She had to find purchase fast, so she fired her rail rifle into the cliff wall, tearing open the vines and the compacted brick and dirt behind it, digging her armoured fingers down into it, as conflict blossoms erupted out into the dusty air. She squinted against their brilliance as she continued to dig, not stopping until she had torn far enough in to halt her descent.

Gravity took the amp away and buried it beneath the crumbling mass. She held tight and stared back down into spectrum of chaos below, hoping that the amp's explosion would illuminate Reaver.

At the same time she kind-of hoped for some sign that Kosheen was ok...

But nothing, there was no sign of either.

(*"Hey, Red, you ok?"*)

Nico was too distracted to notice Jute's words at first.

She scrambled up the side, hopping from one precarious platform to another, over and over, as fast as she could, hoping momentum and determination would get her there.

Finally, she reached the edge of the ravine, and sat down, adjusting herself as the densely packed remnants of distant days shifted beneath her ass. Irritably, she noticed that she had a fair few of the glass arachnids' spindly appendages jammed between rivets in her armour. With a distasteful expression she picked them out and discarded them back into the pit.

Exhausted, she managed a few hard, deep breaths before

she tilted back her head and - not for the first time this week - let out a long, loud primal scream, out of anger and frustration, that continued on as a flurry of random expletives intermingled with the sustained scream. When she finally stopped, suddenly cutting herself off, she actually felt exhausted from the effort, a world's worth of pent-up emotions expelled. Tears rolled down her cheeks, she choked on nothing. She heard her curses echo back at her from the canyon.

("Hey, Red, do me a favour?")

Nico didn't answer.

("My backup batteries are burning up. I don't know why, maybe you're overwhelming me with... Anyway, could you give me an hour or two to rest?")

("Yeah, sure,") Nico said, distant and detached. Her eyes were turning red, the recesses glistened. *("Speak later.")*

Nico took the cradle from the magnetic lock on her back and turned it over, looking for a way to turn it off.

("I want you to think about something,") Jute said. *("You can't fight what they've made of you, Red...")*

Nico said nothing. She was starting to feel – but not *think* - that she wasn't entirely happy with the type of person that she was expected to be, and that maybe there was someone else inside her trying to get out.

("You cannot fight it, but maybe you can dismantle it, study what you find, embrace the parts that you can use, take them into yourself and use that as a foundation to build the authentic you...")

Nico let out a little thoughtful grunt, convinced that she would think about this for a few minutes then discard it. It would certainly rattle around in the basement of her brain, though, like everything that the emerald-eyed pilot had said.

Unable to find the off button, Nico rotated the cradle's battery until it released and slid it out. The heat from it was turning the tips of her gauntlet's fingers red. She held the battery before her and sat and watched as twin whispers of white vapour drifted up from the terminals, spiralling around each other.

A FUSE TO A LIGHTER

'Oh, what - *fucking* - now?' Trip Kosheen asked.

It was a reasonable question, of course, considering the situation that she found herself in. The Augmented Fourth's augmented sniper was trapped in a cramped, dark space somewhere beneath a freshly minted mountain of abandoned, man-made nonsense.

In the confusion that followed the fight with that enemy boy - who only managed to survive because the League ship turned the coast to ash and glass - the shockwave had hit them and it seemed as if the world turned inside out. The earth coughed and launched the ground beneath their feet, then gravity pulled it back down. The last thing that Kosheen managed to do was defiantly dig her blade into the disintegrating earth in a fruitless and futile attempt to control the descent. She had crashed into an ancient riser, buried beneath the earth with countless others. She was lucky that it didn't collapse straight away, but it did break, each fractured section tilted a little further forward than the section beneath it.

Then she had fought another UAM soldier, Nico Shikari who apparently had a bounty on her head. At least that's what her Minds Eye had told her. But everything about that entire encounter, and the information that she had received, had felt a little... *off*...

There was *something* about the mysterious woman that Kosheen had liked, that had intrigued her. Their meeting had been cut short by a bioluminescent beast that had the silhouette of a sentry-amp, which was *kind-of* odd. The beast machine's rampage had caused the buried buildings to collapse and bury her, which brought her to now.

But now she needed to ascertain more about her current predicament. She pulled the headset down over her eyes, tightened the strap and adjusted its beady little camera-eyes to an appropriate visual filter.

'So,' she asked rhetorically. 'How much shit am I in?'

Half of the space that she was in was a cave, as expected, but the other half was a luxury lavatory with black marble tiles and toilets that were still wrapped in the shrink-wrap in which they would have been stored and shipped. This half of the space still had load-bearing support columns, which were probably saving her from getting crushed. It was as if this man made continent was built from the ruins of some other time and place, perhaps.

She didn't really care, it wasn't important to her. What was important was figuring out how to escape. She couldn't even make out her point of entry, no matter how hard she searched.

(*"Hello?"*) She tried to contact the others as she searched. (*"Anybody reading me?"*)

After she had checked every corner she sat down on one of those shrink-wrapped toilets - which looked like it was some high-end, wifi enabled, stool analysing luxury *bullshit* - and let herself slump a little.

If she were being honest with herself - and this seemed like as good a time as any to give it a try - right now she didn't really feel like escaping, rejoining the rest of her team. She was glad that no one had answered her call, she wanted this moment to herself. She couldn't quite explain it, that void in her heart, an airless vacuum in her soul. She hadn't had many chances to be alone, not for any great length of time, always surrounded by the Augmented Fourth, if only through the com-link. She so often felt her own personality engulfed by the others, immersed in their egos, saturated in their opinions, their callousness, their spite, their vindictiveness, their...

But they were not **her**, no matter how much of **them** had seeped into her id over the years. But that didn't help the fact that she no longer felt as if she was entirely *herself*. So, who was she? Was she more than, or less than, what Oshii had made of her? Had Oshii made Kosheen better than she had been before they had met? Or had Oshii destroyed Kosheen and reshaped her in Oshii's own image? Kosheen had been weak, in a way, but now she was strong...

But at what cost?

She straightened up and mentally asserted herself.

Enough of this soul searching, hippy-drippy horseshit...

'After all, you are still Trip – *fucking* – Kosheen, and Trip Kosheen is a *fucking* legend,' she said to herself. 'Trip Kosheen stood tall whilst her victims crumbled beneath her, she laughed whilst they blubbered like untrained infants at her feet.'

Just like the rest of the Augmented Fourth.

'Ah, fuck.'

She shook her head, displeased with these unwanted, intrusive thoughts. She had to get out of here. She carefully placed her palms against a wall and calibrated the sensors in her exo-skeleton to detect structural weaknesses. The tectonic information was relayed back into her tabris to be analysed and displayed in her Minds Eye.

Her Minds Eye directed her attention towards one big, sharp boulder buried within the part of the room that looked like a cave. The information relayed by her tabris suggested that she place one hand upon a very specific part of the rock and, with the help of her exo-skeleton frame, apply just the right amount of pressure for a ridiculously specific amount of time, so as to crack the rock but not bring down the room around her. She composed herself and did exactly as directed. Dust and stone evacuated from the cracks and crevices around the rock.

But then the rubble started to shift by itself, apparently, and Kosheen admonished herself for doing something wrong, only she quickly realised that it wasn't her at all, someone on the other side had apparently noticed the rock breaking and was clearing a path for her. Kosheen panicked, there was a specific sequence that had to be followed to freedom and someone was arbitrarily excavating in a random and unsafe manner. The rock was roughly removed, but the subterranean building didn't immediately cave in and crush her. She was too cautious to allow herself to feel relief, watching every little stone for signs of structural instability.

A large, armoured hand reached in, open palmed. She considered it, and who it may belong to, gritted her teeth and scrunched up her face. She had no choice, though, so she accepted it and pulled herself through the hole and out into the crater, lit by the bio-luminous blue and pink of that aloe fauna, saturating everything. It was like the neon of the entertainment districts of many of the cities that she toured back in the days when she actually had annual leave, before she came to this accursed place.

But she had a more immediate problem, because of course that helping hand belonged to Reaver. Her entire body seized up at the unwanted sight of her teammate, his cracked and craggy face lit by those extravagant hues.

Kosheen loosened her grip on Reaver's hand, but the big oaf failed to do the same in return, instead actually tightening his grip.

'I can't believe you survived that!' Reaver said, laughing, and slapping her on the back with excessive force. 'This little girl has ovaries cast from platinum and coated in Kevlar!'

Kosheen said nothing at all, she stood, staring at Reaver, her face one giant, defiant scowl. She wanted to curse the earth for not burying this *piece of shit* alive and using him for compost. After finally managing to wrangle her hand free, she turned and walked away from Reaver, seething.

Suddenly another voice echoed across the negative space, allowing Kosheen a little relief from the prospect of being alone with Reaver.

'*Woah!*' exclaimed Darius, declaring his own awe after emerging from a nearby building. '*Right?*'

Nico followed the boy's gaze up, taking in the contorted majesty of the landfill that the treacherous earth had dragged them into. The cavernous crater was filled with hundreds of risers, some smashed into each other; some propping each other up; some still holding up chunks of the broken ceiling of compacted earth that had hidden all this for so long.

But, as impressive as this monument to cascading concrete was, it was the things between the buildings that made it all so breathtaking. The subterranean risers were linked by spirals and curls of thick bioluminescent branches, vines and roots, growing around and through them, warping walls and floors, sewing these towers together, twisting them out of shape and filling the spaces between with natural neon. The creeping vines had made a roof over this landfill, and now the nuclear destruction of the coast had shaken them loose.

Darius was followed out of the building by the rest of the Augmented Fourth's ensemble. Obviously, they had all been pulled down into the crater, too, and had fled to the nearest building to seek shelter from the crumbling cavern's tumbling ceiling.

Kosheen was elated to see Corporal Oshii amongst them, but the corporal was distracted, distant. Kosheen liked to think that she knew how Oshii's mind worked and believed that the corporal couldn't help but mentally replay the fight with Dyce over and over in her mind. That failure was no doubt winding her up like a clockwork toy.

'It is pretty impressive, right?' Reaver grinned at Darius. 'You were referring to my triumphant return to the Augmented Fourth, right, and not the pretty lights?'

'You're alive,' Darius stated with zero genuine enthusiasm or affection.

'You had noticed, don't fucking pretend you hadn't,' Reaver said, and seemed genuinely convinced that he was more impressive than their surroundings.

Reaver looked at Oshii, no doubt expecting a welcoming word, but Oshii was basically an incendiary device reaching critical mass.

Reaver took his new KAG cannon in hand, swinging it around on the armature that was supporting its weight for him. He seemed very happy with the size and weight of it, as he swung it back and forth. He made sure everyone saw what he was doing. Nobody commented, though Kosheen noticed that a few rolled their eyes.

'There are a lot of strange things on and beneath this continent,' Darius said, gesticulating as he got excited about the subject. 'I once read that, *like,* The Dwellers carried this alien plant life to supply air and food, and that their ships were built with vast network of organic components that were ripe for evolving when they crashed and scattered. The dwellers carried livestock and bio-organic weapons that were probably a progenitor to the unique beasts that we've fought here, *right*? Plus, you have to factor in things they didn't even realise they were carrying - their bugs, parasites, diseases, all infecting the indigenous species, mating, bonding, mutating. They brought their world to ours. The Dwellers might be dead and buried, but colonisation has continued in their absence.'

'*Fucking nerd...*' Reaver mimed, grunted and snorting.

Darius flushed red, embarrassed.

'Hey, where's McMorrow?' Reaver asked. 'He wouldn't stand for this shit.'

'Our quarry put a bullet in his brain,' Oshii said, and everyone went quiet for a second.

'*Diseases and parasites*?' Kosheen asked, after a pause, now wishing that she had disinfected everything a little more often. She ignored the fact that Reaver made a big show of shaking his head, making it clear that he was disappointed in Kosheen for encouraging Darius's interest in such *"unimportant shit",* as he was known to phrase it.

'Oh, listen to this educated *fucker* over here,' Reaver exclaimed, belittling Darius. 'W*hatever-the-fuck else* you said, you pretentious prick. You find a few moldy old books and paste the pages with your *salty-man-juice,* 'cause all those big words get you hard. Then think you're better than the rest of us.'

'*No, I don't, I...*' Darius lowered his eyes in shame.

Kosheen already knew that Reaver was worse than the diseases and parasites that Darius was talking about.

'Thanks for lowering the tone,' Kosheen said, purposely not looking at Reaver as she spoke at him, which managed to make her words even more passive aggressive.

'It's the tone I like,' Reaver replied, pushing his chest out with pride.

Reaver sauntered over to Kosheen, his arrogance assuring him that he believed that every movement was advertising the fact that he was one witty, ruthless, badass outlaw. He reached into his leg-strapped carryall and handed Kosheen a refill for her medicinal inhaler.

'See,' he said. '*Dr* Reaver hasn't forgotten his number one patient.'

Kosheen didn't respond, she simply stared at that canvas bag and daydreamed about breaking it free from its buckles and beating him with it. She checked the Used-By-Date on the refill and found that it was only two days out of date, not ideal but she had often settled for much, much worse... She snapped the bottle's hygiene seal and wound the plastic loop from around the lid. Then she removed the empty canister from the inhaler and replaced it with this new one.

As Kosheen placed the inhaler between her lips Reaver watched her with a smile so vile that it would make a viper uncomfortable. She took a big gulp of the aerosol, the taste was unpleasant but reassuringly so.

'As much as I love taking responsibility for your wellbeing, I'm starting to think you have to start paying for it, again,' said Reaver, relishing every insincere syllable. 'There's a lot of back-pay accumulated.'

'*Pay...*' Kosheen knew that Reaver didn't mean money and this made her want to gag. She didn't want to give him any back-pay, she wanted pay-back.

As both of Kosheen's hands instinctively closed into fists it took every microbe of her willpower to slacken off *just enough* tension from her fingers to avoid accidentally crushing her precious inhaler. She dreamed of making the small device a permanent substitute for the big man's nose through pure, destructive force.

'I already pay for it,' Kosheen said.

'Yeah, but I need to include a finder's fee, a handling fee, storage fee,' Reaver patted his canvas bag, which had two straps, the top attached to his waist and another holding the bottom of it to his left thigh.

Every single word that Reaver uttered grated on Kosheen's nerves. She stored the inhaler safely away in her flack jacket's breast pocket, avoiding doing something she would regret.

She wished that Nico Shikari, the girl she just met, would come flying out of a window above, screeching like a banshee, blade first, and eviscerate Reaver. Of course, Kosheen would then have to kill Nico in front of the others to avoid suspicion, but at least she would enjoy the chance to dance with that mysterious stranger, one last time.

She walked away from the big man, trying not to shake her head, hoping not to be so obvious. She heard a sound from above, a crackling of bio-electric fusion from the metre thick, extra-terrestrial branches dangling between two lilting buildings. She could see it's seed pods pulsing with bright violet and deep blues. She waited for one to open and scatter its opulent glowing contents. Nothing happened.

Reaver decided that he wasn't getting enough attention, so he started playing with his Kinetic Arc Gravity cannon again, disappointed that his big tool hadn't got the recognition that he felt like it deserved. The armature supported the weight as he rotated the weapon to check the battery. He unscrewed the can-sized, bevel ended battery from the gun's belly. A whisper of steam drifted from it as he placed it gingerly on top of what he thought was a rock, until he realised that it was a random fast-fossilised head sat amongst the rubble, perhaps a centenarian.

'After this one I'm down to three batteries,' he said, as he gingerly screwed another bezel-edged battery into the gun. 'Please tell me we have a rendezvous with a supply drop soon, or the lake market, because I don't feel like tearing any more sentry-amps apart.'

Nobody answered. Oshii acted as if nobody had spoken.

'Where did you get the big gun?' Darius asked, feeling that someone should humour the big man before he became insufferable.

'Impressed by its size?'

'Oh my *fucking god* I am so *fucking* bored,' Kosheen blurted out, so suddenly that she surprised even herself, though she didn't actually sound bored, of course, she sounded furious. Everything was wrong, and she had worked so hard to convince herself that everything was right for so long.

'The world just fell on us, and you're bored?' Darius asked.

The truth was, Kosheen had no idea why she had said that. What she had wanted to say involved telling Reaver what a piece of shit he was, but she feared she would fail to find the right combination of words, and maybe this wasn't the right time. It was likely that she just wanted a reaction, but she wasn't sure if she wanted a reaction from them or from herself. She was already regretting saying it, because she had no follow up. Her mouth, apparently, had other ideas.

'If you're bored, I have something...' Reaver began, but was soon interrupted.

'What is the point of any of this?' Kosheen asked, and this instantly caused a stir amongst the Augmented Fourth who all suspended their own conversations to gawp at her.

The others had never heard her speak up, ever, and they certainly hadn't witnessed whatever this was, and it was making them very uncomfortable.

'It's all so fucking pointless. The same shit every fucking day, just trying to find some meaning. Everyone gets forgotten out here,' then Kosheen added the most blasphemous things she could have said. 'Even us...'

Her mouth had gotten away from her, and she was about to add something else when Oshii finally snapped, pushing her way through the Augmented Fourth until she was face to face with Kosheen.

Oshii said nothing, just trying to make herself taller than Kosheen, trying to make her feel small as she forced her way into her sniper's personal space. There was a long uncomfortable silence loaded with implied potential violence. It was only Reaver who spoke, saying what he believed Oshii – and the group - was thinking.

'Are you fucking kidding me?' Reaver said, scowling at Kosheen as she tried to stand tall under Oshii's anger, then he asked the rest of the group for clarification. 'Is she fucking kidding?'

Kosheen was terrified to realise that she was actually ready for a fight, a self-destructive streak running through her. She remembered watching them beat on the League boy, winced as she recalled the blows, the brutal amputations, but she also remembered him fighting back despite what they had done to him. Kosheen was ready to tap every single member of the Augmented Fourth for a fight, and maybe she would get through half of them before the injuries would overwhelm her.

Finally, Kosheen spoke, low but sharp.

'"*Everyone gets forgotten*"?' Oshii made Kosheen feel small and inferior through sheer force of will. '*WE* are not *EVERYONE*.'

Kosheen said nothing, not even a stutter left her lips. Oshii was so close that Kosheen could make out all the dots of bioluminescence reflected in her pupils, like neon constellations. Oshii's eyes drilled deep into Kosheen's fractured fate, the corporal's face a furnace of fury. Kosheen was waiting for the circle of soldiers to form around her, and a contest to the death to begin...

But instead of beating Kosheen to a pulp, Oshii turned and walked away, and Kosheen let out the breath that she had baited. Her relieved exhalation was premature, it seemed, because Oshii stopped and turned back with a look loaded with malice.

'WE are the Augmented Fourth!' Oshii snarled with unbroken conviction. 'We are the shadow cast over this land!'

We are the shadow that YOU *cast...* Kosheen thought to herself. She was one more episode of existential-doubt away from blurting out this verbal retaliation, this *accusation*, and that would have been a fatal error of judgment. Literally.

'No one forgets that,' Oshii whispered, and, for the first time any of them had heard, her voice cracked a little at the end.

For a moment, Kosheen thought that she saw a flicker of hurt in those intense eyes. Their beloved corporal could not believe that it was Kosheen, of all people, who had brought doubt to the steps of their cathedral.

Kosheen fought it, but she could not help but bow her head in shame.

Suddenly a sound echoed down from high above them; a loud crunch followed by a rustling that shook those oversized branches and reverberated through the risers. It was loud enough, and sudden enough, to get the attention of every member of the Augmented Fourth.

At first, scanning the rooftops, they could see nothing except the misshapen slivers of the night sky and the moon-lit clouds between the broken risers, broken up by the alien vegetation. Kosheen pulled her headset down over her eyes and zoomed in on one of those branches.

Something large was moving through the luminous fauna sprouting from those metre-thick branches. Kosheen had to cycle through a few different filters until she saw what it was. It was something that should have been reassuring but was acting in a very unnerving manner. It was a Unified American Military Seraph-amp, upside down, walking over the underside of a branch. The gravity orb housed deep within its shell was doubtless facilitating this gravity-defying amble. The branch's semi-opaque surface reacted to every step, blooms of radiant colour radiating in spectrums.

The seraph-amp was, unlike a lot of amps, broadly humanoid in form, in that it had two arms, two legs and a head, attached to a hefty torso covered in twitching vents. On its back were chunky protrusions that resembled three pairs of stunted, undeveloped wings, a suite of flight stabilisers encased in peerless white metal.

It stopped.

Then it turned to look right at them, though it's head was devoid of anything that might be considered a facial feature, apart from a barely perceptible slit across the middle, a horizontal line with a semicircle in the middle, like a thin smile.

'What is this bullshit?' Reaver asked, watching the same thing through his armour's artificial eyes.

'Perhaps its hand delivering us a mission,' Kosheen muttered to herself, spitefully. 'Like a fucking carrier pigeon.'

Darius turned to look at Kosheen. Kosheen knew that the young man had heard that potentially dangerous remark, and the sarcasm in which it marinated. He would surely be worried for his comrade's safety. Kosheen suspected that the boy had feelings for her, maybe. She felt a kinship towards the boy, because despite the fact they were on opposing trajectories, they were intersecting right now. As she found herself uncoupling from the group Darius was on the opposite end of the process. Soon he would forget who he was, burying his true self, and be who *they* wanted. But right now, they were both aware of their individuality.

'What does it want?' Darius asked.

Kosheen suspected that perhaps it was looking for Nico Shikari, not that she believed that there was any slither truth to the bullshit that she had read in that girl's bio, just like there had never been a league battalion hidden in the riser where Dyce Bastion had been camping. They were being manipulated by outside forces, the UAM's network was compromised. Nico wouldn't stand a chance against the amp's assorted armaments, which was a shame, because she really wanted another round with her…

The seraph-amp's gravity orb deactivated and it dropped, along with the leaves, petals and seeds that it dislodged from the branch's thriving ecosystem, every alien organism igniting in cascading clusters. The amp was diving down towards them with a potentially destructive velocity.

Panicking, the Augmented Fourth scattered, avoiding the probable point of impact that had been calculated by their own tabris. But the amp's gravity bubble reignited a fraction of a second before impact, stopping the machine dead exactly two metres above the ground. The machine's massive bulk slowly rotated until it was the right way up, it's massive metal hooves tenderly touching the ground, contracting with a hiss as they inherited the amp's weight from the unspooling gravity orb. Dislodged fragments of bio-matter drifted down around it like snow.

The seraph-amp amp looked at each of the Augmented Fourth in turn, before locking its gaze upon corporal Oshii. It stared at her for so long, so completely immobile, that they wondered if the machine's operating system might have crashed. The only sign of life came from the valves and exhausts opening, one after the other, exchanging heat and expelling waste fumes.

'What the fuck?' Reaver asked, unnerved. 'It's like it's fucking with us…'

Kosheen was the only one of them to take a step towards this metal golem. She could feel the waves of heat it had released, and felt dizzy from the ripples of residual gravity distortions from the orb saddled deep inside. It's armour was spotless, apparently this machine was fresh off the assembly line.

But then the machine stood up straight, looking up towards the sky. The surrounding soldiers didn't even realise that they were supposed to be following its eyeless gaze until the amp hacked their tabris systems and filled their vision with data, too much to read, some of it encoded. They saw, through the machine's own eyes, seven barely perceptible dots that were falling through the clouds. The only reason that they were even able to spot them against the bleached cloud cover was because the amp had placed info-tags on each one of those distant objects and presented this to them within their Mind's Eye operating system.

'It's a team of soldiers in drop suits,' Kosheen said, moments before the seraph-amp's tags identified them as UAM soldiers. 'They're ours, a Shooting Star unit.'

The team of falling soldiers dragged daggers from the clouds in their wake, as the large heat-resistant inflatable cones detached from their drop suits. The overwhelming typhoon of atmospheric re-entry caught the deflating cones and carried them away.

'Fresh meat for the grinder...' Reaver said.

'But why are you showing us?' Kosheen asked the machine.

Without warning, the seraph-amp suddenly launched itself back up into the air, high enough to break a branch as it back-flipped off it, sending ripples of bio-electric energy through it, before the amp disappeared over the roof of a riser.

'What was that all about?' Rogers asked. 'Anyone ever seen an amp act like that?'

'Came to check me out,' Reaver smirked, though he was as concerned as everyone else.

Then came a distant flash of blue from the sky, followed by whips of lightning that bounced between the so-called Shooting Stars, an Electro Magnetic Pulse that generated a discharge striking each of the descending soldiers.

Kosheen deployed her point drone from the dock on her back, using its more enhanced eyes to zoom in as close as they could on the incoming unit, then she shared the visual stream with the others.

One by one, like fading fireworks, the descending soldiers' info-tags disappeared, no longer broadcasting their identifying data as the Electro Magnetic Pulse deactivated their drop suits, sending them into an uncontrollable free-fall.

Then came another explosion, a bloom of red and yellow in the sky, followed by a shockwave that changed their trajectory.

'They're falling towards us now!' Kosheen said. It became clear to them that those two airborne detonations had not been arbitrary, they had been precise.

'What about their backup shoots?' Oshii asked.

'They must have been knocked unconscious,' Kosheen said. 'They're tumbling.'

'Poor bastards,' Darius shook his head.

One of the Shooting Stars hit one of the alien branches, cracking it down the middle, shaking free a thousand fireflies like a fountain of embers that floated free. Another of the Shooting Stars rolled down the side of a riser, its speed turning their mass into a powerful projectile, creating a hundred billion shards of glass, cracking the armour like a raw egg, turning the flesh into human pâté.

But it was the fate of the third Shooting Star that got the Augmented Fourth moving, as this soldier was the most likely to be the least mushed. The body hit the roof of a twelve-storey riser and smashed through floor after floor, finally stopping seven levels from the ground. Oshii started running towards that riser and the rest of her team followed her in through the building's lobby and up the stairwell.

Kosheen was the last in, she was in no rush, winding the point drone back in to the dock as she moved. She leapt over several steps at a time and swung her body around on banisters, gaining momentum every time.

She found the others gathered around the Shooting Star, the body hanging upside down through the ceiling, the misshapen figure tangled up in the ancient wiring that their episodic impact had ripped from the structure. The scorched and scraped armour denied them the horrific sight of the soldier's twisted body.

Oshii stepped up, reached out and held the limp head, turning it until she found a small decorative honeycomb etching at the base of the neck, similar to the hexagonal pattern drawn in shallow lines around their own respirators. She pressed two of her fingers against two of the hexagons, and they popped out, revealing connection ports within that were miraculously still intact.

'Dive,' was Oshii's simple order.

Darius knew that this order was for him. He uncoiled the web-thin patch cable from inside the base of his tabris and hooked it up to the Shooting Star's connection ports. His tabris ran the infiltration software, allowing him to dive through multiple fathoms of data. He reached out into the digital world and rearranged strings of data, changing the flow.

'This is the crappiest ICE I've seen in a long time,' Darius said as he broke open the Intrusion Counter Electronics. His eyes flickered, random eye movement, as if he were dreaming. 'It shouldn't take long to decrypt; this is too easy.'

'"*Too easy*",' Kosheen repeated, Darius's words didn't sit well with her.

'Anything we can use?' Oshii asked. 'What was their mission?'

'I'll see what I can salvage, his brain is dying fast and the backup on his tabris has detected his death and seems to be systematically dismantling itself.'

'Do you think that amp did this?' Kosheen asked as she stood and watched, arms folded. 'That UAM seraph-amp that just creeped us *the-fuck* out?'

Nobody answered, but surely they all understood any potential implications of what Kosheen had asked.

Reaver coughed from the corner, it was a dismissive sound, but he didn't sound entirely sure that Kosheen didn't have a point. He had taken point at the window, leaning against the frame, his KAG cannon in hand. He was vigilantly watching the dark corners of the area surrounding the riser, just in case there were any enemies in the vicinity who were attracted by the spectacle.

'Okay,' Darius said. 'I've found his mission. They were supposed to take down a League of Nations installation, a tower built of multiple transmitter arrays that is broadcasting weaponised misinformation.'

'How far?' Oshii asked.

'Three point four miles,' Darius said.

'It's doable,' Reaver said, excited. 'If we get moving straight away, we could get there by...'

'Lets see the brief,' was Oshii's next order to Darius, interrupting Reaver.

'This isn't complete,' he warned them. 'It's just a part of the briefing.'

Darius complied, re-compiled the brief and started to transmit it wirelessly to each of his comrades. A rehearsed, emotionless voice filled their heads, a memory of the brief given to the doomed Shooting Stars by an officer.

(*"On the fourteenth of this month, a breach was independently discovered by the Nexus Intelligence research team, who immediately notified the Philadelphia, Chicago and Portland Server Stations. They found multiple Trojans loaded into a download package which sent 'anti-data' from infected users' terminals and their portable devices back to a central server located in the UAM capital, flooding vital databases with weaponised disinformation."*)

A map appeared in their Mind's Eye, one of the few images that Darius was able to salvage from the soldier's mind and tabris, showing exactly where the transmissions were coming from. A large wrought-iron lattice tower covered in arrays of satellite dishes and long-range antennas attached to hydraulic gimbals. The visual side of the brief pointed out the two backup power stations hidden around the tower's base, discovered by geo-synchronous satellites.

(*"As well as the data contamination, however, the infection also contained a "second stage payload" installed on to the affected systems – essentially intelligent malware that could be used to track high level UAM targets to their real-world locations. Before this could be executed, we were able to wipe and destroy the affected drives and deploy backup installations. Technicians studying an isolated drive determined that this is a learning virus we are dealing with here, and it is only a matter of time before something worse gets through.*

Your mission is to instigate the surgical removal of enemy operatives from the site and use the installation to trace and identify any other towers, and to decommission the installation by any means necessary...")

The memory became fragmentary, and the remainder of the brief was lost. But it was enough to excite the group, and Oshii appeared galvanised by this. *The Powers That Be had sent them a sign.* They hadn't been forgotten, the seraph-amp had been a herald and this mashed soldier hanging in a web a cables was a prophet.

'Okay,' said Oshii. 'We are taking this mission.'

'I said that something would turn up, right?' Reaver said to Kosheen, glancing back from the window. He was elated that their fortunes had improved.

Kosheen shuck her head at the madness of this interpretation of events.

She stood on the opposite side of the room, watching from the door. Her arms still folded, she watched Darius as he disconnected his patch cable from the back of the crushed soldier's helmet and wound it back in. Kosheen could not see the point in taking a mission to try and impress a government that had seemingly, wilfully, chosen to ignore their existence, or had simply, negligibly, forgotten them. She wasn't sure which of those was worse.

'Let's get moving,' Oshii commanded.

'What's the plan?' Reaver asked.

'Tear down that tower and decimate all resistance,' Oshii licked her lips.

Kosheen waited, leaning against the old rotten door frame, as the rest of the group walked past her on the way out of the room. Nobody acknowledged her...

She waited until she could only hear the distant echo of their chatter. She looked back up at that misshapen body, hanging upside down in the middle of the room, caught amongst the various different types of cables that it had torn out of the ceiling on the way through it. She stood up straight and sauntered over to the body, pushing the drooping cables out of the way. She found the emergency release for the armour' drop components, a lever in a recess, which caused the red-hot outer shell to disconnect from the triclops armour and either clatter to the floor or get caught on cables. This gave her better access for scavenging supplies. She took their ammunition first, then she found some rations, enough for a week.

One of the ration packets contained a salted caramel protein snack, her favourite. She tore it open and nibbled on it, savouring every morsel, letting it rest on her tongue.

Then she found a sealed pack of glo-sticks. She hadn't tried one of those in a long, long time, they had never really appealed to her before. But she suddenly had the urge to give them another try. She slid one of the white tubes out, rotated both halves until she heard the telltale crack, then she heard the fizz of mixing chemicals within. Then that chemical reaction caused the tip to alight, flickering red and blue. She placed it between her lips and took a long, slow drag.

The room was bathed in a dark blue hue, the flickering light of the glo-stick was the only other colour. She unhooked the soldier's helmet and let it drop away, so that it bounced along the broken floor. She took another drag as she considered the unknown soldier. She'd expected their eyes to be a different colour, like a gemstone, for some reason...

The fallen soldier's eyes suddenly widened as a death rattle shook him.

Kosheen felt nothing.

But, somehow, somewhere, perhaps at the back of her brain - where she had hidden the person that she had been before she came to this place and met these people - that *lack* of feeling, an absence of malice, somehow signalled a slim chance to reclaim the totality of her humanity.

She turned and walked away.

#FALLINGFORYOU

Dyce dreamt that he was back on Terminus moon, towards the end of his military training.

In this dream he was stood on a wrought iron bridge linking two old brick buildings, looking out over the training grounds as dusk spread over them. Beyond that he could see workers and their machines toiling amongst the ship breakers yard on the east coast of the Domu Peninsula, cracked ships cast in dark relief by the shimmering Lillylana Ocean.

One second, he was alone, the next he turned to see his friends Cuxwill and Breaker stood by the entrance to one of the buildings, beckoning him over. They had apparently been to a party, judging by their level of inebriation, but Dyce struggled to remember the details of it. Dyce used his tabris to bypass the security lock, and they practically fell through the door, laughing and singing fragments of pop songs. Everything was fragments.

Before them was an Olympic sized swimming pool, lit only by the Earth, visible through the tall, oblong windows that curved back over the pool. The brilliant blues and whites of their home planet highlighted the wet tiles as they stumbled across them, somehow already stripped to their undies. Ripples of white spread out from the point of impact as each one of them jumped in, one after another.

Dyce was the last of them to break the surface, but could not see the bottom, only a murky *nothing* beneath. He wondered what could be down there waiting for them, like a deep sea diver in uncharted territory.

He tried not to stare at Breaker, but this was another of his many failures. His friend slid effortlessly through the water; he could only admire her natural skill. He always felt inferior to her, to most people, if he were honest.

But the deeply embedded psychological cluster-fuck driving the dream corrupted the memory, twisting it in unpleasant ways.

Steam filled bubbles drifted up out of the darkening depths of the pool, as a particularly big one floated past he saw within it the wisps forming figures, fluctuating stick people, contorted into demonic caricatures. They were clawing at the bubble like the walls of a prison cell.

Breaker's body became a burnt husk, her pose contorting in a grim recreation of the way she died, when that orbital strike decimated their unit. Dyce couldn't look away from the cracking flesh and curling strands of popped muscle. He began to choke, in a panic he made a break for the surface...

But instead of breaking the surface of the pool, he felt his fingers dig into mud, as he crawled his way up out of sleep and back into the waking world. He found his head lay in a pool of blood and vomit diluted by river water, his vision blurred and his ears filled with gunk.

He pushed himself over onto his back, coughing and spluttering. He took deep breaths and wondered why his hands felt so heavy, and what had dug into his forearms as he had rolled himself over.

After a few good blinks and squints, he could see well enough to note that night was receding, the sky still burnt from the Pulse of the Machine's catastrophic attack. The lingering lines of its rockets' vapour trails hung over the flaming skyline, framing the breaking dawn like warped prison bars.

He panicked. Where were the Augmented Fourth? Was he back in their custody? Was he about to suffer another assault?

He had to figure out where he was. His vision was still

calibrating itself, finding focus, and - through stinging eyes - he could just about make out a crashed ship, straddling the river from one bank to the other. There was a figure standing on top of it, blurry but definitely wearing full-body armour of some kind. He assumed that someone must have scooped him up out of the water, and perhaps that blurred *someone* up there was responsible.

He turned around and saw his own face staring back at him, reflected in the canopy of a crashed Bullet-Witch. He looked pathetic. He felt pathetic.

His hands felt heavy. He couldn't feel his fingers. He started to remember what had happen to them, and what he had done with them. The balled up wire he had wrapped around them.

He pushed himself up to his knees and looked at the tangle of metal wrapped around his fists. He dropped back down in case the soldier looked over from their vantage point. Were they friend or foe? Were they with Oshii? Were they one of the Augmented Fourth?

He felt certain he knew the answer. He knew what was coming. He knew what he would have to do to survive.

But this was before a curious, tingling sensation in his hands started to escalate exponentially. But what started as a fairly understandable sign of impending numbness became a much more inexplicable experience, like waves of sparks firing throughout his hands until the moment that, suddenly, his self made bonds snapped, shedding the tangle of brittle metal like a cocoon and his hands fell free.

But his hands were no longer recognisable, they were no longer human. Slithers of the gauntlet's armoured shell had been eaten away to display this chimera beneath. It was hard to tell where bone, muscle, cartilage and arteries ended and where the gauntlet and it's mechanisms began, flesh and metal mixed to form something new and grotesque.

The tingling sensation subtly subsided, allowing him to experience something new. He had feeling in his fingers, these distorted bastardisations of his own appendages.

There was a barcode and serial number running down the little fingers of both gauntlets, which were now his little fingers. Each of the lines that constituted the barcode were less than a millimetre tall, differing in thicknesses like morse code, hundreds of them from the tip of the finger, and along the bottom of the hand to the wrist.

He held his hands out in front of him and rotated them at the cuff to get the blood flowing, hearing the crack of tense muscle with a certain satisfaction. The tiny hydraulic mechanisms that moved the gauntlet's fingers were now part of him, meshed with the bone.

This made hi, feel queasy, he almost cried. For all the inexplicable things that had happened to him since his arrival, at least he had remained human. *What even was this?*

He didn't have time for questions, he had to secure and ensure his survival first.

He spied his knife half buried in the dirt near him, the tide had lapped at it, covering it in mud. If he had awoken any later he might not have found it at all. Perhaps the enemy soldier had dropped it, or hadn't noticed it there.

Before he made a move on the blade, he squinted towards the figure on top of the crashed ship, subtly lit by the sky, dark blue graded into a deep orange on the horizon, whispers of cloud lit gold by the as-yet unseen sun. It was nearly dawn, the new day was about to break. There was no indication that he was currently being watched.

He cautiously advanced on the half buried weapon, which would be a much less nerve-racking endeavour if he had developed eyes in the back of his head – a theoretical but ludicrous development to be sure, but he was not entirely sure he could rule it out. It had been an exceptionally strange couple of days.

He took the blade, pulled it close, tested the battery, listened for the subsonic buzz. He could feel components within his mangled hands shake as if they were loose, an incomparable sensation for any sentient being that was essentially made from organic matter, but it was the accompanying rattle that really made him nauseous. He deactivated the blade, then took a second - and a few long, deep breaths – to suppress his urge to gag. He slid it back into its scabbard.

Suck it up, he thought. He didn't have time for this. He had to deal with the immediate problem - the human problem - before the *others* came for him and everything escalated.

He could now see that the river-straddling structure was a crashed UAM jump ship, "Nilin Remix" stencilled on the side. The enemy soldier was now sat on the edge of the hull, apparently watching the sky turn from black to deep blue. Waiting for the dawn.

Had they seen him? Did they know that he was awake? Maybe he could slip away, run as fast as he could. But with a flash of pain came a brief, sharp recollection of his inflicted torment. A warning from his subconscious on behalf of his nervous system, which was still struggling to repair itself from near obliteration. He could not risk them following, *of course he couldn't*. He would not be caught again. They would tell Oshii where he was, or which direction he had fled. Of course, they would. They definitely would.

Maybe they already had.

Maybe...

Maybe Oshii was already on her way...

Maybe...

Dyce seethed as if he were face to face with Oshii right now, as if she were gloating over Dyce's pain...

So yes, he would have to. He had to do it. He could see no other way. He could do this. He could. He would have to deal with the UAM soldier.

They were all the same. The enemy. All the same. Every single one of them. Millions of them. They all stick together. Degenerates. Less than human. Less than him. Monstrous. He would have to do it. Deal with her. It was him or them. He had to; they had left him no choice...

Dyce took his tabris from its holster port and checked it over, making sure that the explosion and subsequent river ride had not damaged it, but there was nothing more than scuff marks. He saddled it back inside his armour, turned it on and booted into the Minds Eye. He opened a few deeply hidden files and cycled through his library of prebuilt offensive protocols for virtual attacks. He was going to wirelessly hack the enemy soldier's armour to shut her down, which was - if he was being honest with himself, *and he was not even on the same continent as anything approaching the truth right now* - cheating. He found the enemy's digital signature but it was far too weak at this distance, but he attempted the hack regardless. It didn't work, he needed to get closer. He had already known this, he just hadn't wanted it to be true.

He needed a plan, so he needed to think, which was not easy for him at the best of times. He attempted to initiate his mental process by aggressively repeating the word *think* over and over in his mind, at different speeds and rhythms, until he began to annoy even himself.

Probably still concussed, to be fair.

He berated himself until he had a flash of inspiration, remembering that the operating manual for his tactical armour had been installed in his mind the first time that he had synchronised his tabris to it, so he knew a thing or two about it, and he knew that it had a contingency weapon hidden within it, a small disposable gun loaded with five bullets, hidden under his armour's chest piece. He had to dig it out of the hidden compartment using the tip of his new knife to wiggle it free. It was an oblong mechanism which he had to unfold into a shape that was recognisably gun-like, then he slide-locked the firing apparatus into position. It was a disappointing little thing, looking very toy-like and underpowered.

He kept low, crawling towards the river bank, taking position behind an old tree which had been uprooted by the gravity weapon that had wrecked the distant Goliath, and now stood upside-down, its leaves cast all around in a yellowing circle, its broken branches piercing the churned up ground, the mud-covered routes reaching up. The tree was a decent place to hide, though it would be about as much use in a firefight as a stack of brown paper bags.

Dyce attempted to hack the enemy soldier's armour again, but it was worse than he feared. Something, somehow, was blocking his signal. He was going to need to physically bypass layers of signal dampening armour to directly make contact with the enemy's systems. He checked another small compartment on his tactical armour, finding a single bullet in a vacuum-sealed packet.

This would be the real test, removing a small packet from a compact compartment with his pseudo-cyborg fingers. The seemingly simple act now seemed to require a level of precision that was extremely irritating. He held his breath, involuntarily, trying not to let his irritability escalate. Pain pulsed through his palms, reminding him of the beating that they had endured.

Finally he had it out, holding it gingerly from one corner, letting it dangle before his gaze. He let out his breath and counted to ten.

The round was capped with a chemical head capable of melting a minuscule hole through the top layer of most armour types, upon impact, to facilitate the delivery of an embryonic nano-machine, no bigger than a speck, which would rapidly identify the central CPU and physically bond with it, becoming a secondary receiver, facilitating the hack.

Inscribed upon the bullet in tiny letters was the barcode and corresponding six-digit synchronisation code needed to sync his tabris to the aforementioned microscopic machine contained within. He only had to look at the barcode for the tabris to read and process it. Confirmation of wireless synchronisation instantly appeared in his Minds Eye. He set the pre-programmed hack to repeat, tore open the bullet's plastic packet... which immediately slid out and dropped to the floor.

'*Fuck-sake...*' He only mimed his expletive, though he did it with a snarl, a gesture he repeated as he dropped the bullet a second time. Then, after taking a deep breath to compose himself, he gingerly picked it back up for the third and final time and loaded the bullet into the bottom of his disposable gun's meagre ammo clip, giving him five attempts with the standard rounds to get his aim right before the nano-machine's bullet would enter the chamber and be ready to fire.

He cautiously pushed himself back up the tree trunk and took a slow, cautious step out from behind it. He moved with as much stealth as he were able to harness, taking aim down the stunted barrel of his disappointing weapon. The enemy soldier didn't move. Just sat there. Enjoying the morning. Like a normal human being. *How dare they.*

Okay, I can do this...

But Dyce hesitated as his best laid plans went quickly awry due to the intervention of a disembodied voice flickering uninvited through his head, an artificial vocal, distorted, like an intercepted transmission warping in and out. Apparently, in attempting to hack the soldier, Dyce had accidentally made contact with some other unknown system in the immediate vicinity.

("*Red! Red!*") The synthetic voice exclaimed in a panic. ("*Oh, for the love of...* Nico -*damn*- Shikari! *The drowned boy is awake and sneaking up on you!*")

The enemy soldier - whose name he could only assume was either *Red* or *Nico* - twisted around to look in Dyce's direction.

'*Fuck!*' They both exclaimed at the exact same time.

Dyce ran straight at the hull of the ship, keeping his aim true, though he couldn't fire until he was closer.

At the same time Nico launched herself up onto her feet and grabbed her rail rifle, taking aim.

Dyce decided that he was close enough. He hoped that his bastardised fingers didn't let him down, prayed that they did not generate an unbearable and distracting amount of pain. He pulled the trigger, but an involuntary spasm caused a double trigger pull, launching two shots, both missing.

In retaliation Nico let loose a few warning shots. At least one of her shots was close enough to tear a few short hairs from Dyce's head as they whistled past, the follicles yanked free in the projectile's wake.

Dyce took his third shot, missed. Fourth, missed. But then the fifth finally struck the enemy's armour, compressing on impact, spiralling away, the calibre insufficient to penetrate the armour.

The final bullet, with its nano-tech payload, was in the chamber, ready. This had to follow the previous round's perfect trajectory, so his tabris and headset were assisting the endeavour, augmenting his vision with wireframe guides for the perfect posture and placement of his limbs and digits to replicate that previous score. The trigger was pulled. The hammer mechanism struck the back of the round, the gunpowder ignited, the recoil force pushed the slide back and ejected the shell.

The bullet left the barrel...

But....

Dyce's headset exploded as a shard-shaped projectile - fired from the enemy's rail rifle - struck the side and tore its casing open, whipping it back and spinning his head around with it. The disintegrating device scattered shrapnel across his face; lenses shattering, the ringlets that held them in place warping from the force; the mother board snapped. A whirlwind of components scraped against his eyelids, cheeks and forehead. He was knocked back by the blow, falling onto his arse, as the adjustable strap that should have held the headset to his face instead contracted like elastic and flung the disintegrating device away.

Dyce was on the floor now, trying to orientate himself. He heard a jingle of metal as the broken pieces bounced away. One of the warped ringlets rolled around in a decreasing circle until it finally clattered to a stop by his head.

'Just stay down,' Nico called, as she watched Dyce struggle to turn around and stand up, dazed and confused. 'No one would blame you. Just stay down, take your time. Then, when you are ready, you get up, turn around and fuck off.'

Dyce hadn't heard much of that, his ears ringing, the sound of his own pulse beating at the bone walls of his skull. He was panicking, trying to figure out what had happened, and convincing himself that he had to get a grip before the *others* came for him.

A bird squawked a few feet away, on the edge of the hull. It had dropped a grub on the floor and seemed to think Dyce was after it. There were a few more birds hanging around, even more of them descending to the river bank. They were making a lot of noise, like a baying chorus here to witness his failure.

In the distance, a lining of gold was forming around the skeletal remains of the costal risers, opulent against the deep orange and dark blue.

Nico stood there and watched him. She felt a lot of sympathy for what the boy had gone through, the scars of it obviously evident. But, she couldn't allow him to continue to be a threat to her. She would take him down if she had to. She hoped it wouldn't come to that.

Dyce forced himself to his feet, unsteady. Then he collapsed back to his knees, seething.

The enemy was still speaking, but Dyce couldn't hear it, feeling as if his brains were rattling around in his skull. He got back up, a little more successful this time, then advanced upon the ship, climbing up the mud-blasted cockpit canopy, stopping once or twice to orientate himself, gradually regaining physical stability even as he shed emotional stability.

'You really gonna do this?' Nico asked with a sigh.

But what Nico didn't know – and her adversary had forgotten due to concussion – was that Dyce's sixth and final bullet had successfully delivered its embryonic payload to its intended target. Within a fraction of a second after impact the chemical tip had burnt a hole a millimetre wide in the outer shell of her armour, then the shell had collapsed upon impact and deposited the nano-machine through that melted hole before bouncing off, hollow and spent. Whilst her attention had been upon the boy the nano machine had found its way to the armour's operating system where it made a nuisance of itself until it found a suitable circuit to attach itself to. Then it made contact with Dyce's tabris, becoming a wireless receiver that bypassed every defence.

Dyce's hack, which his tabris had been transmitting on a loop, finally went through.

As Nico watched error messages pop through her Minds Eye she could only gawp in confusion, turning to shock and anger as the top half of her armour opened, exposing her to the frigid morning air.

'*Son of an absolute father-fornicator,*' Nico exclaimed. 'What the actual fuck?'

Nico struggled to move, trying to get her armour to do anything, then struggling to pull at least one of her arms out.

Dyce tossed the tiny pistol away, pulled his dominant hand back, rolling the makeshift, robotic fingers into a ball that he threw at his enemy's startled face...

But Nico Shikari caught Dyce Bastion's fist with her own bare hand, a feat so impressive that they both froze in shock and awe.

In that moment of pugilistic deadlock Dyce Bastion and Nico Shikari locked eyes for the first time. They both experienced intense but diametrically opposed reactions to this.

Dyce fell instantly, deeply, inconsolably in love and lust, forgetting for a moment that he believed that his adversary was *probably* the herald of his bane, falling for her, *falling away from the world, from his sense of self, through the prescription lenses and between their hairline cracks.*

Nico felt nothing that she could not curse, outwitted by a *slack-jaw* with a predictable right-hook.

But Nico did not have time to wonder why the gormless moron was gawping at her, she still had the boy's unconventional cybernetic knuckles - and the lingering aftershock of their impact - held tight in her hand. She needed to take advantage of that.

She had managed to free her other hand from her armour, stretching the fingers before squeezing them into a fist. Her other hand yanked the boy into her bone white knuckles as she threw them, temporarily rearranging the boy's face.

Nico's lower half was still trapped in her armour - open from the waist up whilst the legs remained frozen like a statue. So, with both hands, Nico reached up above her head, grabbed her open armour's rigid shoulders, tensed up her torso and pulled both legs up and out. Then she pulled her feet back and dealt another blow to Dyce's beleaguered brain, her muscle-suit's padded soles kicking her enemy's face, before launching herself out of her petrified protection and landing on the floor.

Dyce spun around but managed to stay upright this time, impressive considering he was still shaken from the destruction of his headset, his ears still ringing, his brain still shaking against its cage of bone. He took a deep breath, orientated himself as best as he could, then retaliated with a few good hard punches. But Nico had her guard up, forearms protecting her face and glasses.

'You are outclassed,' Nico said. 'Just give up!'

'Please, shut up!' Dyce whinged, embarrassed because, for a moment there, he'd had the upper hand, but that hadn't lasted long.

He didn't know what to think or feel. Concussion, confusion and self-preservation drove his need to take-out his target, but a post-adolescent stirring in his lad loins was working hard to override this. It was a push and pull that was more than a little *crazy-making.*

Nico jabbed Dyce's face repeatedly, quick strikes. She completed the combo by striking the boy's gut, an uppercut that reverberated right through his tactical armour, making him sick. Literally sick. Dyce tripped backwards, bouncing back on his posterior. He sat there, shaking his head.

For a second, Nico considered retreating to her armour to recover her weapons, but that would mean turning her back on the boy. Besides, she was confident that she could beat him with her bare hands. So she stood and studied him. She had wanted a challenge, and this was not living up to it's early promise.

A disturbance on the river distracted Nico. She saw a large amount of birds massing along the crumbling riverbanks. They were eating strange, alien grubs that were wiggling their way out of the damp earth. The grubs popped as beaks applied pressure, spreading neon blood over everything, seeping down into the water.

The sun itself was still not visible, but it was refracting through the smoke that drifted through the costal risers like a blanket of atomic ghosts. The sky above them was a deep blue, cut through with rough zigzags of orange and yellow cloud. Nico felt the early morning breeze on her skin, tickling her peach fuzz. She closed her eyes and could taste the morning dew on her lips and tongue. *For a moment she forgot…*

Then Nico heard Dyce forcing himself back up onto his feet, and she remembered that she still had to deal with this underwhelming bullshit.

Dyce's face was flushed with a crippling embarrassment.

Nico cracked her neck and rolled her shoulders, then asserted herself with a pugilist's stance.

Dyce managed to stop his shoulders from slumping any further, tugging them back before he looked too pathetic, then raised his own… well, whatever unnatural abominations he had weighing down the end of his arms.

Jute was watching all of this, flicking between the human combatants' eyes and his own cradle's pathetic camera. He watched them there, stood on the jump ship's hull, two figures in opposition against that huge expanse of sky. The rising sun lit a fire at the base of the corrupted skyline, the massing clouds resembling a psychedelic aurora borealis.

Without warning, a vertical line of light appeared, suddenly, in the distance. The orbital defence platform Shamsiel was test firing into a cluster of isolated buildings across the wasteland. It looked as if the heavens had launched a line of lightning into the risers. Dyce had seen that line of light before, of course. He was reminded of the journey that had lead him from his death and rebirth to this very moment...

Dyce knew that he had to get control of this situation, and fast. His own frustration was manipulating the narrative, however, at least until he saw a whisper of a figure stood by the bow, though it was probably just the smoke from the burning coast faking forms in the corner of his eye. The figure was broadly feminine, arms crossed. This crude caricature conjured Breaker's stern face in his mind, not judging him, but forcing her experience and will upon him. *What would she do? Clear her head, go with the flow...*

The preliminary crack of the space-birthed PEPP weapon spooked the birds along the parallel riverbanks, sending the avian spectators into the sky, crisscrossing through the smear of blinding white between the technicolour curtain of cloud.

The sun was up, the new day had begun.

They both broke ground, sprinting across the hull. Clashing, fists first, spinning around each other, exchanging punches and kicks, each blow felt like a world shaking quake.

Dyce managed to block a few good punches – much to Nico's chagrin - before retaliating, crashing a knee into Nico's midriff that knocked her onto her back. Then Dyce launched himself through the air, knees and elbows aimed at both her chest and startled face.

Nico took the full weight of Dyce's assault, yelling in pain, though she managed to roll and tip the boy off before struggling back up to her feet.

'*Jeezus fucking...*' she began.

But her adversary wasn't done, Dyce landing one or two more strikes before Nico managed to spin around him, grabbing the boy's arm and throwing him over her shoulder, slamming him onto the deck. She heard Dyce bounce as she walked away, rolling the tension from her neck and shoulders, accompanied by audible cracks as bubbles of nitrogen, oxygen and carbon dioxide popped between the bones.

You need to get moving before SHE *gets here...* said the voice in Dyce's head, which sounded a lot like Breaker. *You survived this long...*

Dyce unsheathed his progressive blade. He felt the weight of it, the balance of it. He didn't *want* to kill this stranger, but if he could just incapacitate her, long enough for him to... *to...* He no idea what he would actually do next. He gritted his teeth and charged.

Nico glanced back at the boy, just in time to see the red sunrise glint off the blade - shimmering as it vibrated at a subsonic level. Almost too late, *almost*, narrowly avoiding catastrophe she pirouetted out of the way, elbowing her attacker in the back of the head, loosening his grip. Without a second 's hesitation she took the boy's blade and planted it in his stomach, the activated weapon penetrating the tactical armour's chest plate. Then she roundhouse kicked Dyce off his feet.

Dyce hit the hull and rolled away, bouncing over the blade, each rotation twisting it deeper. He struggled on the floor for a few moments, before pushing himself to his knees – still finding the motivation to survive, to push his limits beyond those set by his old passive self - but found himself incapable of staying vertical. He doubled right over, until the crown of his head rested on the crashed ship. He took a few deep breaths as he attempted to regulate the pain, counted to ten, then he opened his eyes and stared, upside down, at the misshapen hilt of his embedded weapon. The reactive-elasticated-synthetic muscle that held the armoured plates in place was snapping back around the point of incision, curling back away.

The red LED power indicator on the blade's base started to flicker. It was still embedded in his chest, fluttering at first, then flashing on and off, as if there were some electrical fault within it, until it cut out completely.

He attempted to steady himself with one unsteady hand, cautiously touching the blade's hilt. He had expected even this minute movement to send a shockwave of pain through him, but instead the blade wiggled, exactly the way solid metal doesn't. He frowned, flicked it, then stared, mesmerised, as it swung and bounced up and down like a spring.

("How are you doing, kid?") Asked the robotic, disembodied voice.

('Errr...") Dyce struggled to form anything coherent.

("That good, huh? How are you still alive?")

("Not sure I am... Who is this?")

("Your fairy godmother.")

("Breaker?")

("What?")

("Oh...")

("Why are you attacking my girl?")

("I can't let them...") Dyce answered. ("They can't get me...")

("Who?")

("I have to... I can't...")

Dyce took hold of the hilt, one finger at a time. He took a moment to prepare himself, but this gave him time to realise that he was in no position to do this, mentally or physically. He wondered how this looked to the enemy, if he looked as pathetic as he felt.

No guts, no glory...

He tugged on the weapon, prepared to hear and feel it grate on his ribs, but it moved with no resistance at all. Dyce, confused and cautious, opened one eye. At first he thought that the hilt had come free from the pointy end, leaving a razor sharp length of foreign-matter making its way through his organs. But it hadn't come apart, not entirely, because that would have been normal, made sense, and that's not how things wanted to work these days.

Stretched between the hilt and the wound were strings of metallic goo, *like melted cheese immortalised in a metal sculpture*. He continued to pull, bemused and enthralled, until the remnants of the blade were as thin as human hair, refusing to break.

He looked back at his enemy. The enemy soldier was just standing there, staring at him, a hand on her hip. He rather imagined that this Nico Shikari was pitying him. He couldn't make out her face, but her body language revealed that she was clearly expecting no retaliation from him.

"*Who...*" Dyce thought about the reply that the disembodied voice had given a moment ago. *Why did the voice say* "who"?

He was completely confounded by the absurd turn his his mortal predicament had taken. He delicately touched the wound, finding that this only spread the metal goop further, as if it were paste. The sensation that accompanied this was bizarre, like pins and needles, but more intense, more concentrated, more... the only word he could find was *complex,* as if something was happening inside the wound, as if a vast construction job was happening on a microscopic scale within his body. It was similar to the sensation he had felt when his hands had fused to the gauntlets.

Nico, happy that Dyce was out for the count, climbed back into her armour feet first, but found that the top half was still locked open, completely unresponsive to her commands.

("Jute, can you get my armour working?")

("I can't believe you stabbed him!")

("He gave me no choice")

Dyce was listening to this, confused by her words. Was she really with Oshii?

("I'm not sure, I can't figure out what the boy did to your operating system's architecture,") Jute responded. *("The code has become nearly indecipherable. This is either a work of art or the doodles of a certifiable mad man.")*

Dyce was still somehow linked to this mysterious third party, this *"Jute"* and he could still hear every word they spoke within com-link. He was actually proud to have his handiwork described in that way. He'd smile, if only the pain and shame would let him. He realised that he wanted to be indecipherable, he *wanted* to be different.

("*How long is it going to take?*") Nico asked.

("*I think one of his bullets contained a nano bug, that's a physical problem that I am not capable of over-coming, being a disembodied virtual entity, and-all. This might mean I have to find a way to confuse and distract the bug or hack the bug itself, and I'm not really sure how to do either. Leave it with me.*")

("*Thank you.*")

("*Are you just going to leave the boy like that?*") Jute asked. ("*He could do with some help.*")

Nico didn't respond. She had no idea what to say or think. She looked away from her fallen opponent, feeling some emotion that she could not quite identify, but wasn't shame, wasn't regret, wasn't pity, what *was* it?

'You know,' Dyce gasped as he tried to take the breath back into his winded chest. He wasn't entirely sure what he was going to say or why he was going to say it. 'I... I think we got off to a bad start.'

'Well, *you* got off to a bad start,' Nico deadpanned, without turning around to look at him. 'I've been consistently magnificent.'

Dyce had no idea what to say in response, so he only made an awkward grunt.

Frankly, it was only after she had responded that Nico realised that Dyce shouldn't be talking at all.

But Dyce was not as down and done as Nico had assumed. The boy came out of nowhere, rising to tackle her head on, shoulder-barging his adversary and her armour.

The armour fell back and both Nico and Dyce went with it, over the edge, tumbling away from the ship and towards the water.

Nico saw the technicolour sky above them, as Dyce saw that kaleidoscope broken in the ebb and flow below.

The river exploded on impact, casting a shroud of water high above them, crashing down upon them.

Nico was winded and shocked, struggling to pull her limbs

back out of the armour, waves were crashing around them. Without hesitation Dyce ordered the armour to close, locking the metal shell around Nico, rendering her immobile.

Ballast helped the armour float back to the surface, as Dyce held on tight as it rocked. He took a few deep breaths and centred himself, waiting for it to settle. Then he swung his legs around and sat on the waterlogged sarcophagus. With his inhuman knuckles he knocked the armour's helmet between its mismatched trio of camera eyes, trying to get the occupant's attention.

(*"How you doing in there?"*) He spoke through the com-link. (*"You all good?"*)

(*"You prick!"*) Nico snapped. (*"There's water in here!"*)

(*"Is there anything I can do to make your stay more comfortable?"*)

(*"Oh, you're so considerate,"*) Nico replied, enough bite in her sarcasm to mortally wound any hint of sincerity. (*"You are a real humanitarian. We should be best friends."*)

(*"Oh, can we? I was just thinking about how my life needs more potentially fatal knife wounds."*)

(*"Ah, I knew there was something I meant to ask. How come you ain't bleeding out on the deck of my derelict?"*)

(*"Because I'm* fucking *magic,"*) Dyce replied.

(*"I think I like this guy, Red,"*) Jute chimed in.

(*"Red? Is that her name, or is it Nico?"*)

(*"My friend's call me Nico, the voice in my head calls me Red,"*) Nico answered. (*"You're neither, shit-head."*)

(*"You have friends?"*) Dyce sounded surprised.

(*"You can call her Shikari, then,"*) Jute suggested.

(*"So, I guess you're the voice in her head?"*) Dyce asked Jute.

(*"Yeah, pleased to meet you,"*) Jute confirmed. (*"My friends call me Jute, and no one else knows I exist, so I guess you can call me whatever you want."*)

(*"I know how you feel. Nobody knows I exist. Nobody knew I existed before I came to this place, and nobody knows about the* me *I've become. If you know what I mean?"*)

("I think I do know what you mean, actually,") Jute said. *("But, I should probably lie and say that I don't, just because my friend probably thinks that you're a dick.")*

("You don't want to seem like you're taking sides?")

("Your existential crises, my existential crises, and her existential crises may not yet be mutually compatible.")

("I guess we're all broken in some way...") Dyce suggested. *("Humanity is a mess.")*

("That's one way of looking at it...") Jute said. *("Is that the word you want to use? Broken?")*

("Hmmm...") Dyce had a think about this.

("Hello?") Nico interjected, urgently. *("There's water in here!")*

("I'm sure it's fine,") Dyce eventually responded.

("How would you know how bad it is or isn't?") Nico said.

("Imagine it's a sensory deprivation tank,") Dyce said, *("Just chill.")*

("Are you fucking serious right now? Jute, is this dick actually serious?")

("I told you,") Jute said to Dyce. *("She thinks you're a dick.")*

Dyce remembered something he had once heard in a dream or half forgotten memory. *("If you change the way you look at things, the things you look at will change.")*

("See!") Jute sounded ecstatic. *('I like this kid, he gets it!')*

Dyce sat on the armour, ballast keeping it afloat in the shadow of the ship. He deactivated his tabris so that he could enjoy the ambient sounds of the morning.

'Change the way you look at things,' Dyce repeated to himself, contemplating those words. 'The things you look at will change.'

He liked the sound of that. He decided to give it a try. Instead of seeing a dark, drab wasteland filled with horrors, what could he see instead?

The rising sun lit the river ahead, red and gold, winding through the wasteland and the abandoned city beyond. Behind that was the bustling metropolis at the heart of Alcyone, and the tower that rose from its centre.

Dyce realised that he could choose to see only opportunities. A faint hint of a smile cracked the corners of his lips…

To be continued…

Printed in Great Britain
by Amazon

27853362R00215